Be An Angel

Also by Sarah Harrison:

THE FLOWERS OF THE FIELD
A FLOWER THAT'S FREE
AN IMPERFECT LADY
HOT BREATH
COLD FEET
THE FORESTS OF THE NIGHT
FOREIGN PARTS

Be An Angel

SARAH HARRISON

LITTLE, BROWN AND COMPANY

A *Little, Brown* Book

First published in Great Britain in 1993
by Little, Brown and Company

Copyright © Sarah Harrison 1993

A CIP catalogue record for this book is available
from the British Library.

ISBN 0 316 90513 5

Photoset in North Wales by
Derek Doyle & Associates, Mold, Clwyd.
Printed in England by Clays Ltd, St Ives plc

Little, Brown and Company (UK) Limited
165 Great Dover Street
London SE1 4YA

For the girls

Be An Angel

PART ONE
1957–1964

Children aren't happy with nothing to ignore
And that's what parents were created for.

> Ogden Nash, *The Parent*

For the imagination of man's heart is evil from
his youth.

> Genesis 8:21

Really, if the lower orders don't set us a good
example, what on earth is the use of them?

> Oscar Wilde, *The Importance of Being Earnest*

CHAPTER ONE

It had been Bruno Gallagher's conceit to present his new daughter as the main course at dinner. People tended to assume that his wife Elodie, being French, was the fanciful one, but they were wrong. Bruno's origins were Scottish, and he was subject to periodic fits of Gaelic whimsicality. On these occasions his red hair and eyebrows and even the long hairs in his ears and nostrils seemed to crackle and glow with energy like wires attached to an electrical current.

'There you are!' he cried, placing the four-week-old infant, naked but for a nappy, on her bed of braised celery, leeks and turnips. 'Happy as a sandboy!'

The baby waved and clutched, her jaw working.

Elodie looked doubtful. 'I think she is going to cry.'

'Rubbish. She's warm and moist – till recently a natural condition for her. Why should she cry?'

'Bruno – she has no clothes on.'

'Nor did she in here,' said Bruno, cupping his large, freckled hand over his wife's still softly rounded belly. 'My God, woman . . . ' These last words, intended as an affectionate reprimand, became blurred with desire. His hand rose to the waistband of her skirt and wriggled determinedly inside, where it moved like a small animal trapped beneath the cloth.

'You mustn't . . . ' Elodie made an unconvincing gesture of restraint, which ended in her pushing his hand further down until it burrowed happily between her legs. 'Oh! But everybody's waiting . . . '

'Bugger them. It's Christmas.'

It was, Christmas 1957, and a cold one in Quatre Vents, the grey farmhouse on the coast of Brittany. But here in the large kitchen the range glowed red, and in spite of Elodie's prediction the baby remained silent on her edible mattress as her father's mouth latched greedily on to the swollen, oozing nipple which should rightfully have been hers.

They didn't take long – Bruno's voracious sexual appetite had accustomed them to seizing the moment – but the Gallaghers and the Lalandes did not count patience their strong suit at the best of times. Titillated by the smell of the roasting goose, spiced red cabbage, apple sauce, pommes dauphinoise and braised vegetables, they grew restive.

At the head of the table sat Iphigénie, the dowager Lalande, her black hair twisted into a bagel-shaped chignon, her eyes bright in her thick, powdery *maquillage*. With her right hand she clasped the edge of the table, tapping her beringed fingers impatiently. On Iphigénie's right sat her son, Elodie's elder brother Chrétien, smooth and silent, itching for the whole vulgar seasonal charade to be over. Of the adults present only Chrétien, in a bespoke pinstripe, and Iphigénie, in shot taffeta the colour of motor oil, were formally dressed.

On his grandmother's left Blaise Gallagher, aged seven, sat with his elbows on the table, his fingers pushed into his dark hair, his expression one of rugged patience. His elbows, in a grey cotton shirt, poked through the sleeves of his navy handknitted sweater. Beneath the general hubbub Chrétien could feel the soft, bored beat of his nephew's feet on the crossbar of his chair. Between Chrétien and the seat reserved for Elodie, Blaise's younger brother Fabian, in the seat next to that reserved for Elodie, was standing on his chair and shouting repeatedly, 'I'm starving to death! I'm starving to death!' He wore a suit of armour tied on with tapes over his striped pyjamas, and was brandishing a wooden sword. His face beneath the uplifted visor of the helmet was scarlet with the effort of trying to get a rise out of his audience. He was failing because Iphigénie herself was engaged in a rapid and splenetic exchange with her daughter-in-law. Lauren, a New

Yorker, cared not at all for the *folies de grandeur* of the old world, and of her family by marriage in particular. She relished the occasional passage of arms with Chrétien's old battleaxe of a mother, who – she reckoned – got far too much of her own way.

They were conducting their exchange in French, which Lauren (who since leaving the Sorbonne had worked for the Paris-based advertising agency Grix) spoke fluently.

'I don't believe in celebration for celebration's sake, that's all, and neither does Chrétien, though he's too chicken to say so.'

'But you are here, are you not?' snapped Iphigénie. 'Sitting at our table, drinking our wine, preparing to eat our food!'

'And I'm suitably grateful,' replied Lauren, 'as I would be at any time. But I am not, at any future date, going to be made to feel guilty because I want to stay home at Christmas and read a good book in the peace and quiet of my own apart- ment.'

'I'm starving to death!' yelled Fabian.

He made a wild horizontal slash with the sword, missing his uncle narrowly enough to disturb his hair. Chrétien passed a pale, manicured hand slowly over his scalp with an air of pained urbanity. 'Please,' he remonstrated. 'Please.'

'I am here,' went on Lauren, 'because I am married to Chrétien and this is a family gathering at which he feels he should be present.'

Iphigénie glared from one to the other. 'Don't strain yourselves, I implore you!'

Lauren smiled sweetly. 'Don't worry, *belle-mère*, we won't.'

'I wonder,' said Chrétien, 'whether we could hurry them up with the dinner?'

'Darling,' purred Lauren, 'you have such good ideas.'

'Yes!' agreed Iphigénie, reverting to English. She prodded Blaise, so that her long nails dug into him. 'Go, run along, my darling, and be quick as you can. I believe I may be starting a migraine.'

'All right.' Gravely obliging, Blaise got down from his chair and left the room. Fabian, magically restored, sat down and pulled his visor over his face.

'*What* an improvement,' said Lauren.

*

'Blaise!' cried Elodie. 'You startled us!'

'Sorry,' said Blaise, not sounding it, 'only they sent me to find out when dinner was coming. Everyone's going potty in there.'

'Going?' said Bruno. He directed a wide-eyed, mad grin at his son. *'Going?'*

'For a start, Fabian's being completely stupid – hey – ' his gaze alighted on the baby, now covered with a large damask napkin. 'What's she doing there?'

'It's your father's idea.'

Blaise lifted the napkin and peered underneath. 'We're not going to eat that stuff, are we?'

'Why not?' asked Bruno.

Blaise didn't bother to answer. Elodie began assembling the rest of the dinner on two large high-sided butler's trays. Aromatic steam rose like incense, and Blaise's mouth filled with saliva. The open door of the iron range threw a warm red light on to the kitchen, its occupants and the still-sizzling food. Bruno and Elodie gazed fondly down at the baby and adjusted her damask covering. The first thin whips of snow lashed the deep-set window. From the dining-room came the beating of cutlery on the table, but in here, thought Blaise, it was just like the Nativity.

'Right,' said Bruno. 'Let's put the poor souls out of their misery.'

The baby, herself feeling hungry, was winding up to cry in earnest. Her unrestrained hands clutched at the napkin and disturbed it, her tiny red heels spurred at the vegetables and sent one or two rolling off the dish and on to the floor. But then her mother's face, a pale moon marked with a dark, symmetrical pattern, swam into view and, expecting to be lifted, she quietened.

There was a great carved sideboard in the dining-room, created from an ancient bedhead, but it was loaded with files and newspapers, Bruno's typewriter, a record player and a landslide of 78 rpm records, some in, some out of, their paper sleeves, so all the food went straight on to the table. Elodie and Blaise carried the two trays – Bruno brought up the rear with the baby on her platter.

Lauren cried out: 'I don't believe it. More meat?'

Fabian knelt up on his chair again, and Blaise returned to his and sat tranquilly as Bruno lowered the platter and removed the napkin. There was a collective gasp. '*Je vous présente,*' announced Bruno, '*Céleste!*' He gave her name a preposterously French pronunciation.

The Lalandes had not seen the new baby before. She had been asleep in the early afternoon when Chrétien's aubergine-coloured Jag had brought them from Paris, and Bruno had decreed that she be kept under wraps (Elodie mentioned the sniffles) to assist his *coup de théâtre* at dinner.

Lauren stood up, her slim figure rising like a calyx from the swirl of her full red skirt. 'May I pick her up?' she asked.

'If you want,' said Bruno. 'But be careful she doesn't go for your tit, she's due a feed.'

Fabian gave a high-pitched snigger. Chrétien shot him a quelling stare and added: 'And mind your blouse, *chérie*, she may be greasy.'

Iphigénie tapped agitatedly on the edge of the table. 'Bring her here, please! Bring her here to see her grandmother.'

'In a minute . . . oh, she's such a little darling, such a little honey . . . ' Lauren cooed and jiggled the baby. She moved only very slowly towards the head of the table. Iphigénie twitched with impatience. Chrétien smiled indulgently. Fabian snatched a piece of crunchy potato from the dish, dipped it in the apple sauce and popped it in his mouth before anyone could stop him. Blaise stifled a yawn.

Bruno picked up the carving steel and began to sharpen his knife with a ruffianly air. 'Right then – who's for a *tranche* of this noble bird?'

Lauren handed over the baby to Iphigénie and was again brisk and vivacious. 'You bet. Breast and all the trimmings.'

Bruno gave her a lecherous, sidelong look. 'Don't tempt me.'

Fabian grabbed Celeste's hand and waggled it over-vigorously. *'Non, non, non!'* cried Iphigénie, trying to snatch her away. Celeste snickered. Elodie took the baby's shawl, which had been round her own shoulders, over to Iphigénie, at the same time disengaging Fabian's grasp.

'Here, *maman*, wrap her in this.'

Iphigénie shook her head. 'You wrap her in it. It's time to eat.'

Blaise watched as Elodie took the baby and swathed her in the airy pink shawl. The two of them, his mother and his sister, made a pretty sight. Feeling his gaze on her, Elodie glanced up and caught his eye, and made a little kiss-shaped *moue* with her mouth. The baby's snicker became a determined yell.

'Serve me last, Bruno, I must feed her.'

Elodie withdrew to a fireside chair, unbuttoning her blouse as she did so. There she sat, perfectly composed and separate, her long straight black hair falling down around the suckling baby like a screen.

'Blaise!' barked Bruno. 'Pass your grandmother her plate.'

In spite of Iphigénie's proprietorial stance, Quatre Vents belonged not to the Lalandes, but to the Gallaghers. Bruno had made it very plain on his marriage to Elodie that when they visited France, and her family, they would do so on their own terms.

Maximilien Lalande, her father, when he had been alive, had secretly taken to Bruno, but (on the basis of it takes one to know one) had simultaneously recognised a philanderer of prodigious capacity, and warned Elodie more in sorrow than in anger of the trials to come.

Iphigénie had other grounds for objection. She took all men to be goats, so infidelities were only to be expected. She would have preferred her daughter to marry a Frenchman – the family was being overrun with foreigners – but if he had to be foreign then she would rather he were Scottish than English or, God forbid, another opinionated American. What really stuck in her craw was that he was an intelligent man, an academic, who had renounced serious intellectual endeavour in favour of writing bestselling books on – well – human relations. Iphigénie regarded sex with withering contempt: she was outraged that a son-in-law of hers should be making a fortune from peddling his distasteful views on a subject that should have been confined to the master bedroom.

Her married life stood as a monument to her ability to rise above sex. She had kept the amiable Maximilien on a long leash, and he had repaid her by being to all intents and purposes a devoted husband. His *amours* were well distanced from their social circle – his tastes ran to typists, waitresses and shop-girls – so there was never any threat to their union. But this Bruno! Even his name was like a circus animal's, and the man himself a hairy, grinning, mad-eyed satyr with wrinkled collars and loud socks. Whatever he spent his ill-gotten gains on, Iphigénie concluded, it certainly wasn't clothes. Elodie insisted that he had been tremendously brave in the war on some Greek island or other, but then the mad often displayed preternatural courage, did they not? Iphigénie said *ppht!* to that. As Maximilien lay dying of richly-deserved cirrhosis of the liver, he implored her to make an effort with Bruno Gallagher, for Elodie's sake, and she had done so as far as she was able.

The trouble was that beneath the striking dark looks and the assumed gypsy-queen hauteur, Iphigénie was a *petite bourgeoise*: rigid, narrow, grasping and deeply suspicious of anyone who did not share the same values and aspirations as herself. She was profoundly uncomfortable with her son-in-law, so she went on the attack. She told anyone who would listen that Bruno was a scruffy, sex-mad *arriviste* who was not worthy of her daughter. (This last was true in many ways, but not in the way she meant it.)

What she could never forgive him for was the shock of discovering that he had class. A few months after the wedding, when Chrétien took his mother across the Channel to visit the newly-weds, ('That's what's meant by frog-marching,' commented Bruno), there was no escaping the fact that the life into which Elodie had been transplanted was several cuts above what she was used to.

The house purchased with Bruno's tainted money was some

forty miles north of London where the soft tree-studded undulations of Hertfordshire began to give way to the windy austerity of the East Anglian fens. It was a large Victorian grange, embodying all the stern virtues and quirky charms of its period, and it suited Bruno and Elodie so perfectly that they might have been there for ever. Iphigénie smarted. Her own apartment in the Faubourg St Honoré was spacious, and even quite grand, and Chrétien's was undeniably smart if you cared for Bauhaus sparsity and bare floors, which Iphigénie did not. But Hartfield was, as Lauren succinctly put it, a class act.

The Gallaghers made no effort to modify and renovate their house. Even if Bruno had been possessed of the will and the know-how, this was before the great DIY boom of the 1960s. An army of Little Men still ruled the wires, pipes, shelves, attics, tanks and ballcocks of Britain. Hartfield was structurally sound. Lofty and confident, its gables rose like sardonically-raised eyebrows above the surrounding trees. The glint of the sun on its top-floor windows at certain times of day put a gleam in its eye.

With the house Bruno had bought all the accompanying land which included, as well as an acre of tousled garden, a large meadow linking Hartfield with the village of Stoke Broughton. This was known locally as the Craft. A public right of way ran across the Craft, with a stile on the village side and another leading into the drive of Hartfield, which in turn provided access to the lane beyond. Chrétien and Iphigénie urged Bruno to amend this state of affairs as soon as possible, but he said he had no intention of doing so. Apart from the fact that such an initiative would involve him in a lot of messy local politics, he had no objection to the footpath, which was an ancient local freedom and a feature of the parish, pre-dating Hartfield by hundreds of years.

Iphigénie muttered darkly about riff-raff. 'Then they'll feel at home, won't they?' was his response, a notion far too close for comfort to Iphigénie's own view of things.

The garden had a mossy tennis court, a croquet lawn bright with buttercups and daisies, and something which the estate agent characterised as a gazebo but which Bruno called a shed, and quickly appropriated for himself. There were a great many straggling roses and untended flowering shrubs, and the whole area was overrun with grey squirrels which raced, leaped and chittered in the branches, and sat in close attendance during garden meals, awaiting their opportunity.

Inside, the entrance hall was spacious, stoutly panelled, and reached up the height of fully two floors. An imposing staircase led up to a landing, like a minstrels' gallery, with numerous doors and passages leading off it. There were almost as many mice in here as there were squirrels in the garden – more, probably, since they were not so visible – but Bruno and Elodie tolerated them in the same spirit as they tolerated the people who walked the footpath. A coven of feral cats stalked the yard, but never came indoors.

The top floor was reached by a separate door in the courtyard at the side of the house, from which narrow, winding stairs scuttled up to the flat where lived the Doves, the couple who came with the house. Dove was a large man, quiet and slow. Mrs Dove – Evadne – was trim, bright and curvaceous. Her 'Morning all!', 'Don't mind me!' and 'Toodle-oo!' punctuated weekdays like the chimes of a clock. She was in her late forties, and well aware of the effect of her firm breasts, torpedo-like in circular-stitched cups, her bobbing uncorseted *derrière* and her snappy high heels had on Professor Gallagher. It was not intentional. She could no sooner have switched off her cheerful allure than flown.

After that first visit, Iphigénie's last words to her daughter, as the men and Lauren stood talking in the drive, were: 'Keep your eye on the pigeon woman.'

'Who?'

'The housekeeper.' Iphigénie threw a dark glance towards the house, where Mrs Dove was hoovering. 'She is a slut.'

'I'm sure you're wrong,' said Elodie.

Elodie was sure of her husband. She had been a contained, intelligent child who watched a lot and saw most things. She understood early on the huge differences that separated her parents and bound them together. She was, in spite of everything, fond of them both. She looked inward at herself and saw that she was different again. And Chrétien might have been from Mars for all the similarity between him and and herself. From these observations she realised the importance of individuality, and of a tolerance which allowed for individuality in others. When she fell in love with Bruno, it was with her eyes wide open and both feet on the ground. She did not exactly expect the worst, but neither did she expect him to change.

For his part, Bruno thought she was the cat's pyjamas. He never tired of telling her that it had been love at first sight, that he had never seen any woman like her, that all others paled beside her. This was certainly true. Bruno had been thirty when he first saw the nineteen-year-old Elodie walking through the Tuileries, carrying a music case. She was tall, and thin, with big feet and hands. Her pale oval face was framed by long, straight black hair: a heavy fringe came down to her eyebrows. It was 1950, when young women were bursting forth like butterflies from the cocoon of wartime austerity, but Elodie wore a long drab tweed coat, a black scarf, thick black stockings and flat shoes in which she strode along with rangy, graceful strides.

Bruno caught up with her at once and assailed her with little French and even less finesse. 'I just want to tell you you're the most gorgeous thing I've ever seen.'

One long hand in black fingerless mittens flew to her breast; the eyebrows lifted beneath the fringe. '*Pardon, m'sieur?*'

He grasped her by the shoulders, looking her up and down like a recently purchased painting. 'Absolutely bloody gorgeous. You know that?'

She allowed herself to be grasped. She was utterly self-possessed and faintly amused.

'*M'sieur?*'

'Christ–!' He clapped one hand to his brow.

'*Quoi?*'

'Not jailbait are you?'

'*M'sieur?*'

'Be just my luck.' He put the hand back on her shoulder, his eyes on the ground and brow furrowed. *'Quel âge avez-vous, mademoiselle?'*

'J'ai dix-neuf ans.'

'Thank God for that!' She gave a slight inclination of her head, acknowledging his gratitude. He tightened his grip. *'Dites-moi, mademoiselle – voulez-vous coucher avec moi?'*

Her thick black eyebrows rose beneath the fringe. *'Non.'*

He heaved a heavy sigh, and dropped his hands to his sides. 'Fair enough. So what do I have to do?'

'Au revoir, m'sieur.' She sidestepped him and moved on.

He began walking backwards in front of her. 'Tell me, cruel and lovely stranger, do you have parents?'

At this point Bruno had backed into a lamp-post and fallen to the ground, concussed. He regained consciousness in a cubicle in the outpatients' department of a local hospital. He had a blinding headache and felt as though he'd been trampled on by a cart-horse. But on blundering out into the reception area to discharge himself, he saw Elodie sitting on a hard chair among the ranks of walking wounded and their relatives, quietly reading a book, waiting for him.

It was all the encouragement he needed. From that moment on he was not to be denied. He brooked no argument from Iphigénie and Maximilien, whose consent was given more or less by default, and married Elodie in a registry office when Blaise was already a tadpole inside her.

Throughout the courtship Elodie behaved with the same vague, dignified composure with which she had first greeted him, almost as if she were letting the older people play amongst themselves and didn't much care what the outcome was. This apparent indifference inflamed Bruno. In bed she was silently passionate, entwining him octopus-like in her long, strong limbs and sucking him into her with sighs of ecstasy. Out of bed she resumed once more her mantle of serene detachment. Bruno, more used to confusing others, was confused. And this confusion ensured that he remained enslaved, uxorious even while straying, faithful though philandering, for a surprising number of years.

Elodie's pregnancies were an epiphany for Bruno. Entered

into in the most cavalier manner (as a natural, if slightly inconvenient, consequence of sex), they rendered her even more devastatingly desirable. The long, slender body he so adored became different, disguised by rich curves, gravid with fruitfulness and promise. Elodie's pale flesh seemed to glow, marbled with veins through which Bruno fancied he could see the life-force coursing with thunderous sensuality. Her breasts, normally little half-apples set high on her narrow torso, swelled and ripened into Comice pears, the aureoles darkened, the nipples positively straining for attention. As her stomach billowed tautly, the navel popping forward like the button on a stitched sofa, he was quite unable to keep his hands off her. He liked to bath her, kneeling like a nanny on the mat next to the bath while she lay back on his arm in the hot soapy water, her eyes closed and her knees splayed outwards while he soaped her voluptuously, watching the bubbles trickle off the awe-inspiring mounds which cushioned her unborn child. These bathtimes generally ended with Bruno tearing off his clothes and clambering into the bath with his wife, sending water everywhere and grazing himself on the taps, causing small injuries he never noticed until much later.

Unfortunately, pregnancies were succeeded by babies, to which Bruno did not respond so well. If asked, he would probably have said that he loved his children, assuming that the vague proprietary acceptance he experienced was love. But the truth of the matter was that the only strong feeling Bruno had towards them in their early years was jealousy. The lustful idyll of pregnancy ended abruptly in a farrago of broken nights, unpleasant smells, noise and shattered intimacy. With the exception of the last, these were contingencies Bruno was more used to creating himself. He was dismayed when Elodie, though loving as ever, fell asleep in his arms when he had scarcely got started, and even more dismayed when she happily got up an hour later to fetch the baby and put it to the breast. He lay rigid, pretending to be asleep, one furious eye occasionally rolling up to glare at her as she sat propped against the pillows, murmuring sleepily to the child.

Once, during the day, he even appeared in the doorway and

14

asked: 'May I have a go?'

She glanced up at him with exactly the same expression she had used when first propositioned by him in the Tuileries. 'A go?'

He made a jerky, sullen gesture in her direction. 'A suck. There seems to be plenty.'

She smiled. 'Of course you can. When he's finished.'

'Don't I have any rights in the matter?'

She shook her head with a soft little laugh. 'Absolutely not.'

'But it's driving me insane. He's gobbling away at you and doesn't even appreciate it.'

'Don't badger, darling. Please. I shall get all wound up and the milk will be sour, and then—'

'You? Wound up? That's a joke. You're a fucking snow queen.'

'Go away.'

He went. Some fifteen minutes later she called to him, and when he went to the nursery the baby was back in its bassinet and Elodie was sitting on the rocking-chair, bare to the waist. Her head was tipped back and she rocked gently, looking at him through slitted eyes. She had not fully undone her bra and blouse, but simply shrugged out of them so that they lay in rumpled folds around her hips. For Bruno, there was something powerfully erotic in this, as though the clothes had been ripped off her. He was overwhelmed. His legs shook as he went to her and knelt before the rocking-chair in homage. She wore a long chambray skirt, and now she parted her knees and flattened the skirt between them to admit him. It was a simple, practical gesture. She did not touch him, but made herself utterly available to him. With a growling sigh he leaned forward, his hands reaching for her breasts, his mouth following – and then the baby began to cry.

It was a piercing cry of indigestion. Elodie did not move, but Bruno felt her stiffen and saw, on the nipples which filled his vision, two tiny beads of bluish liquid appear in response.

The desire drained out of him. He planted an irritable kiss on her mouth and sat back on his heels. 'Carry on,' he said dully. 'The old bag's beaten me again.'

'Old bag . . .?'

'Mother bloody Nature.'

The baby in question, Blaise, turned out to be something of a hole-in-one: advanced, charming, exceptionally good-looking. The epileptic fit which frightened them all so much when he was three had happened only once since (at school, unfortunately), and merely added to his air of singularity.

Fabian was altogether different. Whereas Blaise had his mother's tall athletic figure, and dark hair and eyes, Fabian favoured his father from the first. It was hard on a new-born infant to have huge hands, a bulging forehead and a cowlick of crinkly red hair, but that was the way of it. Even the most doting aunt found it hard to utter a compliment that did not sound at best ironic, at worst sharply sarcastic. And the paternal likeness didn't stop there. Fabian spent six months turning night into day and rendering Hartfield unholy with his squalls. He remained fiercely unamused by all well-meaning attempts to amuse him while immobile, but once he could crawl he became hyperactive and began a reign of terror in which ironing-boards were collapsed, standard lamps toppled, books masticated and coal scuttles ransacked. His mother handled him best, his father worst. In fact, on several occasions Bruno lifted the child by the braces of his romper suit and seemed about to whirl him round his head and through the nearest window. Fabian, too, was clever, and school went some way to diverting his manic energy, but it was not just coincidence that Elodie had allowed five years to elapse before she next fell pregnant.

The dining-room was quite hot now, and round the table they were all flushed with food and drink and loud conversation.

Bruno rose to his feet and began to sing:

'And it's oh, but I'm longing for my ane folk,
Though they be but simple, quiet and plain folk—'

'Put a sock in it!' shouted Fabian.

16

Elodie looked up and smiled as she settled the drowsing baby, wrapped in her pink shawl, at the back of the armchair. 'Is there any left for me?'

'For you, my darling? The best, the most succulent and delectable morsels.'

'The parson's nose!' shrieked Fabian, irretrievably over-excited. Chrétien cast a beseeching look at Lauren at the other end of the table but she was enjoying herself, laughing at Bruno's antics and tearing some meat off a bone with her fingers.

Blaise rubbed his eyes. His mother, her blouse not properly buttoned, was standing by his father with her arm about his waist as he hacked at the goose with his big knife. The scene was now less like the Nativity than some pagan rite, lit by the flickering flames.

At the last moment he realised what was going to happen, but it was too late to warn them.

Within seconds the family was on its feet and clustered round. A rolled napkin had been pressed between Blaise's teeth. Elodie's fingers were pressed into her cheeks, her face was white. Bruno held her shoulders. Iphigénie became hysterical. Lauren began to stack dishes. Chrétien stood impassively in his place, tweaking the skin on the back of his hand. Fabian ran from the room, roaring with rage and jealousy, as his brother's heels drummed on the floor.

The baby, Celeste, watched the commotion dispassionately with her blue-black eyes. Slipping sideways in the armchair, she belched violently and a scattering of curds fell on the pink shawl. But no one noticed, and she did not cry.

CHAPTER TWO

Celeste was what is known as a good baby – that is, she slept long, cried little and made few demands. She was 'easy' and made everyone feel they could be of use. Blaise was just a touch precocious for comfort, and Fabian would try the patience of a saint. But even the most inept person could change Celeste, or spoon Elodie's mutton broth into her mouth, or wander about the garden with her balanced on their shoulder. 'My daughter,' Bruno would say, as though he were solely responsible, 'has a fortunate nature.'

Lulled once more into a sense of security, Elodie became pregnant again when her daughter was only two. The pregnancy was not as much fun this time, either for her or for Bruno. She was nauseous for the full term, and felt exhausted. The boys, Fabian in particular, ran her ragged. She adored her children, and was a tigress in their defence (which in Fabian's case was required quite frequently), but there were times when she half-wished that Bruno would behave like most upper-middle-class British men and insist his sons went away to be educated so that she could rest and regain her strength. Instead, he ran his socialist colours up the flagpole and insisted they attend the local school.

Stoke Broughton C of E Primary was presided over by Archie Featherstone, a jolly young bachelor who had reckoned himself up to most classroom contingencies until the Gallaghers came his way. Blaise's epilepsy was the first thing. Of course it did not trouble him personally in the least, though it would have been nice to be warned, and not simply confronted with the fall-out from a *grand mal* attack which occurred half-way through Miss Blore's rendering of 'Cargoes'. Miss Blore quite understandably had no idea what to do, and sent for him.

When he arrived the entire class was in uproar, most of the boys rehearsing the colourful version they would pass on that evening and most of the girls hysterical. Miss Blore herself was close to tears. Later Blaise, being unusually bright, was able to rise above it all and even to turn it to his advantage so that the whole school began to regard him as a kind of mystic. But Archie felt constrained to send for the Gallaghers and remonstrate with them.

This proved a bad move. Professor Gallagher lost his temper and asked where was the problem? The school was still in one piece, wasn't it? Miss Blore had eventually finished 'Cargoes' and moved on to 'The Highwayman', or some other such drivel, hadn't she? And the pupils (he spat out the word as though it were a foreign body in his soup) had learned something far more useful than Christmas-cracker verse. Hadn't they? Well, hadn't they?

Archie said that was as maybe, but he should have been informed, some of the children had been quite disturbed by the fit and parents had been ringing up—

'Jesus H. Christ,' roared the Professor, 'just give me their addresses and I'll go round in person and—'

Archie assured him that wouldn't be necessary, it was all over and done with now, he'd set everyone's mind at rest and they'd be better prepared the next time.

Another eruption from Professor Gallagher seemed likely, but at this point his wife – who was French, beautiful and exhausted-looking – stepped into the breach with a few gracefully emollient remarks. She explained that this was only the third attack their son had ever had, and that he was now on medication which should keep the condition completely under control. But they were so very, very sorry, she added, as she escorted her still bristling spouse from the room.

It was not an encounter that Archie had any wish to repeat. Fits apart, Blaise was outstandingly bright and Stoke Broughton had difficulty keeping up with him. With any other

19

family, Archie might have suggested to the parents that a school with a more specialised clientele might have suited the boy better but as it was he instructed Miss Blore and the others to soldier on because they might have a future prime minister in their charge.

The real reason was to keep his powder dry in case the behaviour of the younger boy got any worse. Fabian was at least as clever as Blaise but destined, Archie thought, less for high office than for a top-security wing at Her Majesty's pleasure. The child was a menace: rude, noisy, unmanageable, continually plotting some crime or other against persons or property. He wasn't a bully in the true sense of the word – he didn't confine his attentions to those weaker or smaller than himself. Anyone would do, male or female, child or adult. Since he was rarely fully occupied by the school curriculum, it was a clear case of the devil making work for idle hands.

Like his brother's epilepsy, Fabian had been launched upon the education system without warning. Though, in private, Bruno often referred to his second son bluntly as 'the Antichrist', he gave no hint of his opinion to Archie, who coped manfully for a year or so in the face of outraged parents, a succession of disaffected caretakers and a teaching staff constantly on the verge of insurrection.

The last straw came when the boy used a magnifying glass to set light to the bedding in the pets' corner. The resulting conflagration consumed a whole generation of rabbits and small rodents, and might very well have spread to the rest of the school had not one of the dinner ladies, alerted by the familiar stench of charred meat, spotted the column of smoke and raised the alarm. This time Archie had no alternative but to take issue once more with Gallagher *père*.

In trepidation he phoned Hartfield and was answered by Mrs Gallagher. 'Oh, Mr Featherstone, I'm so sorry! That's terrible. I really don't know – what would you like us to do?'

The French accent and the memory of her pale, drained loveliness put Archie momentarily off his stroke. 'Perhaps one of you could come round and collect him. And come and have a talk with me first.'

'Of course . . . ' There was a pause, during which he could picture her lighting a cigarette with long, trembling hands. She was pregnant again and when he had seen her at the school gate she looked very debilitated. 'Of course. Someone will be there in a moment.'

Archie was comforted by the 'someone'. Perhaps it would be just Mrs Gallagher and the little girl. His heart sank when he saw the Professor's mud-spattered Rolls bounce to a halt outside the playground. But Bruno was all geniality. 'Why does he do it? Why does a dog lick its balls?'

'I don't know. Why . . .'

'Because he can.'

'That's hardly—'

'He's an absolute bugger, isn't he, my son?'

This took the ground from beneath Archie's feet, as Bruno knew it would. He was completely disarmed, so that when Bruno finally left all that had been agreed was that Fabian would be spoken to most severely and not returned to school till the following Monday.

That was the Thursday. On Sunday afternoon, while Elodie took a sleep in the bedroom, Bruno patrolled the garden, carrying two-year-old Celeste. She should also have been taking an after-lunch nap but Fabian, consigned to his room as much for everyone's peace and quiet as his own punishment, had come in and tied the straps of her pinafore dress to the bars of the cot. She was still giving the occasional small hiccuping sob and her face, lying sideways on her father's shoulder, was red and tear-stained.

Bruno felt beleaguered, as he often did when circumstances obliged him to pay attention to his offspring. Now and again he stopped patrolling and glared distractedly at the overgrown shrubs, patting Celeste absentmindedly on the back. In the courtyard he came across Blaise, hitting a tennis ball against the side of the house with a warped racquet. This gave an interesting trajectory to the ball, but Blaise had an excellent eye and was returning it well. When Bruno and Celeste appeared he stopped abruptly, catching the ball in one hand; Elodie did not allow wall tennis here in case its thumping disturbed the

Doves. But Bruno said nothing, so Blaise started up again.

Bruno watched for a moment or two with a bleak expression. His son's dexterity with ball and racquet did not improve his humour. He himself was cack-handed and could scarcely catch. Blaise, counting under his breath, got to fifty and stopped again.

'What the hell am I going to do?' asked Bruno.

'About what?'

'Your infernal brother.'

'Oh, him.' Blaise began bouncing the ball on the racquet, turning the racquet head this way and that to compensate for its irregularities.

'Yes, him. He's got to go back to school tomorrow.'

'I suppose so,' said Blaise, without much interest.

'Well, of course he has! He can't hang around here all day.' Bruno's concern was not for Fabian's education, but for his own comfort and peace of mind.

Blaise understood this. 'He's really awful,' he remarked matter-of-factly.

'Absolutely bloody awful,' agreed Bruno. 'God knows what your mother and I did to deserve it. But there it is. I just wish I knew what I could do to make him half-way civilised so that bunch of staring inadequates at the village school could cope with him.'

Blaise caught the ball and pocketed it. 'Why don't you pay him?'

Bruno drew his brows together and narrowed his eyes. 'Pay him?'

'You know. Give him money each week if he doesn't get into trouble.'

Bruno considered this. He didn't give his children pocket money on any regular basis, and had no idea of the going rate. But the idea had a pure, bright simplicity about it. He shifted Celeste to his other shoulder. 'How much, would you reckon?'

Blaise thought. It was a delicate matter, and one that might well touch on his own financial standing. 'Pound a week?'

'What!' Bruno was scandalised. 'That's daylight robbery!'

'It's got to be worth his while,' Blaise pointed out reasonably.

22

He swiped at a clump of dandelions growing through the stones. 'And yours.'

'It's an outrageous suggestion,' grumbled Bruno. 'I'll think about it.'

Fabian was lying on the floor of his room, reading a copy of the *Dandy* which Mrs Dove had given him. Now he looked up. 'A pound?' he said suspiciously. 'You mean a week?'

'Yes,' said Bruno. 'But only for one hundred per cent co-operation.'

'What if I get into just a bit of trouble? Can I still have fifteen bob?'

'Absolutely not. It's one pound payable on receipt of a clean record sheet, or nothing.'

'Okay.' Fabian returned to the *Dandy.*

Bruno was slightly disconcerted by the swift and ready nature of the transaction. He felt somehow that he had been taken for a mug. But he had made his terms perfectly clear, hadn't he? He moved to the door, and then something occurred to him.

'By the way, I need hardly point out that this applies to your behaviour at home as well.'

'God, honestly!' Fabian rolled over and sat up. 'That's not what you said.'

'It's what I meant. That was absolutely diabolical, what you did to your sister earlier. And it completely wrecked my afternoon. I've spent hours calming her.'

Fabian's pale eyes, the colour of glacier mints, widened in disbelief. 'I think home as well ought to be more.'

'Oh you do, do you?' Bruno reddened. 'Well, let me tell you, laddie, you are in no position to dictate terms! I've got half the village on my back because of your antics and I've had it. Had it! I've made you what most people, let alone most boys of your age, would consider an insanely generous offer, just to conduct yourself like a member of the human race, and you have the barefaced cheek to sit there and engage in horse-trading?'

Fabian stared. He loved it when his father talked like this.

Bruno poked the air with a finger. 'You either agree to what I suggest or—' here a fractional hesitation which Fabian did not miss, 'there will be hell to pay. Understand?'

Elodie had just woken up and Celeste had been returned to her cot when Bruno staggered in, closed the door and lay down beside her with the explosive gasp of a man tried past endurance.

He lay with his back to her, breathing heavily and scratching his crotch, but Elodie recognised his need for attention as clearly as if he'd screamed at her. She leaned up on her elbow and put her hand on his shoulder. 'What is it?'

'Nothing.'

She gave him a little shake. 'No, Bruno – what?'

With a great heave he rolled on to his back. 'I do so dislike having to exercise paternal authority.'

Elodie said sympathetically, 'It must be difficult.'

'There is something so bloody undignified about wrangling with a child.'

Elodie put her arm around him and her head on his chest. 'What were you wrangling about?' She did not have to ask with whom.

'Oh—' He flapped a dismissive hand. 'Cash.'

An awful thought occurred to her. 'He hasn't stolen any, has he?'

'Not this time, no. No, I've been trying to reach an accommodation with him about returning to school tomorrow.'

There was a pause while Elodie digested this. 'An accommodation?'

Bruno moved under her and she felt his hands, large and fiery hot, on her back. 'Don't worry about it.'

She lifted her head. 'But I do.'

For a moment he continued to knead her back, his eyes closed, but as she continued to gaze at him he opened them. 'You mustn't.'

'Then you must tell me. What is this – accommodation?'

He put his hands to his face and rubbed vigorously, half-smothering his answer. She tugged at them. 'I beg your pardon?'

'I'm providing him with a small incentive to behave well.'

Elodie rolled back heavily on to her pillow, throwing up her arms and letting them fall in a gesture of exasperation. 'Ah! You're paying him.'

'That would be putting it extremely crudely.'

'How else should I put it? It is crude.'

She made a move to get up, but he was on to her at once, gathering her clumsily into his arms. 'Don't come on all prim and prissy about it, darling, please. He's agreed. It may even work. Please, please . . . ' He bent his head and began kissing her face and neck with sharp, greedy movements.

She screwed up her eyes, submissive but unmoved. He pulled back. 'Please.'

She looked up at him, her dark eyes shadowed in her pale face, her sensuously sculptured mouth drooping with displeasure. 'I don't know why you're saying please, please like that. You've already made your sordid little arrangement with our son without consulting me.'

'For Christ's sake, forget that!' Bruno had already done so. He pushed up her skirt and placed his palm firmly between her legs, feeling the mossy secret warmth beneath slightly damp cotton. His voice grew thick. 'If there's still room in there, let me in.' At last he felt the subtle change in her which denoted acceptance, felt her grow heavy and languid under him and saw her expression slacken and blur into one of animal self-centredness. This pregnancy had so far lacked the rollicking self-indulgence of its predecessors, but now Bruno remembered all the delights that awaited him under her capacious, rumpled clothes.

With frantic speed he unzipped himself. As he explored her he could feel her feet, like two small independent animals, freeing themselves of her pants. The minute she had done so she wrapped her long legs around him. He gasped. The sensation of her hips between his hands, her body stretched before him and his lower half snugly held, was like driving a fast car recklessly at dawn. His last thought before losing control was that he would always want her.

The accommodation reached between Bruno and Fabian had a

25

profound effect on both his sons. Fabian perceived that, if you played your cards right, virtue need not be its own sole reward. Blaise recognised in himself a talent for what later became known as facilitating – not unprofitable, since his father dashed him generously for services rendered – and achieved a hold over his father and brother which he never chose to exercise but which, by its very existence, gave him considerable quiet satisfaction.

Unfortunately Elodie didn't have long to enjoy these calm waters. She went into premature labour three weeks before her due date, at five o'clock on a Tuesday afternoon when Bruno was enjoying an extended lunch at his publisher's expense. The children were sitting at the kitchen table eating tomato sandwiches. Only Fabian was eating with any real concentration. Celeste was peeling the crusts from her sandwich with a steady hand, the tomato slices cascading to the floor as she did so. Blaise chewed slowly and absent-mindedly, his eyes on an old copy of *Boxing World*. So of course it was Fabian who exclaimed, 'What on earth's all that water on the floor?' Elodie stared in dismay at the large puddle on the tiles. 'Did you pee or something?'

The word 'pee' caught the others' attention. Celeste began to carol, 'Pee-pee-pee-pee, Mummy did a pee', as she laid her crusts in an uneven circle round her plate. Blaise looked up from his magazine. 'Mum? What's going on?'

'Nothing. Don't worry—' Elodie began mopping at the pool with a dishcloth, but as she did so a second gush of fluid rushed out from between her legs and hit the floor with an unrestrained splash.

'Hell's bells!' exclaimed Fabian, impressed, and stuffed what remained of his sandwich into his mouth.

Elodie gave up mopping and tried to smile at Blaise. 'I'm sorry, but it's truly nothing to worry about. It's just the baby arriving a little early.'

Blaise got off his chair and eyed her levelly. 'Is it going to come right absolutely now?'

'Of course not!' Elodie's voice was quite shrill with a bright certainty she did not feel. 'Darling, could you ring Daddy's publisher's office and leave a message about what's happened? It's Repton Lyle, the number's on the board in Daddy's shed.' Blaise ran from the room. 'Fabian, can you go and find Mrs Dove and ask her to come? I think she's upstairs, I heard the radio.'

Fabian at once bawled, 'Mrs Do-ove!', and left the room at speed, still yelling, doors crashing open and left swinging behind him as he went. Celeste, infected by the general unease, stared silently at her mother, squelching tomato seeds in her plump fists. Elodie smiled anxiously. 'Mummy pee?' murmured Celeste.

Blaise returned. 'I left the message.'

'Good boy.' They stood gazing thoughtfully at the floor until Fabian came back with Mrs Dove, marching smartly in her stilettos, her trim figure quivering with excitement and assumed responsibility.

'Oh my goodness. You are under way, aren't you? Here, my dear, sit down.' She guided Elodie to a chair. 'Cottage hospital, is it?'

Elodie nodded, then winced. 'Ugh, I'm so wet.'

'Yuk!' exclaimed Fabian. 'I'm *going.*' He took another sandwich from the plate and left by the back door.

'I don't think we should waste time getting you changed,' opined Mrs Dove. 'I think we should get you tucked up in the labour ward as soon as ever we can. Blaise, lovey, will you stay with your Mum while I go and pack her a few things?'

As Mrs Dove's footsteps tittupped up the stairs, Blaise, his eyes wandering to the Marciano feature, put his arm round his mother. Her eyes at once filled with tears. 'I'm so sorry, darling. It's the shock – it's much too early – I'm afraid in case there's something wrong . . . ' She wiped her eyes, and looked up at her son's impassive face. 'But there won't be, I'm sure.'

'No,' replied Blaise noncommittally. Seeing his mother had now got a grip on herself, he sat down in his place and discreetly turned the page of *Boxing World.* Celeste watched the slippery seeds oozing out from the sides of her fists and clinging there perilously for a second or two before dropping on to her lap. She beamed as Mrs Dove bustled back in, with a bulging suitcase fastened with a strap.

'Right, I think I've got most things in. Blaise, lovey, would you go and fetch Dove, he's up the garden, and tell him to get here quick. He can drive your mum to hospital. Chop-chop.'

'Okay.'

'Chop-chop!' echoed Celeste.

'And you,' said Mrs Dove, leaning over her and kissing her tomato-streaked face, 'are my little sweetie. Dove'll take you there,' she said to Elodie, speaking extra clearly as though labour might have impaired her hearing. 'Then I can stay here and mind things for you.' She must have caught some fleeting expression of Elodie's, for she added: 'He doesn't drive a lot these days but he's safe as houses, had a clean licence for thirty years.'

'Thank you so much, Mrs Dove,' said Elodie. 'What would I do without you?'

Dove's licence had remained clean for three decades because he never drove above twenty-five miles an hour. Even so, he managed to bring into play the full panoply of gears, brakes, horn, lights and signals which his highly-polished Austin afforded. Elodie sat tense and miserable in the back seat (Dove clearly considered the front too familiar), clutching the handle of her case and praying she would dilate no further as they crawled through Stoke Broughton and then along interminable narrow lanes to the cottage hospital.

Celeste watched adoringly as Mrs Dove slipped the halter of her apron over her neatly-coiffed head, and reached behind her to tie the strings. 'Now then, Blaise,' she said, 'why don't you take your little sister out in the garden for a bit while I wash these things up? If she has a bit of fresh air now, I may be able to get her down before your Dad gets back. He'll have quite enough on his plate. Here—' She wiped Celeste's face and hands with the corner of the apron, with brisk, efficient strokes, and then hoisted her out of the high chair and set her on her feet. 'Who's a poppet? There you go. I'll give a call when I'm ready for her.'

Blaise held his sister's hand and led her patiently out of the back door and round the corner of the house. He knew where Fabian would be, and went straight there. They were digging a trench and earthworks in an exceptionally well-hidden spot between some large, gloomy rhododendrons and the spiked iron fence which bordered that corner of the Craft which was wooded and choked with nettles. The trench, whose precise use they had not yet decided, was now of a good depth, and only Fabian's head and shoulders were visible as he worked away like a crazed grave-digger.

'Dove's taken her to hospital,' said Blaise. 'Mrs Dove stayed here to keep an eye on us.'

'Bloody early bed, then,' commented Fabian, a shade breathlessly. 'Give us a hand.'

'I might.' Blaise let go Celeste's hand and dumped her in a sitting position, pointing sternly. 'Pick some flowers for Mummy.' He jumped down into the trench. It smelt dank, and the sides were whiskery with roots and busy with wood-lice.

Fabian chucked a plastic spade in his direction. 'Here.'

'I only said I might,' repeated Blaise, ignoring the spade.

'So what's up with you?'

'You owe me, Titch.'

'Don't call me "Titch"!'

Blaise smiled amiably. 'Okay. Only you still owe me.'

'All right then, there's no need to go on about it!' Red in the face with irritation and from his exertions, Fabian rummaged in his pocket and took out a handful of change. Their heads bowed together as they made the transaction.

So engrossed were they that they did not notice Celeste slithering over the edge of the trench, and she made no sound on the soft loam. She sat there for a moment, unhurt but startled, still clutching the few white dead nettles she had already decided were not for her mother but for Mrs Dove. Her face crumpled, ready to cry. But something about her brothers' back views told her it would be a waste of time, and she began instead to examine a mutilated worm that lay nearby.

A sturdy middle-aged nurse blocked Bruno's way as he entered the nursery. 'May I ask what it is you want?'

'You may,' said Bruno, favouring her with his axeman's grin.

The nurse did not reciprocate. 'Did you want to see somebody?'

'Yes,' said Bruno. 'My son.'

'And you are . . .?'

'Professor Bruno Gallagher.'

The nurse was obviously not a great reader, and was unimpressed. 'Oh yes. Over here.' She threaded her way between the plastic cots in which the new-born infants lay like cucumbers in cold frames. She stopped by one in no way different from any other, and laid a well-scrubbed hand on the rim. 'Baby Gallagher,' she announced.

'Alessandro,' retorted Bruno.

'Pardon? He's only a tiddler, just five pounds, but then he was a little bit under-cooked, wasn't he?'

Bruno stared down, jingling his change. 'Miserably under-sized, and my wife's probably half-dead as a result.'

'She'll be fine,' said the nurse soothingly. 'It's always rather alarming when they come early and quickly like that. But it's not your first, is it?'

'Fourth,' said Bruno, adding with emphasis, 'All born here.'

'Your wife was a trooper, an absolute trooper.'

'Really?' Bruno bent down with his head on one side, in order to stare directly into Alessandro's small, intently sleeping face.

'She's tougher than she looks, isn't she?' continued the nurse. 'I never cease to be amazed at how differently people react to—'

'He's a disgusting colour,' said Bruno.

'Yellow as a buttercup,' agreed the nurse gaily. 'Prems are often jaundiced. We'll larn him.'

Bruno moved away. 'I'm going to say good-night to my wife.'

'The ward will be closed now – but you can have a word with Matron.'

He ignored this. And the young and inexperienced night nurse in the eight-bedded maternity ward was too timid to take issue with him. He went over to Elodie, who was dozing, curled on her side with her hands up to her face like a squirrel.

Bruno's weight tilted the mattress slightly as he sat on the side and placed a hand on her blanketed knees. Elodie opened her eyes. 'So what do you think of him?'

'Not bad. Small. Yellow. Not to be drawn on any of the burning issues of the day. But fine.' She gave a small, silent laugh, turning her head into the pillow for a moment. He bent and kissed her. 'Well done.'

'It was a complete shambles.'

'You may think that. The gauleiter in the nursery accounted it something of a triumph.'

'She means I didn't go completely to pieces. By the way,' she reached out and gave the corner of his jacket a tug, 'you're not supposed to be here. It's after lights out, you know.'

'She said that. But nobody stopped me.'

'The poor girl wouldn't dare. But you must go. I want to sleep and I want you to go home and make a fuss of the others. Blaise was so brave and grown up about all this . . . ' Her eyes filled with easy tears.

Bruno stood up. 'Night-night. Sleep well. Tomorrow afternoon I'll come mob-handed.'

'Only two at a time are allowed—'

But he was on his way.

Evadne Dove prided herself on knowing how to treat a man. It was eleven-thirty when Bruno got back to Hartfield, but she had a nice little lamb casserole in the Aga, a fire lit in the lounge (they would call it the library) and had succeeded in getting that evil Fabian back into bed just in time, so that everything was nice and quiet and cosy. She had achieved this last with much cajoling, some main force and half a pound of iced caramels bought by Dove for himself on the way back from the hospital that afternoon. When Bruno came banging through the back door from the courtyard, Evadne was to be found, oven gloves on and oven doors open, inspecting the fragrantly steaming hotpot. She glanced up, attractively flushed, as he came in.

'Professor Gallagher, congratulations! How is she? And the baby?'

'My wife's rather tired, and the baby is a bit of a runt but holding his own.'

Evadne pushed the oven door shut with her foot and set the casserole on top of the stove. She removed the oven gloves and flapped one well-manicured hand before her face. 'Phew! But he's premature, bless him, not really ready to come. It must be such a terribly rude awakening, don't you think?' She pronounced 'rude awakening' as though it were a phrase of her own, new-minted for the occasion.

Bruno found her utterly charming. 'Whatever are you cooking, Mrs Dove?'

'Nothing much, just a little hotpot in case you were hungry. If you don't want it now it'll keep beautifully till tomorrow.'

'You couldn't keep me from it. But first a drink.'

He went into the library – noting as he did so the fire, the plumped-up cushions, the air of smoothly-engineered order which always followed Mrs Dove's ministrations – and collected the whisky bottle from the trolley.

Back in the kitchen, she had replaced the casserole in the oven and removed her apron. Her hour-glass figure was presented to advantage in a black polo-neck sweater and a straight red gabardine skirt with a fan of kick-pleats at the back which flared out over her shapely calves as she walked. A tassel-shaped black and gold pendant hung between the twin nose-cones of her breasts, and her feet were glossy and trim as polished hooves in black patent slingbacks.

Bruno took tumblers from a cupboard, three of them clutched together with his enormous fingers inside them. 'Join me?'

'Oh, no, thanks very much. I don't mind whisky, but it doesn't like me!'

'Something else? Sherry?'

'Well, only if it's no trouble. Just to wet the baby's head.'

Bruno did not fetch the fino from the library, but took a slightly smeary bottle of Elodie's cooking amontillado from the shelf behind the door. 'This be okay?'

'Lovely, thank you.'

'And where's your husband? Will he join us?' This question expected the answer no, and duly received it.

'There's a match on, and his back's playing him up a bit this evening.'

'Best where he is then,' agreed Bruno. 'Why don't we go in and sit by that fire you've so kindly lit?' He let her go past him through the door, partly for the pleasure of watching her buoyant backside as she walked across the hall. He decided that he was tired, even a little overwrought. It had been a long day, full of heavy demands on his time and attention.

'Not really necessary, I know,' she was saying as he followed her into the library, 'but it can feel quite autumny these nights once the sun's gone, and I thought you might be tired.'

'I am, as a matter of fact,' said Bruno, collapsing heavily on to the sofa and slopping his drink. 'Damn!' He shuffled the glass from hand to hand, licking his hand, and the sides of the glass.

Evadne, bustling over, took a tissue from her sleeve and dabbed at the spillage. She was an artless woman, she meant absolutely nothing by it, and though she noticed that his crotch was beginning to bulge she simply regarded this as being in the nature of things. She really wanted to know about the birth, and the new baby – its weight, colouring, what they were going to call it – but as she opened her mouth to ask Professor Gallagher about these matters he caught her hand, the one with the ministering tissue, and placed it firmly on the bulge.

'What's this?' she asked.

'You know very well what it is.'

'I do, yes, but it's hardly the ticket, is it?' She smiled down at him. He could smell the sherry on her breath. The tassel pendant swung back and forth between them. 'I haven't had my drink.'

'You're a good sport. Be a sport now.' He rubbed her quiescent hand vigorously over his swelling fly. 'Be a friend.'

Just to make talking easier, she sat down next to him. At once he banged his glass down on the side-table, slopping more Scotch over the side, and placed his free hand over her jutting right breast.

'You really have got the most maddening shape,' he murmured, massaging the breast at the same rhythm as his crotch.

Evadne was weakening. Though she wouldn't have put it in-to such words this was clearly all part of her domestic ministry.

33

And all he wanted was a bit of hand-relief after a long and emotionally draining day (she read numerous magazines and had a mind richly-stocked with theories to suit every occasion). Besides, the enthusiastic massage was not unpleasant. Dove was not a massager, nor a talker. It was wham-bang snore-snore a couple of times a month these days. Her hand came to life under his and she began to pluck with small strong fingers, first at the button and then at the fly. Bruno laid his head back, drawing her towards him as her hand laid hold of his mountainous erection 'Good girl, Mrs Dove . . . you're a great girl . . .'

Fabian stood on the stairs in his pyjamas, watching with interest what he could see of the two adults' activities. Mrs Dove, though setting about her task with her usual diligence, seemed substantially the same. But his father was an altered being. Fabian pulled out the waist of his pyjamas and looked down at himself. Nothing. He put in his hand and gave his tail a couple of exploratory tweaks, which also produced no effect. Absorbed, he sat down to watch, and to await developments.

Upstairs in her cot, Celeste struggled with a lump of iced caramel which was stuck in her thick, dark hair. It had been given her by her brother on his way downstairs, to keep her quiet. She wasn't concerned about having sticky hair, but about getting the sweet into her mouth. The more she tugged, the softer and less graspable the caramel became, and the more it spread. Her hands and face were covered in it. She was also very wet. She cried a little, and then fell forward, half-kneeling on the damp sheet, and went to sleep.

CHAPTER THREE

'How do you like your little brother?' people kept on asking.

'I do like him,' Celeste would whisper obligingly with her serious, anxious-to-please expression. This was clearly the correct response because her mother would smile, and so would the people who asked the question, and they would gaze adoringly at little Sandro, their opinions confirmed.

She did like him, of course, but she was at a loss to know why she was always being asked for her opinion. No one had ever elicited it with regard to her other brothers. And they seemed bigger and more distant than ever now, lords of their independent world as she and the baby were captives in their nursery one. Sandro's arrival had precipitated this divide. But then Sandro was precious and delicate, a little brother to be prized and cherished.

Even Iphigénie, who came to stay not long after Elodie got out of hospital, gazed dotingly on Sandro. Her other grandchildren she regarded with a fierce generalised approval, as being the vessels – albeit inadequate – for a handful of her genes. But Sandro, tiny and mewling, succeeded in breaching her armour-plated egotism. Of course this raised yet again the contentious issue of baptism. 'Elodie, you must, it is essential!'

'Don't be silly, Mother, of course it's not essential.'

'It is the right thing to do!' snapped Iphigénie, these days rarely a churchgoer but steeped in the superstitions and prejudices of a Catholic upbringing.

'Insurance, you mean.'

'I mean correct. Christian.'

They were sitting in the library, Elodie on the floor with Sandro lying on her lap, his head resting on her knees. Iphigénie was in a fireside chair. Behind the sofa Celeste also sat on the floor, dressing a bald bear in one of the baby's vests. It was a wraparound vest with tiny ribbons to fasten it; Celeste had done well to get the vest on to the bear at all, but the ribbons had defeated her. She had seen people tie bows, of course, and especially admired Mrs Dove's way of doing it, a kind of lightning dextrous twiddle finished off with a brisk tug. This she copied, twiddling the ribbons furiously, then pressing them together and withdrawing her hands sharply. The ribbons remained obdurately untied, but she did not give up. Her face was pink with concentration.

The time was five o'clock on one of those late September days when winter suddenly strides forward and presses its face to the glass. A log fire leapt in the hearth. A standard lamp and one table lamp were lit, and the edges and high ceiling of the room were already retreating into shadow. The rows of books in the tall bookcases seemed far away.

'Your husband is still working?' Iphigénie preferred to avoid calling her son-in-law by name.

'I suppose so.'

'In that hut?'

Elodie nodded, holding Sandro's hands in her own and patting them softly together.

Iphigénie called: 'Celeste! Celeste? What are you doing behind there? Are you all right? Come and show *grandmère* what you are doing.'

'She's very busy,' said Elodie, 'don't disturb her.' She leaned over the baby. 'We mustn't disturb her, must we?'

Iphigénie looked away jealously. In this mood she always reminded Elodie of a cat which has lost its footing and its dignity, and which retreats with ears flicking sideways and eyes pale with rage. Iphigénie always sat towards the front of a chair, her back very straight and her forearms resting on the arms. In this way she could let her hands hang, so that their increasingly arthritic curves looked almost natural. She had a habit, probably unconscious, of rubbing each thumb rapidly against its neighbouring forefinger. In a quiet room, as now, this rubbing made a little whispering sound. She was never relaxed. 'Where are the boys?'

'Upstairs. Or outside. Don't ask, Mother, it's so nice and peaceful.'

'You don't wonder what they're doing?'

'No. If it matters I shall find out. Otherwise why do I need to know?'

'You are extremely trusting, both of you.'

'Lazy, Mother.'

Iphigénie's face gave a small convulsive twitch, which conveyed that she had forborne to say this.

A silence followed, broken by the sound of footsteps in the hall and a tap on the door. Mrs Dove's head came round. 'I'm popping off now, if that's all right. I've peeled some potatoes for you, they're in the saucepan at the back of the Aga. Aaah . . . ' She spotted the baby and beamed indulgently. 'Look at him, my best boy. May I take a peep?'

'Help yourself.'

Mrs Dove crossed the room, mouthing 'Excuse me' to Iphigénie, who did not acknowledge her.

'Aaah . . . ' Mrs Dove crouched down beside Elodie, and caressed Sandro's cheek with one finger. Her position, though achieved quite gracefully, revealed an inch or two of silky black petticoat edged with lace, and a hint of stocking-top. Iphigénie could also smell the woman's scent, something cheap and sweet like furniture polish.

'He's a love! You're a love, aren't you?' said Mrs Dove. 'I keep telling everyone he's the prettiest baby I've ever seen.' She turned her head to Elodie and asked, 'Is he still keeping well?'

'Yes, touch wood.' Elodie reached behind her and patted the carved foot of the sofa. 'He needs an awful lot of feeding, being so small, so we have very interrupted nights – or I do – but I think we're over the worst.'

Iphigénie stared at the fire, rubbing her thumbs at high speed. Coming as she did from the *pas devant les domestiques* school of employers, she did not consider that her daughter (still less her son-in-law) maintained a sufficient distance between themselves and those who worked for them.

Celeste came round from behind the sofa, carrying the bear in its still unfastened vest. Her appearance presented Iphigénie with a welcome diversion from the cosy discussion of infant management. 'Celeste, there you are! Come and tell *grandmère* what you've been doing.' She leaned forward with a fiercely demanding smile, holding out one hooked hand.

Celeste smiled back, but hesitated, and in the instant of her hesitation Mrs Dove turned round. 'Well I never, there's my favourite girl! What were you doing hiding round there? Have you got your teddy, then, sweetheart? Go and show your nan.'

Iphigénie bristled. Mrs Dove sensibly looked away again. Celeste went over to her grandmother and held out the bear.

'Isn't he a handsome fellow in his jacket,' said Iphigénie.

'It's a vest,' Celeste pointed out.

'And what do you call him?'

'Teddy.'

'Very good. But his vest is not done up. Shall we do him up? He might catch cold.'

'Yes.'

Iphigénie took hold of the tiny ribbons and struggled manfully, for a full minute and a half, to tie them. But it was far too fiddly an exercise for her crooked fingers. Mrs Dove, on her way out, paused and asked pleasantly: 'Shall I do that?'

Celeste at once retrieved the bear and held it up. 'Iss Dove do it.'

She watched entranced as Mrs Dove tied two neat, even double bows and fluffed them up so they looked like little butterflies. 'There we are.'

When Mrs Dove had left the room and Celeste had sat down on the rug next to her mother, Iphigénie said, 'I hope you're keeping an eye on that woman.'

Bruno, returning from his shed, where the paraffin heater had sent him to sleep, met Evadne in the yard as she left by the back door.

'Hallo there,' he said.

'Hallo, I'm just off up.'

'I do like that dress you're wearing. What would you call that?' She glanced down at herself. 'This old thing? It's an old one I got from Bobby's I don't know how long ago.'

'But such a jolly pattern . . . ' He came close to her and skimmed his hand down the side of the dress from breast to hip. 'Of course, it's what's inside it that counts.'

'Well, thank you. Now I must go and get our dinner on.'

'Of course you must.' He slipped his hand to the small of her back and pulled her towards him. She was a little unbalanced in her high heels and tipped forward quite sharply, her breasts pressing warmly against him.

'You should be in films,' he said. 'With your figure you'd have them queuing round the block.'

'Don't be silly, I'm a middle-aged woman.'

'Ripe.' He put his arms round her and kissed her noisily on the lips. 'Ripe.'

'Some say.' She patted his cheek, extricated herself, and disappeared through her own front door.

Striding through the darkened kitchen towards the wedge of warm light that was the library, Bruno slapped his hands together and called, 'Where is everybody? Where's my beautiful wife and my darling children? Let me feast my eyes on you!'

Blaise and Fabian were up in one of Hartfield's attics, the one used for storage, which also housed the cold water tank and a fair-sized colony of bats which came in under the eaves at dawn to roost. Hearing their father's loud voice far below they temporarily suspended their activities, but continued a moment later when there followed the faint sound of the library door closing.

There were two more attics. One was a neglected playroom with a loose-jointed ping-pong table and an old kitchen dresser spewing forth ransacked board games and boxes of magazines and comics. The other was now and had always been the accommodation for Hartfield's live-in couple. It was through the wall between this flat and the storage attic that the boys were currently spying on the Doves. For some weeks, since Fabian had disclosed his findings on the night of Sandro's birth, they had been eavesdropping with the aid of a tumbler, but a couple of days ago they had located a damp patch in the plaster where the tumbler, with minimal pressure, had left a shallow indentation.

In a few short sessions before and after school, when the Doves were at work, the boys had made a peep-hole, using some old grape scissors from one of the attic's many boxes. As Blaise pointed out, they had to be extremely careful to begin with in case the hole turned out to be in a conspicuous position where discovery would be inevitable. Happily it was not. It was in the wall of the narrow passage which formed the main thoroughfare of the flat. This passage had no windows and was poorly lit.

When Mrs Dove found a scattering of plaster dust on the floor she assumed, with some justification, that it must be due to the depredations of mice, and subjected the skirting board to exhaustive examination. Also in the spies' favour was the Doves' choice of wallpaper, an elaborate pattern of trellises, vines and grapes which afforded a perfect camouflage for the peep-hole.

The problem was that nothing terribly exciting happened in the passage. It would have been superb, as Fabian said, if the hole had happened to be in the sitting-room – or, better still, the bedroom. As it was, they saw their subjects only in transit. Even Dove's measured stride took him past in a flash, and Evadne was a mere blur.

'She's back in,' said Blaise, whose turn it was.

'Just after him,' observed Fabian. 'Perhaps they've been doing it in the shed.'

Blaise removed his eye from the hole long enough to give his brother a disparaging look. 'Come off it, there isn't room.'

'You don't need much room. You don't need to lie down or anything.' Fabian had developed a way of talking which suggested he had personal experience of the matters under discussion. 'Anywhere will do.'

Blaise returned to the hole, and flapped his arm. 'There she goes. Just went by.'

'I bet she'll be back in a mo. Here, give us a dekko—' Fabian knelt up beside his brother and pushed him out of the way.

'She's got a really huge bust,' he added appreciatively.

At the beginning of October, Chrétien was to collect his mother and take her back to Paris. He had had a business meeting in Birmingham, after which he and Lauren would spend a weekend in London, doing what Lauren described as 'schlepping round the galleries', looking for pictures to enhance and enlarge Chrétien's growing collection. They were due at Hartfield for Sunday lunch, and to spend the night before returning on the ferry next morning.

On the Saturday Elodie took her mother shopping in the village, leaving Celeste and Sandro under Bruno's supervision. Having made much of the night unholy with his teething cries, Sandro now slept soundly in his pram on the lawn, muffled against the autumn cold and netted against cats. Bruno intended returning to bed. Once the women had left he helped Celeste undress, ran a deep, hot bath in the family bathroom, and put her in it.

She shrieked with delight. Any bath, but especially an extra-curricular one, was her idea of paradise. As she crouched down and her bottom sank into the steaming water, her eyes closed in ecstasy.

'Bubbles?'

'Bubbles!'

Bruno poured in a generous measure of bubble bath, lifting the bottle up and down like the *padrone* of some Spanish sherry cellar. Celeste churned her hands and legs vigorously until the surface of the water blossomed into foam several inches deep.

'Junk?'

'Junk!'

Bruno opened the white-painted cupboard behind the door. A cascade of plastic and rubber bath toys fell at his feet. He picked up an armful and dropped them in the water with a splash. 'Daddy's going to have a rest,' he told her sternly. 'Stay in as long as you like.'

Elodie, walking across the Craft with her mother, looked over her shoulder at the house. She pointed. 'Look – this is my favourite view.'

Iphigénie, watching out for cowpats, agreed without turning that it was charming.

'Not charming, Mother. Handsome. Full of character, *n'est-ce pas?*'

Iphigénie made a non-committal sound. She liked to see her grandchildren, and the baby was enchanting, but in her heart of hearts she was looking forward to being borne away from them all in Chrétien's spotless car, back to her immutable routine in the Faubourg St Honoré – cards, coffee, shopping, Sunday lunch with her son and daughter-in-law, a gallery or theatre every fortnight, an intimate supper with friends mid-week. Even arguing with Lauren had its charms, its own recognisable rules and conventions. This place was a madhouse.

She never, on principle, made the smallest concession to English country life. For today's expedition she wore a plum-coloured fitted suit with a Persian lamb collar; on her head a black Persian lamb pillbox which made her look at a distance as though her hair had been subjected to topiary; on her feet (long, narrow, delicate feet like Elodie's own) black suede laced shoes with pointed toes and Louis Quinze heels. She was not easily beaten. When they reached the road the shoes were scarcely marked.

Elodie swung over the stile, Iphigénie side-stepped gingerly through the gate. As they did so, Blaise and Fabian whizzed past on bicycles, leaning into the precipitous bend from the village, their shouted 'Hiya!'s snatched away by speed.

Iphigénie pursed her lips. 'That boy should not be allowed out on a bicycle.'

'Which boy?'

'You know he is not supposed to. If he falls he could be badly injured. Or cause an accident – be run over – anything!'

'Oh, you mean Blaise.' Iphigénie twitched, she didn't like to be teased. 'We won't stop him doing things. He's only ever had three fits in his whole life and the last one was more than two years ago. He might never have another. Did you know *you* could have one at this very moment?'

'Nonsense.'

'It's true, Mother.' They began walking up the hill at a brisker pace now that Iphigénie was on a surface more suited to her footwear. 'It can begin at any time, at any age. Blaise is a boy who likes sports. He's gifted, you've seen for yourself. Bruno and I would rather he had a normal life doing all the things he's good at.'

'And if he dies as a result of this indulgence?'

Elodie shrugged and then, sensing her mother's horrified disapproval, added: 'It's not going to happen. He's on medication.'

Iphigénie had to be content with this. In truth it was not so much concern for Blaise that had prompted her as a general distaste for the tenor of her daughter's life. She did not understand it and consequently felt a profound and fearful hostility towards it. She did not need to look at Elodie to know that her face wore that maddening expression of chieftain-like aloofness. The old woman did not fully appreciate that the reason she found it so maddening was that Elodie had learned it from her.

Bruno, cosy in the rumpled cocoon of the double bed, slept deeply. The Home Service burbled self-sufficiently to deaf ears. In the family bathroom some twenty yards away Celeste's bathwater was growing cooler by the minute, but being fully absorbed in sucking her sponge and arranging Dunkirk flotillas of assorted craft, she didn't notice until it was quite cold. Suddenly goose-pimply but unwilling to get out, she shouted for help.

'Dad-deee! Dad-deeee!' She was a resourceful child. When there was no response she got cautiously to her feet, waded to the end of the tub and turned on the tap. A jet of icy water hit the surface and sprayed her. She shrieked, and turned it off again. The hot tap was stiff, it took both hands to twist the top, but steam rose comfortingly from the ensuing jet. The bath was already quite deep, so it was a little while before the fresh hot water began to take effect. By the time it did the surface was drawing level with the overflow. When the whole was at an acceptable temperature, it was slopping over the edge.

Celeste, sensibly, had remained standing. The large old-fashioned bath, supported by taloned griffin's feet, stood on a shallow patform. The water trickled over the side and then off the edge of this platform in an impressive cascade. Celeste held the edge of the bath and gazed over.

The water was now getting too hot. Still holding the edge, she waded sideways and tried to twist the tap. But it was stiff, and she was unbalanced by the surrounding pressure of the bathwater. She managed to reduce the jet to a gentle stream, but not to turn it off completely.

'Dad-deee!'

All she wanted now was to escape the bath, the tap and the ever-flowing, steaming water. With considerable difficulty she hauled herself on to the edge resting on her stomach, twisted round (getting a mouthful of hot water in the process) and dropped with a bump to the floor. The bathmat was a sodden rag. The tide had reached the door. Her towel and clothes were on top of the Ali Baba basket but the flight mechanism was now fully activated. Celeste opened the door and scampered, dripping, along the corridor to fetch her father.

Chrétien and Lauren were having a continental breakfast in their room at the Charlesworth Hotel, just off Piccadilly. Chrétien was dressed, and lay on the bed in his shirt-sleeves and stockinged feet reading the *Daily Telegraph*. Lauren sat at the dressing-table in her underwear with a pale pink plastic cape tied round her shoulders, doing her face. On the end of the dressing-table nearest the door was the tray with coffee and croissants. Chrétien held his coffee-cup, from which he took an occasional sip. His wife's cup stood half-full at her elbow.

With a businesslike air she pulled her hair back into a pony-tail and snapped an elastic band round it several times. She peered closely at herself in the mirror, thrusting her jaw forward and tilting her face this way and that. She groaned. 'Jeee-sus. I look like Methuselah.'

'You look wonderful and you know it,' said Chrétien, without looking up from the paper.

Lauren began dabbing on foundation. 'Sure, I look wonderful when I'm fully patched and painted. My mother taught me how to make the most of myself, and that's what I do.'

Chrétien turned the page and folded the paper twice with a brisk crackle.

'The hell of it,' continued his wife cheerfully, 'is having to visit your goddam sister who has four kids, five if you include her husband, and doesn't wear a scrap of make-up but still manages to look fantastic.'

Chrétien shrugged. This was not a new conversation. 'She's no beauty. She has unusual looks.'

'Damn right.' Lauren smoothed the foundation down her neck and upwards and sideways into her hairline, and then took eyeshadow and began work on her upper lids. 'Still, I'm looking forward to seeing them all, and the new baby. Their babies are always so adorable.'

'Yes,' said Chrétien, without enthusiasm. 'What a pity they don't stay that way.'

'Hell's bells and buckets of blood!' yelled Bruno, paddling across the bathroom in his socks and turning off the tap. 'Why didn't you call me? Why didn't you fetch me sooner? Celeste? Celeste! Come here when I'm talking to you – Christ, what a shambles. Celeste!'

'Sorry, I sorry!' Celeste, taking her tone from her father, shouted tearfully from where she stood on the landing, still stark naked and shivering with cold. 'Sorry, Daddy, I sorry!'

'Let's just hope we don't have a collapsed ceiling on our hands – that's all we bloody need with those two arriving tomorrow – why didn't you call me, you foolish child? Here—' He scooped up her towel and clothes and flung them through the door. 'Wrap yourself up in something. Go! *Go!*'

Celeste could not wrap herself up. She was used to her mother or Mrs Dove doing such things for her. She wasn't frightened of her father, but she wanted to distance herself as quickly as possible from his noisy complaints and the mess which prompted them. She grabbed at the corner of her towel and ran down the passage and half-way round the gallery to her room. Once inside she climbed into bed, carrying the bundled towel with her, put two fingers and a corner of the towel into her mouth and wished it were an ordinary day so that Mrs Dove was in the house.

Bruno took every towel he could find and laid them in a patchwork over the bathroom floor. He felt put-upon. After a night with scarcely any sleep (he had in fact woken on two occasions, briefly) he had been left in charge of this sinking ship. And tomorrow it would be all systems go to entertain the Parisian contingent. The only comfort to be had from all this was that the old crow would be leaving.

With the towels in place, he closed the door on the damp bathroom and went downstairs to make himself a pot of tea.

Blaise and Fabian had left their bicycles in the yard and were sitting in the bottom of the trench, which they had lined with an old army groundsheet from the attic. They had also salvaged some boughs from Dove's bonfire to make a movable roof. With these in place, the trench was as well camouflaged as a tiger trap. They were taking stock of their purchases with the aid of Blaise's torch. Courtesy of Fabian's payola they had long since outgrown sweets. This was a haul to satisfy sophisticates: a box of Camembert, digestive biscuits, mango chutney, several packets of Smith's potato crisps, a Fuller's chocolate cake, a copy of *Playboy*, and twenty Embassy. Matches and a knife they kept on site, in an old leatherette record case.

Fabian removed the cellophane from the cigarette packet, while Blaise took out the matches, closed the case and laid the torch on top of it. Fabian opened the packet and shot a cigarette expertly in his brother's direction, before helping himself. Blaise struck a match and lit both cigarettes.

They inhaled deeply and with an air of satisfaction. It was no small undertaking to cycle the four miles to the neighbouring town of Baring, where the local newsagents were not to know that the Embassy were not for their mother. All purchases then had to be stowed in their saddle-bags which made the ride home, much of it uphill, even heavier going. But the sense of a foray successfully accomplished added greatly to the pleasure of consumption.

'I got something else as well,' said Fabian, his eyes narrowing as he exhaled.

'What?'

'Guess.'

'No.'

'You couldn't, anyway.'

Fabian pushed his hand into the pocket of his shorts and drew it out slowly, for maximum effect. He grinned, his eyes gleaming in the torchlight. 'Told you you couldn't!'

Blaise, removing a piece of tobacco from his tongue, betrayed no surprise.

'Okay. Where did you get it?'

'Wouldn't you like to know?'

'Not particularly.' Blaise leaned back against the side of the trench, flicking ash off his cigarette as he did so. Fabian wasn't fooled. He held the whip hand in this exchange. 'I have my methods,' he said, selecting a packet of crisps as though that closed the matter.

Blaise eyed him thoughtfully. 'You mean you stole it.'

'M Y O B.'

Blaise nodded, weary of being always right. 'You stole it.'

Fabian placed the miniature of Gordon's on the groundsheet between them, and took from his crisp packet the twist of blue paper containing salt. 'Bugger, why is this salt always stuck together?'

'Where from?' asked Blaise.

'That drink place on the corner.'

'It's called an off-licence,' said Blaise.

'Who cares? They have all these little bottles on the counter by the till. The bloke was at the back of the shop and I just walked in and helped myself. It was easy as anything. He didn't even know I'd been in.'

'You hope.'

'He didn't! I could do it any time. Honestly.'

'You mean dishonestly.'

'Ha, ha, ha! You're just fed up it wasn't you.' Fabian glanced slyly at Blaise, and nudged the bottle with his foot. 'Try some.'

'No thanks.'

'Go on.'

'I said no thanks,' repeated Blaise with some warmth, adding, 'I don't much like alcohol.'

'Well, bloody hard cheddar, because I do!' retorted Fabian. He unscrewed the bottle and took two large gulps. 'Crikey—' Blaise smiled as his brother's voice cracked and his eyes streamed. 'That's what I call a drink!'

Elodie and her mother walked back over the Craft, carrying their shopping. It wasn't all that much – otherwise, as Elodie had explained to the rebellious Iphigénie, they would have taken the car – but it was enough to make the prospect of a cup of coffee by the Aga an inviting one.

'Are you all right?' asked Elodie, glancing pointedly at the black suede court shoes.

'Of course!' snapped Iphigénie. 'I am not infirm, you know.'

'Certainly not,' said Elodie. 'You are an example to us all, Mother.'

When they got back to Hartfield, any vestigial misgivings Iphigénie might have had about returning to Paris evaporated instantly. Sandro was awake and yelling in his pram, with one of the yard cats hammocked comfortably on the protective net. Bruno, still in his pyjamas, was in the library talking on the telephone. In the kitchen the kettle he had placed on the Aga was boiled dry and white-hot, filling the kitchen with sulphurous fumes. In the drawing-room there was water dripping from the overhead light fitting. Upstairs, the bathroom, carpeted with the contents of the linen cupboard, was saturated and smelt like a dungeon. Celeste was asleep in bed, naked but for a damp towel.

Iphigénie retired to her bedroom. She went to the long window overlooking the side lawn and tennis court and stood there, very straight, her hands at her sides, the tips of her long fingers, trembling slightly, resting on the sill. Raised voices floated up the stairs, the insistent scratch of the baby's crying, the stench of the burned kettle . . . Iphigénie drew a deep breath.

Blaise and Fabian emerged from the trees behind the tennis court and began walking across the lawn towards the house. For once, reflected their grandmother, they appeared to have nothing to do with the uproar in the house. With a sudden rush of tender feeling she rehearsed what she would say about them to her friend, Sylvie Everard, when she returned to Paris: 'Such handsome boys, full of mischief, but highly intelligent . . . and with the grounds that Elodie has, they are out of doors all day long, on their bicycles or climbing trees . . . a perfect life for boys of their age . . .'

When Blaise glanced up she caught his eye and, with a smile that was almost benign, raised one hand to wave. Blaise, charming as ever, blew her a kiss. Fabian stopped, leaned over, and was explosively sick, a shower of liquid vomit spattering on to the lawn and all over his plimsolls.

CHAPTER FOUR

By the time Blaise was eleven, his father's views on state education had altered. He had grown disenchanted with what he termed the 'petticoat politics' of the local school, where female teachers predominated. Even Archie Featherstone was referred to as 'that old woman', and the others as 'the woof-woofs', a reference to their lack of feminine allure.

'Just look at that crew,' he said in a stage whisper to Elodie, when they had taken their seats for the Leavers' Assembly in July 1961. 'You see women like that, and it makes you sympathise with cultures who think females are unclean.'

'That's not fair, Bruno,' said Elodie.

'You're right. It's pitiful that fellow human beings have to labour under such crushing natural disadvantages—'

'Keep your voice down!'

'—but why have they all congregated here, like infections round a wound?'

'Ssh, they're about to start.'

Bruno lowered the whisper a fraction and put his lips to Elodie's ear: 'I swear I can smell their underclothes!'

Archie rose to his feet and the Leavers' Assembly got under way. It was a homely affair as such things went. Arrayed before the eighty or so parents were Archie, his staff (the woof-woofs in their best bibs and tuckers), and a sprinkling of governors, including the butcher, the pharmacist and the Rector, the Reverend Tom Wheeler.

As Archie began to speak of an occasion of hope and

50

optimism, tinged with a little sadness but no regret, Bruno leaned sideways again. 'I see our esteemed sky pilot has elected to wear mufti.' Elodie did not react. Her eyes were fixed on Archie with an expression of calm interest. 'Anyone would think,' went on Bruno undeterred, 'that he was ashamed of his calling.'

It was a fact that whatever Tom Wheeler had worn would not have met with Bruno's approval. He had a hearty dislike of clergymen, all of whom he regarded as sanctimonious free-loaders with an eye to the main chance. This being the case he preferred them in their place, chanting fully robed at the high altar rather than running about in collars and ties trying to infiltrate normal society.

Archie was now announcing that part of the occasion when the school would entertain their guests. A ripple of indulgent anticipation went round the hall. Bruno gave a groan, but converted it into a cough for Elodie's benefit. He found such entertainment tedious and cringe-making. It was not in him to make allowances for youth or unevenness of ability. At the last Christmas service and Nativity which Elodie had forced him to attend, he had sat dry-eyed amongst the dabbing handkerchiefs and muttered: 'When you compare this with that show we saw in town it makes you want to weep!' The show in question was *West Side Story*, but Bruno saw nothing odious, nor even unreasonable, in the comparison. The air of kindly, democratic effort with which the woof-woofs surrounded such productions was another reason for Blaise's imminent departure as a boarder to public school.

A band came on, consisting mainly of recorders and percuss-ion, with a couple of guitars and an elderly woof-woof at the piano. They were followed by the choir – those older children able to hold a tune but not sufficiently musical to qualify for the band – and then Blaise, carrying a cardboard folder covered with orange and green striped Fablon. He took up a seat to one side of the band. Elodie stretched her neck a little to take a better look at him. Archie announced a short programme of music and poetry (the latter written by one of the pupils, Blaise Gallagher) on the theme of Endings and Beginnings.

Bruno folded his arms and glanced challengingly about him. 'At least there'll be something worth listening to.'

'Sssh . . .'

As the musicians struck up with 'Lord, dismiss us with thy blessing', he hissed: 'Where's the Antichrist?'

For the first time Elodie turned a thoroughly disapproving look on him. 'He's not here – this is only for the leavers. Will you be quiet?'

'They can't all be leaving, they're runts—'

'They are performing!'

'Could've fooled me,' responded Bruno grimly. He sank his chin on his chest. As so often when he had fallen out with his wife, his thoughts turned to Mrs Dove. If Elodie was a racing car, then Evadne was a comfortable family saloon, reliable and accommodating. She was never critical. She liked and respected him. She was a man's woman.

His humour restored, Bruno touched the back of Elodie's hand with one finger. She did not react.

Elodie, though apparently giving her full attention to band and choir, was also thinking about Mrs Dove, whose responsibility it was this afternoon to take Celeste and Sandro to a birthday party. Sandro, at two, was a little young but the mother of the three-year-old in question had been pressing, and had suggested that Celeste attend as well to provide a steadying influence. Celeste had not objected, especially since Elodie had taken her to Baring and bought her a blue organdie party dress with a smocked bodice, puffed sleeves and a white piqué collar, and patent leather Mary Janes which caught the light and gleamed against her sparkling new white socks. Mrs Dove was to drive them to the party, and ring up an hour later to check that all was well. Elodie and Bruno would collect them at five.

Elodie had perfect faith in Mrs Dove, but could not help being a little worried about Sandro. There was no comparison between him and the two older boys. They seemed to have sprung fully armed from the womb, and to have become independent of her with alarming speed. Sandro's sweet, gentle, babyish ways were a delight, but not calculated to provide a buffer in the hurly-burly of a birthday party. Elodie glanced at her watch: three o'clock, the time on the invitation.

Bruno caught her checking the time and smiled bleakly to himself. His sentiments exactly.

'Bye-bye then, have a lovely time!'

Celeste, holding Sandro's hand, waved back at Mrs Dove as the front door closed behind her. Her eyes filled with tears. She could still smell Mrs Dove's scent on her dress, from when she had hugged her, and she'd known by the look in her eyes that she understood exactly how she felt. In a large room off the hall there was the noise of the party – music, shrieks, the occasional bang. Celeste felt her brother stiffen. Celeste sniffed, and prepared to be a tower of strength. The host's mother crouched down in front of them.

'Sandro, aren't you a big boy – is this your first birthday party?'

Sandro nodded, and glanced up at Celeste for her endorsement. His eyes were huge and dark, shining with trepidation below his heavy fringe.

'Yes, it is,' said Celeste.

'Well, we're honoured!' said the host's mother. She took Sandro's free hand in both hers, which were smooth and tanned with glossy, pointed red nails. 'And that is such a smart outfit, did your clever mummy buy that in France?' The woman beamed enquiringly at Sandro, who remained mute, so she redirected the beam at Celeste, who lifted her shoulders and let them drop heavily.

'I don't know.'

'Well, it's absolutely super.'

Celeste, feeling she had fallen somewhat short of expectation with her last answer, added: 'Those are real braces.'

'Yes, I can see that.' Mrs Palmer plucked at them with a nail. 'And look at your shoes, Sandro!' Both children did so. 'Proper lace-ups, and tassels on the laces. Who did those up for you? Your big sister?'

Sandro shook his head. 'No,' said Celeste. 'I'm too slow. Mrs Dove did.'

'Good for Mrs Dove,' said Mrs Palmer, standing up to indicate that pleasantries were at an end. 'Shall we go and see what everyone's playing in here?'

She opened the door into the living-room. The Palmers' house was new, and modern and pale. At one end of the long room french windows stood open on to a large patio where the party tea had been laid out on a trestle, and covered with cloths. Beyond the table an expanse of intensively-tended lawn, as smooth and level as a billiard table, stretched away to a distant fence.

In here the noise was deafening. There were a dozen children present and Mrs Palmer's Spanish au pair, Inez, was supervising musical bumps. Inez was not leadership material, and anyway was labouring under the double disadvantage of hay fever and the language barrier. Things were out of hand. Inez sat by the record player removing the needle from time to time while the children rushed about, screaming and bursting balloons, the boys skirmishing and knocking the girls off their feet when the chance arose.

Mrs Palmer crouched again. 'We're just playing some games with music before tea,' she explained, voice raised against the din. 'Afterwards you can all rush about and enjoy yourselves out of doors!' She sailed away from them to give instructions to Inez.

Sandro tugged on Celeste's hand. 'Lester – no. No, Lester . . .'

Celeste gazed down at him. Tears brimmed in his big faun's eyes. But there was no gainsaying the exuberant Mrs Palmer, who was now handing a large tin of Quality Street to Inez.

' . . . if everyone sits quietly on the floor, everyone will get a prize! No, there wasn't a winner, everyone's a winner!'

The children collapsed, still shrieking and chattering, on to the carpet. With an incisive, practised movement like a well-trained sheepdog, Mrs Palmer extracted her son and escorted him over to Celeste and Sandro.

'James, here's Sandro – remember you had lunch at his house?'

James, red-faced and perspiring, stared blankly. 'It was disgusting. We had stew with beans.'

'Couscous,' corrected Mrs Palmer, 'And this is Sandro's big sister, Celeste, she's going to help me and Inez, aren't you?'

Celeste held out the parcel. 'Happy Birthday.'

'Oh I say!' exclaimed Mrs Palmer. 'Say thank you.'

'Thank you.'

It was a book. A wonderful book about mythical beasts, with full-page illustrations by an artist of note. But James, having ripped off a corner of the paper and seen what it was, cast it down absent-mindedly and headed back to the fray.

'Come on, troops!' called Mrs Palmer. 'Tea!'

She shepherded the party-goers out on to the patio. Despondently, Inez switched off the record player and helped herself to a Quality Street. When she saw Celeste and Sandro she came over and handed them, silent and unsmiling, a sweet each.

Sandro clutched his, unopened, in his fist, but Celeste unwrapped hers and popped it into her mouth. Eating was common ground, you did it at home too. Unlike Sandro, she was not a shy or timid child. Indeed she was noted for her composure. Like her mother before her she had learned that an appearance of calm was a good deflector of unwelcome attention. But she was also sensitive to atmosphere – and knew when she was out of place.

She and Sandro were out of place here. The Palmer establishment was in every particular the polar opposite of Hartfield. It was not just its modernity and extreme, clinical brightness. It was the extent to which every item in it, from the bland catch-all framed prints to the nubby, chubby cream sofas, had been selected and positioned exactly, its effect calculated to the nth degree. The orderliness of the living-room, even at this stage of a child's birthday party, was terrifying, and even the most cursory glance around while waiting in the hall left Celeste in no doubt that every other room was the same. It was a house without darkness, without secrets – without texture.

Celeste was far too young to put all this into words, but she knew how it made her feel – as if she were rolling around, unsteady and exposed, like a pea on a polished plate. The garden was a little better, if only because it was out of doors, and she felt that had any of the trees been suitable she might have climbed one, and been able to see the gables of home rising from the trees beyond the Craft.

Mrs Palmer held Sandro by the shoulders and steered him to a slatted plastic chair opposite a plate with his name on. Celeste was about to sit down next to him but was caught in a pincer movement between a fat boy who told her to get out of his place, and her hostess, sho said confidingly: 'I think you're too grown up to sit here, Celeste. Why don't you help Inez keep an eye on these little ones, you can help yourself to what you want. I'm just going to the kitchen to get myself a cup of tea. Inez, would you like one?'

Inez shook her head stolidly. She and Celeste exchanged a look of unforced mutual understanding. They knew their place.

Sandro did not relish the idea of sitting at the tea-table without his sister's reassuring presence. Celeste found herself passing paper plates and picking up rubbish with her brother in close attendance. In spite of his repeated assertion that he was 'helping Lester', he was more of a hindrance than anything, and his constantly questing hands left gobs of egg and chocolate all over the blue organdie. Mrs Palmer did not reappear for some time. Celeste caught sight of her through one of the windows: she was standing by the wall in the huge white kitchen, talking on the telephone and sipping a tumblerful of clear, fizzy liquid. When she spotted Celeste she gave a big exaggerated grin with popping eyes, and wiggled the fingers that held her glass. Celeste grabbed Sandro's hand and fled back to Inez, feeling like a spy.

It didn't take very long for most of the food on the table to be either wrecked or demolished, and the guests began once more to turn ugly. Inez pressed her hands to her cheeks and murmured 'Ay-ay-ay' as chairs crashed back and scuffles broke out. Celeste led Sandro back into the living-room, found the discarded birthday book and sat down on one of the cream sofas to show him the pictures. But Mrs Palmer, fortified by her G and T, returned to the fray bearing aloft a cake shaped like a steam engine and filled with Smarties. The Gallagher children were prised out and obliged to join the others in singing 'Happy Birthday' and encouraging James to blow out his candles.

Nobody wanted to eat a slice of cake there and then, so Mrs Palmer announced that they could all run around on the grass and let off steam while she and 'the big girls' – meaning Inez and Celeste – wrapped up slices in paper napkins to take home. Seeing that Sandro was going nowhere Mrs Palmer swept him up in her arms, bore him to the sandpit at the corner of the lawn nearest the kitchen window and plumped him down with cries of 'There! Call that nothing!' Celeste didn't interfere, but it was no surprise when Sandro returned, grains of sand clinging to his wet cheeks and snotty upper lip, crying bitterly and demanding to stay with Lester.

'He's a clingy little chap, isn't he?' said Mrs Palmer threateningly as Celeste allowed the grit to be wiped off on her dress. 'Still, there's only so much one can do. If he won't, he won't.' With this she swept off to impose 'The Farmer's in His Den' on her unruly guests, summoning Inez to accompany her. She seemed to have lost interest in Celeste and Sandro. They returned to the book.

Blaise held the folder balanced on his spread hand, but he did not look at it. His head was high, and his eyes – a dark brown flecked with violet, as Elodie had often remarked in wonder – were fixed on some point above and beyond his audience, a point that only he could see. His voice had resonance and purity: a thrilling voice, as several of those listening said later. Even Bruno, head still bowed, gave a series of rapid, snapping blinks to show anyone looking his way that he was paying attention to this part at least.

Blaise spoke his own words. Both content and construction were beyond reproach. His audience might not in the main have been intellectuals, but they knew what they liked. Many faces

57

wore introspective smiles, others contemplative frowns. All were rapt. The piece was a poem, entitled 'Hereafter'. It built to a hair-stirring climax.

> *'And do not say, when I am gone,*
> *That all is lost and all forlorn,*
> *But look each unto each and say,*
> *Another dawn, another day!'*

When Blaise finished speaking there was a moment of complete silence during which he remained in position, cheeks flushed, lips parted, eyes fixed on his inner vision, folder open on his hand. Then it was as if he recalled himself to the here and now and closing the folder and running one hand through his hair, he sat down, grave and modest in the face of loud applause.

'He was superb,' said Elodie, agreeing with at least two other parents who leaned towards her to offer congratulations. 'Superb.' She tapped her husband's thigh with the back of her hand. 'What do you think of that, grumpy?'

'Eh?' Bruno feigned waking up with a start. 'Did I miss something?'

'Darling!' Elodie laughed, turning towards the others to show that he was joking. 'Take no notice of him!'

In truth, as the Rector stepped forward to hand out certificates for swimming, art, tidiness and road safety, Bruno found himself quite perturbed. He glanced covertly at the boy who had for the space of a few minutes entranced and then galvanised this cloddish parochial audience. Who was he? What went on? And how had he, Bruno Gallagher, spawned such a creature?

He rubbed his face and groaned aloud. It was beyond him.

'You must have been very proud,' said Archie Featherstone, over cups of tea served by the leavers in the carpeted area.

'I was, very,' said Elodie. Archie glanced at Bruno.

'He likes to strut and fret,' conceded Bruno.

Elodie lifted her shoulders, opened one hand slightly. 'It

runs in the family, you see . . .'

Archie was charmed. And being charmed, emboldened. 'You know Blaise is not the only Gallagher with talent.'

'Oh Christ,' muttered Bruno, through egg sandwich, 'what's the bugger been up to now? A spot of prefrontal labotomy on the nit nurse?'

'Fabian? Ha, ha, ha!' Archie threw his head back and gave a noisy imitation laugh. 'No, no! He's a reformed character.'

Elodie's expression remained placid and unreadable. Bruno was quick to respond. 'I should damn well think so!'

'Whatever measures you took worked like a charm. There's no doubt that nine times out of ten, in the end, parental influence works wonders.'

'Yes. Well.'

'So tell us, Mr Featherstone,' said Elodie swiftly, 'what talent is Fabian displaying?'

In reply Archie put his cup down on a nearby table, relieved them of theirs, and crooked a finger. 'Come.'

As they left the area Blaise appeared. 'Please can I go home now?'

Archie beamed. 'Of course you can, Blaise. And very well done. Your mum and dad are basking in reflected glory.'

Elodie drew her son's head forward and kissed him on the brow. 'You were wonderful.'

'Thanks. Bye.'

Bruno, still wincing from being referred to as 'dad', grimaced.

Archie led them into a classroom and over to the far wall, where assorted artwork had been pinned up. In characteristically democratic style, the paintings so displayed encompassed a wide variety of talents and abilities.

'The brief,' explained Archie, 'was My Dreams.'

'You must be mad,' said Bruno.

'Some of them are very good,' commented Elodie.

Archie nodded. 'They are indeed.'

There was little doubt which two were the most striking. One was a bold impressionistic daub depicting a tunnel of hot colours in which disturbing dark shapes swirled like creatures being sucked into a vortex. The distant end of the tunnel was marked by an eye, yellow and green and veined with red.

Bruno tapped the paper with his finger. 'This bloke has experienced his first hangover.'

Archie bridled. 'Really? You think so?'

'He's got it to a T.'

'That's Fabian's.'

Bruno did not break stride. 'So I was right.'

'And this,' exclaimed Elodie, 'this is remarkable. Who did this?'

The painting she was examining was a carefully-executed representation of a fair-haired woman in flowing white clothes, with wings. The woman was chocolate-box pretty with golden hair, rose pink skin and an hour-glass figure. Her lashes, demurely lowered, lay in long curves on her cheeks. The background was dappled blue and green. But in spite of the saccharine subject matter and its greeting card execution there was a sly sense of irony which made the picture unsettling.

'That's disgusting,' said Bruno.

Elodie shook her head. 'I think it's enchanting.'

'It's also by Fabian,' said Archie triumphantly.

Bruno stared crossly at the painting. 'I must say I find that hard to credit. It's revolting. Twee, banal, cloying. Vulgar.'

'Well done, though,' pointed out Archie.

'That's not enough.'

Elodie brought her face closer to the paper. 'I wonder what it's meant to be.'

'Interesting you should ask that,' said Archie. 'When I asked him what it was called, he told me "The Dove". So there you are. He's not the hard case he'd like us to think.'

'Oh!' cried Elodie, 'what lovely pottery! Did the children make this too?'

Sandro had gone to sleep on the sofa and Celeste had removed his shoes. When the doorbell rang to announce the arrival of parents, it was Celeste who answered, and directed them through the living-room to the garden.

The hall soon filled up with departing children clutching

balloons and take-home bags. Mrs Palmer was now all indulgent smiles, her red-tipped hands casually caressing tousled heads as they milled about, her voice warm and chuckly as she spoke of high spirits but a good time had by all. James, tired of the social niceties, came into the living-room, switched on the TV and watched 'Whirlybirds'.

The Gallaghers did not have television. The noisy processed sound of the programme woke Sandro and he slipped off the sofa and went to sit by James, carefully copying his host's crossed legs, his chin resting on his fists. It was the first time he had voluntarily left Celeste's side all afternoon. She returned to the book. She could already read a little and without her brother clamouring for the pictures was able to proceed at her own pace.

The Gallaghers were last to arrive. The party's official ending time was five, but it was almost quarter to six before they got there. Inez was set to clearing up. Mrs Palmer gave a little token assistance and then appeared in the hall doorway of the living-room holding another gin and tonic.

'Everyone all right? All right, Celeste? I'm sure mummy and daddy will be here soon.'

'I'm all right,' Celeste assured her.

Shortly after that Mr Palmer got home and following a muted exchange with his wife in the hall put his head round the door. 'Hallo, you party people – exhausted by all that merrymaking?' He strode across and ruffled James's hair., 'How you doing, birthday boy? Plenty of loot? Good time had by all?'

James did not reply, but Mr Palmer was not put out. Like Bruno he was fondest of his family when they were leaving him in peace. But that was where the resemblance ended. Where Bruno was idle, scruffy, and disorganised, Mr Palmer was industrious, opportunistic and smart. His outline, with smoothly barbered hair and natty lightweight suit, was so aerodynamically crisp that he seemed hardly to displace the atmosphere of the room.

Leaving, he said: 'What's this, beautiful young ladies lolling on my settee, can't be bad . . . ' but the remark did not seem to require a reply, so Celeste took a leaf from James's book and ignored it.

The Palmers went into the kitchen and there were sounds of glasses, and the fridge, and ice and a tap running. A burst of laughter and Mrs Palmer's voice, ' . . . definitely having an entertainer!'

Inez came in and sat down near Celeste. 'May I see your book?'

'It's not mine.'

'May I look with you?'

Celeste didn't really want to, but she was polite and sensed that Inez, in a passive way, had been her friend all afternoon, so she shunted along and turned the pages helpfully as Inez stared at the Minotaur, the Gorgon, the Loch Ness Monster and others with murmurs of 'Ay-ay-ay'.

This was how Elodie found them. Bruno had remained outside in the car with the engine running.

'Don't worry in the least!' cried Mrs Palmer. 'In fact, they're quite happy. Why don't you and Bruno stay for a moment and have a drink?'

'Yes, do. That would be nice,' agreed Mr Palmer.

Celeste, watching from the sofa, saw him give her mother the strange look which people, especially men, often bestowed on her. She prayed that the Palmers' invitation would be refused, and her prayers were answered.

'No, we mustn't,' said Elodie. 'You've entertained our children for long enough and we must get home and make sure the boys aren't up to anything.'

'Fat chance!' said Mr Palmer, meaning only to be facetious and missing his wife's warning look.

Celeste needed no second bidding. She helped Sandro with his shoes and hauled him, complaining bitterly, from in front of the TV and into the hall.

'He doesn't want to go. Don't you want to go home?' asked Mr Palmer, bending over and breathing gin into Sandro's face. Sandro shook his head.

Mrs Palmer pressed take-home bags on them. Sandro wouldn't take his, so Celeste held it.

'Thank you so very much. They've obviously had a marvellous time.'

'No trouble.' Mrs Palmer patted Elodie's arm. 'They've been good as gold.'

'Come along then,' said Elodie. She shook Sandro's hand and looked down at Celeste. 'Celeste – what do you say?'

'Thank you for having me,' said Celeste.

Back at home, Sandro was put straight into the bath. Celeste was divested of the blue organdie and put back into her usual summer uniform of cotton shorts, Aertex shirt and plimsolls. The Aertex shirts were her brothers' cast-offs, gone soft and almost colourless with use.

While Elodie bathed Sandro, Bruno sat in a basket chair by the library window. He held a newspaper, but his eyes weren't following the print.

Celeste didn't disturb him. She wanted to be on her own. She kept a look-out for Blaise and Fabian, but only because she wished to avoid them. Their smiling faces looking down at her, and their hands holding hers, meant only one thing: secrets. She'd had to keep so many in her young life that the maintaining of a discreet silence had become a habit. She very seldom volunteered information, and if asked directly about some sensitive matter either ignored the question or said she didn't know. There had even been a time about a year ago, when Mrs Dove had told Elodie she thought Celeste might have hearing difficulties, and there had been visits to the doctor which had only proved the opposite.

Celeste went round the house and across the courtyard. From an open window she could hear the Doves' television announcing the news. There was a faint smell of frying. Celeste had eaten almost nothing at the party, and was hungry. One thing the big boys could generally provide was food; they kept a stock of it, regularly replenished.

'Hallo, sweetheart!'

Celeste looked up. It was Mrs Dove, leaning out of her kitchen window. She wore a red gingham-patterned apron over the white blouse which had smelled so nice earlier. She grinned and opened and closed both hands at ear-height, like glove puppets.

'How was the party, then? I gave a ring and Mrs Palmer said you were being the life and soul.'

Celeste wasn't sure what this meant, but it sounded like a compliment. 'It was okay.'

'Only okay?' Celeste nodded. 'Aah . . . Fancy an apple fritter?' Celeste nodded again, more vigorously. 'Come on, then, door's open.'

By the time Celeste had climbed the stairs the fritters – three of them – were in a bowl on Mrs Dove's yellow formica kitchen table, with a spoon and fork alongside and a thick sprinkling of caster sugar.

'We've had ours,' said Mrs Dove, removing her apron and hanging it on a hook on the back of the door. 'I was just washing up.' She sat down by Celeste and watched her eat, with evident pleasure.

The sound of the television was switched off and Dove came in. 'Eating fritters?' he said in his rhetorical way.

'Yes,' replied Celeste.

'That's the style,' said Dove. He addressed his wife. 'I'm popping out for a bit.'

'Rightie-ho. Have one for me.'

'Eating all my fritters . . . ' muttered Dove by way of a lighthearted farewell.

Mrs Dove lit up a cigarette and talked to Celeste about nail-care problems. When Celeste had finished eating, she said: 'I'd offer you some more, only that's it.'

'Thank you.'

'Does your mum know you're up here?'

'No.'

'You'd better run along. And if you can't eat your dinner, blame me!' Mrs Dove gave a peal of cheerful laughter.

'Can I go to the loo?'

'Course you can, darling, help yourself. You know where it is.'

Celeste went along the passage to the bathroom. This gave her an opportunity to glance in at the other rooms. First was the lounge (it was okay to call it that), where she quite often went, to eat Nuttall's Mintoes and listen to Mrs Dove's Russ

Conway LPs. She liked it there, surrounded by what Mrs Dove called her 'nice things'. These things had acquired a special importance for Celeste because of the value Mrs Dove placed upon them. These were not the large, vague accumulations of stuff that the Gallaghers had – hundreds of books and jungles of plants, and constellations of strange pictures – but particular items of whose origin, provenance and cost Mrs Dove could give precise details.

'See this little fellow?' she'd say, of a china boy in a cap and cutaway jacket like Oliver Twist. 'See him? I love him. I saw him in a shop in Portsmouth when we were driving back from Christmas with Ed and Madge, and the minute I saw him I fell for him. He was quite pricey – five pound odd – but these pieces are very collectable these days. Not that I'd ever let him go. He's my best boy. Aren't you?' And she would kiss the china boy, and then polish him lovingly on her sleeve, or her skirt, while Celeste watched, entranced. She hoped that one day she would have a room like this – neat and cosy – where all her possessions could be touched and handled as Mrs Dove handled hers.

Next came the bedroom – she'd never been in there, but it always looked the same, the bed sculpturally smooth beneath rose-pink candlewick and Mrs Dove's feather-trimmed mules by the bedside table.

The bathroom was at the end of the passage. You went up two steps to it, and inside everything was there, all matching, bath, basin, loo and tiles all in a colour Mrs Dove referred to as 'pinky-beige'. The floor was spongey white tiles, and there were bath and pedestal mats that looked to Celeste as if they were made of chopped string. The Doves had recently had the bathroom freshly fitted out. Celeste approved of everything. At the end of the bath was a shelf positively groaning with bubble bath and bath salts and body lotion and talcum, and the rack across the bath carried not just two face flannels but a long brush, and a loofah and a sponge.

Celeste pushed down her shorts and pants and sat on the lavatory, where the water was always scented and blue. It was when she'd finished, and was just about to press the handle on the cistern, that she heard something. It was a mere snippet of sound: the tail end of a laugh.

She froze, and withdrew her hand. Distantly at the other end of the passage she could hear Mrs Dove singing as she ran a tap and clinked crockery. But in here there was an unnaturally deep silence which Celeste was afraid to break. She rolled her eyes to scan the room without moving her head. It was the last thing she saw: the little ventilation grille high in the corner above the loo. The moment she saw it, she smelt something too – faint, but unmistakable – cigarette smoke, shockingly noticeable in the dainty atmosphere of Mrs Dove's bathroom.

Stealthily, fearfully, Celeste withdrew, walking backwards, feeling for the door and slipping through, pulling it shut behind her.

And as she scampered back along the corridor to the kitchen she felt the slither and hiss of secrets, following her.

CHAPTER FIVE

'Of all the requests, from all the men, in all the joints in town!' Lauren laughed out loud in disbelief.

'I don't know why you should find it so extraordinary,' said Bruno, nettled. 'It's standard practice.'

She wiped away an imaginary tear. 'For some, yes. But I never thought I'd see the day . . .'

'It has nothing to do with us. It's what Blaise wants.'

'Of course.' Lauren composed herself. 'The dear, sweet boy.'

Bruno turned his head away, breathing hard. 'Spare me.' When he faced front again his expression was menacingly polite. 'Look, can we just be businesslike? Are you or are you not prepared to be my son's godmother?'

'I am. I'm honoured!' Lauren bit on her napkin and shook her head in apology.

Bruno saw nothing amusing in any of this. It had to be gone through. In order to expedite the matter he had brought Lauren to the dignified and expensive Boulestin where she had not stinted herself on either food or wine. He had held back the reason for his invitation until after she had finished her syllabub and ratafias. He rather liked the idea that the restaurant's other lunchtime patrons were glancing at the two of them and wondering what their relationship was. Her typically unfettered laughter might be misconstrued by the onlookers, especially as he found himself unable to join in.

'Hey—' she reached over and touched his hand. 'I'm sorry. Really.'

Bruno replied as though he hadn't heard her apology. 'It's

quite simple. If Blaise wants to go through with this, he needs godparents.' He raised his hands, open-palmed. 'It's as incomprehensible to me as it is to you.'

Lauren placed her crumpled napkin on the table and rested her chin on her linked fingers, prepared to be serious. 'You're wrong about that.'

'What?'

'It's not incomprehensible to me. I had religion badly at his age. It's very common.'

'Not in my family.'

'But Bruno,' Lauren shook her head fondly, 'that's why, don't you see? It's a reaction, a kind of rebellion. Good luck to him, I say. What's more, he's had the guts to come right out with it and ask to be baptised. Most kids his age would be content to moon about in corners with a Bible and a crucifix.'

Bruno swished the last of his brandy round his glass, looking gloomy. 'I should never have sent him to that poncey school.'

'Why ever not? He loves it there.'

'Exactly.'

'So you want him to be miserable?'

'Don't be ridiculous.'

'I just don't know what you're trying to say. Relax, Bruno. Lots of fathers would be thrilled to pieces over something like this.'

'I am not "lots of fathers".'

'Tell me about it.'

'Then stop treating me as though I were! You know my views on all this hog manure that's served up in the name of religion. You can hardly expect me to be skipping like a calf neath the cedars of Lebanon when my first-born falls for it.'

'May I have some more coffee please?'

Bruno ordered it, and another brandy for himself. He sighed heavily. 'Anyway, he must be indulged. But I didn't want to be raking around among my acquaintances for people with suitably pious backgrounds. It's too bloody embarrassing. So I thought if you and Chrétien would do the honours, it could be kept civilised and in the family.'

'I'm not sure your criteria are quite what the prayer book intended.'

'What does it matter? I'm only concerned to satisfy the head count.'

'You may be, but the priest may want to vet the godparents. I thought you needed *two* godfathers.'

'Too bad.'

'It will be, for Blaise, if you choose people who haven't been baptised at all. I understand the C of E's quite tolerant. They'll let Roman Catholics be godparents, but not complete heathens.'

Bruno looked alarmed. 'And what are you?'

The waiter came and Lauren sat back to allow him to refill her cup and replace Bruno's brandy. When he'd gone, she smiled. 'My mother saw I had the best of everything. I got baptised.'

'What about Chrétien?' Lauren made a face indicating that it was a silly question. 'Thank God!'

'You've got a nerve thanking Him, when you've spent your whole adult life saying He's a discredited entity.'

'So you'll do it.'

'Sure, why not. I can't speak for Chrétien.'

'You and I both know that where you go, he willingly follows.'

'I know no such thing,' said Lauren. 'I'll mention it when I get back, but you must ask him properly, yourself.'

When they'd finished and stood up to go, Bruno made an uncharacteristic fuss over taking her coat of red bouclé wool from the waiter and helping her on with it himself. He hoped the remaining lunchers – predominantly men – were still watching. Lauren was the all-American smart woman, bright and confident (she was now a rising star on the creative staff of Grix), her natural exuberance nicely modulated by Paris chic. Any man looking on would admire her, thought Bruno, would wonder how Bruno had got her, how he managed her, what the secret was. Bruno pictured himself saying, 'Oh, just my son's godmother. . .'

He kept his hand under her elbow as they crossed the dining-room and ascended the stairs.

Outside it was cold and wet. Lauren pulled on a pair of black leather gloves and turned up the big collar of her coat so that it framed her silvery blonde head. 'That was a very nice lunch. Delicious.' She put her hands on his shoulders and kissed his cheek. 'Thank you, Bruno.'

'Thank *you*.'

'Bye, now.'

'I don't suppose you've got an hour or two to kill?'

She gave him a look that both rebuked and encouraged him. 'I'm on a tight schedule when I'm over here these days. I have to go see some baby food manufacturers to discuss ideas.'

'Let me come,' suggested Bruno. 'I've always had a yen to be in advertising. I bet I'd be good at it.'

'You think so?' She raised her eyebrows. 'Baby food?'

She kissed his cheek and walked away. Just before she turned into Floral Street she did a little soft-shoe shuffle, her briefcase held out before her like a top hat. She was telling him how crazy it all was, but that she was part of it. Bruno grinned. She was a great girl.

In the taxi on the way to his publisher's office in Kensington High Street Bruno was in good spirits. He gazed out of the window as the cab crawled round Trafalgar Square towards St James's, part of the outer rim of the slowly-turning wheel of traffic of which Nelson's Column was the hub. He was far enough along with his latest book to ensure that the meeting with Maurice Repton (one of the redoutable old giants of British publishing) was not fretted with any awkward enquiries about its potential delivery date. He had enjoyed an excellent lunch with a glamorous woman of whom he cherished high hopes. And at this precise moment, with the rain spattering on the taxi windows and London just beginning to light up in the late afternoon gloom, he was untraceable: free as a bird.

Elodie did not feel free, though she thought perhaps she should have done. This autumn she had more time to herself. Sandro had begun morning school, and Blaise and Fabian were away during term time. Acquaintances in the village said how strange this must feel, and she suspected they were watching to see how she would make use of all this time. The truth was, she had no idea. Her life was her family – Bruno and the children. It did not even extend to any great interest in the house. She loved Hartfield, it was her setting, the place where she felt at home, but Mrs Dove kept it clean and Dove tended the garden, so there wasn't much for her to do.

She noticed, suddenly, her lack of friends. This observation was without self-pity. She didn't feel the need of them. She and Bruno were not part of the Stoke Broughton social circuit. They were happy to accommodate part of the summer arts festival in their garden, and to let the school and the Cubs and Brownies have occasional use of the tennis court. When parents called for their offspring Elodie would offer them drinks or coffee, but Bruno had resisted returning invitations to dinner or cocktail parties: the social effort involved was simply too great. So in the end the village people had given up on them.

Now, with unaccustomed spaces in her day, Elodie realised that she had no handy network of local contacts to fall back on. She did not especially want one, but the lack of it surprised her, made her look at herself in a new way. Was she so different? So unusual? What did other women do with their time, and did they really enjoy whatever it was they did? She came to the conclusion that she had a great capacity for idleness. She could sit and dream, or read, for hours, untroubled by conscience or the need to be busy. With four children in the house this capacity had been something of an asset. It gave her a serene availability. She was always a lap to sit on, a hand to hold, an ear to bend. People marvelled at her patience, at her ability to ride the shocks that motherhood is heir to. You never saw Elodie become ratty, or snappish. Tired, yes, but even her worst weariness (as Archie Featherstone had noted) had a luminous quality as though her outer casing had been worn thin to reveal the glow beneath.

Her new-found solitude, and the elegiac note that autumn always struck in her, made her aware of her solitariness. When, at three o'clock, she wandered across the Craft with Sandro to collect Celeste from school, her hands pushed deep in the pockets of her long tweed coat, she was almost stunned by the noise and vitality of the playground, and the other mothers, shouting to each other and their children from car doors, exchanging information and opinions, making arrangements, endless arrangements . . . She couldn't wait to get back to the cluttered emptiness of Hartfield, where all this village busyness was contained in the huddle of roofs on the far side of the Craft. She wasn't guilty, so much as objective. What were the alternatives to all this drifting, dreamy wasting of time? Like a fiddle pizzicato beneath a plaintive flute melody, the brisk tap of Mrs Dove's footsteps were an unsettling counterpoint to her reveries.

Bruno, nearing the second draft of his book, entitled *I Thee Worship* (it was about sex in marriage), was buoyant and restless, looking forward to that pleasant period of browsing, sluicing and shoptalk which characterised life between projects. His happy mood contrasted sharply with her own lassitude. She began to have something close to out-of-body experiences, when she would suddenly entertain a picture of herself as another might see her. Her degree of detachment frightened even her. One afternoon she was standing by the library window, arms folded, gazing across the Craft towards the church tower. Her mind was a blank. She was possessed by a familiar muffling lethargy. But when someone appeared by the gate at the far side she saw, with shocking suddenness and clarity, her own still, straight figure in the darkened window, arms folded, shoulders slightly hunched, her pale face starkly framed by flat, black hair, her eyes two vacant holes. She had to shake her head to rid herself of this image, and immediately left the window so that she would not be seen.

Unlike Bruno, she was deeply moved by Blaise's conversion. She herself was unreligious, having early on been bored to distraction by the drily conventional Roman Catholic rites of passage inflicted on her as a child by Iphigénie: crowded, droning masses in the local church and the sentimental embarrassment of her first communion. She did not even mind that Blaise was about to be received into the Church of England.

If Iphigénie had displayed the slightest signs of belief, or even of lively curiosity, things might have been otherwise.

Elodie was not wholly indifferent to the music, the incense, the sense of occasion. But for her mother the whole business was simply part of the rigid infrastructure of middle-class life, and Elodie had vowed not to inflict the same passionless bowings and scrapings on her own children. But Blaise's decision to be baptised touched and awed her with its quixotic courage. How quickly one's children became separate and startled you with their individuality. She felt humbled. She recalled events over the years which might now be interpreted as pointers to Blaise's inner life. His mature acceptance of the epilepsy which now, thank heavens, had gone into abeyance; his calm when she had gone into labour with Sandro, his reading of the poem at school, his ability to cope with Fabian at his most outrageous. Elodie found she had tears in her eyes thinking of this boy, this son, who had somehow always been a man.

'Don't for Christ's sake tell me you're going the same way!' Bruno had pleaded. 'One religious maniac in the family is more than enough!' She wished he would have a little more respect for Blaise's decision, rather than treating it as an hysterical pubescent impulse to be grudgingly indulged. But Bruno accorded respect to no one: it was not in his nature.

The baptism was arranged for early December in the parish church. Blaise, but not Fabian, would come home for the weekend. Fabian was annoyed not to have the weekend off, but since he had no interest in the proceedings it had been decided to keep him at as great a distance as possible.

'Go on, be a sport, I want to come!' he shouted at Bruno over the phone in a call box. The conversation itself was illicit, since phone calls home were only permitted in emergencies or times of the direst family crisis, and had to be booked through, and taken in, the secretary's office. The payola having ceased, Fabian had been rusticated twice already for smoking, and for distributing unsavoury magazines: one more infringement would result in immediate expulsion. He did not particularly want to be sacked – he enjoyed school and its limitless scope for manipulation – but neither was he prepared to curtail his activities on account of a few petty regulations.

'Not this time,' replied Bruno in a fairly reasonable tone of voice; he did not know about the ban on phone calls. 'This is just for the people involved.'

'Don't brothers count?'

'Don't play that card with me, Fabian, you know very well you're not interested in all this—'

'That's where you're wrong, I'm *madly* interested.'

'You know what I mean. It's not long till the holidays, and you've got work to do. Do it!'

'Damn and blast the lot of you!' barked Fabian and slammed the phone down.

So it was arranged. Bruno had spoken to Lauren and Elodie had written to Chrétien as a formality. She had also been to see the Rector, who had been quite exaggeratedly joyful over the whole thing, presumably on the basis that there was more rejoicing in heaven over one lost sheep, and so forth. He had been understanding about there being only one godfather, and that one a Roman Catholic, but striking while the iron was hot, he enquired whether Blaise would subsequently be taking confirmation classes. Elodie responded with a cool stare and the declaration that the decision would be entirely his.

Iphigénie was predictably triumphant. Though she would have preferred Blaise not to be baptised an Anglican, she was prepared to accept it as a much better state of affairs than had existed.

'Now you will have the others done, of course!' she wrote in her fussy handwriting, as though advocating the doctoring of cats, but no such assurances were given. Such a step was out of the question in Fabian's case, Sandro was not of an age to know his mind, and Celeste . . . who knew what Celeste thought about such things? Or if she thought about them at all. She was her usual practical, rather serious self, more concerned with the making of the special fruit cake and helping Mrs Dove make up beds for house guests.

'I think it's lovely, I really do,' said Mrs Dove to Celeste as they sorted out the airing cupboard together one wet weekday morning during half term. 'That big brother of yours is going to break a few hearts before he's through.'

The connection between these two remarks was too obscure

for Celeste to grasp. Instead she asked: 'Will you come?'

'I don't imagine so,' replied Mrs Dove, using one of those adult phrases which Celeste correctly interpreted as conveying a slight miff. 'Not to church. I'll be back here getting the tea on. But I'll wet his head when you all get back if I'm invited.'

'What's that?'

'Raise a glass, drink his health. I haven't had bubbles up my nose since Madge's girl's wedding.' She sucked her teeth cheerily. 'That was the prettiest wedding I've ever seen, the dress was that sort of Victorian style with the high neck, and the bridesmaids wore tangerine silk with little pantalettes peeping out underneath, it was a picture . . . Where are we putting underblankets?'

Celeste rushed to the pile and patted it. She was warming to the conversation. Bridesmaids she knew about. One of the girls at school had recently been a bridesmaid and had made it quite plain that nothing before – and very likely nothing to come – could compare with it.

'When do you think Blaise will get married?' she asked.

Mrs Dove leaned over her and patted her cheeks. They had come full circle. 'Who knows, lovey. He's got a lot of wild oats to sow before then. Twenty years younger and I'd be in the queue myself!'

Celeste had not given much thought as to whether she herself would like to be baptised, but this was only because she was preoccupied with other matters. For one thing she was worried about her mother, who was sad, and seemed lonely. Celeste wanted to cheer her up and keep her company, but it was as if she were wrapped in a cocoon of her own thoughts, so that even when she smiled you felt her mind wasn't on it. Celeste was used to being on the edge of people's attention, but this was different. She'd always known that her mother was there if needed, a constantly replenished source of comfort and security. Now it seemed that even when Elodie was there, in some odd way she wasn't.

This created a small shadow on the periphery of her life, not desperate or dreadful, but enough to make her feel sad last thing at night, and when she woke up in the morning. She turned more and more to Mrs Dove, who was always very much present with a smile, a hug, and a stream of comforting endearments.

Celeste had many responsibilities, which weighed heavily on her. Now that Blaise and Fabian were away for weeks at a time, she was the sole guardian of the trench and its secrets. Not that in reality there was much chance of anyone uncovering it. Over the past year the boys had no longer camped out in it for hours and it had become merely a repository for contraband goods and material. It was overgrown, and the tough sinewy branches of the rhododendrons had reached out over it. Even Celeste found it quite a job to get to it, but she tried to do so once every day to check that everything was still there.

There was an old tin tuck-box of Bruno's with 'B.J. GALLAGHER' on it in white paint. This contained the boys' cache of cigarettes, drink and magazines with pictures of ladies with gigantic bosoms, whose appeal Celeste was at a loss to understand. The leatherette record case, now measled with mould, was the really important thing. Inside it were some money, bits of paper and photographs in a yellow Kodak folder. Celeste had never seen the photographs and did not know what the bits of paper were, but Fabian had impressed upon her that much depended on all of it remaining undisturbed and undetected.

'If Dove starts mucking about with any of these bushes or anything,' he told her, 'and we're not around, for Christ's sake move the stuff.'

'Where to?'

'Anywhere. Even chuck it over into the edge of the field till the coast is clear.'

It worried her a little that both the tin box and the record case were quite large and she might not be able to chuck them quite as readily as Fabian suggested. From time to time she struggled down into the trench and tested their weight. She decided it would be difficult, but not impossible. And since she was growing all the time, and the boxes weren't, she foresaw the task becoming steadily easier.

Her main problem was finding the right moment to conduct her tour of duty. In the summer and early autumn it had been no problem to go out in the garden either just before or after having her breakfast, when her father was still in the bathroom and her mother occupied with Sandro. But with the days growing shorter and school occupying most of the daylight hours opportunities were fewer, and there were weeks when she only managed two visits. Not only that, but Sandro always wanted to accompany her, and could not understand her uncharacteristic refusal. It hurt her to turn him away, especially when his big dark eyes shone with tears and his chin quivered heartbreakingly. From time to time she gave him little things of her own to make up for her desertion – a teddy, a giant pencil, a china duck – which he accepted with wistful resignation.

She struck an unexpected snag when she was coming in for her breakfast one morning and met Mrs Dove in the yard. 'Hallo, young lady, whatever have you been up to? Just look at the state of those shoes!' Mrs Dove took her by the shoulder and spun her round. 'And it's all over your skirt, too! Whatever have you been doing, digging to Australia?'

On this occasion Celeste had to opt for a guilty grin and a promise not to walk the mud all over the house for Mrs Dove to clear up. But there was a manifest need for a good story in future, especially with the weather getting worse. So Celeste started a trench of her own, behind the stable block. It was hard work and not very deep, but she encouraged Sandro to help and used its supposed secrecy as a pretext for her solitary outings, telling him he had to keep cave.

All this was quite tiring. Celeste was not by nature a devious child. On the contrary she was trusting, trustworthy, sincere and loyal. But her allegiance to her brothers made heavy claims on all these qualities, claims she felt obliged to meet in full. She tried not to think of what might happen if she, and consequently they, were found out. She saw herself as a peacemaker, keeping everyone happy.

'She's such a funny old-fashioned little thing,' Mrs Dove said to her husband. 'Got the cares of the world on her shoulders.' She pulled a humorous face. 'Not like the rest of them.'

*

'Jammy bugger,' said Fabian to Blaise as they read their respective letters from Elodie. They were hogging a radiator just outside the second-year common room.

Blaise looked up. 'What's eating you?'

'Godparents!' Fabian spat it out. 'Hah!'

'What's wrong with that? When you're baptised you need godparents.'

'I bet you don't. I checked. Aren't you "as are of riper years"?'

Blaise lowered his letter and smiled. It was partly this smile – warm and sweet, but also tinged with melancholy – which gave people the feeling they were in the presence of someone special.

'You have been doing your homework, Titch.'

'Well, aren't you?'

'I don't know. Honestly. But that's not the point, people like to be asked.' Blaise watched his brother walk away. He was not disturbed by what had passed between them. He was calm and confident. His sights were set. The question of godparents was a mere side-show as far as he was concerned, something to keep the family amused. He knew himself to be a man apart.

CHAPTER SIX

The Reverend Thomas Wheeler – Father Tom as he preferred to be called by his flock – told Bruno and Elodie that these days baptisms in Stoke Broughton were generally conducted during the course of a normal matins or parish communion.

' . . . so that the congregation has an opportunity to welcome the new arrival,' he explained genially over Scotch and soda one Saturday lunchtime at Hartfield. Father Tom was a small, energetic man whose favourite definition of a priest (mercifully not aired in front of Bruno) was a 'labouring Christian'. His confidence was not easily dented, which was just as well given the kind of glum, silent scrutiny to which his host was currently subjecting him.

'It does give the occasion a greater relevance,' he added. 'And it is more usual nowadays – the accepted form.' He glanced questioningly at Elodie. 'But there again, it all depends on your son.'

'We have spoken to him about it,' said Elodie, 'and we think we would all prefer a private ceremony, as long as that will cause no offence.' Father Tom made an open-handed gesture of assent, so she continued: 'He's away so much at school now, that is where he will be attending services most of the time, so . . . ' She tailed off with a lift of the shoulders.

'Yes,' said Father Tom. 'Of course, there is a case for saying it would be more appropriate to hold the service in the school chapel. If that's what you wanted to do I certainly wouldn't stand in your way.'

'No!' said Bruno bluntly. 'This will do fine.'

The day of the baptism was sunny and cold, with a sharp overnight frost, the first of the year. A glittering day that put a crisp edge on the steeple of the parish church. The Gallaghers and the Lalandes chose to walk across the Craft. Thistles, molehills and cowpats were brittle and spangled with white. Three horses stood in the corner of the neighbouring field, and raised their heads in unison as the party came into sight.

'I did say I'd drive you,' said Bruno testily to his mother-in-law, 'but you wouldn't have it. If you remember.'

'I had no idea it would be so cold,' said Iphigénie in a faint, musing voice as if he hadn't spoken. 'Everything is frozen. I may turn an ankle.'

'Here,' offered Chrétien, 'take my arm. It's not very far.'

The terrain took its toll: they began to spread out. Blaise, manly and handsome in his school suit of dove-grey herringbone tweed, with a white shirt and navy silk tie, was at the front with Celeste. Next came Bruno, disgruntled and hands in pockets, followed by Lauren trying to catch up with him. Then Chrétien accompanied by his mother. Finally Elodie, deliberately dawdling so that Iphigénie would not be last, with Sandro alternately skittering about and hanging on to her hand.

There were the usual disparities in dress. Iphigénie and Lauren had taken the opportunity to dress up to the nines. Iphigénie was sleek and imposing in black beaver lamb and a turban of maroon jersey, embellished with a jet and garnet brooch. Lauren was Christmassy in a scarlet suit with black piping, worn over a white polo-neck sweater and topped by a black velvet cap with a tassel. Both women wore black high-heeled shoes, Iphigénie's suede, Lauren's patent leather. Celeste had on the sort of classic English children's coat which Elodie adored, a double-breasted raspberry tweed with a velvet collar. Bruno had added a tie to his weekend ensemble of grey flannel bags, Viyella shirt and corduroy jacket. Chrétien wore a non-business suit (plain navy, as opposed to striped) with a matching tie and handkerchief in dark red with tiny grey spots, and had put a pink carnation in his buttonhole to mark the occasion.

Sandro, orbiting his mother with jumps and dashes, was as unmistakably Parisian as his grandmother, in a black and white checked suit and a black jumper. Elodie from time to time lavished on her youngest and prettiest child a certain rogue fancy for picturesque clothes as though, realising that childhood did not last, she was fighting a rearguard action against what was to come.

Elodie was swathed in a long, russet-coloured cashmere cloak with a fringed hem and flat brown boots. 'Pocohontas as I live and breathe,' Bruno had said. Her hair was brushed back off her face and hung in a sleek black waterfall down her back. She wore neither make-up nor jewellery. In spite of his facetious comment, Bruno today was quite sure that he adored her. She accompanied his life like a fine, continuous violin note, distant and unobtrusive, but haunting. Once or twice he glanced over his shoulder, and took a reviving sip of her cool, plain beauty.

In the lane those at the front waited, so as to move on together and reach the church in good order. 'I shall never,' said Lauren to Bruno, 'understand this British obsession with walking. I can't believe we all hiked across that field in our best clothes – well, some of us in our best clothes – when we could have travelled in warmth and comfort.'

Bruno laughed and put his arm round her shoulders. 'Blame Elodie, it was her idea. Here, let me warm you up. You're looking wonderful, by the way . . .'

In reply to a question from Chrétien, Blaise said: 'Not nervous, no. But I still wish it was over.'

Celeste gazed up at him. 'Why?'

'Well . . . ' Blaise pushed his hands into his pockets and looked back across the lane at the rest of his family. 'You know.'

'Not really.'

'It's just to do with me, isn't it. I wish it didn't have to be this big thing. Nobody else has any idea how I feel and I don't suppose they're interested.'

'Surely there is a need for people to mark the occasion – and for others to bear witness,' said Chrétien, wondering of exactly whom this was true. 'And as for not being interested, you will be my only godson.'

Elodie and Sandro held the gate for Iphigénie and they all began to walk on. Celeste put her hand in Blaise's. He seemed somehow noble today. Perhaps this was the beginning of a better time, without secrets.

Chrétien fell in beside his sister. 'How are you, Eli?' He spoke in French. 'We don't see you often enough. You should come and stay with us, now the children are at school. Both of you, of course, but if Bruno is working, come on your own.'

'I couldn't.'

'Why not? He's not helpless. And you have the superb Mrs Dove.' Elodie was silent. 'Think about it. Are you going to Quatre Vents for Christmas?'

'I suppose so. We always do.'

'Then why not come to us afterwards? The New Year is such a disheartening time. It would be good for all of us.'

A car approached and Elodie reached for Sandro's hand. 'I'm not sure. The children will still be on holiday from school, and Fabian and Blaise have these great trunks that have to be packed . . . I think I need to be here.'

'That,' said Chrétien, 'is just why you should absent yourself. Bruno and the housekeeper can manage. He is their father after all.'

'You're forgetting you invited him, too.'

'Yes, but we both know he doesn't really like to stay with us. He doesn't like to stay with anyone. He likes to be in his fortress with the drawbridge up and the portcullis down, and to make occasional forays when the mood takes him.'

'Preferably,' pointed out Elodie, 'with someone waiting for him at home.'

'So? He must learn self-sufficiency. You will think about it?'

'I'll think about it, yes.'

'Excellent.'

As the party went through the lych-gate into the churchyard with its guard of great old elms and yews, Celeste glanced up at her brother's face. She found that she almost blinked, because it was so bright, not just with excitement, but with a fiercely burning determination. Blaise has a face like a knight, she thought, except that King Arthur told his knights to be humble.

The church of St Michael and All Angels was highly regarded amongst people who knew about such things. At the turn of the century, when the building had been subjected to extensive cleaning and renovation, the north wall had been found to be covered with elaborate graffiti from the time of the Black Death. Figures in various stages of physical decline and emotional anguish were depicted in fine, deep strokes in the stone, as well as a still-recognisable representation of the mediaeval settlement, and some written observations of a dourly ironic cast. One of them, translated from the Middle English in the parish guide, read: 'Help us, O Lord, in the time of our tribulation, for what has this place done to displease you? Let us stand upright again so that we may bring our harvest offerings and sing your praises as before.' A straight trade-off, as Bruno had remarked.

Father Tom met them in the porch. He greeted those he knew, shook hands energetically with those to whom he was introduced, and placed an encouraging hand on Blaise's shoulder.

They assembled round the font. The ladies of the parish had placed a tall copper jug of autumn foliage and amber chrysanthemums at the base of the font, and there was a large, sweeping arrangement of copper beech and white chrysanthemums on a wrought-iron stand to one side of the bell tower steps. The faint thrum of the boiler could be heard, like the engine of an ocean liner, but the radiators were positioned in such a way as to heat the feet of those sitting in the central portion of the nave, and nothing else. Father Tom's breath hung before him like ectoplasm as he enjoined his small congregation, for Blaise's sake, to approach their task with proper seriousness.

From above their heads, on the cornices of the rugged stone columns of the nave, roughly-carved angels and gargoyles gazed down pop-eyed. The angels were the architect's intended embellishment. The gargoyles were the invention of bored thirteenth-century artisans who had used one another as models. One had a grossly protruding tongue, another picked his nose, a third tugged at his cheeks with stubby fingers to produce a hideous grin. Each face radiated a subversive vitality.

' . . . they that are in the flesh cannot please God, but live in sin, committing many actual transgressions,' warned Father Tom, reading from the Book of Common Prayer (Blaise's choice, he himself preferred a more up-to-date idiom). Bruno, glancing rebelliously upward and catching the eye of a gargoyle, was flooded with gratitude and relief. Across the centuries, a kindred spirit mouthed: 'Sod this for a game of soldiers.'

Mrs Dove had taken charge of the catering. Though she would have liked to be at the church, she regarded the provision of the christening tea as a sacred duty and one which she was uniquely qualified to perform. Elodie was a marvel with all things savoury, but she was not one of nature's cake-makers, so Evadne had taken it upon herself (with Celeste's assistance) to construct the celebration cake, a traditional confection of fruit, nuts, marzipan and royal icing, with many twirls and flourishes. It was a labour of love. She looked forward to the gratitude and admiration of the whole party, and especially that of Blaise, who had such lovely manners and could be relied upon to say something charming.

The dining-room at Hartfield was long and narrow. At one end there was a door and hatch leading to the kitchen, where meals were normally taken. At the other end tall windows reaching almost from floor to ceiling afforded a view of the lawn, the tennis court, and the shrubbery beyond. When the lower half of these sash windows was open in fine weather the older boys often came straight through this room from the kitchen and vaulted out rather than taking the longer route via the back door and yard. When there was a thick red oilcloth over the table to protect its polished surface they would actually run along the top, stretching up half-way to touch the heavy brass electrolier.

Beneath the hatch was a high serving table with a hotplate, and at the far end, next to the windows, an upright piano complete with candle-holders. In spite of the fact that only Elodie could play, and had not done so for years, the piano was a folly of Bruno's. He had seen it advertised for sale in a pub in Camden Town, and bought it on the spot, with some idea of entertaining his family with renditions of 'Roamin' in the Gloamin' ' and 'Nelly Dean'.

Apart from the table and ten assorted chairs – four matched, the rest an eclectic mix of elegant antiques and basic utility – there was little other furniture in the room; its shape made it impossible. But the walls and mantelpiece were crowded with pictures, hangings, weapons, mirrors and ornaments. A nightmare to dust, as Evadne had often pointed out to friends. She set out the food on covered plates and breathed lovingly on the Sheffield plate tea-pot before rubbing it with her sleeve.

'Almighty and immortal God,' said Father Tom in a chatty, democratic voice intended to draw the sting of the elitist language, 'the aid of all that need, the helper of all that flee to Thee for succour, the life of them that believe, and the resurrection of the dead; we call upon Thee for this person, that he, coming to Thy holy Baptism, may receive remission of his sins by spiritual regeneration. . .'

Celeste hoped, and indeed on this occasion prayed, on hearing the word 'sins', that the secrets of the slit trench would be included in any forgiveness currently being handed out. Blaise at this moment was so splendid, so dignified, it was impossible to connect him with the squalid cache of contraband she had guarded so conscientiously. She stood on one side of her mother, Sandro on the other. He was not behaving well, making thrumming noises with a small metal car and occasionally dropping it with a loud clang on the stone flags. Elodie took no notice. Celeste leaned round and scowled at him and he lowered his head so that his heavy fringe shielded his eyes. With one finger he spun the wheels of the car.

Celeste herself was enthralled. She felt keenly the sense of occasion. When, like Bruno, she looked upwards, it was past the ugly grinning faces of the gargoyles to the sweeping fan-vaults of the roof. She blinked, awed, at the motes of coloured light streaming from the west window, where St Michael (resplendent in silver armour and an elaborate filigree halo) held court with his angels (less bellicosely clad in conventional robes of white) amongst green hills studded with flowers. When she looked at Blaise, who had stepped forward to answer some solemn-sounding questions from Father Tom, she was struck again by the resemblance between her brother and the chevalier saint. Both were clear-eyed and calm-browed. Both gazed serenely into some unreachable private distance. Neither looked ready to brook doubts or backsliding. If anything, Celeste reflected, Blaise was the more impressive of the two.

'Wilt thou be baptised in this faith?' asked Father Tom.

'That is my desire,' replied Blaise. The way he spoke made Celeste shiver, so that Elodie looked down at her and mouthed, 'Are you cold?'

Evadne finished laying the table – except for the asparagus tarts and smoked salmon sandwiches, which were to remain in the fridge till the last minute – and went to light the fire in the drawing-room. She allowed that this was the drawing-room, as opposed to the lounge/library next door. In a smaller house and in different circumstances it might have been referred to as the parlour, but at any rate it was discernibly a room for withdrawing into on those occasions when only the best would do. Withdrawing was not something the Gallaghers went in for a great deal, so the room was generally rather cold and gloomy. Evadne put a match to the fire and then bustled about, placing her hand on radiators, flicking the corner of her cotton apron over polished surfaces, adjusting lampshades. It was nice the way the room came to life as the pale new flames began to leap in the hearth; it would be cosy when they all came back.

She put a couple of logs on the blazing kindling and went into the hall. The champagne glasses stood upside down on the high-sided butler's tray. She examined them one at a time, and gave a couple of them a brisk extra wipe on the apron. She sang under her breath: 'What do you want if you don't want money, What do you want if you don't want gold?' She liked Adam Faith, he had bedroom eyes. For no very good reason this made her think of her husband, who had been instructed to drive over to the church in the Rolls to bring back the halt and the lame, as Professor Gallagher had put it. She did hope that Dove would not go completely silent at the party, it made him seem stupid and it reflected badly on her. He was not a stupid man, just a deliberate one. He was already complaining about having to drink champagne, which gave him an acid stomach. She had decided not to tell him that Professor Gallagher had got a dozen pints of Frobishers in the scullery – let him be pleasantly surprised, and make an effort to show it.

Evadne removed her apron, folded it and put it in the tea-towel drawer. Then she marched briskly back into the drawing-room to see how the fire was doing. It was only half past three, but already the uncovered windows were darkening and she could see a couple of small lights in the village. The fire had reddened nicely and she put a few lumps of coal on to keep it in, so that when she heard them arriving back she could top it with a nice big log and get a blaze right up the chimney. Then she lit the art nouveau lamp in the corner. It was a bronze and ivory dryad carrying a water pitcher. Evadne had thought it altogether too much of a good thing to begin with, but it was growing on her. The dryad was a plump girl, artfully draped. Contemplation of her prompted Evadne to glance at herself in the mantel mirror. She dabbed at her hair, and then turned sideways, smoothing her violet wool dress over her stomach and hips, straightening her belt and lifting her chin. She was quite pleased with what she saw.

With a brief backward glance she moved in the direction of the windows to draw the curtains, and stopped short with a gasp. A face looked back at her from beyond the glass, mocking her vanity with a slitty, knowing smile, eyes narrowed above the pulsing red spark of a cigarette.

Her hands flew to her cheeks, her heart pounded with shock

and embarrassment.

'Fabian! Whatever are you doing here?'

Celeste held her breath as Father Tom dipped his hand in the font and drew the sign of the cross on Blaise's forehead with his thumb. She knew she was watching something desperately important, and terribly secret. More secret by far than the contents of the slit trench. More secret even than the sly laughter and the smoke behind Mrs Dove's bathroom wall. For this was Blaise's own private secret, which nobody else could know.

' . . . and do sign him with the sign of the Cross, in token that hereafter he shall not be ashamed to confess the faith of Christ crucified, and manfully to fight under his banner against sin, the world, and the devil, and to continue Christ's faithful soldier and servant unto his life's end.'

Celeste felt her neck and cheeks prickle with pride and dread. She shivered again, and Elodie squeezed her hand as if to say, 'Not long now.' But Celeste could have stayed here for ever.

'Our Father,' said Father Tom, and now they all joined in, except Bruno who was feeling the cold and shifting discontentedly from foot to foot. Celeste looked at Sandro, but even he had his eyes shut and his hands pressed together under his nose, the toy car between his palms.

'Surprised?' asked Fabian, sauntering in through the back door, which Evadne was holding open. She watched him go by as if he were a ghost. 'I can see you are,' he said with an air of high good humour, opening the fridge. 'What's in here? I'm ravenous.'

His greedily questing hand recalled Evadne to herself. 'Don't touch any of that, it's for the party!' She banged the fridge door shut. 'I'll make you a sandwich.'

'Cheese and chutney, thanks.'

Fabian leaned back on the edge of the table, ankles crossed. He wore a school suit similar to Blaise's, with the jacket buttoned and the collar turned up. His black lace-up shoes and his trouser bottoms were soiled. His reddish hair stuck up in points. Unlike most red-haired people, he had a high colour, in which his light-lashed eyes were a startling china blue. He did not share Blaise's precocious physique nor his good looks, but his presence was powerfully unsettling. Evadne had to remind herself that this was a naughty twelve-year-old schoolboy and that was all.

Having something to do helped her regain her composure. She was, after all, in charge here. She glanced sharply at him as she sawed bread and spread butter. 'Have you run away from school, then?'

'No.'

'What's that supposed to mean?'

'What it says. I haven't run away. I've come to my brother's christening.'

'But you haven't got permission, have you?' Evadne took the chutney jar out of the cupboard and banged it down on the side.

'No.'

'You're going to be in the most awful hot water, you do realise that?'

He shrugged. It was not just a bad boy's display of bravado. He didn't care. Evadne cut the two rounds in half with a single savage stroke, dumped them on a plate and handed them to him.

'Cheers. Any chance of a cup of tea?'

'You can have one when I've made it. They'll all be back soon. And I wouldn't like to be in your shoes, I can tell you.'

Fabian attacked the sandwich with gusto. 'It'll liven up their dull little lives,' he said round a substantial mouthful. Before Evadne could think up a suitably withering response the telephone rang in the library. 'That'll be the school,' he said, and took another mouthful. Evadne, flustered, hesitated. 'Let it ring,' he suggested. 'I mean, what can you say?'

Furious with herself and with him, she moved the kettle on to the centre of the plate, partly to cover the insistent ringing. Fabian, sandwich in hand, pushed the kitchen door shut with his foot. 'That's the way. You're a sport.'

'I am not a sport!'

89

'Okay, keep your hair on.'

'I shall tell your parents the very second they get back, and they'll ring the school.'

'Of course.'

'I just hope you realise that you will have ruined your brother's special day!' Fabian's derisive snort sent a spray of crumbs half-way across the kitchen. 'Spoiled his special day? Don't be bloody ridiculous, it'll make it for him. He'd wear a hair shirt if he could get hold of one.' He wiped his mouth on his sleeve. 'The worse I am, the better he'll look.'

'You don't care about anybody or anything but yourself, that's your trouble,' muttered Mrs Dove. She was angry and off-balance. Even if Blaise's day wasn't ruined, hers certainly had been. 'And go and get out of those filthy shoes!' she snapped.

Blaise and Celeste apart, they were all anxious to get away after the service. The less devout among them came back to life as they emerged from the church porch and began laughing and complaining humorously about the cold. Elodie bent over with her arms around Celeste and Sandro and said, 'You were both so good! Now we're going to have a party tea.'

'Tea!' yelled Sandro, heading for the gate at speed, but Celeste could not even think about tea. She was still spellbound. All she wanted was to look at Blaise. Father Tom had detained him just inside the church door and was talking to him with smiling earnestness. Blaise looked serious. Of the two, Blaise looked the grander and more important.

Bruno slapped his hands together and stamped his feet. 'Hell's teeth, talk about mortifying the flesh! Ah, there's Dove with the motor, now who's for the ride home? Mother, I take it you will, and the two smalls had better go.' He put an amorous arm round Elodie. 'What about you, toots?'

'Yes, I think I'd better.' She stepped out of his embrace and held out her hands to the children. 'Mrs Dove has been on her own quite long enough.'

'Can I come, miss?' asked Lauren, 'before I get pneumonia, miss?'

Elodie laughed. 'You poor thing. Come along.'

Wearing an expression of foolish fondness, Bruno watched them go. Now the ghastly bit of the proceedings was out of the way he was looking forward to some refreshment. 'Come on, Padre!' he bellowed. 'We're wasting good drinking time!'

'Mummy!' shouted Sandro from the kitchen door which led to the dining-room. 'Fabian's in here eating our tea!'

Celeste was almost knocked over as Mrs Dove came rushing through from the hall, and nearly collided with Elodie, who swept Sandro aside to see for herself.

'Mrs Gallagher, he just got here, he doesn't have permission, but I thought I'd better wait for you all to come back—'

Lauren, eyebrows raised in amusement, came into the kitchen and stood with her back to the Aga, removing her gloves. Seeing Celeste's white, shocked face, she winked at her. 'Never a dull moment, huh?'

Iphigénie entered with Dove in attendance, and at once divined a crisis. 'What? What is going on?' Mrs Dove and her husband exchanged a rueful glance.

'Apparently Fabian is here,' Lauren told her mother-in-law.

'Fabian? But he should be at school!'

'No! Really?'

'There is no need to be sarcastic. Where is he?'

Lauren waved a casual hand. 'With the food, where else?' Iphigénie's gaze fastened on the dining-room door, which was ajar, and from beyond which voices could be heard. 'But don't let's interfere, hm?' added Lauren. 'Let's all go through and talk amongst ourselves like well-behaved people. Where's Sandro?'

'He went in with Mummy,' said Celeste. She felt almost sick with unhappiness. Everything had been perfect, and now it was spoiled.

'Best place for him,' said her aunt, 'let him stay. Is there a fire in the drawing-room, Mrs Dove? Come along then, *maman*, let me take your coat . . .'

Celeste and Iphigénie allowed themselves, very unwillingly, to be ushered from the room.

The Doves stood in the kitchen, the hiss of the kettle to one side of them, the muted, frantic sound of voices on the other. 'They won't be all that long, the rate that lot set off,' said Dove. He wore a beige suit and a shiny green tie. Evadne could not get him to wear new things.

'Never mind, it's not our problem,' she said with a firmness she was far from feeling. 'Here, you can help me get the bits and pieces out of the fridge.'

Sandro sat as good as gold on an upholstered carver's chair, listening to the argument.

'I don't know what has possessed you!' said Elodie in a soft, desperate voice. 'You will be expelled!'

'Don't get so worked up. I'm not.'

'But why not? What is the matter with you? Can't you see what a silly, reckless, bad thing this was to do?' None of her adjectives quite expressed what she wanted to say, which had to do with misrule and disturbance and Bruno's rage.

Fabian sat looking at her. He held a choux bun containing cream cheese in one hand. 'Look – okay if I eat this? Only it's going soggy, and I can't very well put it back because my hands are dirty—'

'Eat it! Eat it!' Elodie flung her hands in the air and let them fall on her head and drag down over her face.

Fabian lifted his feet in grey wool socks. 'I took my muddy shoes off,' he said. 'Wasn't that good of me?'

Elodie moaned. He put the choux bun in his mouth, whole.

There was a tap on the door and Mrs Dove put her head round. 'I thought you'd like to know, Mrs Gallagher, the others are back. Just passed the window.'

'Oh . . . thank you, Mrs Dove.' Elodie picked Sandro up. He was too big to be carried really, but she felt that holding him gave her a sort of authority. 'Fabian, go upstairs to your room.'

He stood up, one cheek still bulging, and dusted his palms together. 'Why? I'm not worried. I want to see everyone. That's why I came.'

'Well, it will not be appreciated!' said Elodie.

The Doves had retreated to the no man's land of the hall. As

Fabian followed his mother into the kitchen, Bruno burst in at the back door with an exuberant shout. 'We're here, we're here! Let the atrocities commence!'

Sitting on the edge of the striped drawing-room sofa, with one hand on Lauren's knee, Celeste heard her father's cheerful bellow turn into a roar of rage. Fear, boiling hot and icy cold, rushed through her and manifested itself in a sudden trickle between her legs. Everything was horrid. She began to cry, and was at once enveloped in Lauren's arms, and her scent, Diorling, which Celeste could never again smell without feeling wretched, just as Mrs Dove's made her feel safe.

It was after one in the morning when Blaise came into Fabian's room. 'Idiot,' he said, sitting down on the bed. 'What did you think you were doing?'

'Coming to your christening, O holy one. What La Dove called your "special day".'

'Did Dad hit you?'

'Not likely.' Fabian sat up. 'He's all talk and trousers.'

'You'll get the sack tomorrow when he takes us back.'

'I suppose so.'

The two of them sat there in the dark, reflecting on this. Fabian spoke first. 'So what was it like, then, this afternoon?'

'You're not interested, so why ask.'

'No, I am, honestly. I'm here, aren't I?'

'That's got nothing to do with it.'

'But anyway, what was it like?'

Blaise turned his face towards his brother. 'Fabulous,' he said. Fabian could make out the shine of his eyes. 'It was fabulous.'

Grudgingly, Fabian had to admit he was impressed. Blaise had managed to rob the word of its slang associations and return to it some ancient and wonderful meaning. 'Glad to hear it.'

'But you,' said Blaise, in a quite different voice, cold and sharp, 'are just so bloody stupid. Stupid, hear me?' He gave Fabian a push which sent him keeling over sideways so that he fell out of bed. 'Stupid!'

After Blaise had gone Fabian lay rigid where he had fallen. He told himself that he would not sleep all night. It was something they'd done when they were younger to score points off each other, both a penance and a display of power. For hours he scarcely moved. His neck, shoulders and legs became first uncomfortable, then painful, then unbearable. When he eventually crawled back into bed it was with the humiliating knowledge that Blaise would not have done so.

In the morning he was up first, and was seated in the hall, fully dressed and ready to go by the time the others came down for breakfast. His mother, aunt and sister tried to talk to him but he was monosyllabic, his nose and mouth pinched with a look of bitter disgust. As they waited in the courtyard for Bruno to back the Rolls from the garage, he turned to Blaise. 'Hey. Holy Joe.'

Blaise turned a calm, unruffled face towards him.

'Nobody,' said Fabian, 'calls me stupid.' He spat on his brother's shoes.

Celeste, watching this exchange from the shadows of the kitchen corridor, felt a pulse of horror. Momentous things had happened over the past twenty-four hours, and only some of them in church.

CHAPTER SEVEN

Celeste sat on a rock with her mother and watched as Sandro, in a blue duffle coat and wellingtons, made friends with an elderly couple at the water's edge. The three figures were quite distant, for it was low tide and this was a typically Breton beach, vast and ancient, across which the Atlantic breakers raced and plunged until they spread themselves exhausted on the moon-coloured sand.

It was January the second. The weather was clear and windy, the horizons etched razor-sharp against skies that were baby-blue one minute, purple the next. From time to time when the clouds passed over they scattered handfuls of icy rain that pricked Celeste's face, and then the sun would come out again and make everything glassy bright, though not much warmer.

They had come to a familiar place, where a huge outcrop of smooth, tumbled rocks stood at the edge of the beach between the dunes and the flat sand. Around the base of the rocks were little inlets and coves which in the summer made perfect picnic places, and in the winter afforded some shelter from the booming wind. Celeste loved the rocks. No matter how often she and the boys clambered over them there was always some new place to find, a strange and enchanting bolthole, a different vantage point. When the tide was high and they looked down from the garden of Quatre Vents the rock-mountain was just a black glossy hump, like the head of a sea monster, round which the waves churned and broke. At low tide, when Celeste sat on one of the natural thrones half-way up, she liked to imagine the sea creature which must have flickered and lurked around the rock when it was submerged.

She had climbed up the rocks this afternoon, a little earlier; she always did, it was a kind of rite which had to be observed. Usually Elodie came too, giving Sandro a hand, but today she had wandered back and forth on the empty, wind-combed sand, looking as if she was searching for something. Sandro had climbed as far as he could and then stood there, calling pitifully that he was stuck until Celeste had come down to him. She didn't quite trust herself to help him climb any further, so they descended together. Now he was off making new friends, and Celeste sat on the rock with her hood up and her mother's arm around her. The wind came from behind the rocks at their back. They could see the devastation it left in its wake as it rampaged across the beach like an invisible marauding army, whipping up the sand into wild wraiths and tearing off the tops of the distant waves. Shadows of clouds fled before it like sad, driven ghosts. Over to their left, where the dunes rose in a succession of false crests to the narrow coast road and the wooded cliff beyond, the shaggy tufts of long grass and dry winter thrift showed alternately green and silver as the wind flattened and released them.

The sky darkened and some rain spattered down. For a moment it was bitterly cold and Celeste turned her face inside her hood and pressed into Elodie's coat. The coat was an inside-out fur, smooth and patterned with coloured embroidery on the outside. It had a pungent, spicy smell which Celeste liked. She had heard her father say, with wrinkled nose, that 'the damn thing wasn't properly cured', but of what she had no idea. Huddled up like this, with her mother's hand absent-mindedly rubbing her arm, she hoped that the elderly couple by the sea would keep Sandro amused for ever.

Of course it was they who were amused by him. They were Danish, on holiday at St Supplice, the town just around the headland to the east. When they had set out for their after-lunch walk it had been with the intention of leaving civilisation behind. And they had at first been rather dismayed when this small figure, in his navy duffle and red boots, had come scampering through the edge of the water towards them.

'I'm Sandro,' he told them. 'I live up there.' He pointed in the direction of the cliff top. They looked, obligingly, and saw a long grey and white stone house with small shuttered windows all at different levels and an uneven slate roof.

'What,' said the man, 'and you're down here all on your own?'

'No, Mummy and Celeste are sitting over by the rocks.' He pointed again, but this time they could see nothing.

'We're going for a walk to keep warm,' explained the woman. They began to move on and he fell in beside them, stopping and starting, rummaging in his pocket for something.

'Stop a minute!' He was imperious. They obliged. 'Do you want these?' He held out a handful of shells in a damp and gritty red wool glove. 'I've got a collection.'

'That's very kind of you,' said the woman. 'If you're sure you can spare them.'

'I've got lots. I covered a box with them.'

'That was very clever.'

'Mummy helped me.' He held up the shells. 'There you are then.'

The woman took them, and she and her husband examined them with appropriately admiring comments.

'Very nice. That is kind of you. Thank you.'

'I don't live there all the time,' explained Sandro. 'We live in England most of the time, but we come here for Christmas and in the summer.'

'Ah!' smiled the man, nodding. 'We thought you must be English.'

'I am,' said Sandro. 'But Mummy's French.'

'So you speak French, do you?'

'Yes, I can. But I don't want to.'

A mountainous cloud sailed across the sun. The sand turned grey, the sea inky, the cliff black. The woman shivered. 'It's too cold to stand about! Shall we walk back with you to your mother?'

'If you like.'

Sandro slipped in between them and put his hands in theirs.

It was the action of a child who had known nothing but uncritical affection. The Andersens had no grandchildren of their own, and they found it almost overwhelmingly sweet and touching. They glanced at one another over his head but did not like to let their eyes meet for fear of the defenceless emotion they would find there.

The cloud rolled on its way and Celeste saw Sandro approaching, between the two old people, across the bright, wet ripples of sand. They were coming quite slowly. At every third or fourth step Sandro would give a little hop and swing on their hands, making them laugh.

Celeste looked up at her mother. She had her face turned towards the sea, but Celeste could tell she hadn't seen Sandro or the others coming. 'Mummy . . . Mummy, Sandro's bringing some people.'

'What's that, my darling?' Elodie looked down at Celeste as if recalled from a great distance. She looked where Celeste pointed. 'Oh dear, I don't want to talk. Be a kind girl and fetch him, would you?'

Celeste jumped down off the rock and began running towards Sandro and the Andersens. Once she was out of the lee of the rock, the wind pounced and she almost lost her balance. She called to Sandro, but her voice was snatched away. The three of them were so taken up with each other that she was almost upon them before they noticed her. 'Sandro, come on, Mummy wants you.'

The Andersens smiled indulgently and released Sandro, but he pretended not to have heard, and jumped up and down on the spot, staring at his feet. Mrs Andersen leant over and placed a gentle encouraging hand on his back. 'Off you go, now. Is this your big sister?'

'Yes, I am,' replied Celeste. She went up to Sandro and grabbed his wrist. 'Come on.' She towed him away, feeling his slight resistance as he waved goodbye to the Andersens. But as soon as they reached Elodie he climbed on her knee and complained of being cold.

'Are you?' she laughed. 'Have we been here too long?'

'Yes, can we go home now?'

Elodie stood up, sliding Sandro gently to the ground. Celeste jumped down on to the sand. Now that it was decided they should go home, she too felt cold, but she didn't want to leave. She could have stayed here for ever, snuggled up with her mother on the rock seat, with her brother a dot in the distance.

The two weeks in Brittany since Christmas had been amongst the happiest Celeste could remember. She felt safe, peaceful, and needed. Not in the way that Blaise and Fabian needed her at home – to run their errands and keep their secrets – but needed just for herself. Elodie wanted her near all the time, as if for reassurance. Sandro was still the baby, of course, and demanded attention, but his demands were self-centred and quickly gratified; a kiss and a hug, and he was off until the next time. Celeste was content to be there constantly, providing the comfort which her mother so obviously required.

For everything had changed at home. With Fabian's expulsion had come the realisation that the safety-net of tolerance so long enjoyed by the Gallaghers, and taken for granted by them, was no longer there. There were some things the outside world would not put up with.

Bruno's fury with Fabian for going AWOL from school was as nothing compared to his rage with the headmaster for sacking him. He seemed to think that his own perturbation was somehow worth more than anyone else's, and should therefore be accepted in lieu of all other forms of punishment. He was stung to think that another man should have the right of punishment over his flesh and blood and so, by implication, himself.

'Supercilious, self-righteous arsehole!' was his maddened comment on returning from school with the unrepentant Fabian and his personal effects. 'Who the hell does he think he is?'

'A responsible headmaster, perhaps?' suggested Lauren, who was staying an extra day at Hartfield.

'Don't you start. I don't know how he has the brass neck to ask me to take Fabian away, as he so euphemistically put it, when Blaise is there practically running the place and

displaying all that's holy bar stigmata.'
'Perhaps that's why.'
'What's that supposed to mean?'
'Perhaps Mr Caldecote thinks it's unfair on Blaise to allow Fabian any more licence.'
'Unfair?' They were in the library, and at this point Bruno grabbed the whisky and poured himself a large measure. 'Unfair? It's a bloody sight less fair to banish Fabian just to spare Blaise embarrassment.'
'I only meant that—'
'Besides which, I thought the godly were supposed to relish a bit of a challenge, a cross to bear, all that eyewash?'
At this point Lauren had given up.

Usually, Christmas in Brittany notwithstanding, nothing could deter Elodie from entering into the spirit of things at Hartfield, getting out the Coleport Advent china with its border of holly and ivy and installing a ten-foot Christmas tree in the hall. Bruno regularly poured scorn on all this wasted effort. The two activities were as much part of the season as brandy butter and Iphigénie's migraines. But not this year. Cold reality had intruded on the operatic charade of family life, and made them all feel sombre and irritable, unable to put on a good show even for each other.

Only Fabian seemed unaffected. There was in his manner no hint of guilt or remorse; his unspoken message was that it was up to others to decide what happened next. When Bruno upbraided him with the upset and inconvenience he had visited on everyone, he countered by pointing out the saving on fees, a matter which had prompted strong words from his father on more than one occasion.

'Don't imagine,' said Bruno, 'that just because you've been thrown out of that place you're going to sit around here on your backside all day.'

'I didn't,' said Fabian. 'I'm not stupid.' This last remark was not quite the run-of-the-mill retort it seemed, but Bruno was in no mood to notice fine nuances of expression.

'I intend speaking to the head of the school in Baring – I shall spare him nothing, of course – and you'll start there after Christmas.'

'Fine by me,' said Fabian and sauntered off, leaving Bruno seething.

In the past Celeste had sometimes wished that her older brothers were not quite so united, they had seemed to form an impenetrable barrier between her and the rest of life. Now that they were increasingly separate and distinct she felt, instead of relief, a sort of panic, as though their demands on her might become even more urgent and complex.

One dark afternoon just after school a hard hand grasped her arm in the kitchen passage. 'Hi. Come with me a tick.'

Even if it hadn't been an order, Celeste would have had to comply. The cruelly tight grip steered her out of the back door and into the yard. 'Ouch, you're hurting. What do you want?'

Fabian let go of her arm. He had grown several inches, and looked down at her from his new height like someone with a flyswatter watching a sleepy wasp. 'I want to go and check the trench. Coming?'

She had no choice. 'All right.'

He walked away and she half-ran to keep up with him. The strain of being a slave to two brothers was as nothing to the strain of this vague complicity with one. The shadow of wrong-doing hung about Fabian and infected her with a guilt not her own. His lack of remorse became her burden.

As they left the lights of the house and walked across the grass beside the tennis court the deepening darkness pounced, so that Celeste reached for her brother's hand and found only the sleeve of his pullover. But once they had pushed through the shrubbery their eyes were accustomed to the dusk, and the dim, misty Craft was still grey, with the white scuts of startled rabbits bobbing away like will o' the wisps.

'Right,' said Fabian. 'Let's take a dekko, shall we?'

Again, it was not really a question. Celeste stood shivering as he hauled the branches away from one end. She wished that her mother or Mrs Dove would come to the back door and call loudly for her, but she had not been missed.

Fabian lowered himself into the trench and looked up at her.

101

He was no less threatening now that his head was on a level with her shins.

'Everything still here, is it?'

'Yes!' She nodded vigorously.

She was by no means as certain as she sounded. It was some weeks since she had carried out an inspection. But the last time she had done so everything had looked undisturbed. In fact, she had got so used to the look of the record case and the black tin box that they now seemed as organic and permanent as the root fibres, damp soil and leaf mould which surrounded them.

Fabian ducked his head and disappeared for a moment. Beyond the Craft the church floodlight was switched on so that the spire appeared, suddenly, a fantastic space rocket against the darkening sky. Its startling brightness made Celeste shrink and stiffen like an animal caught in the head lights, as though the whole village could see what she and Fabian were up to.

He reappeared, and jerked his head. 'Come on, then.'

She obeyed, unwillingly. Refusal was unthinkable.

Down in the trench it was dark and clammy, with a dungeon-smell. Fabian was squatting near the trunk, fiddling with something that made a clicking sound. She could hear his breathing, even and concentrated. 'Blast,' he said finally. 'Flaming torch won't work.'

She didn't reply, not wanting to colour his mood in any way. 'Here,' he said, passing her the torch. 'We'd better take that up and get some more batteries.'

'Okay.'

She sat holding the torch in both hands, feeling the damp seep through the skirt of her corduroy pinafore dress. Fabian opened first the trunk, then the record case, and rummaged through them, identifying things by touch. She found that she was holding her breath in dread, in case anything was missing. But after a couple of minutes he said, 'Right. Come on, then,' and hauled himself out of the trench. He lowered his hand to help her up. She took it. His arm was thin and hard and with a single yank he hoisted her out. Now he was replacing the branches. She noticed that he was carrying a small oblong package.

'Come on,' he said. 'I've got it.'

She didn't want to see, but she stumbled after him through the bushes and back past the tennis court to the dubious safety of the house. In the courtyard, and feeling a bit braver, she whispered 'What is it?'

'Wouldn't you like to know?'

Once they were in the back passage they could hear Bruno and Elodie talking in the kitchen. Celeste could see now that the package was one of the paper folders full of photographs. But Fabian grabbed his parka, unzipped one of the pockets, and stuffed it in, closing the zip. 'Later,' he said, his eyes like blue stones in his foxy face.

But she never saw the photographs. And shortly afterwards Fabian told her that he'd emptied the trench, so her services in that department were no longer needed. This development was a relief, but still served to remind her of the changes that had recently taken place. Until now, almost her whole identity, her *raison d'être*, had been connected with the trench and its contents. She had borne the strain of responsibility gladly because it meant she was needed and depended upon. Now, suddenly, that chapter of her life was at an end and she was not sure what would follow. She felt cast adrift, rudderless and fearful.

They had left the dark, undecorated house six days before Christmas. The custom was for a tree and basic provisions to be delivered to Quatre Vents by the local tradesmen to coincide with their arrival. Once there, it was all systems go to air and make beds, prepare food and dress the tree before the arrival of the Lalandes from Paris on Christmas Eve.

Before they left Celeste gave Mrs Dove her present – a cross-stitched dressing-table mat which she had made herself at school. Mrs Dove was delighted with it. 'It's so pretty, and all your own work! And I've got something for you, you can open it now if you like.'

They were in the kitchen of the Doves' flat, and Mrs Dove took something out of her tea-towel drawer. It was a square package, yielding and rustly, and carried with it a whiff of Mrs Dove's scent. She had told Celeste the name: Aréthuse. The wrapping papper was scarlet, with brown reindeer and gold sledges all over it.

Celeste admired it. 'Can I open it?'

'Of course! There's not much point in you taking it all the way to France in its paper is there? And besides, I've got my mat.' She stroked it appreciatively with her long, elegant fingers.

Celeste undid it carefully. Inside was one of the loveliest things she'd ever seen, slippery pink satin adorned with a frou-frou of silken frills and flounces and a large pink and white flower made of tulle with a cluster of pearl dewdrops at its centre. She was struck speechless.

'Like it?' asked Mrs Dove. 'It's a handkerchief sachet.'

'It's just what I wanted,' said Celeste. It was a formula, but she could not find the words to express her pleasure.

Mrs Dove laughed indulgently. 'It's never that, but it caught my eye.' She watched as Celeste stroked the satin, the ribbons and the gleaming flower. 'You know what it's for, do you?'

Celeste shook her head.

'It's to put your hankies in, when they're all nice and clean and folded. It keeps them dainty and smelling nice.' Celeste was entranced. 'Open it up,' said Mrs Dove, 'there's something else inside.'

Celeste did not know where to begin opening the sachet. It seemed a shame to disarrange it. Mrs Dove leaned over and tweaked lightly with her pearlised peach nails at one end of glossy ribbon. 'There you are.'

Reverently Celeste delved inside the sachet's slippery folds and felt two objects which she withdrew. She breathed deeply at the sweet scent they brought with them. This was not Aréthuse but lavender, lemon verbena and rose petals, caught in a little bag of cotton lace secured with violet ribbon. And then there was a hankie, but she knew she would never bring herself to blow her nose on it. It was a tiny square of white cotton with a border of lace, and the letter 'C' embroidered in pink silk in one corner.

How could mere words express her enchantment? 'Thank you very much, Mrs Dove,' she said. 'It's lovely.'

Mrs Dove bent and kissed her cheek. 'Only the best for my best girl.'

Celeste knew that, no matter what else she got for Christmas, nothing could be better than this. She could not even bring herself to show the sachet to anyone for fear of in some way diminishing its magic. She realised properly, for the first time, how much she loved Mrs Dove. It was as though she had been given a vision of herself as grown-up, separate and beautiful, a thought which she had never entertained before. It was a little frightening, but wonderful.

Carefully, she placed her three other hankies in the sachet. They could not compete with the lace one, being childishly patterned with coloured Bambis and Dumbos, but it was nice to feel that she was keeping them 'dainty' as Mrs Dove had suggested. When Elodie was piling things on her bed to take to France she kept the sachet hidden, and laid it carefully between two cardigans when the case was packed.

Once she had concealed the sachet she knew that she had constructed another secret – this time her own – which, although not a guilty one, she would have to guard if she did not want to be quizzed about it. While Mrs Dove had regularly given her presents for birthdays and Christmas in the past, Celeste knew on some deep level that this one was different. It was more expensive, more exclusive, more special. It might give rise to discussion which she did not know how to deal with.

When they left, crammed into the Rolls with Blaise in the front with Bruno, and Sandro on Elodie's knee in the back, the Doves waved them good-bye in the yard, and Mrs Dove blew a kiss. Celeste knew the kiss was for her, and had to press her face to the car window for a little while to hide tears of desolation and, for some reason, dread.

Christmas itself had been curiously tense. The weather had been, as it was still, wild and capricious. Shafts of bright sunshine would dart through the clouds and refract on the salt-rimed windows of the farmhouse, to be followed minutes later by hissing sleet and tumultuous winds. The French caretaker, M'sieur David, was full of bad news about window frames and roof-tiles and suggested to Bruno, not for the first time, that he would be well-advised to a) let the property and b)

dig into his pocket and spend money on the fabric of the house
before things got any worse and cost him a real fortune.
M'sieur David was a dapper little man with a Napoleonic
haircut designed to conceal baldness, and a liking for coloured
shirts with white collars. He was not in the least cowed by
Bruno, whom he regarded as the archetypal mean Scotsman.
Bruno saw M'sieur David as a typical nit-picking arrogant Frog.
But each recognised that if they were to lock horns in earnest
their reciprocal prejudices might inflict real damage, so they
tended to be polite. 'I don't want a bunch of strangers here,'
Bruno said in his competent, execrably pronounced French.
'This is our home.'

'Your second home,' pointed out M'sieur David.

'Our other home, yes,' agreed Bruno. 'I'm not aware there is
any limit on the number of homes a man may own, and do as
he likes with.'

'Absolutely not. But there remains the question of
maintenance. This house was built to last, but it is in a very
exposed position. Time and the weather are taking their toll. I
would be failing in my duty, Professor, if I did not point out
that there has been very serious deterioration in the past few
years.'

'I shall form my own opinion while we're here,' said Bruno,
showing David to the door. 'And act accordingly.'

Celeste and Sandro, who were making models with some old
candle-ends on the living-room floor, watched with interest.
These exchanges between their father and any of his regular
sparring partners were oddly comforting. Predictable. Evidence that the pattern of everyday life, in some areas at least,
was continuing as it had always done.

Bruno slammed the door against the icy gust which
accompanied M'sieur David's departure. 'What are you two
staring at?'

'Nothing,' said Celeste.

'You,' said Sandro.

Bruno laughed a mad laugh and waved his arms above
his head. 'I'll huff and I'll puff and I'll blow your house
down!'

They watched him go through into the kitchen, and returned to the candlewax.

But the exchange with M'sieur David was the only thing that did remain the same. Most of the time Celeste felt the underlying differences that made her cold, like the scurrying draughts that fled about the stone floors.

Of course the motions of Christmas were gone through. The fire blazed, the tree came to life under Elodie's ministrations, the range in the kitchen gave off good smells and the presents were heaped on the deep windowsills beyond which the distant grey sea, blurred by rain, raced and roared.

Quatre Vents had always seemed like a fortress with its thick grey stone walls and its commanding cliff-top position, but this Christmas it felt more like a prison to Celeste, a place where they were all cooped up willy-nilly. Fabian and Blaise kept bikes here, but they didn't go out on them together any more. Blaise spent a lot of time in his room and Fabian alternately drew cartoons of the various inmates, or went out on solitary expeditions along the cliff path or on the beach. When he was indoors and at a loose end he was a nuisance, provoking the younger children and arguing with Bruno.

When Chrétien and Lauren arrived with Iphigénie it was a relief to have other people there to draw the immediate family's attention away from itself. Even Iphigénie's headaches and complaints were a welcome diversion from the divisions that were appearing elsewhere.

At Christmas lunch Bruno got extremely drunk and told everyone what they already knew, that he was not cut out to be a father and it would very likely drive him into an early grave. The grown-ups pretended to find this amusing, but Blaise got up and left the room and Fabian growled, 'For goodness' sake, spare us!' for which he was sent out. Sandro began to cry and Elodie took him on her knee. Celeste sat very quietly, staring at the remains of her pudding and wishing it could all be over.

Which very soon it was. On December 27th the Lalandes left. They asked Elodie to go with them, but she refused. However, when the due date for the rest of them to depart came round, New Year's Day, Celeste found that there had been one of those night-time alterations made, and she and Sandro were to stay on for a while with their mother. The reason given was that Bruno had to make last-minute adjustments to *I Thee Worship*, and would oversee (unlikely as this seemed) the return of the older boys to their respective schools. Such an arrangement was quite unprecedented in Celeste's experience and she could not help feeling a thrill of sheer horror as the Rolls set off for St Malo with only her father and brothers on board. How would they manage? What would they say to each other? Would Bruno and Fabian get even as far as the boat without fighting?

'Will they be all right?' she asked Elodie as they ate their supper of scrambled eggs in the kitchen, with the tireless wind thundering outside.

Elodie glanced at her, looking almost frightened before she smiled and said, 'Of course. Why shouldn't they be?'

'Daddy can't cook.' It was not chief among Celeste's worries, but the only one she felt able to put into words.

'No, but Mrs Dove will look after them,' pointed out Elodie. 'And she'll help with Blaise's trunk and everything. They'll be fine.' She looked more closely at Celeste's flushed face. 'You mustn't worry, twopence. It will do them good to be without us for a little while.'

Celeste's anxieties were not allayed by this remark. The very idea that her mother should say that something was 'good for' her father was strange. She wondered what else was going on that she did not see or understand. The thought of Mrs Dove looking after them caused her real pain.

'How will we get home?'

'We're going to fly!' said Elodie, widening her eyes encouragingly.

Sandro gaped. 'Are we *really*? Going to *fly*?'

'Yes. We'll get a taxi from here to the airport, and then fly to London, and Daddy will pick us up there and drive us home.'

'Smashing!' said Sandro. 'We're going to fly!'

Once the strangeness wore off, Celeste's worries faded, she began to enjoy this unlooked-for idyll with her mother. She did not ask when they were going back, and Elodie never mentioned it, so the days rolled by and the house became a fortress again, safe and strong against the battering wind and rain.

But not against the telephone, which crouched, squat, black and incongruous out in the narrow hall with its rush mats and arrow-slit windows. When, very occasionally, it rang, its harsh persistent summons made Celeste's skin prickle, and she noticed that her mother moved quickly to silence it and find out the worst it had to offer.

The first time it was Bruno, calling from home to say they had arrived safely, that he was doing damage to a large Scotch and that the boys had already started on the fish pie made by Mrs Dove. Elodie had laughed with relief, and put Sandro and Celeste on to say hello. Their father sounded loudly genial, as he generally did with a drink in his hand. When she put the receiver down Elodie hugged Celeste and said: 'There you are, you see? They're managing perfectly.'

The next two calls were from Chrétien. The first was to say thank you, and to ask again whether Elodie wouldn't consider coming to Paris. The children could be put on the plane in the care of Universal Aunts and would probably thoroughly enjoy it. Lauren would take time off, she and Elodie could do the town, shop, go to galleries and theatres, have long leisurely lunches in old haunts . . .

Celeste, sitting nearby during this call, saw her mother's face assume the wistful smile which signalled retreat and refusal. She spoke in French to her brother. Celeste could understand only a little, but the meaning was crystal clear. She was so grateful and so sorry but she couldn't. All she wanted was a quiet time here, and then she would have to go back to Hartfield with the young ones in time for the school term. She really wasn't in the mood for Paris.

Chrétien's second call concerned Iphigénie. This time Elodie looked harassed. 'Is it serious? I mean, does the doctor say it's serious, you know how she is . . . really? Yes. I see. Should I—? No, I suppose not. I must say I would rather take the children home first . . . Right. If you're sure. I'll write to her of course, but do keep in touch.' She replaced the receiver and sat with blank, inward-looking eyes. Then she collected herself and answered Celeste's unspoken question. 'It's *grandmère*, she's ill. But it may be nothing.' Impulsively she opened her arms to Celeste and folded her tight in them. 'Poor *grandmère*.'

Celeste breathed in the cool, clean smell of her mother's hair. 'Is she in hospital?' She wasn't very interested, but she liked being in Elodie's arms.

'No. But she may not be able to live by herself any more.'

She squeezed Celeste a little tighter and kissed the side of her head in a way that made Celeste sure that here was one more bad thing to worry about.

She was sorry, but she could not be all that sorry for something which made Elodie need her. Often, during the next few days, sitting by the fire, or round the table, or battling with the wild winds on the beach, Elodie would embrace her with a kind of distracted gentleness and say 'My darling' or 'You are my good, good girl', but it was not the same as when Mrs Dove said such things.

Then came the call from home. It was in the early morning. Elodie was still in bed and Celeste and Sandro were sitting on the horsehair sofa in their dressing-gowns, eating cornflakes. The wind had dropped a little, and fitful sunlight put glints on the gunmetal grey of the sea. Celeste didn't like it, it made the house seem less of a fortress. When the telephone rang she jumped nervously.

Sandro ran to answer it.

'Hallo, Daddy, we're having breakfast. No, just cornflakes. Mummy's in bed . . .'

Celeste ran along the passage and up the short flight of stairs to the main bedroom, the only one on a separate level. Elodie was deeply asleep, her hair in a long, loose plait that made her look like a schoolgirl. Celeste would have liked to watch her for a while, but she knew her father became furious if time was wasted on the phone. 'Mummy! Mummy! It's Daddy on the phone!'

It was like pressing a button on an electric toy. Elodie was out of bed and down the stairs, still almost asleep, her eyes

barely open, her long thin arms wrapped around her against
the cold. Back in the living-room Sandro was still talking.
' . . . we're going to fly home in an aeroplane and you're going
to meet us—'

Elodie took the receiver from him, holding his head against
her for a moment in apology. 'Bruno?'

Sandro wandered back to the remains of his cornflakes.
Celeste sat down on the sofa and watched her mother. She felt
again the trickle of foreboding she had experienced when
waving good-bye to Mrs Dove. She feared that their quiet, safe
time was coming to an end. When Elodie replaced the receiver,
she knew it.

'Oh . . . ' Elodie let out a long, quivering sigh and lowered
her face into her hands. In this attitude she looked even more
like a young girl, pale and thin, her shoulders hunched, long
feet bare and vulnerable on the floor. '*Oh, mon dieu!*'

Sandro, quite unconcerned, pattered off to the kitchen in
search of the next instalment of breakfast.

'What's the matter?' asked Celeste.

Elodie lifted her head from her hands, revealing a face scored
with anxiety. 'It's your brother, Fabian. He's done something
very bad—' She shook her head, on the verge of tears, and then
rose. 'We shall have to go home now.'

It seemed to Celeste that her mother had gone from despair
to grim practicality in the space of a minute. She ran after her,
back to the bedroom, and stood in the doorway as Elodie tore
the band from her hair and began pulling clothes from the
cupboard.

Celeste spoke in a tiny voice. 'What's he done?'

It was obvious Elodie hadn't heard. Just now she could hear
nothing. Her lips moved silently as she dragged her striped
nightshirt over her head, and began to dress hurriedly in
yesterday's clothes which hung over the chair. The low-
ceilinged uneven room, which had seemed so tranquil when
Celeste had come in to waken Elodie, was now spoiled. The
warm bed looked untidy and neglected, the rug was rucked up,
all was disturbed by whatever had happened on the other

111

side of the sea.

'What's he done?' asked Celeste again.

For a moment she thought her mother had still not heard her. She buttoned a shirt, shrugged on a jacket, gave her hair a few savage crackling strokes with the brush – and then stopped abruptly and gazed at Celeste across the room with the bleakest, saddest look Celeste had ever seen.

'I'm afraid Mrs Dove is going to leave us,' she said.

Celeste stared. It was not what she had been expecting to hear. Not what she had ever expected to hear. She rejected it. 'But what's Fabian done?'

Elodie pulled her case from under the bedstead and began putting things in. Even now she was a meticulous packer, shoes neatly nested at the bottom, jewellery in a cloth roll, make-up and wash things in matching green and white bags. Elodie's style of dress was entirely her own, but her packing came from Iphigénie.

The sight of the two bags reminded Celeste of the beautiful handkerchief sachet and pierced her to the heart. A sob swelled and burst in her throat and tears coursed over her cheeks. Elodie rushed to her and scooped her up. She went to sit on the edge of the bed, wiping Celeste's tears with the corner of her jacket.

'No, no, don't cry, darling. You mustn't cry, please. It's not as bad as all that, really. We should never have let those silly men go home together, they're not good for each other. They need us there to make them behave, don't they?'

Celeste nodded, speechless with unhappiness. Elodie rested her chin on her daughter's head and stroked her hair. 'It's Mrs Dove, isn't it?'

Celeste nodded again and another sob tore out of her. Sandro appeared in the doorway carrying a model fighter-bomber. Elodie held out her hand to him.

'What's the matter with Lester?' he asked in a tone of bright curiosity.

'Well, we've got to go home,' explained Elodie. 'And Mrs Dove is going to leave us, so Celeste is sad.'

Celeste now succumbed completely to her weeping. Sandro

broke free and ran the plane repeatedly along the edge of the bedside table until its undercarriage wheels buzzed like hornets. 'I don't see why,' he said. 'Mrs Dove's stupid.'

The novelty of the flight home was wasted on Celeste. During the course of it she went through a complete circle of emotions from desolation via wild and unfounded optimism to fury and back to desolation, though to all intents and purposes she had sat still, and been an exemplary traveller. By the time they reached Arrivals at Heathrow she was mentally and physically exhausted. To make matters worse, Bruno had obviously decided that a good show must be put on and behaved with terrifying joviality, all bear-hugs and chocolate bars.

'You may find this hard to credit but I've missed you, you little beasts!' he announced, picking them both up at once and aiming a kiss at each of them. He found Sandro but missed Celeste, who was heavier. He dumped them back on the ground and kissed Elodie with greater accuracy and feeling, to which, Celeste noticed, she did not respond.

The weather in England was bitterly cold and dank, the air sodden with mist which put a halo round the road lights and forced them to have the windscreen wipers on all the way. The adults' conversation was on two levels. One was tense and muted, conducted between half-open lips and to the accompaniment of brief, urgent glances. The other was artificially loud and designed to soothe the children in the back. It did not achieve this aim, since Sandro was not worried anyway and Celeste was far beyond being soothed.

When they got back, everything seemed treacherously normal. As she climbed stiffly from the back of the car, Celeste glanced up and saw that the lights were on in the Doves' flat, though the windows were closely curtained.

Mrs Dove did not come down to greet them. As they stood in the hall and Bruno took their cases up the stairs, Blaise emerged from the library, carrying a book. He looked aloof and serious. He kissed Elodie and Celeste and gave Sandro a push on the head.

'Where is he?' asked Elodie.

'Upstairs.'

'I can't believe he would do this.'

'Really? Can't you?'

Celeste took off her coat and crept into the library. The curtains had not been drawn and there was no fire in the hearth. The illuminated church spire was ghostly in the mist beyond the Craft. A plate with crumbs and streaks of red sauce lay on the hearthrug, underlining the absence of Mrs Dove. She would never have let it remain there.

She heard her mother and Blaise retreat into the kitchen, and Sandro scamper up the stairs. She curled in the corner of the sofa and waited for the end of the world.

It didn't end. And nobody told her anything. She and Sandro had gypsy bread at the kitchen table, and baths, and went to bed early. Bruno insisted on reading to them. Fabian never appeared. When the light went out, the house was quiet, but Celeste knew people were talking because doors which were never normally shut were opened and closed below.

The next day Elodie said she could pop up and say good-bye to the Doves, who would be off in the afternoon. She tried not to think about that as she went up the stairs and knocked on the door of the flat. But when she saw Mrs Dove, who had never looked prettier, in a white broderie anglaise blouse with a red cardigan and black slacks, she began to cry all over again. Dove, who had appeared in the background with a hangdog expression, melted away again.

'Here, come on, that'll do,' said Mrs Dove. 'Do you fancy a Crunchie bar?'

Celeste couldn't have cared less, but the Crunchie was comfortingly normal. The flat looked bare. The furniture was still there, but all the little touches – the pictures, the knick-knacks, the tins and jars and plants and mats and calendars – had all been Mrs Dove's.

'Why are you going?' asked Celeste. 'Please don't.'

'Believe me, sweetheart, I don't want to,' said Mrs Dove. 'It's the last thing I want. What am I going to do without my best girl? Still, we'll keep in touch, won't we?'

'But why do you have to?' persisted Celeste.

'It's your Fabian,' said Mrs Dove. She put on an American accent. 'This house just ain't big enough for the both of us.'

'Why not?'

There was a silence. Mrs Dove was sitting opposite Celeste at the kitchen table as she had so often in the past. She seemed to be assessing Celeste. Finally she said: 'The little tinker's been spying on me.'

Celeste felt her face flood with guilt, hot and red. She had known. She took a huge bite of the chocolate to stop herself saying anything.

'He's been spying on me and taking pictures of me,' went on Mrs Dove. 'And I found them. I can't be doing with that, lovey, I'm sure you understand even if he is your brother. I didn't say anything to your dad at first, well – ' She paused as if to add something, and then gave her head a little shake and went on, 'Anyway, I didn't. I had a word with Fabian about it. But he never said sorry, you know how it is.'

Celeste nodded. Suddenly she couldn't bear any more. She put the remains of the Crunchie on the table and got down from her chair.

'Bye-bye then, best girl,' said Mrs Dove, and bent to embrace her, but Celeste was hell-bent on flight, now. Dove reappeared in the narrow hall and began to say something, but she didn't wait. That was the last time she ever saw him, standing in the doorway looking baffled and a little hurt as she rushed away with her nasty, rotten, wicked secret.

As she came out of their door Fabian came through from the direction of the tennis court. 'Hi,' he said. 'Been saying good-bye?'

'Yes.' There was so much she wanted to do and say – too much, she could manage none of it.

'I never showed you those photos, did I?'

She shook her head. 'It's all right, I don't want to see them.'

'You don't want to know what all the fuss is about?' He was standing right over her now, she could smell the trench-smell on his jumper.

'No.'

'She found them, but I got the best one . . . ' He fished in his shirt pocket and pulled out a dog-eared square of card. 'Take a look.'

'No!'

He laughed and grabbed her hair, panning the snapshot back and forth in front of her eyes. 'Want to know the best bit? No one believes this, but you will. Precious Blaise took these.'

He released Celeste roughly, so that her head jerked back and hit the wall. Trembling with shock, she ran into the house and up to her room. She closed the door and opened the top drawer in her chest of drawers, taking out the pink handkerchief sachet. She held it over her face as though the Aréthuse were ether and would bring oblivion. But she could not blot out the brief glimpse she had had of the photograph. Mrs Dove, all white and fat and bare . . . and her father's hunched head and shoulders, like a creature drinking her blood.

PART TWO
1987

A woman will always sacrifice herself if you give her the opportunity. It is her favourite form of self-indulgence.

W. Somerset Maugham, *The Circle*

I married beneath me – all women do.

Nancy Astor

There ariseth a little cloud out of the sea, like a man's hand.

I Kings 18:44

CHAPTER EIGHT

Celeste had no trouble finding a place to park her red Metro. The street was on the borders of Camberwell and Dulwich, too far out to be metropolitan, too grand for suburbia. It was broad, leafy and confident, flanked by detached Edwardian three-storey villas, each with its attendant elm or monkey-puzzle tree. She glanced at her watch: ten to nine. The journey here from the house in Parsloe Mews had been fairly painless because she'd been travelling against the prevailing traffic. She was going to be absolutely on time. Everything was organised. She'd rung her boss, Henry Porterfield, and told him she wouldn't be in till lunchtime. A pressing family matter, she'd said, which while it may not have been the whole truth was certainly not a lie.

The house, when she found it, looked much the same as all the others except it was obvious it had been converted into something other than a private dwelling. She caught a glimpse of a large new extension in fresh brick at the back, and one of the downstairs windows had the unmistakable white louvre blinds of an office. A discreet silver plate near the door displayed the partners' names, and several large cars were parked in the tarmacked area which had once been the front garden.

It was a beautiful spring day. The first shy sprinkling of blossom fluttered overhead and the sky was the tenderest blue. But Celeste could not prevent herself from thinking that somewhere, not very far from here, dead babies were being burned.

*

'I don't intend making a habit of this,' said Lauren, putting on her earrings and fluffing her hair with her finger tips. 'I hope you realise that.'

Bruno leaned forward from the pillows to take a noisy sip of his tea. 'My dear, of course. Habit is death to passion.'

'Forget passion, I'm talking tacky.'

'Tacky?' Bruno pretended to be aggrieved. 'I thought it all went rather well.'

'Don't be disingenuous. You know what I mean. You may be used to cheating, but I'm not. Tacky is how I feel, especially just now when Elodie is obviously depressed.'

'You're right, it's all getting very tedious.'

'She's unhappy, and if she ever found out about this it would destroy her.' Lauren took the jacket of her aquamarine suit from its padded hanger and slipped into it, the silk of the lining and the silk of her white shirt whispering expensively together. 'I look on Elodie as a friend. This situation doesn't make me feel good about myself.' Bruno snorted. 'Be like that, but till now I can honestly say I've never done anything to hurt either another woman, or my husband.'

'But this won't hurt them!' Bruno swept aside the quilt and got out of bed with the slight lurch dictated by rheumatism. 'Not if they don't know about it.'

'I know about it, and that's plenty.'

'I hate to point out the obvious, but you and Chrétien are not what you might call inseparable these days.'

'That's none of your business. We have a very sound marriage, based on mutual respect, and I have no wish to jeopardise it.'

'He lets you stay over here in this flat for weeks at a time—'

'He trusts me! As Elodie, God help her, trusts you.'

'She's never trusted me further than she could throw me, she's just pragmatic about things. It's a very French quality. Your husband's the same.' Bruno put on his shirt first, something he had started to do since developing a paunch.

He allowed a silence to develop, during which Lauren

removed their cups with ostentatious briskness and took them out to the kitchen. As she returned and began straightening the bed, he said, 'I must say I think this attack of conscience is a bit misplaced. A dozen or so extremely pleasant interludes in, what, fifteen years? And which no one else need ever know about. Where's your sense of style?'

Lauren gestured at her surroundings. 'Right here. And here.' She indicated her clothes. 'My apartment, my possessions – anything you like. But style does not take in personal morality. Excuse me.' She stalked out again.

He went to the door, fastening his trousers over the Y-fronts he refused to relinquish in favour of boxer shorts. 'Jesus wept, woman, I didn't realise you were such a suburbanite at heart.'

She was slotting documents into a briefcase that stood open on the sofa. Now she snapped it shut and walked slowly over to him, her eyes narrowed. 'See here, old man.' Bruno grinned. 'Don't trade insults with me. I'm an expert.'

'Don't I know it. Look – ' He caught her wrist just as she was turning away again. She did not resist but simply stared down at his hand until he removed it. 'You have nothing to reproach yourself with. It's all been very civilised, a coming together of two close friends from time to time for the purpose of . . .'

She returned his gaze steadily and in her eyes he saw what he had expected to see, that she was too honest to let this pass.

'It was a little more than that, and you know it.'

'Ah, so you admit it!' Quickly, before she could move away, he kissed her, and then returned to the bedroom, sitting down on the edge of the bed to put on his socks. She hesitated and then went to collect her briefcase, calling back to him: 'Help yourself to anything you'd like. Liberty Hall.'

'Thank you, I will.'

She appeared once more in the doorway, briefcase in hand. Lacing his shoes, he glanced up at her, eyebrows raised. 'Still here?'

'I'm sorry. I didn't mean that.'

'What?'

'You're not old.'

He grinned. 'Yes, I am. But I'm bloody good for my age.' He

chuckled to himself, and next time he looked up she had gone and he heard the front door of the flat close behind her.

He was in no hurry to leave. He had told Elodie he might be spending the night and would have appointments today. So he was not expected, and he was incommunicado, his ideal state of affairs. Besides which, he liked it here. Lauren, now an executive director at Grix, had been responsible for the decor of the dockside flat and thought it was not the sort of place he'd have considered buying himself, he had to admit that it had a lot going for it in terms of comfort and convenience.

The kitchen was simply a corner of the vast living area that looked out over the Thames. Below the acreage of double-glazing which afforded one of the best views in London, the wall of the converted warehouse dropped straight into the water. If you put your forehead to the glass you could see the row of iron hauling-bars jutting out from the brickwork, a testament to the building's previous role as a warehouse. There was a busy flow of river traffic out there in the pale spring sunshine, but in here Bruno enjoyed a sense of perfect privacy. There were no draughts, no intrusions, no noises. There was no clutter. Just this elegant large space, a sort of play area for adults. Bruno thought about the night before as he poured himself more coffee from the chrome cafetière. Lauren had been perfectly correct, he was an old man, and she was no spring chicken herself; they were both well past their sell-by dates. But by golly they had fucked each other's brains out last night. No matter what they had both said, he would be extremely surprised if this was the last time.

Bruno picked up his coffee and wandered out of the kitchen. He took the mobile phone off the wall and sat down on one of the low mushroom-pink armchairs near the window. He tapped out the number and hummed 'Wild Rover' to himself as he gazed out over the river.

When Elodie answered he had no difficulty in evincing great good humour. 'Darling? It's your errant husband.'

Celeste rang and entered, as the notice by the door advised her to do. She passed through an outer lobby with a black and white tiled floor, and through a heavy glass-paned door into a hall hushed by deep cloud-coloured carpet and fragrant with the scent from two large flower arrangements, one on an antique side-table beneath a mirror, the other on a desk facing the door. There was no one at the desk. To the right of it a flight of stairs led up to a half-landing where more flowers stood on a windowsill. The place had a churchlike tranquillity.

A tall woman, beautiful and soignée, materialised behind the desk. 'Good morning. How may I help?' She spoke with a faint German accent.

'My name's Celeste Gallagher. I've come to collect Miss Bryce-Atkinson.'

'Ah, yes.' The woman glided round the desk. Her straight charcoal-grey skirt ended just above the knee to reveal breathtaking legs. In her high heels and important hair-style she dwarfed Celeste. 'Do come through and sit somewhere more comfortable while I fetch her for you.' She walked past Celeste, bathing her in a waft of expensive scent, and opened a door. 'Make yourself at home. The magazines are up to date,' she smiled charmingly. 'Would you like some tea or coffee?'

'I shan't have time, shall I?' asked Celeste pointedly.

There was another smile, this time edged by a professional glitter. 'Mr du Toye likes to have a word with his patients before they leave.'

'All the same, no coffee, thanks.'

'Right you are.' The woman waved a long, graceful hand on which sparkled several delicate rings. 'There's a bell by the fireplace if you change your mind.'

She drew the door to behind her. Celeste went to the window and sat looking out at the street. A woman was walking past, pushing a buggy loaded with supermarket carriers. Usurped by the shopping, the woman's small child trailed and whined, and finally scrambled up on the low wall between the pavement and the parking area of the house. He ventured a few uncertain steps, arms windmilling, then stopped and wailed. Impatiently his mother returned to him, grabbed him by the arm and hoisted him down, administering a stinging slap as she did so. His yells crescendoed as they disappeared. Silence descended once more.

The moment she'd said good-bye to Bruno and replaced the receiver, Elodie wished she hadn't done so. He'd explained that he was just about to walk out of the club to a meeting, so she couldn't even call him back. She felt more isolated than if she had never heard his voice. She half-lifted the receiver again for a moment, as if she might still be able to catch him, but there was only the dull fly-buzz of the empty line.

There was an American expression that Lauren sometimes used about people she worked with: 'sidelined'. 'He's a complete gook. He's been sidelined,' she'd say with cavalier brutality. Now Elodie felt sidelined. It was nothing new, in fact it was a chronic condition. She blamed herself for it. Somewhere along the line she had allowed it to happen, and it had proved irreversible.

Crossing the hall on her way to collect Iphigénie's breakfast tray, she caught sight of herself in the oval mirror between the library and drawing-room doors. The glass had a slight ripple that momentarily distorted her reflection as she moved past it; it made her feel like a ghost.

In a series of vague, involuntary gestures she touched her hair and clothes. She had intended having her hair cut a few years ago. The long straight locks, now speckled with occasional wiry strands of grey, no longer flattered her. They made her look witchy, she told Bruno. 'No, they make you look fey,' he said, 'I absolutely forbid you to chop them off.' She had indulged him, compromising by wearing her hair up during the day, but this made her look gaunt. If she tried to brighten her face with make-up (which she had never before worn) she looked like a clown. If she wore shorter skirts, paler colours, more jewellery, she felt grotesque. The panache which for fifty-odd years had enabled her to carry off her plain unadorned look with triumphant success had deserted her utterly. A crippling lack of confidence bowed her shoulders and dulled her eyes. She was not coping.

Outside her mother's room she stopped and drew a deep breath before opening the door.

Iphigénie sat up against her bank of pillows with her eyes almost closed. Elodie could remember the babies doing this – just a gleaming slit showing between their lids and lower lashes. They had been asleep, but in Iphigénie's case it was hard to tell. One had to tread carefully. Elodie did not hesitate or stare, but tidied the tray and moved it off the bedside table on to the chest near the door. Then she touched her mother's hand. 'Mother? Are you awake?'

Iphigénie nodded and heaved a deep, rattling sigh. Her false teeth were the most substantial thing about her these days. The small white slit between her lids widened gruesomely before the glaucous irises swam into view.

Bruno in his anthropological mode had often remarked that a smile was a token not of amiability but of anxiety, frustrated hostility and appeasement. As Elodie smiled her first smile of the day at her ninety-three-year-old mother she knew this to be true.

'You ate your breakfast!'

'Of course.'

'Do you want to get up now?'

'I don't know . . . '

This was one of the many exchanges Elodie dreaded. Iphigénie was in robust health by nonagenarian standards. She was becalmed in the still waters of extreme old age, not moving much, but not sinking either. Sometimes Elodie feared that she would live for ever, still eating, still quibbling, ticking over but non-operational, until she drove her daughter into an early grave. But none of this prevented the old lady from intensive internal debate about how she felt, at every turn. Of course they both knew that really she wanted to get up and would in the end do so. The lure of the television (bought to keep her amused) and the possibility of gossip, or fuel for gossip, was a powerful one. On the other hand it was in her interests to seem to be harbouring one or two undisclosed malaises. It kept people on their toes and assured her of their best attention at all times . . .

Elodie said: 'I'll take the tray down while you think about it.'

'I probably shall,' warned her mother in her chirruping voice, surprisingly resonant for a woman of her age. 'But I must just . . .'

'I'll be back in a minute,' said Elodie.

Downstairs Wendy Potton had arrived for her three hours of strong tea and conversation interspersed with a little light cleaning. The days were gone when it was possible to advertise with any expectation of success for a 'live-in couple'.

'Give me that,' she said to Elodie. 'How's your mother?'

'Oh – fine,' said Elodie. Wendy was about as different from Evadne Dove as it was possible to be. She was a bulging, uncared-for wife and mother in her early thirties with a bleached frizz of dingy-rooted hair, a pimply, heavily made-up face and a bad case of BO. She came to work in jeans and a tee-shirt, which offended Elodie. She did not wish to see Wendy's great winking bottom and knock-kneed legs squeezed into stone-washed denim, and her splayed and drooping breasts and spare tyre barely contained by pastel cotton. They brought out more than a trace of her old coolness and hauteur.

'Wendy, could you clean some of the silver today, please? Just whisk through downstairs and then do as much as you can manage.'

'Sure,' said Wendy, 'why not?'

Iphigénie thought Wendy was wonderful. She had (with justification as it turned out) been suspicious of Mrs Dove, but Wendy posed no such threat and was always ready to indulge in idle and scurrilous chat. She curried favour with the old lady quite shamelessly, buying her the chocolate snacks she adored (though they ruined her appetite for meals other than breakfast) and reading aloud to her magazine articles on marital problems. Elodie hesitated to take issue because Wendy was keeping her mother amused, and Wendy knew it.

As she went back up the stairs to help Iphigénie start the day, she looked forward to the weekend when Celeste would be here. It sometimes worried Elodie that her only daughter was so willing to come back and help at weekends. Did it, she wondered, denote a shortfall in Celeste's social life? She did hope not. But her visits were so welcome, such a help and support, that she hadn't the courage to put her off.

She went into Iphigénie's room and began the long process of assisting her parent to get up, bathed and dressed without seeming to do so. In fact there was nothing Iphigénie liked better than being made a fuss of, while claiming to dislike fuss.

'Is Mrs Potton here?' she asked as they went along the passage to the bathroom.

'Yes, she is. She's going to clean the silver this morning.'

'Good. She can bring it into the library and talk to me while she does it.'

'I'd much rather she was in the kitchen.'

'You can put down some newspaper.'

Elodie turned on the taps. 'We'll see.'

'None of those crystals – they left a powder all over my skin.'

Elodie tested the water and helped her mother in, averting her eyes from the ancient body that was skinny, pouchy and hairless, like the new-born offspring of some species of rodent. Every day she managed to perform an astonishing number of intimate and personal tasks for her mother without studying her too closely. The waxy, flaccid flesh, the freckled hands, horny nails and stringy limbs were an inescapable reminder of her own future. Sure as worms, as Bruno was wont to say.

'I'll be back in a minute,' she said, and went out, leaving the bathroom door ajar. Iphigénie's gruntings and splashings followed her along the corridor. From downstairs the prattle of the local pop radio station accompanied Wendy's whip-round with the spray polish.

The door swung silently open and the German woman reappeared, smiling broadly. 'Here she is.'

Celeste rose as Louise came in. She wore a very short black skirt, a white cotton shirt and a loose jacket in black and white houndstooth check. She was made-up and her short, feathery hair was freshly washed. They said hallo and kissed. Celeste took Louise's overnight bag.

In the hall a black cleaner in espadrilles and a check nylon overall was just laying a basket of salmon-pink roses on the desk.

'Oh, my goodness,' cried the German woman, 'you mustn't forget these!' Without acknowledging the cleaner she swept up the roses and presented them to Louise.

'No, thank you,' said Louise, 'you keep them.'

'But they're so lovely.' The woman put her face down to the flowers and breathed in extravagantly, eyes closed. 'Such an exquisite scent.'

'If you like them,' said Louise, 'have them.'

She walked quickly out of the inner door. Celeste had to put on a turn of speed to prevent both doors closing on her as she followed with the overnight bag. She called after Louise, 'Hey! I'm parked the other way – sorry!'

Without comment Louise turned and walked swiftly back in the direction of the car, tears streaming down her face.

As she made the bed – mercifully dry – and picked cautiously over the clothes her mother had worn the day before, Elodie glanced at the massed ranks of family photographs on the chest of drawers. The only up-to-date one was an enlarged snapshot of Celeste, standing with her arm round Iphigénie in the garden last summer. The others were carefully selected to show individuals at the time of their lives which Iphigénie found most appealing. Chrétien and Lauren, Elodie and Bruno, on their respective wedding days, shining with optimism; Blaise in his black cassock, handsome and windswept in the churchyard of his first parish in Lancashire, accompanied by three-year-old Molly in oilskins and sou'wester; Fabian at the wheel of his E-type, grinning foxily from beneath the peak of a Lennon cap, a cigarette protruding from the hand which rested on the rim of the steering-wheel; and Sandro in his art school days, all black shirt, big fringe and burning dark eyes, the suggestion of a spot on his chin.

Elodie gazed at her children. Children no longer, grown-up, successful, even Fabian – most of all Fabian, if you counted success in material terms. Sometimes she longed for a little of the dependence, the neediness, of their childhood. Even the horrible problems with Fabian had been excitement. She had been at the centre of things then, galvanised by real emotions, not sidelined.

When the boys came home to visit now they were lordly, bestowing on her the gift, as it were, of their new and dazzling selves, patronising her in the nicest possible way, bringing presents that had more to do with them than with her. She did not include Celeste in all this because in a way Celeste had never left. Their relationship, gentle and undemanding, had continued uninterrupted. Elodie picked up the picture of Blaise and Molly. Her grandchildren – Molly was now twelve, and Nathan nine – were a delight. But she didn't see enough of them.

'Elodie! The water's going cold!'

In the bathroom Elodie held up her mother's towel to screen her as she rose, a withered Venus, from the bath. At the weekend Celeste would be here, and she would do this for her.

The house which Celeste owned, and shared with a friend, Alexa, was in Parsloe Mews, just north of the park. It was a schizoid street, unsure of its identity. It laid claim to being Lancaster Gate by virtue of the Royal Lancaster Hotel in whose shadow it lay, but if you turned right out of its entrance you were, incontrovertibly, in Paddington.

The drive back was not as quick as the one down, partly because they were on the tail-end of the morning rush-hour, and partly because Celeste was making an effort to drive smoothly and slowly. Her heart ached for Louise, who was so beautiful and brilliant, and yet who sat next to her stone-faced, the tears trickling down her cheeks. From time to time she would dash away the tears with her wrist; the cuff of her shirt was stained with make-up, pale apricot and grey. Celeste longed to express, if nothing as presumptuous as sympathy, at least a little sisterly solidarity.

'How are you feeling?' she asked as they crossed Vauxhall Bridge.

Louise cleared her throat shakily. 'Not too good. Doped.'

'That'll be the anaesthetic,' said Celeste. 'When we get back you must go straight to bed and sleep it off.' Louise said nothing, so she added cautiously: 'And how about – you know – in yourself?'

For a moment she thought Louise would not reply to this, either. She turned away sharply to look out of the window, then turned back and said, 'I don't regret it, if that's what you're getting at.'

'Well – that's good.'

'So why,' went on Louise in an outraged tone, 'do I feel so fucking miserable?'

Though Celeste knew the question to be rhetorical, she gave some serious thought to its answer. 'Post-operative shock?' she volunteered. 'Your system's experienced a trauma, after all, no matter how much you wanted it.'

'I suppose so . . . ' Louise swiped at a fresh onslaught of tears. 'I just wish to God my bloody womb would stop crying.'

By eleven o'clock Bruno was bored with the flat. He rang his editor, Max Lindberg, and asked what he was doing for lunch.

'Meeting you, as of now,' was Max's reply. Bruno Gallagher's heyday might be some time ago, but he was still a good deal more than just a dependable unit in the Repton Lyle backlist. He was one of a group of elderly but unpredictable writers with interesting reputations, referred to affectionately by the sales force as the Loose Cannons. They might not always have a new one on the stocks, but they had high media profiles and a cavalier, cultured way with them which helped to foster the impression that Repton Lyle conducted its business in book-lined rooms over glasses of vintage port.

'Where shall it be?' asked Max. 'My treat.' He had in fact been due to meet an old crony, the books editor of a moderately respectable tabloid, at the Groucho Club, but Bruno was his favourite loose cannon and he had already scribbled a 'cancel' note in his diary.

They settled on the Savoy Grill, which suited them both nicely. Repton Lyle's budget could easily run to it, the food was better than at either the Groucho or the Athenaeum, and Bruno was a sufficiently regular patron (and his output sufficiently contentious) to merit a special table.

Bruno liked the sensation of being made room for. 'I'll book,' he said. 'You pay.'

*

While Iphigénie took her after-lunch nap, Elodie called Porterfield's.

'Hallo, Fiona, it's Celeste's mother here.'

'I'm sorry, Mrs Gallagher,' said the cool young voice at the other end, 'she's not in today. May I take a message?'

'No, it doesn't matter. Did she say why? I mean, is she ill?'

'I really have no idea. Would you like me to check with someone?'

Elodie began to say that wasn't necessary, but was at once aware that she was talking to herself, the receiver stifled by a hand at the other end.

'Mrs Gallagher? Apparently it was a family matter.'

'Oh, I see.' Elodie tried to sound as though she had realised what the matter must be. 'I'm sorry to have disturbed you.'

She toyed with the idea of ringing Celeste at home, but rejected it almost at once. If there really was a 'family matter' and she didn't know and hadn't been told about it, then she was obviously not meant to know. Either that, or it was a lie told for Celeste's own personal reasons. She had better leave well alone. Sidelined again.

'Wouldn't you be more comfortable in bed?' asked Celeste. 'I put clean sheets on mine this morning.' She did not add that she had done so specially.

'No, thank you. I'm fine.' Louise was sitting on the edge of the sofa, looking anything but fine, rummaging in her shoulder bag. Celeste's tabby cat, Pooter, sat next to her purring smugly. 'He gave me some bombs . . . Here they are. Can you read his writing, because I can't.'

Celeste took the two small plastic bottles and studied the labels. 'This one's an antibiotic, two right away and then one four times a day. These are painkillers.'

'Great. I'll have a handful.'

'To be taken when needed, maximum of six in a twenty-four hour period.'

'Six then.'

'Two. How about a cup of tea or coffee to wash them down?'

Louise laid her head back and closed her eyes. 'I'd kill my granny for a Scotch.'

'Sorry, no alcohol allowed.'

'And no operating machinery, so that's all my fun ruined . . . ' Her voice broke off unsteadily and she turned her face away. Celeste took the pills, and Pooter, and went to put the kettle on.

Being alone in the house on a weekday morning would normally have been a rare treat to be savoured, but the circumstances put paid to that. As she stood in the kitchen she was uncomfortably aware of Louise in the other room, aching and angry and in tears. Celeste felt momentarily mutinous. They had both been put in an impossible position. Almost everything that was happening was bad, and wrong, and she was part of it. She had acceded, colluded, become an accessory after the fact. Even her sympathy was unwanted.

She put out her hand to the kettle and brushed her wrist on the jet of boiling steam from the spout. But in deference to Louise, whose suffering was of an altogether higher order, she bit back her yelp of pain.

At four-thirty Elodie and her mother had afternoon tea in the library. The breaking up of the day into short bites, marked out by naps, and the preparation, consumption and digestion of food, was something Elodie remembered from her children's infancy. It was a process which used time and imposed a routine on an otherwise terrifyingly formless existence. But with the babies there had been the undiluted joy of satisfying their needs and watching them bloom and unfold as a direct result. Iphigénie had needs, but they were far outnumbered by her requirements – which she let it be known were only ever partially met. Added to this was Elodie's knowledge that, at this stage in her mother's life, the most conscientious care amounted to no more than a holding operation. Iphigénie sat near the fire watching children's television. Her mug of tea (safer than a cup) stood on the hinged table over her lap. She was eating a digestive biscuit, which she dunked in the tea with a quavering hand and transported, dripping, to her outstretched lips. Elodie sat near the window. She tried to ignore the biscuit operation, but the slurpings and smackings that accompanied it were audible through the cheery prattle of the TV.

Outside, rain was falling from a bright sky. A rainbow stood over the village rooftops, appearing to end somewhere behind the church tower. A woman Elodie vaguely knew was walking across the Craft towards Hartfield, accompanied by her bounding black labrador. When she reached the stile Elodie was quite certain their eyes met, but just as her own hand jerked into the beginnings of a wave the woman looked away and entered into an over-elaborate dumbshow with the dog, encouraging it to jump over the stile. She didn't so much as glance in the direction of the house again, and was soon out of sight. Elodie knew what it was. From being an attractive curiosity she had become slightly embarrassing – a recluse with an unreliable husband and an ancient parent to care for. From the first she had made no effort to establish a position in the local community. Now it was too late.

Bruno and Max Lindberg emerged from the Savoy in the late afternoon, wrapped in a warm glow of self-congratulation. They had decided that the work in progress, a pseudo-scientific treatise on sexual attraction entitled *Chemistry for Beginners*, had Number One written all over it.

'I love it,' said Max, 'and the reps'll go wild.'

'Gives them something to get their teeth into, doesn't it,' agreed Bruno, 'and it ought to be worth "Start the Week" and "Bookshelf" at least.'

'Sod them,' cried Max. 'This one's for telly.' Bruno climbed into a taxi and Max stood looking in at him, his hand on the door. 'By the way, how far along are you?'

'Quite far enough,' replied Bruno. 'You get the cream of your young hypers on the job, okay?'

'I'm here,' said Fabian. 'Where is she?'

'In the living-room, asleep on the sofa.'

'Everything okay?'

'I'm no expert, but as far as I—'

'I'll take a look.'

He went through into the living-room. The black Ferrari was parked at a slight angle on the cobbles of Parsloe Mews, gleaming shark-like in the rain. Celeste closed the front door and followed him.

He was standing by the sofa with his hands in his pockets. Louise did not look her best. Her eye make-up was smudged and her mouth was open. There was a small damp patch on the cushion beneath her cheek. Her breathing vibrated gutturally on the edge of a snore. 'Did he give her anything to take?'

'Yes. They're in the kitchen. Do you want to see them?'

'Just out of interest.'

Celeste fetched the pills and gave them to him.

'Yeah, perfectly standard. He's a good bloke, du Toye, knows his onions. Did you see him when you went there?'

'No. Louise spoke to him before she left, but I only met the receptionist.'

'Ursula, did you?' Fabian's lips drew back in a predatory grin. 'The Valkyrie. I bet she keeps him up to the mark.'

Celeste spoke in a whisper, to make him lower his voice. 'Fabian, Louise was crying on the way back. She couldn't stop.'

'That's fine. It's a biological reaction as natural as bleeding. I'd have been a hell of a sight more worried if she hadn't cried.'

He sat down on the edge of the sofa, glancing round the room as he did so. 'Where are my flowers?'

Celeste tingled with anxiety. 'I don't know . . . What sort were they?'

'Bloody great bunch of orange roses.'

'Perhaps they were delivered when I was out.'

'Don't be daft, Lester, I sent them to the clinic.'

'She must have forgotten them.'

'What a prize waste of money.'

Celeste took the pills back to the kitchen and put them in the cupboard above the fridge. She dried the things on the draining board and put them away, making a few ostentatious noises as she did so. She was careful to close the door on Pooter when she'd finished.

Louise was sitting up, with Fabian's arm across her shoulders. Her head lolled backwards, her eyes were swollen, and her cheek was red and creased where it had pressed on the sofa cushion. She looked barely conscious.

As Celeste came in Fabian said, 'She'll be right as rain. We'll go back to my place when she's woken up a bit.'

Celeste perched on the arm of a chair. 'I thought she could stay the night here. There's a clean bed made up, and I'm not going anywhere tonight.'

Fabian raised an eyebrow. 'Really? How did you allow that to happen?'

Celeste ignored this. 'It might be better for her not to be hauled off somewhere else just now.'

'For Christ's sake, she hasn't had open heart surgery! A termination at sixteen weeks is nothing. A quick hoovering-out.' Celeste flinched. 'And du Toye's the best there is.' He gave Louise's shoulders a squeeze without looking at her. She was as unresponsive as a doll. 'She'll soon perk up.'

'I think she needs to get into bed and sleep it off properly,' said Celeste.

'She can, at my place.' He took in Celeste's stubborn look with obvious exasperation. 'Look, be an angel and get me a drink. I've braved colleagues, patients and rush-hour traffic to be here, and I most emphatically do not need advice on how to treat a healthy young woman who has just received the best attention money can buy. Hm?'

As Celeste left the room Fabian removed his arm from Louise, and she saw him glance at his watch.

CHAPTER NINE

Alexa, who shared the Parsloe Mews house, thought Celeste was mad and told her so.

'I didn't know I was that exciting,' said Celeste drily, rolling two pairs of tights and putting them in the pink satin sachet.

'Just tell your right reverend brother that something came up.'

'You don't understand.'

'I do. I understand that you're martyring yourself on the altar of duty when you could be having a beezer time with Josh. I mean, what did he ever do to you that you're so mean to him?'

'He never did anything to me,' said Celeste ruefully, folding her nightshirt and pushing it into the bag. 'Nor I to him. That's just it. Neither of us felt the urge.'

Alexa moved aside as Celeste pulled open her sweater drawer. 'So what? You can go out with the poor guy, surely, without it being Mayerling for Christ's sake!' Celeste laughed. 'Well can't you?'

'I suppose so . . .'

Alexa picked up the mobile phone and thrust it at Celeste. 'Then phone Blaise and tell him you're already booked.'

'But I'm not. Or I wasn't when I said I'd go. And I'm honestly not fussy about this charity ball. Besides, it's Tessa I'm going for, not Blaise. What with the children and all her other responsibilities she doesn't get any time to herself, and this weekend school means a lot to her. Far more than a long night at Grosvenor House means to me.' Celeste picked up her bag

136

and her waxed jacket and went out of the bedroom and down the stairs.

Alexa followed, still remonstrating. 'You spend all that time mopping up after Fabian—'

'All I did was pick Louise up and bring her back here. It was the least I could do.'

'Come off it, the fall-out went on for weeks. He was no damn good and you know it.'

'He's a plastic surgeon, Alexa, he can't just take days off when he feels like it.'

'No, of course. I forgot,' said Alexa with heavy irony. 'But the old-boy net is so handy for late abortions.'

'I'm going.' Celeste opened the door. 'Please, please don't forget about Pooter.'

'How could I when he hates me so much? That's the only ex-tom in town to have taken assertiveness training. It's a pity you didn't go along. Have a nice time.'

As she headed towards Bishop's Bridge Road, Celeste was so cross that she had to pull over for a minute or two to regain her composure. She was fond of Alexa, but their house-sharing relationship was based on mutually accepted differences which only occasionally surfaced. When they did, they left a wake of ill feeling.

Celeste, at thirty, was the older of the two by a year but to outsiders the gap looked larger. Alexa was deputy head of features on a magazine entitled *Maxima*, aimed (as Celeste knew by heart) at single, self-supporting AB women in the 25–40 age group. Alexa herself might have been the model for this rather daunting readership. She was a fit, smart, ambitious young woman, with excellent legs and a mane of fashionably tumbling hair. She was never lost for words or for company. Like Pooter, but unlike Celeste, Alexa knew how to say no. Or at least she knew how to say no to requests for favours and unwelcome calls on her time. Men were another matter, though Celeste was far too tactful to say so.

Celeste herself was also AB, single and self-supporting, but she earned considerably less than Alexa for dong the sort of job nice girls have always done. Porterfield's was a recherché jewellers specialising in the repairing, remodelling and marketing of period pieces. They operated behind a discreet black door in Jermyn Street. In their spacious, businesslike reception area on the first floor only a single choice item was ever on display. Customers were attracted by word of mouth and subsequent receipt of the Porterfield's catalogue, gold lettering engraved on glossy blue covers. Inside the catalogue, many of the pieces were displayed on models who, Henry Porterfield insisted should be 'real women, our sort of people, not bimbos'.

This had opened the way for Celeste to be photographed from time to time, usually in pearls, which were shown off to advantage by her flawless, creamy complexion (one of the compensations, as she saw it, of being stout). She did not go in for low-cut dresses, though had she done so she would have been able to parade a devastating cleavage, but unfortunately her generous bosom and broad shoulders were balanced by equally generous (Bruno said child-bearing) hips. Her legs were stocky, her forearms strong, her hands capable-looking. She rarely wore make-up and considered her face completely unremarkable, round and predictable as the face of a clock, framed by her dark hair in a well-cut but unadventurous bob. Her eyes were grey, and her mouth wide but rather set, as though she were perpetually demurring about something.

Alexa wore natty suits with short skirts, and walked to work in Reeboks with her power heels in a bag over her shoulder. Celeste took the tube, wearing high-necked blouses with needlecord or chambray skirts and low-heeled courts. Alexa had a crimson cashmere throw and a winning way with cabs. Celeste had a Barbour jacket and a folding brolly. Alexa drove a classic customised mini, the care of which was entrusted to a muscular mechanic off Praed Street. Celeste had taken an evening course in car maintenance which the Metro had not yet tested.

Alexa's firmly-held view (often expounded at length for Celeste's benefit) was that a girl owed it to herself to play the field and adhere to the fun ethic: take what one could get, grab the going while it was good, live life to the full, and so forth. Privately Celeste thought she detected a hint of desperation in all this. She herself might be too accommodating where her family was concerned, but when it came to the opposite sex she would not pretend to pleasure and excitement she did not feel. Otherwise, how could one fully appreciate the real thing in the event of its coming along?

This accounted for what Alexa saw as her ungrateful treatment of the attentive accountant, Josh. He squired her to dinners and parties, escorted her to the opera and ballet and had even invited her to go skiing with him (she had invoked her mother and grandmother as an excuse). Celeste had no wish to offend Josh, but she could not pretend that her association with him was an emotional roller-coaster, or a riot of sensual delights. In fact she felt almost nothing for him, except a vague regard for his basic decency: scarcely a basis for the devil-may-care hedonism advocated by Alexa. If she was absolutely honest with herself (and she was rarely anything else), going to look after her nephew and niece for the weekend was marginally less tedious than wearing a hired frock to support Rain Forests with Josh.

In West End Lane, just after Kensal Rise tube station, she saw a parking space and slipped into it. Her visits to Sandro at the restaurant he ran with a friend were generally on impulse, for she was seldom invited. She had put money into Fare Do's at its inception, and suspected that Sandro thought she was checking up on him. He was wrong about this: Celeste didn't expect to see her money again. It was Sandro who insisted on referring to it as a loan, she who regarded it as a helping hand and perhaps a good investment.

She certainly wasn't disposed to be critical. On the contrary, she was filled with admiration for what the boys had done. Even after four years she was still struck by how the narrow frontage of the restaurant, with its dark green paintwork and plain gold lettering, stood out among the surrounding shops, bookies and estate agents. The door stood open and the scalloped edge of the green and cream striped awning fluttered gently in the breeze. Jack, the Chinese help, was sweeping the step, wearing a spotless unbleached apron over his T-shirt and jeans. He was the latest in a succession of genial, hardworking Chinese mature students who had worked at Fare Do's: the first, three years ago, had been so pleased with the pay and conditions that he had passed on the job to a cousin of his who was coming over, and the cousin had passed it to the present incumbent. All had introduced themselves by their Chinese names and then asked to be known as Jack.

'Morning, Jack.'

'Hallo there, Miss – ' Jack found 'Gallagher' excruciatingly difficult to say, and left a polite glottal stop in its place.

'Is my brother there?'

'Yes, Miss – They are in the office. Having a row.' Jack beamed unmaliciously. Celeste's heart sank. 'Thank you.'

She passed the restaurant entrance on her right and went up the steep narrow stairs to the first floor. The door to the office was closed. On the frosted glass panel were stencilled the words 'FARE DO'S, PROPS A. GALLAGHER & M. SHAND'. Above was suspended a card in the form of a Manhattan pedestrian sign, currently turned to read, 'Don't walk'.

From the far side of the door Celeste could hear the lively fugue of voices in argument. Not allowing herself time to reflect, she knocked. The voices continued unabated. She knocked again and this time depressed the handle at the same time. The door was locked. The voices rose as if to drown out her interruption, and she caught the words: 'If you're so all-fired creative, here, take the books' – there was a bang – 'and cook them yourself!'

She took advantage of the tiny pause which followed to knock again on the glass panel. At once, as if he had crossed the floor at a bound, Michael rattled back the bolt, swung open the door without looking, and snapped, 'For God's sake, can't you read?'

'Yes, but I didn't think it meant me,' replied Celeste spiritedly.

Michael banged the heel of his hand on his forehead. 'Celeste – I'm sorry.'

'That's all right, you weren't to know.'

140

'That's what talking about money does to a person.'

'Lester, is it really you?' Sandro looked genuinely delighted to see her. 'You came in the nick of time!'

'Really?'

'Mmm . . . ' Sandro embraced her enthusiastically.

'All she's done,' said Michael, returning to his desk and shuffling papers together, 'is postpone the learning of a salutary lesson.' He did not expect, and the other two did not intend, that this spiky innuendo would be taken up. All three recognised that with Celeste's arrival the altercation was at an end.

'I must get back to the engine room,' said Sandro. 'Why don't you come down and have a cup of coffee?'

Michael sat down and ran both his hands over the smooth grey stubble that covered his head. His eyes were red-rimmed and underlined with dark scoops of tiredness. 'Include me out. Work to do. Besides,' he added, 'families need quality time together, I'm always reading about it.'

Celeste followed Sandro back down the stairs and through the restaurant where Jack was now starting to lay up the ten tables for lunch, taking freshly laundered mint-green cloths from the cupboard beneath the sideboard and spreading them diagonally over the floor-length white cloths already in place. On top of the sideboard stood ten plain glass flutes, each containing a single gardenia framed by its own dark green leaves. On the table by the door where Michael took bookings and welcomed customers, there was an almost spherical clear glass globe filled with white canna lilies. The walls were covered with pictures, some of them Sandro's own, some of them framed photographs *'d'un âge passé'* (Celeste recognised one of Iphigénie's grand wedding), some of them paintings by friends and some framed prints. On a comparatively modest amount of money they had achieved an effect that was charming and comfortable and which also had an air of permanence. They reached the kitchen: basement at the front, ground-level at the back. Sarah Brough, Sandro's assistant, was grating courgettes into a Pyrex mixing bowl.

'Hi,' she said, 'fancy a job?'

'I don't mind,' said Celeste, 'what shall I do?'

'She's not here to work,' said Sandro, 'she's going to have a cup of coffee. Do you want one?'

'I suppose I may as well enjoy the sensation of letting one grow cold at my elbow,' said Sarah, grating furiously.

Sandro winked at Celeste as he spooned grounds into a red enamel jug. She smiled. They both knew about Sarah, a divorcee in her late thirties with rather harassed and neglected good looks. She was a Prue Leigh-trained cookery writer who had let her career and her marriage slip, and was now beginning the long hard slog back. Her uncertain temper was due to factors unconnected with those present and was not to be taken personally by either.

'Many in this lunchtime?' asked Celeste.

Sandro rocked his head. 'So-so. But tonight's full right through.'

'So business is good?'

'Terrific. I don't know why Michael gets into such a tizz about it all.'

'He does look exhausted.'

'It's his own fault. He lets himself be tyrannised by figures.'

'But everything is all right?'

'I refuse to have this conversation with you as well.' Sandro poured water, hissing, on to the grounds.

'You think he's going to tell you with me here?' said Sarah acidly over her shoulder.

'Believe me, Sarah,' said Sandro, 'if we were going under you'd be the first to go.'

Sarah blew at her fringe. 'Shall I begin on the filo cases?'

When he'd poured them all coffee, Sandro took a gulp of his and then fetched pheasants from the fridge and began jointing them at the table with swift unnerving strokes of the knife. Chunks of unwanted meat were carelessly discarded into a large bin on the floor, the first trickles of what Celeste considered a dreadful daily avalanche of waste. Sandro told her how Michael had discomforted a no-show: when Michael had called the man's home number the babysitter had let slip the name of the rival establishment where her employer and his party were eating, so Michael was able to ring up and ask to speak to him . . . Sandro hooted with laughter as he described the incident. Even Sarah smiled as she shaped the filo rounds over china ramekins. Celeste was pleased he was happy.

He had kept his charming looks. People of both sexes found him enchanting. Many commented on his resemblance to the tennis star Pat Cash, though Sandro was finer of feature and physique. He even wore, for work, an elasticated towelling headband, around which his luxuriant dark hair sprouted in farouche spikes. Michael was the business brain and suave, savvy *maître d'*, but when Sandro came up from the kitchen as he sometimes did late in the evening he was undeniably the star, a young princeling come from the battle with his apron stained, his sleeves rolled up and his face and throat shining with sweat. That he was a good cook helped, but it wasn't essential. As Michael, very drunk, had once said to Celeste: who could fail to love him?

'Michael really let him have it, didn't he?' He addressed Sarah, as he ran the knife under the tap.

'The arrogant sod had it coming to him.'

'It's so inconsiderate,' said Celeste. 'I can't understand it.'

'Of course you can't, Lester,' said Sandro, 'because such a thing would be entirely foreign to your nature. But take it from me the world as it passes through these doors is largely made up of arrogant sods, and rude sods, and drunken sods and sods who've left their wallets at home.'

'Don't forget the wives,' Sarah reminded him. 'Cows, what are they?'

'Cows,' agreed Sandro. It was a well-rehearsed and enjoyable litany. 'Fat cows, badly-dressed cows, whining cows and ignorant cows.'

'And nymphomaniacs.'

'Disallowed. Intelligent and attractive ladies in their prime who find me irresistible.'

'Ha!'

'Well,' said Celeste, rinsing out her coffee mug. 'Time I was off.'

By the restaurant door, Sandro asked: 'Where are you off to?'

'I'm going to stand in for Tessa over the weekend. She's doing a counselling course.'

'God, you're so good, Lester. Why can't we all be as good as you?'

'I'm not good. I'm perfectly happy to go.'

'That's what makes you good. It's ages since I made the effort to see family. There's really only Sundays and they're so precious . . .'

She kissed his cheek. 'You don't have to justify yourself to me.'

'Have you seen anyone else lately?'

'Fabian.'

'Me too, he brought that new girlfriend of his here the other night. Pretty to die for, how does he do it?'

'I've no idea,' said Celeste. 'It's one of life's great mysteries.'

'Oh, and Lauren brought a couple of clients for lunch, which was decent of her. They weren't too bad – not braying arseholes, anyway, and we could do with a bit more expense-account trade.'

Celeste glanced at him as she opened the door. 'You would tell me, little bro, if you had any worries?'

'I shall pretend I didn't hear that.'

She kissed him fondly as he stood on the step, tousled and appealing, a royal wedding tea-towel tucked into the ties of his chef's apron.

'If you need help, all you have to do is ask.'

'I would, Lester. You know me.'

Yes, thought Celeste as she waited at the lights on the Finchley Road, she did know him. But why did they all, family and friends, think they knew *her*, when the fact was that they knew nothing about her at all? She didn't even know herself. She was only sure that the Celeste she saw reflected back from other people was neither the whole picture nor the true one.

After lunch, Celeste and her nine-year-old nephew Nathan walked through Sumpter Yard to the Abbey. They were going to deliver a message to Blaise from the Mothers' Union, a representative of whom had just called at the house. Molly, three years older, had gone into town with a group of friends to 'hang out', as she put it, in the Graveney Centre, a new shopping precinct which boasted every conceivable attraction from a McDonald's to a Jean Exchange. Nathan was at a loose end and had elected to keep his aunt company on this not strictly necessary errand. They were nice children – bright, personable and aware. Celeste was not sure they really needed anyone to look after them. She had the uneasy feeling that it was they who were being good with her, making room for her in their full lives and making allowances for her lack of relevant experience. All she had done so far was microwave the moussaka from Tessa's freezer, wash up, and take a call from her brother saying that he'd be out till early evening but could be found in the Abbey if he was needed.

Nathan was wearing one roller skate, scooting along on it and then swivelling to a stop till she caught up. He had his mother's clear, light, English looks. His hair was cut *en brosse* in response to fashion, and he wore a purple tracksuit embellished with the Lords of the Universe cartoon characters.

The Abbey rose above them like a great ship of grey and yellow stone, a scattering of inland gulls dotting the roof between its stern gothic towers.

'Which door do we go in by?' asked Celeste.

'Don't worry, I know.'

Nathan scooted off along the path and round one of the massive buttresses. 'Round here!'

'I'm on my way.'

When she caught up with him he was crouched down by a small side door, unlacing his roller boot. There was a notice on the door: 'Abbey Staff Only'.

'Do we count as Abbey staff?'

'Sure.' He discarded the boot and looked down at his odd feet: one in a trainer, the other in a yellow sock. 'Yikes. Better take off the other one.'

'Won't you be cold?' asked Celeste before she could stop herself. Predictably there was no answer.

When he'd removed the trainer he put both hands on the black iron ring to lift the door latch. It was heavy and intractable and his whole face bulged red with the effort.

'Can I help?' asked Celeste, putting her hands over his. 'I don't suppose I'll make much difference, but—'

The latch rasped on the other side and the door swung open. They were in a small passage, separated from the body of the Abbey by a wooden partition. One or two macs and scarves hung from a row of pegs on the near wall, and at the far end was a green-painted door.

'Behind the green doo-oor!' Celeste sang in a stage whisper.

'Pardon?'

'Don't know what they're doin' but they laugh a lot, behind the green doo-oor!' repeated Celeste. 'It's a song. Grandpa sings it.'

'He's weird,' said Nathan. 'By the way, there's no need to whisper.'

She followed him down the passage. He was silent in his socks and she was conscious of the loud, busy squelch of her sensible crepe soles in his wake.

The door opened into what Blaise frequently referred to as the den of thieves, but was in fact the immensely respectable (and under Blaise's supervision, lucrative) commercial wing of the Abbey: a bookshop, gift shop and tea-room manned by volunteers of impeccable character who managed to convey the impression that profit was the last thing on their minds.

Being Sunday afternoon, and with the onward march of spring, there were quite a lot of customers. The tea-shop was doing a brisk trade in fresh filled rolls and small queues had formed at both the cash desks in the shopping area.

'Where's he likely to be?' asked Celeste, gazing round.

'Over here.'

Nathan led on, threading his way between the customers and the display stands. At one point he stopped and fingered one of a jar of pens inscribed with the name of the Abbey. 'I had one of these but I lost it. I'm going to get another.'

'I'll get you one,' said Celeste. 'How much are they?'

She observed the brief struggle between acquisitiveness and training. Training won. 'It's okay, thanks.'

On the far side of the bookshop, stairs led up to a gallery

some thirty feet above the Abbey floor. At the foot of the stairs was a hinged wooden bar, which Nathan unlatched and held up for Celeste to pass through. 'He'll be up here.'

Celeste trudged up the stairs, which were almost vertical. At times like these she wished she had accepted Alexa's pressing invitations to accompany her to the gym. By the time she was half-way up she was labouring for breath. Nathan, having bolted the bar back in place, had caught her up but was following at a discreet distance, his pace politely adjusted to hers. She stopped and looked over her shoulder. 'Do you want to go on? I'm holding you up.'

'Don't worry, you're nearly there,' he said encouragingly.

'Just as well.'

She reached the top panting, her legs trembling and her vision dancing with dark spots. It was a good half-minute before she had recovered sufficiently to take in her surroundings. When she did, she saw an image of Blaise so dramatic that for a moment she thought she might have succumbed and be en route to a better place. He was standing by the gallery rail, his back to her. Beyond him was the vast stone-draped emptiness of the Abbey's upper reaches, its man-made cliffs of granite, its peaks and arcs soaring into dark, secret eyries, pierced by windows through which the uncertain April light bled in drifts of startling colour. Against this backdrop Blaise stood, dressed in black, his arms uplifted wide, his head tilted back as though invoking a Higher Power, his whole frame taut with a thrilling tension.

Celeste did not dare move. Nathan was to her right, leaning up against a table and doodling with a paper and pencil. It was only when he looked up and called 'Dad!' that she recollected herself. As she walked forward Blaise relaxed his outstretched fingers, then bent his arms at the elbow and brought his hands down to his head. Still massaging his scalp he turned and she saw on his face the last trace of the yawn which had accompanied the stretch.

'Dad, Mrs Callender from the Mothers' Union came round and wonders if you're still all right for Wednesday and can you give her a ring,' said Nathan, with the total recall and flatness of tone of the habitual messenger.

Celeste put a hand to her breast. 'Just as well he told you – I couldn't have.'

Blaise came over to her. 'Those stairs are the best aid to cardiovascular fitness I know.' He dipped his head to kiss her cheek and she experienced a dart of anxious pleasure. Then he put an arm through hers and led her to the balustrade. 'Catch your breath and look at this. One of the loveliest views in England.'

Nathan ran ahead of them and leaned forward on his folded arms on the top of the balustrade, lifting his feet up behind him so that Celeste flinched, but Blaise said nothing. The Abbey opened up around them, cavernous but curiously alive as if the great stones had been worn smooth by constant leaping and plunging. Her heart raced, and not just from the plod up the steep stairs. Blaise's arm was round her shoulders, his other hand lay gently on the nape of Nathan's neck. The three of them were suspended in mid-air. From up here the shop and cafeteria assumed their rightful proportions, humbled by the surrounding grandeur.

'Astonishing, isn't it?' said Blaise softly.

Celeste nodded.

On the return journey Celeste insisted on going last. When she emerged into the shop Blaise was in animated conversation with a fellow canon, and two of the bookshop ladies were in close attendance, waiting their turn. Once, as she talked, he put out a hand and touched the wrist of the nearest lady to show that he knew she was there, and would not be long. Celeste saw the woman's expression soften, charmed. By such small human gestures were soldiers recruited to Christ's banner. Nathan tugged at his father's sleeve and was scooped up effortlessly with one arm and held against his side. Her brother was a star in the diocesan firmament. A gilded person who warmed and lit the place where he was. Tall, vigorously strong and robustly male, with the physique of a sportsman and the presence of an actor – not so much a man of God as a man for God, embodying the best of what men could be, someone they could offer up as theirs, but better than they were.

Knowing he would be a while she walked through and stood at the foot of the main aisle looking towards the high altar. Communion was an intoxicating event when Blaise was the celebrant. Even in his last parish in the suburbs of Birmingham, in a grimy church battered by vandals, and with an initially tiny congregation stultified by years of boredom and neglect, his services had galvanised people with their vivid simplicity, brilliantly delivered.

A public-school chaplain whom Celeste had encountered at an otherwise boring dinner party with Josh had known Blaise. 'Oh, yes,' he had said, smiling with a hint of rueful envy. 'He's a born communicator. Charisma is a dreadfully overused and undervalued word in these days of telly-evangelism, but Blaise has it in spades. It really isn't fair on the rest of us toilers in the vineyard.'

She studied her brother's face. It was the face of one of the more merciful Roman soldiers at the foot of the cross: rugged, questioning, altogether human. A rugby accident at school had broken Blaise's nose and left him with two small scars where an enthusiastic opponent's studs had raked his left cheek. It would have been hard to find a man upon whom the priest's vestments looked more devastatingly incongruous. He seemed to bear them as a mild yoke, a symbol of the allegiance he owed to his stern and gentle Master. At baptisms when he carried 'the world's newest Christian' – a favourite expression of his – in his arms to present it to the congregation, die-hard old-school Anglicans grew pink and misty with emotion at the sight.

At the end of the Eucharist he would kneel at the altar and stretch his arms along the edge of the table. His strongly-veined hands and broad shoulders were like those of a Billy Budd spreadeagled to receive the lash. After a long, still moment he would draw in his arms, bend forward and curl tight as a foetus on the ground before the cross. Despite the discreetly bowed heads, every eye was drawn to this hunched figure, the negation of pride and essence of humility.

It was this extravagant self-abasement which convinced Celeste that Blaise, for all his priestly gifts, was a martyr to the cardinal sin of vanity.

As they returned from the Abbey they almost collided with Molly, hot from the telephone. 'Pin back your ears, you lot. You are never going to believe this! Ta-rah! Uncle Fabian's getting married!'

CHAPTER TEN

The hotel where the Gallagher contingent stayed before the wedding had been recommended to them by Louise's parents. 'Completely reliable, caters for all tastes', was how Brigadier Bryce-Atkinson had described it, by which it was understood that it suited none perfectly. The Cableford Phoenix, formerly the Cableford Arms, was part of a chain but pretending hard not to be. There was near desperation in the management's attempts to seem unique and individual, and to capitalise on the hotel's being within easy reach of both Gatwick and Heathrow. The décor was all-purpose country-house, a bizarre mix of mid-Atlantic plaids, twee chintz, portraits of racehorses and artificial potted trees. The doorman was tricked out like a refugee from a Ruritanian operetta in gaiters, a green velvet frock-coat with frogging, and a cockaded hat. The receptionists wore sharp pink suits with cutaway jackets and bow ties. The bar staff, despite the glassy-eyed animals' heads that adorned the walls, were dressed for a Paris bar of the *belle époque*, with striped shirts and long aprons. Service was attentive in a beaming, generalised way, the result of intensive formatting to the Phoenix Hotel standard of customer-friendliness. Celeste had never visited Disneyland but she was sure the two places must have a great deal in common.

At dinner on their first night most of the party gathered for dinner in the hotel dining-room. Absent were Iphigénie, who was in the care of a nurse for the weekend, Fabian, who was dining at the Bryce-Atkinsons', and Molly and Nathan who had opted for room-service sandwiches in front of the TV in their room. Blaise, having finished his poached turbot with a mousseline of crab, had gone up to look in on them. Sandro raided various other people's plates and pronounced the food unexceptionable.

'By which I suppose you mean inferior,' said Bruno, who was doing damage to a gigantic peppered steak. 'Or dull.'

'It's perfectly fine,' said Sandro, 'by hotel standards. Looks good, taste somewhat sacrificed to appearance, but that's okay.'

'You're not eating, though,' said Elodie, nodding at his barely disturbed chef's salad.

'He doesn't,' said Michael. 'That's cooks for you. In between tasting what they're working on and stoking up on junk food they don't get round to eating sensibly.'

Tessa, mopping up Cumberland sauce with a heel of bread, said cheerfully: 'I can think of nothing I'd less rather be. Catering for the family nearly finishes me, let alone for a horde of total strangers.'

'It doesn't bear thinking about,' agreed Lauren. She entered the lists only because Bruno's stockinged toes had slipped beneath the hem of her skirt and were burrowing deep into her crotch. 'Now tell me how you guys are managing to play hooky for two days.'

'With difficulty,' said Michael dourly.

Chrétien frowned playfully. 'For heaven's sake, *chérie*, do you want to ruin the celebrations for them?'

Sandro reached for the bottle. 'Even restaurateurs need a holiday sometimes. Sarah's in charge. She'll love it. It'll take her mind off her private life and she'll very probably stage a coup in our absence.'

'She can and welcome,' said Michael.

Bruno finished his steak and slapped his midriff appreciatively, using this as a cover for removing his foot from Lauren's crotch. 'Right then, what's for afters? Let me at it.'

Sandro said: 'I predict a sweet trolley loaded with things that are all different colours and embellished with sauce chantilly.'

'Pardon me?'

'Ersatz cream to you and me, Dad. The question is,' Sandro

lifted a finger to indicate the importance of the question, 'can they boil the perfect egg?'

Michael groaned. 'Don't be such a pseud!'

There began a lively discussion about the difficulty – or not – of getting boiled eggs right. Chrétien inclined his head towards Celeste. 'What are your views on all this?'

'On eggs?'

'Aaah . . . ' Chrétien pretended to think about it. 'No.'

Celeste smiled and shrugged. 'It's a nice family get-together.'

'Let us hope so. You are happy with the match?'

'As if it made one iota of difference what I think!'

'I'm interested to know.'

'I think they may surprise us,' she said carefully.

'You don't think Fabian has simply collected an attractive and accomplished wife so that he can move on to other things?'

'No, of course not!'

'Of course not.' Chrétien dabbed his mouth with his napkin. 'The very idea.'

Blaise arrived back.

'How are they?' asked Tessa.

'Having a whale of a time,' said Blaise, sitting down and nodding at the wine bottle which Bruno hung over his glass. 'Thanks.'

Elodie leaned her head back, her hands to her throat. 'I think I shall have an early night myself. It is such a luxury to be in a hotel, to have nothing at all to do—'

'You have nothing to do at home!' said Bruno with exaggerated disbelief.

'I mean nothing that *has* to be done,' she explained, looking round gently for support.

'That's right!' agreed Tessa. 'No cooking, no washing, no cleaning, no diplomacy – marvellous.' She laughed, but cast a conciliatory look in Blaise's direction.

'Thank you, darling,' said Elodie.

Bruno harumphed. 'I had no idea my simple needs were such a burden.'

They all groaned. 'Shut up, Dad, for heaven's sake,' said Sandro.

Blaise took his mother's hand. 'I think you should feel free to admit that it's a blessed relief to be away from *grandmère* for a while.'

'If she won't, I will!' Bruno held up his arms as if surrendering. 'I admit it! I admit it!'

Elodie fiddled with her spoon. 'She should be here, really.'

'No, she shouldn't, *maman*,' said Blaise. 'She wouldn't really enjoy it. She'd be uncomfortable and exhausted and the result would be that you wouldn't enjoy it either.'

Elodie continued to look troubled. 'And neither would anyone else, for crying out loud,' said Bruno. 'She may be as old as the hills and becoming mercifully infirm, but there's no one who can hold a candle to your mother when it comes to spreading a blight.'

'That's not fair,' said Elodie, but laughing. 'She can't help it.'

'No,' agreed Bruno, 'it comes naturally to her.'

Seeing that Elodie was not offended by these remarks, everyone laughed. Blaise put his arm round his mother's shoulders and kissed her cheek. Lauren watched speculatively. He was a gorgeous hunk, and had she been twenty, or even ten years younger . . . Of course the priestly uniform did no harm. He rarely wore lay clothes. Perhaps he knew how good he looked, on this hot night, in the light grey suit over a grey shirt and dog-collar. The innate desirability of the proscribed, she reflected . . . She felt Bruno's toes resume their investigation of her crotch and smiled winningly at him, thinking of Blaise.

'You know what I want?' she said. 'I want everyone to describe what they'll be wearing at the wedding.'

After general barracking Tessa gamely embarked on a description of her turquoise and white – and, she stressed, very reasonable – outfit from her favourite local shop in Dane Street near the cathedral close. Michael and Sandro peppered this account with penetrating questions as to style and finish, so that the whole exchange became a set-piece entertainment and the waiter with the sweet trolley (which was just as Sandro had predicted) had to stand for some time before catching Bruno's eye.

'What about you, Blaise?' asked Lauren. Blaise was

conducting the ceremony. 'Something special for the ring-master?'

'I do have a rather beautiful cope,' admitted Blaise.'

'He does,' said Tessa, 'and it's a nightmare to iron.'

Celeste did not consider herself among those required to give an account of their wedding ensembles. Everyone knew what she would be wearing: she was chief bridesmaid.

'Steady on,' her father had said in his bruisingly frank way. 'Matron of honour, surely.'

'No,' retorted Elodie, meaning to put him in his place, but making things subtly worse. 'You have to be married to be matron of honour.'

Whatever her title, Celeste feared she would not look her best in the dress. There were two other bridesmaids – Molly, and Louise's cousin Isobel, an exquisite child of six. The tiny page was Isobel's brother Jasper, still young enough to tolerate the pudding-basin haircut inflicted on him by his parents. Louise had chosen a simple 1920s' look in cream eggshell crepe. Jasper was to wear a smock of the cream crepe, with brown velvet breeches and cream stockings with flat pumps. The girls' dresses were simple and flowing with cap sleeves, drop waists and a soft draped sash that tied on the hip. The skirts fell to just below the hem at mid-calf. Sheer cream stockings and cream court shoes with Louis heels and instep straps took over below the hem. On their heads they were to wear narrow satin headbands with a cluster of mimosa-like white flowers at the temple. Celeste and Molly would carry sprays of cream and white flowers and Isobel a pom-pom arrangement looped over her wrist for safe keeping. On first seeing the designs, along with that of Louise's ravishing lace wedding dress, Celeste had known that they were stunning and original and that she would resemble nothing so much as an animated pillow. She even thought quite fondly of the tangerine silk and pantalettes so much admired by Mrs Dove at Madge's girl's wedding.

Louise had asked her if she was happy, but beyond a few faint demurs which seemed to beg for reassurance (readily provided) she could not bring herself to declare her misgivings.

The waiter with the dessert trolley bowed over her left shoulder and asked if he could tempt her with anything. She would have loved a slice of mocha meringue with whipped cream, hazelnuts and hot chocolate sauce, but the thought of the sleek, dropwaisted dress deterred her.

'Fruit salad, please,' she said. 'No cream.'

The Bryce-Atkinsons having discreetly withdrawn, Fabian and Louise stood in the drive by the hot, shining flank of the Ferrari.

'Come on back to the hotel,' suggested Fabian. 'I've got an extremely pleasant room there, courtesy of your old man, just going to waste.'

'I won't, if you don't mind.' Louise glanced back at the house. 'Mummy's building up to an emotional *crise*, and I think I should indulge her.'

'I'm only talking about a nightcap.'

She touched his large nose with her forefinger. 'Really? That's all right then.'

Without so much as a glance at the house, he placed a hand on her breast.

'Don't!' She dragged his hand down, but it sprang up again.

'I really like you in these clothes.' She was wearing sand-coloured cotton trousers and a man's white shirt. 'A hint of cross-dressing. Can't you get married in this?'

'I wish I could. My father seems to think he won't have done his duty unless the whole business has virtually bankrupted him.'

'He should have let my lot pitch in. Or me. I'd have helped.'

'Don't be ridiculous. If there's one thing more important than conspicuous spending on these occasions, it's tradition and protocol. Besides, I'm their one and only, this is how they wanted it.'

Fabian slipped his hand inside the unbuttoned neck of her shirt. 'So you're going to look tremulous and virginal . . .'

'No.'

'Regal and commanding?'

'No.'

'Filmy and angelic?'

'Stop that!' She batted his hand away. 'Daddy'd go spare if he saw you doing that!'

'Some people,' said Fabian, 'have led very sheltered lives.'

Driving back to the hotel, he felt on top of the world. He had the pleasing sense of crossing the achievements off his list, one by one. He had made – was indeed making – a packet. His dream car (replaced annually) glided and cornered beneath his touch like a fish in water, something pliant and organic rather than a thing of metal and chrome. In little more than thirty-six hours he would have acquired a beautiful, clever wife, her steel tempered in numerous pre-marital conflicts, who would be entering the union with her eyes open, her feet on the ground and her expectations of fidelity realistic.

Fabian's own expectations were high. He had not finished yet, not by a long chalk. As the warm night gradually engulfed the benign home-counties countryside between Chertsey and the Cableford Phoenix he reflected again upon his only problem, the race against time. He already had a grumbling ulcer, high blood pressure, and an alcohol and nicotine addiction that made his own doctor despair, but he had no intention of altering his life and was reconciled to the idea of it being short. Louise would outlive him by twenty, perhaps thirty years. On the very rare occasions when he experienced a small stab of guilt about his treatment of her, the probability of his early demise soon made him feel better. She would still be relatively young, attractive and well off. There would be ample time for her to marry again, this time with some stable and clean-living man who would provide her with security through the second half of her life.

These thoughts did not occur to him in any spirit of altruism. Fabian was entirely self-centred. He wished to achieve his goals, and carry on to new and headier ones without having to worry about his conduct or other people's feelings. Since the day Blaise had told him, so coldly and scornfully, that he was stupid, he had dreamed of a moment very like this – gliding along a country road in a fast car, with all the threads of his success perfectly taut and balanced at his fingertips. And the day after tomorrow Blaise, the handsome, holy devil, would have the privilege of conducting his younger brother's wedding ceremony. They would all be there to celebrate not just his marriage but to acknowledge his material and professional success: the whole sodding tribe from his crazy parents to the gay cook and his boyfriend, the American nymphomaniac and her tight-arsed husband and poor old Lester, intent on steering a middle course and doing no one any harm. Christ knew what she was going to look like in whatever confection Louise was dressing her in.

Fabian tapped in a CD and placed a cheroot between his strong yellowish teeth. The triumphalist strains of 'Thus Spake Zarathustra' filled the car. His pale eyes glinted in the small flame of the lighter. He wasn't finished yet, not by a long chalk.

Plastics had been the perfect choice, a licence to print money. He hadn't been a high-flier in medical school, or at least not in the academic sense. But in spite of the girls, the booze, the partying – and yes, the drugs – he had always kept enough back to get the work done. He'd emerged not brilliantly, but creditably. He'd slogged through the twilight intermediate years, watching the consultants, the guys who'd made it, and fuelling his ambition with huge doses of high-octane envy.

It had got him where he wanted to go. He was now the junior partner to Mr Frederick Gervase, just off Harley Street. His name was on the plaque. The Ferrari basked in a reserved parking space. Annette, his secretary, was a lush career woman in her fifties who had been round the track a couple of times – most recently with a disgraced billionaire – and who wore Jean Muir to work. The practice did no NHS work.

Still grinning, he craned his neck to glance at himself in the mirror. He was perversely pleased by his ugliness. He didn't give a damn about how he looked, but was making a small fortune pandering to those who did. And it took so little! At a party the least glance, the gentlest brush of his hand, could persuade a woman – or increasingly these days, a man – that there was some part that needed improvement or alteration. If he waited, the phone call would come. Most interestingly, he had learned that his troll-like appearance – the rough red hair, the mesmeric pale eyes in the choleric complexion – turned potential clients on. The women especially. He might be a no more than competent plastic surgeon, but he was a preternaturally gifted salesman.

He swung into the hotel drive and pulled up in front of the glass door, blocking the exit of several other cars. One of the Ruritanian doormen appeared as if by magic. 'Park it for you, sir?'

'If you would. Not miles away.'

'No, sir.'

Fabian glanced at his watch. It was ten o'clock. The family would have had dinner and dispersed, he had avoided them beautifully. He crossed the hotel foyer and entered the *belle époque* bar. He did not look around for anyone he knew, his instinct was always to allow others to come to him. At the bar he ordered a large Bell's, no ice, and asked to see the manager.

'I'll try, sir. I don't know whether he's in his office just now,' said the barman cautiously. 'Can I help at all?'

Fabian allowed a tiny pause to elapse, as though considering the proposition. 'I'm afraid not.'

The barman placed the Bell's in front of him, and passed the water jug and *hors d'oeuvres*, both of which Fabian ignored.

'May I ask what it's about, sir?'

'No,' said Fabian silkily. 'You may not. May I have a cigar?'

Having furnished Fabian with a cigar the young man disappeared and returned five minutes later with the manager.

'Mr Gallagher – what may I do for you?'

Fabian removed the cigar and blew a stream of smoke over his shoulder. 'You could begin by explaining to your staff that you're always available to the hotel's patrons. We won't call them guests, at this price.'

The manager gave a wintry smile and nodded at the barman to get on with his work. 'We have a number of young trainees, sir. They mean well but don't always get it exactly right.'

'Perhaps they shouldn't be released on to an unsuspecting

public until they do.'

Another wintry smile. 'Perhaps, sir. Now then, how may I help?'

'I called a few weeks ago to hire your banqueting suite for a stag night.'

'The Buchanan Suite? Yes sir.'

'I ordered the top price menu. I wanted to check that the service would be on a par with the price.'

'We provide our most experienced staff for private functions, sir. There will be a steward and two girls on the bar—'

'No girls.'

'Don't worry, sir,' said the manager indulgently. 'They've seen it all before.'

'I dare say. But I'd rather have barmen.'

'Then I'll see what I can do.' The manager took a slim pad from his inside pocket and made a note. 'Am I to assume that that goes for the table staff as well?'

'You are.'

The manager scribbled again. 'Right you are, sir.' He put the pad away and replaced the cap carefully on his pen. 'I hope you received my letter confirming the booking?'

'I'm sure I must have done.'

'You have the large room which has its own bar, and is soundproofed, though we would ask . . . ' He tailed off under Fabian's pale glare. 'We've also reserved you the use of both cloakrooms in that wing, plus a green room for your cabaret entertainers.'

Fabian raised his eyebrows. 'Green room?'

'It's a large double bedroom with all the usual offices and a mini-bar.'

'I see.'

'That is our usual arrangement. Drinks and refreshments ordered by the entertainers automatically go on to the hirer's bill, so we leave it to you to reach an understanding.'

'Just as long as we're left alone after dinner to enjoy ourselves.'

'Of course sir. Bar staff only after dinner. And you have the suite till one a.m., I believe.'

'Something like that.'

Fabian had long promised himself a night of unfettered bad behaviour prior to his wedding. One of the two strippers he had seen before. The other came with glowing references. He had heard the comic at a sports club dinner a year ago, and knew he was guaranteed to make the veins stand out on a few foreheads.

'Second thoughts?' Blaise leaned up on the bar next to his brother. 'What is that, whisky?'

Fabian nodded. 'Thanks.'

'Make that two, and whatever you'd like.' Blaise held a twenty-pound note aloft. 'Good dinner with the prospectives?'

Fabian's shoulders lifted slightly. 'A man's gotta do . . .'

'I hope you're going to be good to Louise as long as you both shall live.'

'I'm making a bored housewife of her, aren't I? If you'd told me ten years ago that I'd be doing this, I'd have split your lip.'

'How charminigly you put it.'

'That's the kind of guy I am.'

The whiskies arrived and Blaise pocketed his change. 'I've been thinking,' he said, 'about this war party of yours tomorrow night.'

'Oh yes?'

'I think I'd better dip out after dinner. I don't want to put a damper on the proceedings.'

'Why should you?'

Blaise flicked his dog-collar. 'You know very well why.'

'Come off it, Blaise, discard the paraphernalia for once.'

'I prefer not to.'

Fabian rolled his cigar across his mouth, eyes narrowed. He looked, thought Blaise, exactly like one of the gargoyles in Stoke Broughton church.

'You can't fool me,' he said. 'It'd take more than a bit of locker-room humour to shock you and who knows, we might need the services of a man of the cloth.'

'I'd hate to inhibit you.'

Fabian gave a derisive snort of laughter. 'Look, I don't care whether you come or not but for fuck's sake don't be mealy-mouthed about it.'

For a second they locked eyes. Fabian thought that he might have gone too far. Blaise's face wore that expression of bare, polished anger which still had the power to scare him. He shrugged. 'You must suit yourself.'

'Yes,' said Blaise. 'I think that would be best.'

The following day Celeste, in spite of her misgivings about the dress, was caught up in the feverish pre-wedding excitement. In the morning she drove to the Bryce-Atkinsons with Molly and submitted to the dressmaker's final adjustments. Jasper and Isobel, who were staying, had been dealt with first and released into the garden.

'I think this is going to be one of the prettiest weddings I've done,' the dressmaker told her.

'I'm sure the bride will look ravishing,' agreed Celeste.

Today Louise was effortlessly glamorous in faded jeans, canvas baseball boots and a red tee-shirt that slipped off one shoulder. When the fittings were at an end and Molly had gone down the garden with Mrs Bryce-Atkinson to talk to a pony on the other side of the fence, Louise made Celeste a coffee.

'Did I ever thank you properly?'

'Whatever for?'

'Mopping me up after what is politely known as my termination.'

Celeste blushed hotly. 'I didn't do anything.'

'No, you did. You were there, which was more than Fabian bloody well was. And I think you may have been first in the firing line when the stick was being handed out.'

'I don't remember.'

'That's nice of you,' said Louise drily. 'Thanks, anyway.'

'I do hope,' said Celeste, reaching out and taking her hand, 'that you're going to be very, very happy.' The hand lay, acquiescent as a child's, in hers.

'You know what,' said Louise. 'So do I.'

After lunch Celeste made two phone calls. One was to Hartfield on Elodie's behalf, the other to Alexa.

The nurse sounded a little harassed. 'She's a very demanding old lady, Miss Gallagher.'

'Yes, she is,' agreed Celeste. 'Frankly, it's best to indulge her as it's just for a short time. Make life easier for yourself.'

'And a rod for Mrs Gallagher's back when she gets home!' responded the nurse tartly. 'No, I think I must be firm and keep to our routine. My chief problem is not speaking French.'

'But she speaks perfect English.'

'Not to me.'

'Oh dear, you mustn't stand for it,' said Celeste. 'Speak English and just ignore her if she won't do the same.'

'It's a little difficult,' complained the nurse. 'She is nearly a hundred.'

Celeste had to agree it was a little difficult. 'It's not for long, though,' she added, hearing the faint weary sigh on the other end.

Alexa was an altogether more cheerful experience. 'I'm shaking down with that cat of yours. Beat him on the half-hour and keep him hungry.'

'You love him really.'

'What about you?' Managing to get away with only half the organisation?'

'Don't be silly. I'm not doing a thing, it's a holiday. I had a swim with the kids this morning before breakfast—'

'While their parents were in bed, I bet.'

'Tessa was, but she deserves it. Blaise was out running with Michael.'

'And how's the demon king?'

'He's being as good as gold. They've got this horrid stag party tonight, but we shall have a nice quiet dinner and an early bed.'

'You wish. Something's bound to come up, and most of it semi-digested.'

'Don't be disgusting.'

Alexa made a hooting sound. 'A stag night is so old-fashioned it's practically radical chic. I think we should run a feature on it.'

'As long as you don't ask me to write it,' said Celeste.

Only Blaise and Chrétien joined the others for dinner in the Buchanan Suite at eight o'clock. Bruno was not invited, for obvious reasons. Michael had a slight summer cold, and this was used as an excuse for him and Sandro to slip out for supper at a country pub. 'Fabian can't honestly have expected them to go, surely,' said Lauren to Celeste as they sipped white wine in the bar. 'They'd be like vegans at a barbecue.'

'I suppose he didn't feel he could leave them out.'

'Garbage,' said Lauren. 'He just likes putting them on the spot.'

Celeste agreed with this assessment, but permitted herself only a non-committal smile. Mature observation had not affected her early training: no matter what she thought in private, she rarely criticised her brothers publicly.

With most of the men absent, and Molly and Nathan in their place, dinner tonight had a different feel. Bruno, morose and taciturn at being left out, indulged in occasional bouts of terrifying jocularity for the children's benefit.

'So who's going to be first to disgrace themselves at this society wedding tomorrow?' he asked loudly, glaring at Nathan.

'I assume that's rhetorical,' said Lauren.

'You are,' said Nathan.

'First prize to the young man with the chicken and chips! And who next?'

'Me, I hope,' said Nathan. 'If I'm allowed a drink.'

'I told you,' said Tessa, 'you can have one glass of champagne to drink the health of the bride and groom.'

'I take it that means I'm allowed more than one,' said Molly.

'Not necessarily.'

'Oh, go on,' said Lauren, 'of course she can. She's going to be the belle of the ball, aren't you, sweetie? All those dashing young men are going to be plying her with booze and bad intentions.'

Elodie leaned across the table to Nathan. 'You can have a sip or two out of my glass, I promise you.'

'I tell you,' blared Bruno, 'it'll take more than pious hopes to keep that marriage afloat.' He made a pushing motion with his right hand. 'I name this ship *Titanic*. May God help her and all connected with her.'

Elodie lowered his hand with hers. 'That will do, darling. *Pas devant les enfants.*'

'Don't bother, Gran,' said Molly. 'It's not as if we don't know about Uncle Fabian and his many women.'

'Molly!' gasped Tessa.

Lauren gave a shriek of laughter. 'Will you listen to it! Out of the mouths!'

'The point is,' said Celeste, in Molly's direction but with a wider audience in mind, 'that that doesn't matter any more. Fabian may have had lots of girlfriends and Louise may have had lots of boyfriends, but tomorrow they're saying that they want to be together and stay together for the rest of their lives. For better for worse. For as long as they both shall live. And we're all going to be there to celebrate and say we want that as well. To encourage them. That's the point.'

She stopped, aware that she sounded moralising, and also that her small audience was watching and listening with an unprecedented degree of attention. 'Sorry.'

'Don't apologise, my darling,' said Elodie. 'You are absolutely right.'

Tessa gazed sharply at her children, eyebrows raised. 'She is. Your Aunt Celeste is quite right. And Molly – that's enough.'

Bruno gazed round restlessly for the wine waiter. 'We stand rebuked.'

Celeste blushed. 'I didn't mean to rebuke anyone. I just thought we should—'

But Lauren was already describing a campaign for jeans in which a girl in full bridal fig ran from the church at the last minute, hoisted her skirts to reveal faded denims, and was borne off on the back of a Harley Davidson by a man with stubble and studs.

Celeste was only half-listening to this when she saw the very man, apparently, whom Lauren was describing. He appeared in the doorway of the restaurant, hands in pockets, one hip cocked, and stared about him in a slow, concentrated way as if fully conscious of how out-of-place and potentially unwelcome he was, and determined not to be hurried.

Lauren was suggesting animatedly that it was every bride's fantasy to be carried away from the altar by what she described as rough trade.

The gaze of the man in the doorway swept up to and over Celeste like the beam of a torch, brief, searching and impersonal. She blinked. One or two other diners were looking his way, but now the head waiter had noticed him and was gliding over with a politely enquiring expression.

Tessa said her hat was like an inverted cup and saucer and she was going to put her hair up. Bruno spun a knife on the table and said it was for the person whose neck hadn't been washed in the past week.

The man in the doorway greeted the head waiter with a hand on his upper arm, a smile, a thumb jerked in the direction he'd come from. He wore his confidence as he did his scuffed leather jacket, like two fingers raised to the hotel, its patrons and all its works. Celeste knew that the embarrassment she felt on his behalf was quite unnecessary. This man didn't know the meaning of the word. A burst of laughter recalled her to the table, to her own plate where the last neglected mouthfuls of chicken chasseur and green beans had congealed.

' . . . in a world of her own, aren't you?' Lauren was saying. Celeste realised everyone was looking at her again, and blushed.

'What? Sorry.'

They all laughed again, Bruno loudest. 'I'd offer you a penny for them,' he said, 'but I know they won't be worth it!'

CHAPTER ELEVEN

When the phone by Celeste's bed rang in the small hours she jumped as if electrocuted. Disoriented, she reached the wrong way into the empty darkness and felt only the unslept-in half of the double bed. The ringing was clamorous and urgent. She turned the other way, felt for the lamp switch and pressed it. At once the whole room was brilliant with light as two bedside lamps and one on the dressing-table came on. Half-blinded she at last made contact, clumsily, with the receiver, and knocked the telephone itself to the floor with a crash. 'Hell's bells!'

'Celeste?'

She hauled the phone back on to the table, her eyes still screwed up against the light. 'Yes, this is me.'

'Look, be a love and pop down here for a mo, can you?'

'Pop down – Fabian, is that you?'

'It is. Come on, Lester, get your arse down here, there's a good girl.'

She began to focus. She could hear that Fabian was drunk, and was laughing, sharing his laughter with someone on his end of the phone, not with her. For her there was the usual peremptory edge.

'But what time is it?' she squinted at her watch.

'What does that matter?'

'Fabian! It's a quarter to two!'

'Is it really? Time flies when you're having . . . ' His voice tailed into more laughter, muffled as he put his hand over the receiver. Then he was back, sharper. 'So are you coming or aren't you?'

'Why should I?'

'We have a damsel in distress. She needs a bit of TLC and womanly sympathy.'

'Don't be ridiculous, Fabian.'

The Buchanan Suite was in a new wing, protruding from the rear of the hotel between the garden and the car park. Two sets of heavy swing doors divided it from the main building. Between the two was a payphone, presumably that from which Fabian had called her. The moment Celeste pushed her way through the second door she was buffeted by a humid wave of alcohol and tobacco fumes, and a hubbub of voices pitched to compete with the thumping background of rock music. There were doors marked 'Ladies' and 'Gents' to her right, and another, standing open, a little further along to her left. She walked to this door and looked in.

It was only a moment before Fabian was at her side, but in that moment she took it all in. This was a tribal rite. Men fired up or laid low by drink were spread about the room, in various states of disarray, on, over and under the furniture. A naked woman moved among them like some deranged looter on a battlefield, her hips and breasts swaying with rehearsed lasciviousness to the beat of the music. The taped voice sang breathily of a lover with a slow hand. The three dining-tables arranged in a horseshoe resembled a desecrated altar, the cloths stained red and trailing on the ground, glasses and candlesticks tipped on their sides, food spattered everywhere. Pieces of bread, cigarette ends, ties, shoes and crumpled paper napkins littered the floor. There was the unmistakable tang of vomit in the air. On the far side of the room was a small, cluttered bar. One bored-looking middle-aged waiter stood behind it and two more, younger and less certain, stood in front of it, carrying metal trays and cloths. The attitude of these two reminded Celeste of parents at an out-of-control children's party, panicked but paralysed. Most of the men were now in shirt-sleeves. Several were spark out. Another had his flies undone and was playing with himself, to vociferous encouragement from those nearby. The naked woman, whose shape was beyond anything Celeste had dreamed possible, advanced on him, and the men's voices rose in a roar, drowning the music.

Fabian's face, red and grinning, came between her and the rest of the room. His hand on her arm was hot and his breath was pungent. 'You took your time.'

'Where's Blaise? And Chrétien?'

'Gone, hours ago. Come on.'

He pushed her roughly into the corridor as the voices swelled and broke like a wave around whatever was happening. Celeste wanted to see, but he closed the door and manhandled her along the corridor and through another set of wing doors. They were now flanked by what were obviously bedrooms, each with a number on the door. It was cool and hushed here after the Buchanan Suite, and a woman's sobs were eerie and persistent in the silence.

Fabian knocked on the door of a room half-way down, the source of the sobs. It opened while his hand was still raised, as though they'd been expected. Celeste experienced another jolt of surprise, for as the sobs grew louder it wasn't a woman who confronted them but the man she had seen earlier in the dining-room.

'This is my sister,' said Fabian. 'Can she come in and have a talk with Dallas?'

'She can,' said the man, with a slight emphasis on the first word. He had a soft, flat voice with what Celeste thought of vaguely as a London accent. The unseen woman continued to cry, dramatically, determinedly.

'Fine.' Fabian squeezed Celeste's arm. 'There you go, then.'

Celeste gathered herself. 'But I've no idea what's going on.'

Fabian laughed, though the man was stone-faced. 'Let me put it this way. Dallas is being paid the rate for her not terribly demanding job, but things got a little out of hand and she's taken offence.'

'Come in,' said the man. Celeste stepped inside and the door was closed between her and Fabian. Between her and retreat.

The only light in the room was the lamp on the dressing-table. The weeping woman lay on the bed with her back to the door, the printed cotton counterpane draped over her. One pointed bare shoulder and a fuzz of permed fair hair caught the light. On the bedside table stood a half-full tumbler, and a crowded ashtray with a newly-lit cigarette resting on its rim. The man also held a cigarette, and drew on it deeply as he stared at Celeste. She felt again the hardness of the stare, as though nothing could touch him, as though everyone were grist to his mill.

'You'll have to excuse me,' she said, 'I still don't really know why I'm here.'

'That makes two of us.'

'Fabian said something about—'

'Your brother is he, Gallagher?'

'Yes.' She glanced quickly at his face, but it was unreadable.

There was something exaggerated about his appearance, as there had been about the stripper's in the other room. His chest seemed to bulge through the open jacket of his suit. His hips were narrow but his legs were thick, the thigh muscles visible through slightly too-tight trousers. The cigarette was a roll-up, but the hand holding it might have been a surgeon's – was more like a surgeon's than Fabian's – shapely and sensitive, the back of it marred by a burn scar.

She had the sense of being in a foreign element. But whereas he, in the hotel dining-room, had stood astride the difference and played it to his advantage, she felt badly wrong-footed.

'So what can I do?' she asked.

Abruptly the crying stopped and the girl on the bed rolled on to her back and whined: 'You can piss off!'

'Shut it, Merrill.'

'And you!'

'I thought her name was Dallas?' said Celeste.

'Stage name.'

'Oh.' Celeste went round to the other side of the bed. There was an armchair heaped with clothes, some of them costume – a red satin cape, a glittery bodysuit, a black and silver basque – and she perched on the edge of the seat. In her haste she had pulled on a tracksuit over her pyjamas, and was wearing her stretchy slippers from Marks and Spencer. She knew she looked out of place. But she was beginning to feel oddly excited at the prospect of helping the girl and of being seen to do so by the man, who had sat down on the dressing-table stool with his hands loosely laced between his knees, waiting. The girl, who couldn't have been more than eighteen or nineteen, gave her a hostile look from black-smudged eyes. It was hard to tell whether she was pretty because her face was all smeared and swollen. Her chest still jerked and twitched with the after-math of the crying, like a toddler fallen asleep after a tantrum.

Celeste spoke firmly. 'Why don't you tell me all about it?'

'And who the fuck are you?'

'My name's Celeste.'

'Oh yeah?' The girl sat up. Celeste thought she might be going to hit her, but all she did was wrap the counterpane tight beneath her armpits and reach for the glass. 'Oh yeah?'

'It's my brother's party. I'm sorry if things got out of hand.'

'Out of hand?' The girl pulled an ugly grimace of disbelief. 'He fucking raped me!'

Celeste was shocked. She looked across at the man. His face was expressionless, but he lifted his big shoulders in a shrug that told her it was true.

'Don't you do that, you dirty bastard!' hissed Merrill. 'What did you do to stop him? Bugger all!'

Celeste put her hand on the girl's wrist. It was very thin and delicate. The hand had long, perfect red nails, but one of them had come off, revealing the blunt, bitten ends, like a child's, underneath. For some reason this gave Celeste confidence.

'We'd better get you to a doctor,' she said.

'It was a doctor that did it,' said the man in his toneless voice. Celeste was still burning with shame when he added, 'Besides, she was asking for it.'

'Bastard!' wailed Merrill and began to cry again, covering her face with her pathetic, uneven hands and scattering ash on the bed. 'That's not true, and you know it, you bastard!'

'She's right,' said Celeste. 'Nobody asks to be raped.'

'She does in her act,' he replied, stubbing out his cigarette on the inside of the metal rubbish bin and dropping the dog-end. 'Besides which, she's under-age and it's all undeclared income. Bet your mum and dad don't even know what you're up to, do they, sweetheart?'

'Mind your own bloody business.' Merrill swallowed the rest of her drink and slammed the glass down on the table.

'I see,' said Celeste. She entertained a brief, mad picture of herself describing this scene to Alexa. 'So what should we do?'

'I've told him,' said Merrill. 'I want my jug-money.'

'Jug-money?' Celeste glanced at the man. 'What's that?'

'The girls pass a jug round half-way through the evening. A collection for the optional extras. Simulated lesbian stuff. Stuff with the customers.'

'Not including rape,' suggested Celeste.

'That's right,' agreed Merrill. 'Hear that, wise guy? Not including rape!'

'As I see it it's not a question of money,' said Celeste, 'but of making sure that you're all right, and that – whoever it was—'

'The cunt!'

'– is made to pay,' concluded Celeste.

'That's right,' said Merrill again, stabbing the air with her cigarette. 'Made to pay. I want two-thirds of that jug-money for what happened to me.' In warming to her theme she had cheered up considerably. Celeste, too, was beginning to feel less helpless. They seemed at last to be getting somewhere. She looked across at the man.

'Actually that sounds reasonable to me,' she said. She was beginning to get the feel of the exchange, to see what was possible. Her moral judgement was suspended. She was dealing in the available currency. 'How do we arrange that?' she asked.

Merrill tamped out her cigarette viciously and jerked her head in the direction of the Buchanan. 'Her. Yolanta.'

'The girl who's still in there?'

'Girl? Give me a break!'

'But she's raising objections.'

'Among other things,' said the man, deadpan. Celeste

realised he had made some kind of joke, but there was no invitation to laugh.

'I'm sure we can sort this out,' said Celeste. 'Would you like a cup of tea?'

'I could murder a cup of tea,' said Merrill. 'Stuff's in the cupboard.'

The man opened the cupboard at the end of the dressing-table and took out the tray. He put it on top and carried the jug kettle to the bathroom to fill it. As he stood at the basin Celeste glimpsed a spectacular mess of make-up, tissues, underwear and damp towels. Then he turned the light out, returned with the kettle and plugged it in.

There was a brief silence as the kettle began to hiss. In spite of the bizarre circumstances, Celeste did not find the silence awkward. She was aware of having successfully crossed an invisible barrier. She might not be one of them but she had shown that she was not one of the others, either.

'Will – what's her name – Yolanta?'

'Her name's Ruth,' said the man.

'Will Ruth have finished her act by now?'

He glanced at his watch, and she saw that the left hand too was scarred. 'Should have done.'

Celeste got up. 'I think I'll go and waylay her. Sort something out. Keep me a cuppa, won't you?'

'Sure.'

Full of confidence, she paused at the door. 'I'm so sorry, I realise I don't know your name.'

'Joe Cook.' He held out his hand and she shook it. His grip was firm, but light, like his voice.

'And are you the—' she sought the right words, 'the girls' manager?'

'You got to be joking. These mares aren't my problem. I'm the comic.'

Celeste encountered Ruth/Yolanta emerging from the Ladies. She was barefoot, huddled in a white trenchcoat mac and carrying a bundle of strappy clothes and a riding crop.

'Ruth?'

'That's me. Mind if I don't stop, I've got one more change to do.'

'No, please,' Celeste fell in step with her, 'I don't want to hold you up.'

'What are you doing here, anyway?'

Celeste made a lightning assessment of the options. 'I'm a friend of Joe's.'

'Really?' Ruth pushed through the swing doors and gave her a wide-eyed sceptical grin. 'You do surprise me.'

Celeste took the plunge. 'Just before you go back in, can we sort out the cash side of things?'

'Oh yes, I get it . . . ' Ruth stopped, and the smile faded and hardened. 'You're the gofer. Look, love, the kid's a beginner. She thought she knew what she could get away with but she was wrong. She'll live. And she's learned something she won't forget, either.'

'I realise that,' said Celeste. 'But in the interests of keeping everyone sweet, do you think she could take a bit extra out of the jug-money?'

'No,' said Ruth, 'I don't. It'a a small do, there's not a fortune there by the time the comic's had his whack. And I'm doing extra because of her tossing a wobbly. Fair's fair.'

She had her hand on the door handle. Celeste caught the sleeve of her mac.

'Ruth. Please.'

'I said no, love. What's it to you anyway?'

'It was my brother that did it.'

Ruth tipped her head back and laughed heartily, opening the creases on a neck that wouldn't see thirty again. 'Fine. Why don't you go and ask him for it then?'

She swept into the bedroom, leaving the door open behind her. Celeste put her head in. 'I think I will,' she said and shut the door with a bang.

She was so angry that she hadn't actually considered what she was going to do. She was back in the Buchanan Suite before anxiety struck, and happily Fabian was taking his wallet from his jacket pocket in the pile by the door.

An insinuating sound something between a jeer and a sigh

greeted her intrusion. She grabbed his arm.

'Fabian. I want a word with you.'

'My pleasure, old girl. But not in here.' He grinned over his shoulder at the others. Out in the corridor there was the sound of someone throwing up in the Gents.

'Why do you do this?' she asked.

'Why? Because it's there.' She knew that he was not nearly as drunk as he seemed, not nearly as drunk as the others.

'You're going to feel terrible tomorrow.'

He opened the wallet. 'Fifty quid says I don't.'

She whipped the notes from his hand. 'Fifty quid will sort out your little bit of bother.'

'Come off it, Lester!' She could see she had actually wrong-footed him for a second. 'I got you down to administer tea and sympathy, not extort money with menaces.'

'I've done the tea and sympathy. It's not enough, Fabian. That poor girl says you raped her.'

He leaned back on the wall, head down, shoulders shaking with mirth. 'For Christ's sake, that little scrubber? She loved it.'

Celeste remembered the harsh sobs in the quiet corridor, the tear-smudged make-up, the bitten nails. 'No, she didn't. You owe her this.' Celeste wagged the money in front of his eyes. 'In fact you owe her twice this.' She held out her other hand.

He took a single fifty out of the wallet and slapped it down on her palm. 'Fine. Take it. I don't give a shit as long as I can enjoy the last half-hour of my bash.'

'I'm sure you don't,' said Celeste. 'Thank you.' She turned to go, and then turned back and added: 'If I had anything to do with it, you'd go to court for this.'

'Celeste, please!'

His fierce laughter followed her as she went through the swing doors. Outside the bedroom she encountered Joe Cook coming the other way with Ruth, who was dressed in an academic gown and a black silk teddy.

'Just going along for the last set,' he said. 'So what gives?'

'I spoke to my brother,' Celeste told them. 'Here.' She peeled off three tens for Ruth and two for him. 'That's for your trouble.'

Suddenly they were warmer, happier. They both laughed. Joe Cook said, 'All *right*,' and Ruth handed him her money saying, 'Put that somewhere warm and dry for me, will you?'

'Gotta go,' he said to Celeste. 'And cheers.'

'No problem,' replied Celeste. 'I'll get her a cab, shall I? Send her home.'

'Nice one.' He touched her upper arm lightly with his hand. 'And don't worry about your brother. I see it all the time. It'd never stand up in court.'

The next day Celeste was buoyantly cheerful in spite of lack of sleep. She ate a cooked breakfast with Molly and Nathan at eight o'clock and watched as the surviving stags, walking wounded, tottered whey-faced to their tables and slumped over grapefruit juice and black coffee. Of those who had still been indulging during the Merrill incident only Fabian appeared unscathed, his colour high, his eyes bright and his manner abrasively chipper.

'What does your brother run on?' Chrétien asked Celeste. 'Blaise and I bowed out after dinner and even so I am a little disenchanted with life.'

'I don't know,' she replied, and added innocently: 'Perhaps it was a quieter evening than we think.'

'I think not.' Chrétien wagged a finger. 'Have you seen the rest of them?'

Celeste laughed.

At this point Fabian came over to them and pressed a quick, hard kiss on her cheek. 'You're looking almost pretty today, our Lester. What have you been up to?'

'Wouldn't you like to know?' she said.

In the vestry of St Mary the Virgin, Blaise prepared to perform the wedding ceremony of Fabian Gallagher, bachelor of the parish of St Mary the Boltons, and Louise Frances Bryce-Atkinson, spinster of this parish. He liked being a guest artist, and enjoyed from time to time the smaller, more domestic proportions of a parish church. Maximum effect for minimum effort.

He wore a shining white cope, the back embroidered with stylised ears of corn, poppies and cornflowers, the front with a gold cross rising from golden corn. The only other occasions on which he'd worn it were Easter, Harvest Festival, and a recent choirs festival at the Abbey. The cope sat heavily on his wide shoulders. When he raised his arms it hung in a gleaming inverted arc. He laid the ribbon of his prayerbook smoothly down the gulley of the opening page of the ceremony. In the main vestry the choir – six small boys, as many elderly ladies and three men – shuffled and whispered. Battle-hardened though they were, they had a sense of occasion this afternoon, and not only because of the large and predominantly heathen congregation embellished with the extravagantly rich and fashionable. His own presence, he knew, trailing clouds of cathedral glory, contributed much to their excitement, and he would see to it that they were not disappointed. The incumbent, though invited to participate in a satellite capacity, had declined on the grounds that he needed a weekend off.

The church was now full. The organist, an old school friend of the bride, was playing the Andante from Handel's Water Music at a level just sufficient to keep the burble of voices in its place. There was, too, that delightful susurration of expensive fabrics, and net on hats, and the sweet fragrance of much expensive scent. Blaise liked everything about it.

He went through to the choir. They were all prinked up and keen, the women with newly-set hair, the men groomed, the little boys with clean hands. As Blaise smiled and greeted them winningly he reflected on how different was this team of eager amateurs from the jaded pros at the Abbey. There the junior choristers sang like angels but thought like mercenaries, and the lay clerks envied the junior choristers. Nor did it help that twice in the past year the coats of the lay clerks had been rifled during evensong, and many hundreds of pounds and a score of credit cards taken. The Abbey choir took the view that everything would be fine if it weren't for the congregation.

One of the ladies touched his arm. 'We're going to have to get used to singing everything at the proper speed this

177

afternoon,' she said wickedly. 'Mrs O'Toole does take everything at a slow march.' The others all smiled in acknowledgement of this. 'And she forgets last verses,' added one of the boys.

'In that case,' said Blaise, 'I shall look forward to hearing you let rip.' There was a ripple of dignified, worldly laughter. He pocketed their easily-won friendship and moved on. 'Now I must go and see whether or not we have a bride. Not a bad notion at weddings, in my small experience.'

He felt them glancing at one another delightedly as he held aside the dusty curtain and stepped through the door into the south aisle.

Sandro, who was chief usher on the groom's side, was walking towards him, looking charming in his dove-grey morning suit and silk stock, his hair becomingly dishevelled. 'Blaise – she's arriving.'

'I'm on my way.'

They walked down the side aisle together. Elegantly coiffed and hatted heads drew together, commenting on them. Such a splendid family, a pride, so handsome and talented.

Sandro looked up at Blaise. 'You look marvellous, but I suppose you know that.'

Without turning his head, Blaise said, 'Don't vamp me, little brother.'

'Why not? Everyone's got his price.'

Blaise reached the main door. The flood of sunlight edged his fine head with fire and struck sparks from the gold threads in his cope.

'Oh, certainly. But mine is well beyond your means.'

With that he stepped forward into the church porch and stood, flanked by lilies and roses, to greet the bride on her wedding day.

Elodie felt peculiarly detached from the proceedings. She told herself that this was because it was again the wedding of a son, which she had on good authority was not the same as the wedding of a daughter. And there was no sign of Celeste getting married . . . But at Blaise's wedding her emotions had been stirred. There was something almost noble about the marriage of her dazzlingly handsome son to the likeable, capable, ordinary Tessa. It was wrong to think like this, but she couldn't help it.

The same could not be said of Fabian. As she watched the couple making their promises she reflected on the many and curious manifestations of sex appeal. In the bright pool of light at the chancel steps the central group made an interesting triptych. Blaise, given extra inches by the top step, looked wonderfully impressive, his dark buccaneer's face startling above the shining stooks on his cope. Louise, glancing up at him, embodied for that moment the appropriate soft radiance of all brides everywhere. This ferociously independent, uniquely stylish, crop-haired young eighties woman was just for now a lovely girl in white, given in marriage by her father, and promising to love, honour, cherish, and – yes, obey, her future husband, Elodie's second son.

As for Fabian he was his uncompromisingly ugly self, made still less attractive by the presence of his best man, Frederick Gervase, who was tall and charming-looking. Fabian's vulpine profile seemed to Elodie to wear a trace of its habitual cold grin. She raised her eyes to the altar to take her mind off it. But a couple of minutes later his voice, loud and abrasive, said 'I do' in the almost facetious tone that only Fabian would use in church, and she flinched so that Bruno glanced down at her in surprise.

As the happy couple led their train of attendants and register-signers between the choir stalls to the strains of 'The Arrival of the Queen of Sheba', Chrétien put his hand on his wife's neatly-suited waist. The atmosphere, the sunlight, the music, the smiling faces made him feel uncharacteristically sentimental. Lauren, half-turned towards the aisle, looked briefly over her shoulder at him and smiled. *'Je t'aime,'* he mouthed. In response she made a 'what brought this on?' face and leaned back slightly from the waist to whisper to him.

'Celeste looks pretty, did you notice?'

'Not really.' He gazed uxoriously at his wife's smooth powdered cheek and moved his hand so that one finger lay crooked beneath her bottom.

Lauren ignored him and began to move forward to take her place in the happy procession moving out of the church.

When Celeste looked in the cloakroom mirror before joining the reception line the reflection she saw was familiar, but different. The same components somehow added up to a new whole, as if her molecular structure had been changed. Even the dropwaist dress, the pale tights and the headband appeared quite a success. She felt confident, even pretty. Without saying anything particularly clever she managed to be fun and sparkly and to draw people to her side.

The marquee was a pale buttermilk yellow, pleated and flounced like a desert sheikh's pavilion and festooned with cream, yellow and flame roses and freesias so that the scent was quite wonderful. On this hot afternoon the whole of one side was looped back so that the guests could wander in and out on the Brigadier's immaculately tramlined lawn and admire the herbaceous borders and shrubbery which glowed in disciplined profusion in the hot afternoon sun. A combo of army bandsmen from the brigadier's old regiment, currently at Camberley, sat just inside the marquee and played selections from the great shows. The buffet was so pretty and fresh and delicate it seemed a pity to eat it, but everyone managed to force themselves, and to return with loaded plates to the elegant round tables with their floor-length ivory cloths and centrepieces of freesias and stephanotis. Celeste had two helpings of most things, and enjoyed them free of guilt.

Between the food and the speeches Frederick Gervase approached her. 'Can it be Celeste?' he enquired in a smiling drawl from his great height.

'Hallo, Freddy.' Daringly she placed a hand on his shoulder and offered her cheek to be kissed.

'This is such an agreeable occasion,' he said, letting his hands rest for just a moment on her shoulders. 'And you, if I may say so, look peachy.'

'Peachy?' she laughed. 'What does that mean?'

'Delicious,' said Freddy. 'May I get you another glass of champagne?'

'Please. I'd love one.'

By the time Freddy had procured the two fresh glasses he and Celeste had been summoned to take their places with the other principals for the speeches and toasts. Fabian's speech was snappy and epigrammatic, hinting at a misspent past now put behind him, and a blameless future stretching ahead. Freddy's was elegant and droll, adorned by courtly compliments. Celeste did not think she just imagined a special flourish of his glass in her direction as he commented on the grace and beauty of the bridesmaids. She smiled back, slightly tipsy and wholly, unjustifiably happy.

When Fabian and Louise left at six o'clock, the black Ferrari trailing a drag of pink and silver balloons, Celeste was gazing into the sun and did not even see the bouquet until it landed, waxy and fragrant, in her arms.

Joe Cook, driving his white van to a British Legion Hall in Thurrock on Saturday evening, wondered how the posh wedding had gone. This was highly unusual for him, because he rarely gave a thought to a gig once it was over. And he certainly had no interest in the smart-arse doctor who'd paid him his money. But he found himself thinking about the woman, the sister, who'd come down in the middle of the night to talk to Merrill. She was nothing to look at, but Joe had spent so many evenings in *ad hoc* changing-rooms, most of them nothing like as salubrious as that at the Cableford Phoenix, with gorgeous girls of gravity-defying physique, that he actually understood the meaning of the phrase 'looks aren't everything'. There had been something weird and wonderful about Miss Gallagher, well-stacked in her tracksuit, with her boarding-school vowels and capable jolly-hockey-sticks manner and innocent round eyes. She was something a bit different. And not short of a bob or two, he was prepared to bet. He pulled a rueful face as he turned off the motorway. Given half a chance, he'd have been in there.

CHAPTER TWELVE

The invigorating effect of the wedding weekend stayed with Celeste for months. She even found the resources to finish with Josh, though kindly did not tell him about Freddy Gervase. He had called her twice. Alexa, whose social and emotional life was undergoing one of its regular upheavals, commented on her good humour. 'What have you got to be so cheerful about?' she asked, slightly miffed. 'If I was you I'd be going apeshit.'

'No,' said Celeste, 'if you were me you wouldn't be. Apeshit is something I don't go.' She was helping Alexa pack for an early September holiday in Crete. Alexa had been to France in May, but this third week was an escape from the fall-out of her crashed affair.

'Why don't you come with me?' she asked Celeste, not for the first time, as she ironed a pair of burnt-orange silk culottes. 'We could have a blast.'

'No, I really won't, thanks.' Celeste folded a pink shirt. Her shirt-folding was nothing short of an art form. 'I don't want to. I like the autumn.'

'It isn't too late,' Alexa persisted bossily. 'Nothing to it. Just ring the bold Henry and tell him. After all you are entitled to holiday, which I'm quite sure you haven't taken.'

'I have actually taken most of it,' Celeste reminded her.

'Oh, well, that,' said Alexa ruefully. 'I'm not in any way diminishing it, but I'm not sure compassionate leave for your grandmother counts.'

Iphigénie had died in August. She had timed her departure

with fiendish accuracy to the moment when Bruno and Elodie were driving back to Hartfield after Fabian's wedding, so that they arrived to a Greek chorus of the nurse, the doctor and Wendy Potton, all looking distraught and piously put-upon. Bruno, appalled by the fuss, retreated to his shed with the synopsis of *Chemistry For Beginners* and remained there for the best part of several days, leaving his unhappy wife to face all the chores of bereavement alone.

Elodie had rung Celeste and implored her to come. Celeste dutifully approached Henry Porterfield and asked for a fortnight off, which he willingly granted. She remained at Hartfield until the funeral, and it was not easy. Bruno was childishly cantankerous, as though his mother-in-law's death had been expressly contrived to cause him inconvenience. Elodie was more than usually debilitated. Celeste had constantly to refuse her mother's offers of help, and bully her father into doing his share. She phoned friends and relatives, registered the death, cleared her grandmother's room and arranged for the body to be flown to France for burial next to Maximilien. 'It'll be the first time he ever lay next to her for more than one night,' commented Bruno unhelpfully. Fabian and Louise were incommunicado in Thailand, but Celeste informed the Bryce-Atkinsons, just in case the happy couple should get in touch. Her tasks were not made any easier by the presence of Wendy Potton, all prurient woe and acrid armpits, who seemed to have assumed, unasked, the mantle of chief mourner and most injured party.

'We really got on, your gran and me,' she confided moistly to Celeste over Nescafé and Kit-Kats. 'She was fantastic for her age. I don't know why people go on about old people, they got so many memories and that. I really respected her, your gran.'

Celeste smiled non-committally and began to rinse her own cup under the tap in the hope of shifting Wendy, but it was not that easy.

'I'm really going to miss her,' she went on. 'This house isn't the same now, she was such a character.'

There was no mistaking which way this particular wind was blowing. Celeste dried the mug and put it back on its hook with such force that it swung briskly for several seconds.

'She and I used to have such talks,' went on Wendy relentlessly. 'That was the trouble with that nurse, she didn't talk to her.'

'That,' said Celeste, 'was because my grandmother pretended she didn't speak English.'

'She never!' Wendy shrieked with laughter. 'The little devil! No, we used to chat away nineteen to the dozen.'

'It's very sad, but she had a wonderful innings,' said Celeste. 'And she spent her last years here, where she wanted to be, in the bosom of her family.' If she hoped by this remark to make a point about the pecking order of bereavement she was disappointed. Wendy was endowed with the sort of hide which could deflect such points without as much as flinching.

'It's the end of a chapter,' she said mournfully, snapping off another finger of Kit-Kat. 'The house feels really empty without the old lady.'

Celeste gave in. If it had been up to her alone she might not have done so, but there were her parents to think of. 'Of course,' she said, her jaws tense with the effort of false amiability, 'we all so appreciate your kindness to *grandmère*. And I hope this won't make any difference to the way you feel about working here.'

Wendy rose to her feet, munching and dusting crumbs from her rolling bust and stomach. 'No, no,' she said, placing her mug in the sink for someone else to wash, 'don't you worry. We soldier on. You have to, don't you?'

Celeste certainly had to. Though Blaise had come down and placed himself in charge of taking everyone to Paris for the funeral, there was no getting away from the fact that she was in the emotional front line. Or perhaps it was just that she had the uneasy feeling that only she completely understood the extent to which her mother had been affected. Elodie seemed to have gone a little peculiar, and Bruno was not being the stay and support she was entitled to expect.

The funeral, even by the standards of the occasion, was depressing. The late August afternoon was overcast but hot – stale, charmless weather in which they all languished in their dark clothes. Like all funerals of the very old it was poorly attended. At the graveside, among the petrified forest of headstones in the drab churchyard where Iphigénie's husband was buried, were ranged on one side the Gallaghers and Lalandes, and on the other a curious group comprising Iphigénie's former housekeeper, her doctor, her lawyer and the sole survivor of her luncheon-and-cards circle, now bent double over a walking-frame. There were also two stout, choleric, ancient men, erstwhile business colleagues of Maximilien who must have heard of his wife's death over the twilight tom-tom, and come to pay their respects out of shared guilt for years of goatish complicity. Elodie was thin and pale as a ghost on Blaise's arm, Bruno was scowling and fidgety, making it obvious that he was only attending on suffrance. The priest, in a black biretta, swooped and muttered through the service on automatic pilot. All Celeste felt, as the small coffin was lowered into its narrow resting place, was a great relief. She was therefore surprised, as they left the graveside, to see that Sandro had been crying. She went and linked her arm through his.

'Cheer up. She had a long life and quite a happy one in a perverse way. She certainly always suited herself.' He shook his head speechlessly and dashed at his eyes with his free hand. She kissed his damp cheek. 'Mm? Sandro? What is it, really?'

'I don't know . . . I'm sorry. It's – intimations of mortality or something.'

'Oh well,' she cuddled his arm, 'that's allowed. But you've got a long way to go yet. You've got to get those three Michelin stars, at the very least.'

They had fallen slightly behind the others, who were now climbing into the cars, watched with glum indifference by a handful of passers-by.

Sandro disengaged himself from her arm, rummaged for a handkerchief and blew his nose. 'I didn't mean me,' he said. 'I meant Michael.'

Celeste's heart stumbled and missed a beat. Sandro must have seen the effect of his remark upon her, for he took her arm again and together they walked to the waiting cars.

It was only towards the end of Lauren's elegant buffet that

Celeste regained sufficient composure to broach the subject again.

'I'm sorry for being such a broken reed back there,' she said to Sandro. 'How bad is it? And what can anyone do to help?'

'Nothing, really.' She saw his eyes fill again, but he got a grip on himself, took a deep uneven breath and cleared his throat. 'He found out a year ago, but he didn't tell me. People go for years without becoming ill, and he didn't want to worry me. Now he's actually got it, and it's twice as bad because I had no warning.'

'Oh, love—' Celeste put her hand over his wrist, stroking the back of his hand with her thumb. 'This is dreadful. But how bad is he? I'm always reading about long, long remissions. You're going to have to think positive.'

'Whichever way you look at it, Lester, he's under sentence of death,' said Sandro, turning upon her the full, pleading poignancy of his large eyes. 'And I'm going to be on my own. It's easy to talk about thinking positive, but I don't know that I – that I can . . .'

'I know. I'm sorry. Platitudes are no help,' said Celeste. 'Let's have a proper talk when we get back, and Michael too. Have you told the others?'

He shook his head. 'I've missed my chance with Mum, I can't possibly inflict it on her now. Same goes for Dad. They've always behaved as though if they ignore it – me and Michael – it'll go away. And Fabian's view is that it goes with the territory, I've heard him say so.'

'You should certainly tell Blaise,' said Celeste.

Sandro pulled a wry face. 'His line of business, you mean.'

'Yes,' she replied, adding quite acerbically, 'besides, he *ought* to know, he's your oldest brother and in the best position to help. As for me: what can I say, except that you know I'm always here.'

He lifted her hand and kissed it. 'Love you, Lester.'

On the return flight Celeste sat next to Blaise.

'So how are you?' he said. 'It's so odd to be just us, no spouses and offspring. Like the old days.' He made those days sound like an idyll of harmony and innocence.

'I'm fine,' she said, 'but Mother isn't.'

'It's perfectly natural,' said Blaise. 'She's temporarily without a focus for her life. Tessa's going to invite them both up. I'm impossibly snowed under as usual, but it will give them a break. It's at times like this I wish Father had never sold Quatre Vents. They could have gone off there together and had some peace and quiet.'

It seemed a waste of time to point out that Bruno had sold the house because he was no longer in the least interested in getting away with his wife, nor in visiting her relatives. And if Blaise had any sense of the part he had played in bringing this state of affairs about he never showed it.

'Will you be able to cope with Father?' she asked.

'He'll become more civilised if he's treated in a civilised way,' said Blaise, with a sweet reasonableness which made Celeste's blood boil.

'He's exceptionally b. minded at the moment.'

Blaise smiled indulgently. 'He's hardly going to change the habit of a lifetime over a little thing like a death in the family. He's getting through a difficult time the only way he knows how. By being twice as difficult himself.'

Celeste glanced over her shoulder. The stewardess with the drinks trolley was attempting to interest Bruno in her wares. It was clear from his attitude – half-out of his seat, surveying the cans and miniatures with a disdainful expression – that he was being awkward. The stewardess's professional smile was a work of art. Celeste turned back with a sigh. 'I suppose so.'

The trolley reached them and Blaise ordered himself a whisky and Malvern, and Celeste a diet Coke (the 'diet' part not specified by her). When it moved on, she said cautiously: 'Has Sandro spoken to you?'

'No. But if it's about Michael, I guessed. He's obviously unwell and he's lost a lot of weight. He could always run me into the ground but when we went out before the wedding he was nauseous after half a mile.'

'It's so *awful*. What are we going to do?'

'Pray.'

Celeste thought this an extremely soft option, but forbore to say so. 'Sandro's devastated.'

Blaise took a reflective sip of his Scotch and narrowed his eyes at his plastic glass. 'This may sound hard – and if it does I apologise – but this experience could turn out to be of immense value to Sandro.'

'Blaise, for goodness' sake!'

'He may surprise us all. Call up hidden reserves that neither he nor the rest of us knew were there. It happens. It's not only the dying who discover unexpected courage. God pushes people and they fly.'

Celeste looked out of the window and reflected on this as they dropped through the dingy eiderdown of cloud towards Heathrow.

August, dull and muggy, had shuffled to its end. Fabian and Louise returned from Bangkok and took up residence in a palatial modern flat in a block in St John's Wood, just north of Regent's Park. Fabian said that it was possible to hear the lions roaring at feeding-time. Blaise, up to his eyes in initiating admission charges at the Abbey, contacted Celeste to say that Elodie had accepted their invitation, but that Bruno had pleaded pressure of work.

'Actually,' said Celeste. 'I think it's a good thing for her to get away from him for a while. And it'll be easier for you and Tessa too.'

'Not if she insists on behaving as if he were a recalcitrant adolescent who's likely to burn the house down in her absence. She's going to be like a cat on hot bricks the entire time which will completely defeat the object of the exercise.'

'Perhaps *you* could persuade him—'

'Hopeless, a complete waste of time, he's determined to be contrary.'

'I'm sure she'll stop worrying once she's actually with you.'

'I very much doubt it. Sadly, I think we'll have to admit defeat on this occasion.'

Oh no you don't, thought Celeste. 'I've got an idea,' she said. 'Why don't I go up to Hartfield and stay with him while she's away? I can easily commute from there and then she'll know he's being looked after.'

'That,' said Blaise coolly, 'would be a saintly act.'

'My pleasure,' said Celeste.

It didn't end there. A few days later Tessa rang, sounding more than usually harassed. 'Celeste, I feel simply awful about this. I was going to drive down and pick your mother up but the wretched Retreat House Management Committee have had to bring their AGM forward to the Friday for reasons too tedious to go into, and it's the service of blessing for pets on the Sunday which means I'm going to be baking for the five thousand on the Saturday. QED, I'm completely lumbered. I don't suppose I could possibly prevail upon you, if you're going to be there, to pop mother-in-law on a train? If she catches one in the early afternoon then I'm sure one of us—'

'That's all right,' said Celeste. Tessa could never be accused of shirking. 'I'll run her up to you. It's a weekend, I'd enjoy it, and it'll get her holiday off to a good start.'

'I dropped a hint to Bruno, but it wasn't taken up, you know what he's like.'

'I do,' said Celeste. 'Don't worry, I'll bring her. Then everyone's happy.'

The stay at Hartfield was one of the reasons she had declined Alexa's invitation, but she had not said so for fear of incurring her friend's usual accusations of spineless doormatting. She did not feel in the least like a doormat. There was still, like a tiny pilot light at the back of her mind, the delightfully empowering memory of getting Fabian off the hook; and also that of Joe Cook's hard-to-impress blue eyes as they warmed briefly in her honour, and the feel of his careful, scarred hand encasing hers as they said goodbye.

As so often happened after the obligatory holidays of August, the weather improved, so that Celeste's drive north into the fens with her mother was blessed with fresh blue skies across which bosomy clouds sailed voluptuously, trailing their shadows across the broad fields.

'Now you're going to have a smashing time,' said Celeste.

'Father and I will be absolutely fine, and you're not going to give us even a passing thought. No news is good news, okay?' She flashed a brief smile at Elodie, who sat very straight and squaw-like in the passenger seat, with her hair in a plait over her shoulder. There was a poignancy for Celeste in this holiday reversion to a younger style. In it she could read the extent of Bruno's carelessly crushing influence on her mother.

They turned on to the dual carriageway and Celeste got up speed. A crow, pecking at a dead fox on the hard shoulder, lumbered up into the air like a tattered black binbag. 'Poor thing,' sighed Elodie, sounding unutterably sad.

Celeste played her trump card: 'Freddy Gervase called me the other evening. Do you remember him – Fabian's partner?'

'Of course I remember him!' Elodie exclaimed with barely concealed surprise and delight. 'Darling, that's—' it took her only a few seconds to reject the various adjectives which had spontaneously occurred to her and adjust her remark to the rather lame: 'What did he want?'

'He was inviting me to have dinner with him on Saturday week.'

'Dinner! What fun!' said Elodie and turned to gaze out of the window with an air of the utmost contentment.

Celeste was pleased that her mother was pleased. But it wearied her a little to be reminded of all the hidden hopes and expectations concerning herself. It was not simply that her parents wanted to see her married. It was more complicated than that. They wanted evidence of her lusty normality (Bruno would probably have liked a few stained sheets) and then they wanted her to go on being her amenable and available self. They wished to be relieved of the burden of her virtue while still reaping its benefits. These were the facts of the matter as Celeste, quite without rancour, saw them.

'Look,' she said, touching Elodie's hand. 'We're almost there.'

Ahead of them, still some miles away and rising above the surrounding buildings as though it rode on their backs, was the Abbey.

Be An Angel

*

'My main concern,' said the Dean to Canons Gallagher and Mates as they stood just inside the west door surveying the sign that advertised admission charges, 'is that people should understand where their money is going and what it's for, without us appearing to bang on excessively about bricks and mortar.'

Derek Mates agreed. 'We mustn't lose sight of the fact that a visit to a cathedral is at least in part a spiritual experience.'

'If you'll forgive my saying so, Dean,' said Blaise in a tone which did anything but beg forgiveness, 'you worry unnecessarily about emphasis. These are entrepreneurial times. People understand bricks and mortar. They appreciate a practical approach. And as for your point, Derek, surely the Abbey is an instance of the material and spiritual being one and the same thing – inseparable. A chap's not going to have much of a holy moment if he's standing in a pool of water being showered with falling masonry.'

The Dean laughed. 'Your usual graphic touch, Blaise. You're right, of course.'

'There's some truth in what you say,' conceded Derek.

'Why thank you,' said Blaise.

'But,' went on Derek, 'public relations is going to be vital over this initial period.'

'Of course. As ever.' The Dean began to rock back on one leg, arcing the other foot from side to side in front of him, a sign that he was about to take his leave. 'Yes. The important thing is to keep talking. Communicating. Not to appear just to have stuck the signs up and retreated. What we say to the visitors is going to be a hundred times more valuable than any carefully-worded justifications in print.'

'Absolutely. Absolutely,' said Derek Mates.

'Right,' said the Dean, executing a drop-kick with an invisible ball. 'I'm off. Fur and feathers tomorrow, yes? And Jenny and I have the radical Rector of the Witton-in-Rise group coming for dinner.'

'Well,' said Blaise, 'our Lord dined with tax-collectors.'

191

The Dean, who had intended no slight to the Reverend Rammage, and who was never quite sure when his Canon Treasurer was making fun of him, threw his head up, took two steps backwards, gave a short snicker like a nervous pony, and departed.

Blaise and Derek Mates walked through the Abbey towards the south door. There were plenty of visitors about, gazing up from guidebooks, lighting tapers in the side chapels, bending close to read worn inscriptions. A few sat on the wooden chairs, staring towards the high altar, resting their feet and letting their brains, uncoupled, drift free. The sound of voices was like water falling on to stones, a continuous, uneven ripple, resonant but indecipherable in the huge space. When Blaise caught someone's eye he smiled and said 'Hallo, nice to see you!' as if this were his house and all had been invited.

There was a gypsy family hovering near the entrance to the south porch. The big trailers with their attendant dogs, litter and scrap iron appeared regularly on the bridleway at the foot of the cathedral meadows at this time of year as the travellers moved into the area for potato-lifting and pea- and fruit-picking. The farmers welcomed the cheap, tough labour. The chattering classes with their sympathetically-modernised manses and manors became extra security-conscious and said well, these weren't real gypsies, not true Romanies, but they had a right to live, just so long as they gave no trouble. The locals said they were a bunch of bloody old dids and the sooner they were off out of it the better.

The woman by the Abbey door could have been any age between twenty and fifty and had a thin, sagging body and a shock of wild, dull hair. In a battered carrycot on wheels sat a large stained toddler mauling a frozen Skyrocket and surrounded by several plastic supermarket carriers bulging with crisps, sliced white bread and bottles of highly-coloured soft drink. Two other children, a boy and a girl of junior school age, loitered nearby. The boy wore a thick, matted jumper, jeans and plimsolls, and the girl a frilly sundress over a frayed, lime-green tee-shirt. All four of them had the slightly scurfy, black-nailed, grey-faced look of the seldom washed and unhealthily fed, though the children had feral eyes, agelessly calculating.

'Good afternoon to you!' cried Derek with great heartiness.

'We got to pay to go in there?' asked the woman.

'Yes, I'm afraid so,' said Derek. 'If we don't raise the money there won't be an Abbey to go into.'

'I wanna go in!' shouted the boy. He sounded as if he always shouted, as if there were no other way of getting attention.

'Can't go in, can't afford to,' said the woman. The toddler dropped his lolly stick over the side of the pram, and Derek darted to pick it up.

'If you want to take the weight off your feet for a bit,' he said, 'why not just come and sit here in the porch? It's nice and cool and there'll be a choir practice in' – he consulted his watch – 'ten minutes, so you'll have some music to listen to.'

The woman ignored this and, with a sure instinct for whose opinions mattered, turned to Blaise.

'Why we got to pay to go in? We never used to have to pay.'

'Well,' said Blaise silkily, 'you do now.'

'It's not Christian, that,' said the woman. 'You ought to be giving bloody money away not coining it in.'

The boy made a sudden sally for the door but Blaise, without taking his eyes from the woman's face, stuck out an arm and caught him.

'Sorry. This is not an adventure playground, nor a picnic site nor a community centre. It's an historic place of worship.'

'And sod you too,' said the woman.

Derek watched with dismay as Blaise turned the boy with one hand and steered, or rather pushed, him back in his mother's direction.

'Good afternoon.'

The woman leaned forward. Even out here in the sunshine she gave off a strong, gamey smell. 'Sarcastic bugger. Don't forget – I know your face.'

'And I yours, madam,' said Blaise, walking briskly away towards Sumpter Yard.

Derek Mates caught up with him. 'If you don't mind my saying so, I think you want to be awfully careful taking that line with people – any people,' he said.

Blaise gave him a sidelong look. 'Don't worry. I will be.'

Derek's blue Fiesta was parked on the corner of Black Lane, the narrow cobbled street which led into Sumpter Yard.

'I'll see you tomorrow at the Pets' Blessing.'

Blaise raised a hand as the Fiesta bumped noisily away from the kerb. He didn't go straight away into the Yard, but turned right, walked a few yards and leaned on the stone wall overlooking the Abbey meadows. Pale, heavy cows grazed, moving barely perceptibly over the lush grass, which was now dying back, revealing the subterranean humps and ridges of some long-buried Stone Age settlement. Half a dozen great trees, oaks and chestnuts, provided the meadow with precious shade. But beyond them, and beyond the barley field where a harvester trundled and flailed like a gigantic insect, and beyond the distant glitter of the gypsy trailers at the bottom of the long hill, stretched the fens. Blaise felt a deep attachment to this part of England. He felt with keen pleasure its undertow of barbarism and blackheartedness. Witchcraft and wickedness crawled along the dykes and slithered up the drains into the most unlikely homes. 'Child abuse' was rare, but incest was commonplace. Soon, with the onset of autumn, the fading light and rising mist, the area would revert to type. The travellers would move on, the tourists would retreat. The great trees in the meadow and in the close would lose their leaves and the Abbey would be left exposed to the shrieking north-east wind that had the bite of Russia on its breath. And, thought Blaise, pushing back off the wall and heading for home, exposed to evil. For evil lived here, in the bleak and tardily civilised flatlands of this diocese. It crouched at dinner-tables and squatted in meetings, it scuttled and sniggered among the gracious houses of Sumpter Yard, and from time to time it found a host, and clung to that person's back for months at a time so that that person carried a darkness around in his head and spread it wherever he went.

Glancing back at the Abbey Blaise saw the gypsy woman and her children, still hanging around on the grass. Prowling and prowling, he thought, like the hosts of Midian in the hymn which had so impressed him as a boy. She must have sensed his eyes on her for she turned to look at him, and shouted something, stabbing the air with her finger. Blaise entered the shadowed seclusion of Sumpter Yard with a confident stride.

Tessa was hanging up washing. She thought, 'the king was in his counting-house, counting out his money,' as Blaise undoubtedly would be now that the visitors were paying. But there was precious little chance of the queen eating bread and honey in the parlour. And oh, for a maid!

The Black House (named, like Black Lane, after the Franciscan monks who had once lived here) was the oldest in the close, and the finest of its kind in England. It was a Tudor building, the outside plasterwork densely crosshatched, the upper story bulging threateningly over the pavement of Sumpter Yard. The red-tiled roof, scabbed with moss and lichen, undulated waywardly between a coven of crooked chimneys. Tourists, peeking discreetly into Sumpter Yard, exclaimed over its picturesqueness. But the oldest part of the house, a low-ceilinged room whose narrow, arched window admitted little light, pre-dated the mediaeval monastery, and was chilly even in summer.

Tessa was aching with tiredness, not just from the cooking itself but from her resistance to it, which tightened her shoulders and gripped her temples in a vice. She was a poor wife for a gifted and ambitious churchman like Blaise. The strain of being the good sport everyone thought her gave her migraines, and occasional burning pains in the solar plexus which she feared might be an incipient ulcer. The feminist writers she read warned against the common female failing of sublimation. It did awful things to your psyche and your physique. But what was the alternative? To make endless scenes, and weep and complain? The feminist advisers didn't live with Blaise.

She'd come to hate the Abbey. Sometimes, driving back from somewhere, she'd look up at it from the foot of the hill and liken it to a bad tooth, grey and hollow, in an otherwise wholesome mouth, its bad roots poisoning its surroundings.

These were guilty thoughts, because she knew how much Blaise loved it. Once she'd seen him standing in one of the side aisles, his hands flat against a pillar, his eyes fixed on the fan-vaulting strung like a stone cobweb high above his head. His whole body, his attitude and expression, were informed by a passion and intensity which she had never been able to arouse in him. At such times her own faith seemed a small, tame thing, scarcely worth the name. A matter of cake-baking and list-making and flower-arranging. No matter how often she reminded herself that 'who sweeps a room as for thy laws makes that and the action fine', she could not rid herself of the picture of something grander and fiercer, something which Blaise had and she did not. And she felt diminished.

The washing, pegged, drooped motionless in the afternoon heat. Everything was infected by the lassitude of this seasonal no man's land. Glancing over the levels she saw the glitter of car windscreens catching the sun on the dual carriageway: the road to London, a hundred miles away. When she was very depressed she would tell herself that all she had to do was get in the car and drive down that road to freedom.

She sensed Blaise behind her and turned, smiling, to greet him.

'How are the great British public taking it?'

'You know them. With equanimity, just as I forecast.'

'Good.' She touched the washing as she walked back towards him. 'I've made six dozen fairy cakes, three sultana loaves and N sponges. I ought to be bathed in a glow of domestic satisfaction.'

'Evidently you're not.' He seemed about to add something, but half-turned his head and raised a hand, listening. 'I believe they're here.'

She hurried through the cool drawing-room into the hall. She could hear the bang of a car door, Celeste's voice saying, 'Hang on, I'll take that.' In her mind's eye as she went to the front door she carried the image of Blaise's face as she had passed him. With the arrival of his mother and sister it had assumed, for a split second, the unreachable cold vacancy of a statue.

CHAPTER THIRTEEN

Celeste and Bruno shook down together, as they always did.
She presided over a routine as close as possible to that
which he was used to, not so much for his sake as for her
mother's, whose pitch she did not wish to queer. She tried to
encourage Wendy to greater efforts without disaffecting her,
and embarked on various minor domestic projects such as
tidying out the airing cupboard and scraping the black mould
from the corners of the less accessible window-frames. These
occupied a proportion of each evening. They also reminded her
of those long hours of complete contentment spent doing the
same kind of thing with Mrs Dove. She had the pink silk sachet
with her, as always, though it was now becoming threadbare,
and one night when her father had been particularly pettish
she took it out when she went to bed and sat stroking it and
thinking about the past. It was extraordinary how everyone,
the sinned against and the sinning, had managed to bury it as
though it had never happened. Perhaps guilt and pain were
easier to bury than a nagging sense of loss.

On the Saturday of the middle weekend she had dinner with
Freddy Gervase. He took her to a restaurant in Mayfair so
exclusive that for a few hours she felt herself to be beyond the
reach of ordinary life and its demands. Indian summer had
scarcely given way to autumn, but she made a cold evening the
pretext for wearing a burgundy velvet suit which had always
flattered her.

'You're looking quite lovely,' said Freddy, as they sat in

197

green leather armchairs with their drinks and the menu.

'Thank you,' she said. Force of habit prompted her to add: 'This is a very kind outfit.'

'On the contrary, any dress would be enhanced by you,' said Freddy gallantly.

'Don't be silly, Freddy.'

'No, I mean it. And you must learn to accept compliments when they are due. By the way, I do recommend their cold artichoke soup. It's like white velvet.' As he said this he allowed his eyes to linger on Celeste's throat. She was conscious of being in the company of a noted ladies' man (an old-fashioned expression which suited Freddy) and it was remarkably pleasant.

He amused her all through dinner with stories about patients. The stories were indiscreet, but told with a gentleness and affection never present in Fabian's treatment of the subject. Over coffee he said: 'We should have dinner with Fabian and Louise some time, the four of us.'

'Should we?'

He raised his eyebrows. 'Celeste! That was almost vinegary.'

'I'm sorry, it wasn't meant to be.'

'Don't say that, I enjoyed it.' He swished his brandy around. 'Besides, it suits me. I should obviously like to have you to myself.'

At about the time Celeste was enjoying a hazelnut and praline ice cream with mango coulis in the company of Freddy Gervase, Joe Cook was dying a death by a thousand cuts in the sergeant's mess of an army depot near Hythe. In fact, by ten minutes into his act he had already died and passed into a hopeless purgatory, waiting for the moment he could decently get off.

His audience was mainly bandsmen, but he couldn't imagine them playing any of those jaunty, triumphalist marches that had the girls smiling and waving in the street. A more miserable, misanthropic bunch of sods it would have been hard to imagine. It must have been that army bonding you were always hearing about, thought Joe: they'd ganged up on him.

He realised now as he stood there, microphone in hand, the sweat even beginning to soak through the underarms of his suit, that he had never stood a snowball's chance of a laugh. There was something about him they didn't care for, something he couldn't do a frigging thing about.

'This nun went to see a Paki doctor,' he began wearily. He'd taken them to the outer limits of his material – racist, sexist, blasphemous, so filthy it made his stomach turn to hear his own voice spouting it – and with each turn of the screw it had been he who had got more boxed in, while they just drifted free, with that look of sadistic indifference on their smart-arse, short-back-and-sides, little boys' faces. Joe wanted to chuck in the towel, but he needed the fee and didn't want to give them the satisfaction.

'He says: "A lady in your position shouldn't be suffering from this complaint, Sister Bernadette" and she says: "I'm a bride of Christ, young man, how would you know what my position is?" '

There wasn't even a covert smirk. In even the worst audiences there was generally one bloke who didn't run with the pack, who stifled the odd snigger if only out of pity or embarrassment. But this lot were trained to stick together. Trained to kill.

Joe loosened his tie. 'Is it just me or is it bleeding hot in here? Tell me something, how do you manage in them tight trousers? I mean, I've seen ballet dancers with more room in their tights than you got in there – where d'you put it? Eh? Whisk it round three times and ram it up your arse? Or what?' He was getting aggressive with them, which was tantamount to begging for mercy. The mess, which hadn't seemed a bad place when he arrived, no worse than most and a sight better than some, began to shrink around him like a condemned cell. He felt as if his audience – well, hardly 'his' – might leap forward like unrestrained killer dogs the moment he stopped speaking, and tear him to bits for their own sport; as if his only chance was to keep talking as he edged towards the door. This made working the overnight lorry parks look like very heaven. Joe was a regular at the lorry parks, one of the few comics on this circuit with the bottle to go on, fill the time, and get off in good order. The audience there had made many a professional entertainer weep, and sent him home early, a broken man. They were the punters from hell. On the other hand, they were passive. They might not laugh, but they were too exhausted to heckle. A proportion of them were foreign and had no idea what he was on about. They just sat there, staring and belching.

This lot were different, they were vicious. They'd taken against him and now they scented his fear. Joe could smell it himself. He was obsessively clean and the sour dampness of his shirt made his gorge rise. The mike felt slippery in his hand. He began to wish he'd shaved off his stubble, had a haircut and removed his earring before coming.

'A story for the married blokes,' he said, now on automatic pilot, ticking off the sections of his act in his head, aiming for the bare minimum which would earn him his £100. 'You know what it's like, getting a blow-job off the wife – like shitting bricks, right, so what do you do?'

There was a group of soldiers at the bar, ordering drinks and carrying on a conversation at the normal level, with their backs to him. Normally he'd have drawn attention to them, made a few cracks at their expense, initiated an exchange they had no chance of winning – but this time he was on a hiding to nothing, and they knew it. As yet another punchline sank without trace he thought wildly of doing a song as a last resort. A Yamaha keyboard stood under a cover in the corner of the room but he couldn't play it and this was not a setting in which audience participation was likely to be forthcoming. Room full of bandsmen and he'd have to sing a capella . . . On second thoughts, he'd had enough self-inflicted humiliation for one evening. A couple more gags, then he'd tell them they'd been warm and wonderful, and sod off home. 'Know about the South African policeman who saw a kaffir being swallowed by a crocodile?'

He soldiered on. Funny expression that, he thought. I might die laughing. Approaching the tag of the story he saw one bloke – the leader of the pack, a great big barrel-chested NCO with little piggy eyes – revving up for a heckle. There was always one: one bastard the others took their cue from. Joe speeded up the story a little, reached the last few words, paused momentarily and delivered himself of them with a grim relief.

'So he says: "You're under arrest, Sambo, you can't use an endangered species for a johnnie." '

He went hot and cold. Two voices had spoken – his own, and that of the pig-faced NCO. Shit! He'd been tagged. The line got the first laugh of the evening, but it was the death rattle of his act. It was comedian's lore that you saved the best till last and what had happened? He'd been tagged on his penultimate gag. Now nothing could save him. There was still a ripple of self-satisfied laughter running round the room. The men were grinning sycophantically at the NCO, showing that they appreciated his cleverness. Joe had nothing left to lose. If he never got another gig in this place it'd be too soon, and the thing about the army was they were always moving and didn't mix much with anyone else so they couldn't slag him off to other bookers. He laid down the mike on a chair. The audience made a wary, mocking 'Oo-hoo-hoo' noise and he experienced a small fizz of hopeful adrenalin. For the first time he had their attention. Or half of it. The other half was with their man.

He stepped forward, past the first row of tables. There were more 'Oo-hoo's and some scraping of chairs as people moved as if making space for a fight.

'Tell me something, sir,' he said.

The NCO pointed at his own chest and glanced around exaggeratedly as if asking, 'Does he mean me?'

'Yes, you, sir. I want to ask you something.' The NCO stood up. He wasn't tall, but he was built like a brick shithouse. Same sort of build as Joe himself. Older; probably a bit fitter; but with a lot to lose here.

'Go ahead,' said the NCO. 'Wouldn't want to refuse the condemned man.'

More laughter. Joe took another couple of steps forward. The audience, closing round him, was different now. It wasn't a bear-baiting any more, it was a prize-fight. They had a more open mind about it. They wouldn't be broken-hearted if the sergeant got knocked down.

'I just wondered, sir,' said Joe in a soft, conversational tone, 'whether you bled at the mouth once a month?'

There was a tense, sniggering pause. The NCO's colour deepened but he wasn't admitting defeat – yet.

'You'll have to do better than that, Sunny Jim,' he said. 'Haven't you heard about us? We're the professionals – and that includes insults.'

There was some laughter, and someone behind Joe in the front row gave a cheer. He decided to be more specific.

'I hear you're all magicians here, so what is it you play, sir, the one-handed organ?'

The second half of the joke was drowned out by laughter as – too late – he realised what he'd said. Musicians was the word he'd wanted. *Musicians.*

The NCO stepped out from behind his table and swaggered towards him for the kill. It had been handed to him on a plate.

'Magicians? Wish we were, sonny, wish we fucking were. If we were fucking magicians maybe we could have conjured up a fucking comedian!'

Joe pulled up at the first lorry halt he came to. Apart from the tea truck there was just one other vehicle there, a container lorry for a dairy produce chain. He bought a pint of tea and a bacon roll and leaned against the warm bonnet of the van, watching the car headlights slash the darkness on the road. He was knackered. Knackered and depressed and angry, the worst possible combination. No adrenalin to coast home on, just the humiliation of accepting money for crap. Joke money at that. He threw the last piece of the greasy roll into the bushes behind the van. He wished he'd had the courage to stuff the envelope back into the fat red hand of the quartermaster who'd paid him. But he needed it, and they knew he needed it. So without meeting the bloke's eyes he'd grabbed it and got the hell out.

The van didn't have anything built in for music, but he had a small radio-cassette player that he kept on the floor by the passenger seat. He liked classical, easy listening compilations of stylish standards. Often the drive home after a gig, with a tape playing, was the best part of the day. Not tonight. Even

James Galway had lost his power to soothe.

The driver returning to the container lorry spoke to him. 'Evening.'

'How you doing?' replied Joe, automatically. As the lorry roared and hissed into life, and crunched its way out of the lay-by, he reflected that the driver might have been in his audience on any one of a dozen recent occasions, staring and drinking and waiting to be impressed. Here in the lay-by it was all the late-night camaraderie of the road, but once you were the hired hand you could forget it.

Joe returned his mug and got back into the van. He left the door open for a second while he lifted his jacket off the passenger seat and felt in the breast pocket for his pay envelope. Ripping off the end he peered inside and gave a little nod of disgust. They'd docked it. Only a hundred here, and badgering his agent would do no good. The army would just say he'd been a waste of space. Retrieving the cash would cost more in time, effort and telephone calls than the sum was worth.

Joe slammed the door and glanced at himself in the rearview mirror. His face, dimly lit by the inside light, was grooved with tiredness. Not the simple, physical sort, but soul-weariness, self-disgust and disappointment. His shirt-sleeves were rolled up and his forearms, braced on the steering-wheel, were covered in a dense, paisley-like pattern of tattoos: snakes, ivy, banners, legends, thorny roses and art deco lilies.

Those fuckers had to go for a start, he told himself as the van, shaken with a noisy ague, waited to turn out into the stream of London bound traffic. It would mean going private and digging into his modest savings again, but it would be worth it.

Chiefly for her sister-in-law's sake, Celeste drove up to the Abbey to collect her mother. When she arrived in the early afternoon Elodie was upstairs taking a nap and Tessa had seized the opportunity to nip round to the Retreat House on some errand or other. Blaise opened the door to her wearing cricket whites, explaining that he was due to captain an Abbey eleven against the choir school at three o'clock, in the last match of the season.

'As we've got a minute, let me show you our brand-new administrative hub,' he said. He took a key from the row of hooks in the hall and led the way back into Sumpter Yard and into the old Chapter House next door. It was Saturday, so the clerical staff were not in, but in a small side-room the electronic money-counter muttered and clanked to itself over the previous day's takings. Shrouded keyboards and blank VDUs stood about on white laminated desks, the steel feet of which had had to be propped up in places to compensate for the unnevenness of the ancient floors. There was a curious smell, a compound of fresh paper and office machinery, and the ancient dank stone that lay just beneath the emulsion and beige corded carpet.

'I thought you'd like to see,' said Blaise, 'we're very proud of all this. Frankly we're so far ahead of the field in this area we're practically out of sight.'

'And does that make a great difference?' asked Celeste doubtfully.

'An incalculable difference!' Blaise embarked on an exhaustive run-down of the advantages. Celeste, not really listening, stared at him. His skin looked very dark against the white shirt and pullover. A feathering of black hair showed at the neck of the shirt, and on the backs of his hands, thickening on his wrists and becoming dense at the point where his forearms met his rolled-up sleeves. These days she found something repellent in her brother's good looks.

They went back into the house through an interconnecting door, a massive slab of oak strapped with black iron hinges, which opened into Blaise's study. He locked the door behind them with a second, pantomime-size key. On the desk an answering machine showed a winking light.

'Excuse me one moment.'

While Blaise listened to a man's voice delivering a lengthy message about funding for what he referred to as 'the God spot' on local radio, Celeste looked about her. The study bore testimony to taste, sensibility and visual judgement of a high order. The carpet was a warm terracotta, the curtains a rust and gold William Morris print. In deference to the room's ancient, crooked proportions it was under-furnished – a superb beechwood desk, two leather armchairs, a couple of handsome lamps and a defiantly non-ecological chess table of ebony and ivory inlay. On the sill of the deeply-recessed window were various *objets trouvés*, including stones and coins which Blaise had picked up on walks. There were no family photographs and nothing, apart from books, to indicate the calling of the occupant. The books occupied one wall. On another was assembled a collection of modern paintings, all but one exuberantly impressionistic. The odd one out was a male nude figure leaping forward off the canvas, feet and hands thrust forward as if pouncing, head low and glaring, the whole form violently foreshortened by the artist's perspective. The painting was both arresting and unsettling – not really, thought Celeste, the sort of thing one would expect to find in the study of a reverend gentleman.

'Who's that painting by?' she asked when Blaise had written down his message.

He came and stood at her shoulder. 'Don't you know?' She shook her head. 'It's Fabian's.'

She sensed that he expected a reaction to this, as though he were reasserting the old pattern of fear and collusion.

'I might have guessed,' she said. 'It's so nasty.'

'Nasty?' Blaise stepped forward and peered at the painting more closely, caressing the painted face gently with his finger. 'I must say I think that's a little unfair. The subject may be disturbing – and why is it? – but you can't fault the execution.'

'I'm not an expert,' said Celeste. She glanced round. 'Don't you have anything of Sandro's?'

Blaise continued to examine the painting minutely. 'No, actually. I know little bro was the one with artistic pretensions but he never had half Fabian's style and imagination.'

'You mean he didn't set out to shock.'

Blaise turned to her, eyebrows raised. 'You're very contentious this afternoon.'

'I'm only voicing my opinion.'

'My own, for what it's worth, is that Fabian had the greater talent. And in the final analysis neither of them chose that

205

direction, so the argument is academic.' He glanced at his watch. 'I must go, they can't start without me.'

They went into the hall. Tessa was back. They could hear her voice and Elodie's drifting down the stairs. This prompted Blaise to say: 'She's been fine. I haven't seen as much of her as I'd have liked, but I suspect the change has done her good.'

'I'm sure it has.'

'Excuse me. I must retrieve my cricket bag.' He disappeared in the direction of the kitchen, calling, 'Celeste's here!' on his way.

When he returned, Celeste asked: 'Should you be playing cricket?'

'Why ever not?'

'There are risks, surely.'

Blaise's expression became cold. 'Good grief, Celeste, all that's gone away long since. I'd hardly be driving a car if there was still any danger. I can't even remember when I last thought about it.'

'I see.'

'I've been off the medication for years. Once you can show a certain number of years drug- and fit-free you're judged to be out of the wood.'

Celeste looked into his face. She felt this to be an important confrontation, though she couldn't say why. The bedroom door had opened wider on the landing and she could hear her mother saying, 'It's been so lovely, I've enjoyed it so much.'

'I do think you ought to be careful, Blaise,' she said. 'I'm always reading how epilepsy can be triggered again after years of being dormant.'

He put his hand on her shoulder with slightly unnecessary pressure. 'It's very sweet of you to worry about me, but there is nothing to worry about, I promise you. You take too much upon yourself, do you know that?'

At that moment Elodie came down the stairs with Tessa carrying her bags, and Blaise smiled as he stepped forward to say good-bye to his mother.

Celeste's return to London was not happy. When Alexa opened

the door of Parsloe Mews, one look at her face told Celeste that something awful had happened.

'Celeste, I'm so, so sorry, I don't know what to say—'

'Say it anyway.'

'It was a complete accident, there wasn't a thing I—'

'Oh, no.' Celeste dropped her bag on the floor and closed her eyes for a moment. When she opened them again, she said: 'It's Pooter, isn't it?'

Alexa nodded miserably. 'I'm so terribly, terribly sorry.'

'It's all right.' Celeste went into the kitchen. She filled a kettle, running the tap so hard that she was sprayed with water. She was conscious of Alexa's dithering distress behind her. 'These things happen.'

'Please don't be like this, Celeste, it honestly wasn't my fault.'

'I'm not being like anything. I believe you. It's hard to protect cats. Impossible, actually.'

'Can I tell you what happened, will you let me do that?' Alexa sat down at the table and fumbled with a cigarette packet and a lighter, inhaling deeply. 'I got a cab home last night, I left the door open while I collected some extra cash from the bedroom, he was in the hall, and the cabbie came to the door. He must have been spooked by this strange man, and he shot out. It was just fate that there was a car arriving at that moment. He was terribly upset, poor man, we all were, but even I could see there was nothing he could have done—'

'Oh for God's sake, Alexa, stop going on and on about it!' Celeste whirled round. 'I don't want to hear! I understand! I accept your apology! And it was only a bloody cat!' She left Alexa aghast at the table, and rushed upstairs where she collapsed on the bed and wept bitterly for her cat, and herself, a corner of the duvet cover stuffed into her mouth to stifle her sobs.

Sandro, too, was near tears, and wishing he could be anywhere but in the kitchen, listening to Sophie, his seventeen-year-old waitress, relaying a customer's complaints. '. . . and he said the pheasant is leathery, please may he have a chef's salad with blue cheese dressing instead, and something off the bill.'

'No!' cried Sandro. 'He can have the damned salad with the

horrible dressing, but I will not, will *not* take anything off the bill! Why should I? The man's eaten like a pig, and behaved like one too, and absolutely no one else has complained about the pheasant.'

'Actually, they have,' said Sophie, owlish and exact behind her large spectacles. 'That woman who usually comes at lunchtime said to me that it wasn't as nice as usual. She said she was only mentioning it because the standard here was so consistently high.'

'Bullshit!' cried Sandro, his voice breaking. 'That's just whining bullshit!' Sophie glanced around nervously at the others for support. Jack dried a saucepan as though his life depended on it. Sarah was spooning lemon sorbet into brandysnap baskets and topping each one with a sliced strawberry and a mint leaf, with a steady hand.

'Well, what shall I do?' asked Sophie of the kitchen in general.

'Tell him to go to hell,' snapped Sandro. 'Tell them all to go to hell!'

Sarah stood back. 'Take these up, Sophie, will you?'

'Okay.'

When she'd gone, Sarah said: 'Let's do the salad then.' She began shredding red oak and endive into a white bowl. Jack washed up energetically. Sandro wiped his eyes on his apron. He went and stood next to her, one hand pressed down on the sealed lid of the bowl of blue cheese dressing.

'I don't know what to do.'

'Give him his salad, reduce his bill. Take the line of least resistance. It's easier for everyone.'

'*Bloody* man! I don't mean him.'

'Michael?'

Sandro looked away for a moment, fighting for control. 'He goes into hospital tomorrow. I'm frightened.'

'Don't be. He's going to have a good rest and get the treatment he needs.'

'But Sarah, I can't cope!'

'Yes, you can,' said Sarah bracingly, taking the bowl from him, dextrously prising off the lid and spooning dressing on to the salad. 'You can, because you've got to. There, that's for

Sophie when she comes down.'

At one a.m. Celeste was in bed, but not asleep. When the phone rang she snatched it up, full of vague fears and anxieties.

'Lester, is that you?'

She leaned back on the pillows. 'Yes. Hallo, love.'

'How are you? How were the parents?'

'Everything went smoothly.'

'And you? You sound a bit funny.'

'Well, it is the middle of the night.'

'Christ, I've woken you.'

'No.' Celeste was about to add that there had been no chance of that, but checked herself. She could tell from Sandro's voice that it was her sympathy that was wanted, not an account of her own inconsequential troubles. 'How is everything?'

'Terrible.' There was a snag in his voice. 'I need your help, Lester.'

Celeste closed her eyes so tightly she felt she was bruising her eyeballs. When she opened them there were dancing lights against her vision. 'If there's anything I can do, I will, you know that, love.' There was a deep, quivering sigh at the other end. 'Sandro? Come on, spit it out.'

'It's just that Michael has to go into hospital tomorrow – you know – for a while anyway – and I'm dead worried about the business . . .'

Celeste hesitated. Her addled, small-hours brain gathered itself. 'Don't be. Go on doing what you do best, that's what keeps the business going.'

'But the books. Michael does all that, he's brilliant at it – and we've had a few problems lately.'

'You mean personally, or financially.'

'Well, both, they're the same thing really at the moment.'

'I'm so sorry,' said Celeste. 'It really is the root of all evil. And you don't need to be worrying about it just now.' No response was forthcoming from Sandro, so she asked: 'I'd like to come and visit Michael while he's in dock, can I do that?'

'Yes, yes of course. We could go together.' Sandro's voice had a childlike eagerness.

209

'Is that a good idea? I don't want to intrude on your time together.'

'Not at all, I'd like it.'

'Right.' The conversation seemed to be slipping around in Celeste's grasp like a cake of soap. She felt as though she had offered various answers without fully comprehending the question. And perversely she thought she might fall asleep at any moment if Sandro didn't get off the line. 'So you'll give me a ring,' she said, 'and keep me posted. They're generally very relaxed about visiting these days.'

'Lester, will you keep the books?'

The question was perfectly clear now. 'What?'

'The books, while Michael's in hospital. It's not all that arduous, but I have absolutely no talent for it and I don't want to make things harder for Michael when he comes back. And after all,' he added, with a trace of his childhood cuteness, 'you are a sort of partner.'

In the mornings, Joe was a different person. He always had a hard shower when he got in, no matter how late it was, so that he woke up feeling fresh. And he always made certain before leaving his flat in the evening that everything was clean and tidy. That way the day dawned restful and civilised. First thing – it would be around ten-thirty – he did some exercises, pulled a few weights. Then he went through to the kitchen in his tracksuit, picking up his post on the way, fed his cats, threw open the windows if it was sunny, made a cup of tea and a piece of toast and Marmite and read *The Times*, usually to the accompaniment of Radio Three if it wasn't too radical. He scarcely drank. Even if he'd liked the stuff it would have been impractical with the mileage he did for gigs. The van was an open invitation to every bored plod on the road, without him being over the limit as well. But he was a heavy smoker and suffered these days with a morning cough of Vesuvian proportions. It bothered him a bit, obsessed as he was with his future plans.

This particular morning he knew he'd got to put some bones into the day or it would collapse around him. He had no gig for the evening, and his post comprised a final poll tax demand and a snotty letter from his agent, Victoria, saying that their professional relationship was not as productive as it once had been and perhaps the time had come for a thorough review.

'Too right it has, sweetheart.' He scrunched the letter up and threw it into the waste-paper basket. Then he picked up the phone and dialled his doctor for an appointment.

CHAPTER FOURTEEN

Celeste was shocked by Michael's appearance. The fact that his morale was surprisingly good made his physical deterioration even more distressing, like sunshine glinting off a car crash.

'We're quite an upmarket crowd in here,' he remarked. 'Professional types to a man.' He lowered his voice. 'A touch right-wing for my tastes, but beggars can't be choosers.'

'Don't go offending anyone,' warned Celeste. 'It's not as if you can walk away if they turn nasty.'

'Offend?' Michael laid on his breast a hand on the back of which the long bones stood out delicately like the veins on a leaf. 'I'm wounded that you should think me capable of offending anyone, Celeste. Me, the mildest of men.'

During this little exchange Sandro had been staring round the ward, anywhere but at Michael. Celeste had realised almost at once that her brother had not the emotional resources to deal with this disaster. His love for Michael was two-thirds emotional dependence. She could well understand why Michael had kept the news of his illness secret until the last possible moment: telling him must have been like beating a puppy. Sandro was overcome with self-pity at the thought of being alone, his request that she help with the restaurant's books was the old cry of 'Carry me! Carry me!' in a thinly disguised adult form. She had been brought along this afternoon purely and simply to ease the awkwardness and oil the conversational wheels. She felt a rush of rage at her brother's inadequacy, and at the hand she herself had taken in creating it.

Abruptly, she said: 'I expect Sandro's told you I'm helping him with the books while you're in here.'

'Oh, no!' Michael grimaced in disapproval. 'You mustn't. Sandro, you shouldn't have dragged Celeste into this. I told you just to keep them up to date and bring them in for me to look at.'

Sandro grinned rather wildly at both of them. 'But you knew that would never work. I'm useless with money, as you never stop reminding me.'

'Then this was the time to learn,' said Michael sternly.

'No, it wasn't. Not when I'm worried sick about you and finding it hard to concentrate anyway. Celeste offered, didn't you? You said you were happy to do it, didn't you?'

'Of course,' said Celeste, and added pointedly: 'Although I'll need your help to begin with.'

Sandro stood up. 'Christ, is there somewhere I can have a smoke here?'

'Out of this room, turn left, right out of the ward and there's a disgusting little room with orange tweed armchairs near the lifts.' Michael watched him go. 'You'll ruin your health with those things!'

'I won't be long.'

Michael rolled his head on the pillow and gazed at Celeste. For the first time his manner exactly matched his appearance. 'I can't pretend,' he said, 'that my reasons for not wanting you to delve into our books are entirely altruistic. We're experiencing what are euphemistically known as liquidity problems.'

'I understand. Don't worry. I shall be a mere functionary. I'll write things down and add things up and suspend judgement.'

Michael sighed. 'But you're not a mere functionary, are you, and we both know it. Sandro referred to you as a shareholder, and he's right.'

'No, I'm not,' said Celeste firmly. 'I'm more of a – what do they call it in the theatre?'

'An angel?'

'Exactly, an angel. And it wasn't very much.'

'Enough to get us going, and don't think I don't remember that every day.' Celeste noticed he didn't say 'we'.

213

She shook her head. 'You're bound to have ups and downs, it's only natural. Restaurants are a volatile business.'

'Sandro wants to experiment, to be up there with the best, among the awards and the stars and the quality write-ups,' said Michael fretfully. 'And he should be, he should be. He's gifted, and he can't see why tedious things like rates and electricity should stand in his way. But we've always run the place very close to the mark, there isn't much of a margin of error.'

'It always seems to be full,' put in Celeste.

'Yes, because we keep the prices unrealistically low. I feel we should go for a *prix fixe* menu at a viable rate and coast for a bit, consolidate. But the lad wants to be Anton Mosimann, or Marco Pierre White – no, wrong temperament, he's too sweet for that.' He smiled, and Celeste saw all his pride and dread illuminating his face.

She took his hand in both hers. 'I know this is the silliest thing in the world to say just now, but don't worry. I'll hold the fort till you're back. I'll keep an eye on the boy wonder. Everything will be all right.'

He lifted his hand, still wrapped in hers, and kissed her fingers. 'I wish I shared your optimism. But thank you.'

Sandro came back, his composure regained. He was wearing faded jeans with a white tee-shirt and a soft black leather gilet, scored and supple with age. Round his neck was a blue and white spotted handkerchief. His step was quick and light in Timberland boots. He looked like an especially charming fairground hand. Several weary heads turned slightly to look at him, and faces faded with illness brightened. Celeste, seeing Michael's expression of pure love and yearning, lowered her eyes. That look stabbed her to the heart and made her burn with shame. Michael was dying, her brother was facing unimaginable loss, and she was consumed with envy.

When she looked up Sandro was seated opposite, his folded arms resting on the edge of the bed, and Michael was touching the side of his face very lightly with one wasted hand. 'I was saying,' she said with jarring forced cheeriness, 'that Michael doesn't have a thing to worry about while he's in here. We'll keep the show on the road between us, won't we?'

*

It was the middle of October. Fabian liked the autumn. It was the season he felt most at home with. He enjoyed the freshening temperature, and the shortening days, and the crackle of energy he derived from both. He welcomed the ebbing of the tourists from London, and the downward drift of amber leaves that exposed the bones of the trees and blurred the formal patterns of the city parks. The short drive from St John's Wood to the consulting rooms – he would never have considered walking – gave him infinite pleasure.

Louise caught the bus across town to Bloomsbury, where she was assistant marketing director for a firm of specialist art publishers. She was good at what she did, but it was the sort of work, like Celeste's, which Fabian could not regard as anything but a paid hobby. The Thai girl came in after they'd gone and did all that was necessary to maintain the apartment and its contents in mint condition. Fabian had bought it because it was central, stylish and had a storybook view over Regent's Park which meant very little to him, but would greatly enhance its value to the foreigners who would buy it in three years' time at a massive profit. It was then his intention to buy something vast and distinctive in Hampstead, with a garden shaded by mature trees. Trees gave a place presence, *gravitas* – a feeling of richness and history. This was why he preferred to mark time in the flat, which had only a balcony, rather than settle for some supposedly characterful house with a narrow strip of intensively cultivated ground, overlooked on all sides. Fabian wanted land to spare, and it had to be in a part of London where the mere thought of its real estate value would make his acquaintances sweat with envy.

The consulting rooms he shared with Freddy Gervase occupied the basement and ground floors of a corner house about half-way down Portland Place on the Harley Street side. Fabian drew up immediately in front of the wide door, jumped lightly out and handed his car keys to Spiro, the doorman. Spiro, who wore a black silk suit and a white tie, like a gangster, grinned broadly and headed for his daily dose of *folie de*

215

grandeur. Fabian knew very well that Spiro made a wholly unnecessary tour of the block before leaving the car in its appointed space below ground at the rear of the building, but it didn't trouble him. He liked to arrive and walk straight in.

The door to the consulting rooms was on the left of the wide, carpeted outer hall. It was a white door with a heavy brass knob and a peephole so that Claire, the receptionist, could check out callers. A plastic surgeon's clientele included a more-than-average number of deadbeats and no-hopers, but one had to develop a nose for genuine undesirables and the impecunious. For instance, one learned early on that those seeking tattoo-removal pressed their suit with the most urgency and the fewest funds.

Fabian slipped his key into the lock and entered. Claire was at her desk. She looked up and smiled.

'Good morning, Mr Gallagher.'

'Good morning, Claire.' Claire was only twenty-two, but with a keen appreciation – unusual among her contemporaries – of how to dress for work. Fabian found something acutely sexy in her gorgeous, lissome figure (she was an ace at Real Tennis, apparently) constrained by a severe navy suit and white silk blouse. She wore Gucci low-heeled courts with tiny gold chains on the instep, and small real pearl stud earrings. Her hands were a thing of beauty – as smooth and pale as cream, with perfect nails, simply polished. Her voice had the bell-like tones of private boarding school, and Pimm's parties and Peter Jones. The voice, in fact, of privilege.

Fabian stood close to the reception desk and grinned down at Claire. One day, for sure, she would come his way. Claire smiled benignly back. It was impossible to discomfort her. 'Who's in at the moment?'

'Diana and Annette.' The latter was Freddy's secretary. 'Iris hasn't arrived yet.' Here she referred to the practice's nurse. 'And Miss Anstey's not due in till ten today.' Miss Anstey was the collagen clinician who, along with Mrs Layne the skin camouflagist, occupied separate rooms on the basement floor. Miss Anstey and Mrs Layne (neither of whom were of the 'Ms' generation) only came in two days a week.

'I'll pop down and see Annette,' said Fabian. He leaned forward a little. 'Did you have a nice weekend?'

'Super, thank you. I went to a TA Ball down in Sussex. They had the Midnight Blues playing, do you know them?' Fabian shook his head in mock wonderment. 'No,' went on Claire forgivingly, 'well, they are quite fantastic, everyone went absolutely mad. I've never been at a do where the dance floor was simply packed all evening. It was only when I got home at three-thirty that I realised my poor feet were an absolute mass of blisters!'

'Oh dear, poor old feet,' said Fabian, tilting his head to look at them under the desk. 'How are they now?'

'Fine!' laughed Claire, waggling them a little to show how fine they were, 'completely encased in elastoplast!'

'So,' Fabian stage-whispered, 'they should feel pretty much at home here.'

Claire laughed heartily at this and Fabian cantered down the stairs.

The basement was the boiler room of the practice. In area it was the same size as the consulting floor, but it accommodated many more rooms and activities. To Fabian's left as he reached the foot of the stairs were the rooms of Miss Anstey and Mrs Layne, and two floor-to-ceiling cupboards, not much smaller, in which were kept non-sensitive medical supplies and stationery. A little further along on the left of the hallway was a cloakroom, and facing him a large comfortable sitting-room which the women used as a snug in which to drink coffee and (when Mr Gervase was not in) to smoke. On the right after the sitting-room was the kitchen, large and well-appointed, but not used for very much except to brew coffee and tea and microwave the occasional calorie-counted ready meal. Finally, to the right of the stairs, were the two secretaries' rooms, linked by a connecting door. Fabian went into the furthest of these.

Annette had just picked up the telephone. 'Mr Gallagher's rooms. Yes. Yes. Well, I will check of course, but my recollection is that Mr Gallagher is completely full for that period. Would you hang on for one moment?' Annette put her hand over the mouthpiece and looked up at Fabian, who was now standing by her desk.

'Referral from Patrick Reeves. Not on, surely?'

Fabian shook his head. 'Not after that last fiasco. What does he think I run here, a charity?'

Annette gave a smile of exasperated agreement, because she was a good-hearted woman who considered that, no matter what the evidence, it was her duty to think the best of her employer. She removed her hand from the mouthpiece.

'Hallo? I'm sorry, my feelings were correct. It's simply impossible. And I wouldn't want to commit Mr Gallagher any further ahead, his appointments book is completely full for the forseeable future. Yes, I'm sorry. Thank you so much. Good-bye.'

She replaced the receiver. 'Phew!'

Fabian placed a hand on her shoulder, where the soft, scented flesh was warm beneath her black dress. 'Another consummate performance. Thank you.'

She began tapping on her keyboard. 'It's what I'm here for.'

'Mail interesting?'

'Not really. Do you want to see?'

'Also not really. Let's take a dekko at the appointments list.'

He scanned it. 'This new patient – upper arms – who's she from?'

Annette stood up and gazed at the list, searching her memory. 'That chap in Epping, I believe. Yes, I'm sure of it.'

'What is he playing at? I shall do my best to dissuade her. If she remains adamant, I rely on you to make the financial prognosis as gloomy as possible.'

'Don't worry, I'll do my best.'

Fabian moved away, still holding the list. Annette tweaked it from his hands with her finger and thumb.

'Excuse me, Mr Gallagher. There is a copy in the consulting room.'

'Naturally.' Fabian relinquished the list. 'How could I ever have doubted it? I'll see you upstairs in fifteen minutes or so.'

On the stairs Fabian encountered Freddy coming in the other direction. 'What the devil are you doing here?'

Freddy laughed and rested his lanky, graceful frame against

the banister. 'I work here, remember?'

'It's not your day. Bugger off. Unless, that is, you'd like to take charge of another of Patrick Reeves's bungled sex-changes. Or some matron shaking her upper arms in dismay.'

'No, thank you.' Freddy glanced at his watch. He was dressed, as ever, with exquisite elegance – a dove-grey vicuna suit with a blue waistcoat, a self-striped white lawn shirt, and a grey and blue silk tie in a Windsor knot. His feet, in handmade black Oxfords, were as narrow as a dancer's. He carried with him his own particular fragrance, comprising sandalwood soap, strong mints and expensive cloth. Fabian preferred to be able to overwhelm this scent with a Havana, and was annoyed not to have one to hand, especially as it was officially his day at the consulting rooms, when the smoking ban on the lower floor was lifted.

'Actually,' went on Freddy, 'the symposium's off, so I took the opportunity of getting Diana to bring forward a few patients to ease the congestion on other days.'

'Ease the congestion?' Fabian grinned. 'Do me a favour. Where is the golf this Friday? The Belfry? Sussex? Spain?'

'I shall ignore that,' said Freddy genially. 'Excuse me.'

Fabian placed a hand on the blue waistcoat. 'When are these movable feasts of yours turning up? I wouldn't want any confusion.'

'Don't worry,' said Freddy, 'after lunch.' He stepped away from Fabian's hand and down the stairs, adding over his shoulder, 'Which, incidentally, I'm taking with your sister.'

'Get your cheque book warmed up,' said Fabian. 'Our Lester eats like a horse.'

'I'll come back with you if I may,' said Celeste as they emerged from The White Parakeet into the sunlight. 'I want to see Fabian. Do you think he'll still be there?'

'I should imagine so,' replied Freddy. 'His appointments list looked like a page from the OED.'

They were only in Great Titchfield Street, and so began to walk, at a leisurely pace, back in the direction of Portland Place. It was something which Fabian would never have done, and which strengthened Celeste's growing affection for Freddy. In the past month they had been out together often, and she had come to realise that beneath the high polish and practised charm was a really nice man – a kind man, who always considered her comfort and convenience before his own. She was enormously flattered by his attentions, and her enjoyment of his company was not spoilt by any undue protestations of passion. He had kissed her on the last evening they had spent together but it had seemed more like the kiss of a loving friend than an enflamed suitor. And it was as Freddy's friend that she thought of herself. The scenario was an attractive one: 'We're going to be friends all our lives,' she thought. 'Even when Freddy has made a dazzling match I shall still be there, and I shall be friends with his wife, too, and perhaps a godmother to his children. I shall taken them to the pantomime at Christmas, and the Trooping of the Colour, and Freddy and I will have these pleasant meals in town, oh, about once a month, and I shall be invited to parties and for weekends and always be welcome. And if there are any little hiccups in his marriage he'll tell me about them and I shall be warm and witty and wise and send him back to his wife to sort things out and make them even better than before . . .'

'I wonder,' said Freddy as they paused by a crossing, 'whether you would consider marrying me?'

To her horror, perhaps because of the line her thoughts had been following, Celeste's reaction to this was an involuntary yelp of laughter. The crossing light turned green and several people behind expected them to step forward, and consequently bumped into them. Freddy held her arm firmly and refused to move. 'What on earth does that mean?'

Celeste pulled herself together. 'Nothing. I'm so sorry. It must have sounded so rude, but you took me by surprise.'

'Did I? But we're both far too mature for candlelight and a solitaire diamond.'

'But it's only been a month!'

'Too mature – in my case – for unnecessary waiting, as well.'

'Waiting?'

'Yes. It can't be all that much of a surprise, surely.'

While Celeste considered this the light turned red again and an elderly couple with a giant poodle on a lead came and stood by them. Celeste rewound and played again the last four weeks. Had she missed something? Had she been unusually obtuse? Or should she never have submitted to that friendly kiss?

'It is actually,' she said. 'A complete surprise.'

A youth in baggy jeans, unlaced trainers and with the word 'BAD' cut into the hair above his left ear, joined the elderly couple.

'I am proposing to this lady,' announced Freddy. 'I thought you might like to know.'

They obviously did, because now the light changed again, but nobody moved. The youth turned his back to them as though looking out for someone he knew. Celeste blushed fiercely.

'Freddy!'

'I expected the answer to be a foregone conclusion,' went on Freddy, 'but it appears I was wrong.'

Celeste stepped closer to him and glanced up at him, her face scarlet. 'Freddy, these people don't want to hear about it.'

'I think it's lovely,' said the woman. 'Good luck to you both. You make a lovely couple.'

'Soppy old bat,' said the man affectionately.

Celeste turned towards them and met the fascinated stare of the youth, who at once began walking away and was almost run down by a taxi.

'Look,' she said, 'that's very sweet of you, but I haven't answered him.'

'Go on, then,' said the man with mock roughness. 'Get on with it or I'll never get her home.'

Freddy placed his hands on either side of Celeste's face and turned her gently towards him again. 'Yes,' he said. 'Come on, Celeste. My darling Celeste. Speak up.'

She was suddenly dazzlingly aware of all that was being offered to her – love, comfort, security, and the lifelong company of Freddy with his famous charm and fabulous income. Her head swam, her knees weakened, but her heart remained resolutely unfluttered.

'I'm so sorry, Freddy,' she said. 'But no.'

The woman let out a disappointed 'Aaah . . .'

'Come on,' said her husband, 'show over.'

Freddie removed his hands. 'A perfectly proper response to a first proposal made under unusual circumstances,' he said.

The elderly couple were half-way across the road, their huge poodle in tow. 'Thanks for your support!' called Freddy.

Mercifully the couple turned right on the far side of the road and Celeste hurried to put as much distance as possible between them. Realising she'd left Freddy far behind she stopped and turned to wait. The youth was standing on a traffic island staring at her. 'I said no!' she shouted, with a note of elation in her voice. 'Did you hear that? No!'

By the time they reached the consulting rooms the smoothly amicable status quo had been restored and Celeste's moment of elation had evaporated. Her refusal had seemed scarcely to ruffle Freddy's feathers: it was obvious he saw it as no more than the first step in a ritual dance which would end in her capitulation, and the end of their delightful friendship.

'That was a lovely lunch,' she said. 'I'm sorry about—'

'Ssh! Not another word. I insist.'

As soon as they were in the reception area she went straight over to the desk and asked: 'Claire, is my brother still here?'

'He's finished consulting, but I believe he's downstairs. I'll buzz him for you.'

'Thanks.'

Celeste stood by the desk, making a more-than-necessary production out of picking a piece of cotton off her skirt. Freddy laid his hand briefly on her shoulder. 'I'll be in touch.'

She watched as he went into the consulting room which faced her beyond the desk, and picked up the appointments sheet off the blotter. The interior decoration of the rooms had been a joint effort: Fabian had taken charge of the consulting room and made it a svelte space in black, grey and scarlet with white blinds, a smoked glass desk and a black lacquer Chinese screen decorated with a crimson bird of paradise. Personally,

Celeste would have hated to go in there with a bulbous nose, or unsightly port-wine marks, it was a profoundly unsympathetic décor. The waiting room had been Freddy's province and was far more to her taste, with a pale pink and green print on the curtains and covers, light pine and basketwork for the tables and chairs, a silvery-green carpet on the floor. One could live with that, she thought, and was reminded of the recent conversation.

Claire replaced the receiver. 'He says to pop down, he's in the sitting-room.'

'Thank you.'

Fabian was sitting with the ankle of one leg resting on the knee of the other, revealing an expanse of yellow silk sock. He was reading *Private Eye* and let out a sharp, barking laugh as Celeste entered.

'Fabian, I know this isn't exactly – but I wanted to have a word—'

Still grinning and without looking up, he lifted an index finger to put her on hold. Celeste obediently sat down in another of the armchairs. The room displayed all the characteristics of a staff bolt-hole: it was furnished and decorated in a sort of neutral, common-denominator style, and had hardwearing corded carpet on the floor. The two occasional tables, the coffee-table, mantelpiece and window-sills were crowded with an eclectic army of objects, presents from grateful patients. The objects, Celeste knew, ranged from the shockingly expensive to the dirt cheap, but since all were ugly (the really nice things went upstairs) it was impossible to tell which was which. A massive brass Buddha rubbed shoulders with a red Venetian glass; a set of pink and green onyx chessmen marched towards a pair of carved ebony candlesticks which would not have been out of place in Dracula's castle; snuffboxes, table lighters, china figures of winsome children, plant pots, ginger jars, potpourri bowls, clocks, cats and chinoiserie jostled unsuccessfully for attention, defeated by their setting. Over the fireplace, which Annette and Diana kept cheerful with a large arrangement of dried flowers and grasses, was the one thing Celeste rather liked. It was a child's picture, framed, and with the laborious legend: 'Mr Galager Thank you for helping My Mum'. The picture was of an animated figure, presumably female since the lower limbs were covered by a triangular skirt, with wild corkscrews of hair and stick-thin arms. The face was sliced by a gigantic smile, above which the dots of eyes sat like a couple of currants in a doughball. Whenever Celeste saw this picture she found her eyes wandering to the figure's torso to check for signs of a brave new bosom. Breast augmentation accounted for about a quarter of Fabian's work. But the unknown parent remained resolutely frozen in the prepubescence of her child's imagination.

Fabian tossed aside *Private Eye* with a final 'Ha!' and fixed his eyes on Celeste.

'Sorry about that. Most amusing story about that MP from Norfolk, Tim Catchpole. He had it coming to him.'

'Poor man,' said Celeste. She wondered whether Fabian had been the source of the story. It would not have been the first time he'd dished the dirt on no-longer-useful acquaintances to diary and gossip columns.

'Far from poor,' said Fabian, 'and speaking of which, how was lunch?'

'Very nice. The White Parakeet.'

'He loves that place. It's so exclusive it's peering up its own arse.'

'The food's lovely,' said Celeste. 'Look, Fabian, I—'

'Has he proposed to you yet?'

She felt as if he'd smacked her, but some long-past learned response helped her ride the shock. 'Yes, he did. I said no.'

She was pleased to see his eyes widen, just momentarily, before he said: 'Jesus wept, our Lester, that's perverse even by your incomprehensible standards.'

'No it's not, it's the most straightforward thing I've ever done.'

'Why? You imagine you're going to get a better offer or something?'

Another slap. She blinked. 'That's not how I look at it.'

'It's how most people would look at it.'

224

'I'm not interested in most people. Or you, Fabian. It isn't your business.'

'I only asked.'

'And I answered.'

'Not really. Go on, what's the objection to Freddy? The poor bloke's about as eligible as you can get, short of advertising. Eligible to the point of desperation.'

Celeste ignored this. 'I don't love him. I like him, very much, but that's all.'

Fabian took a cigar from the Burmese teak box on the table next to him and lit it, holding it between his yellow teeth and keeping his eyes steady on her through the first puff of smoke. 'What, you think he loves you?'

To her fury, she blushed. 'I suppose so,' she muttered.

Fabian shook his head and chuckled genially. 'He just wants to get hitched and you were lucky enough to be in his sights at the time. Do yourself a favour, Celeste, and oblige him.'

Celeste gathered herself. Real anger, hot and passionate, hammered in her chest. 'You're so old-fashioned, Fabian. It honestly never crosses your mind, does it, that I might enjoy my single, independent state, and that it might take an awful lot more than a desperately eligible middle-aged doctor to lure me away from it.'

He looked at her steadily, watching her as she spoke, knowing that in spite of her brave, furious words, his own had hit home. 'No,' he said, 'it doesn't cross my mind. What was it you wanted to say anyway?'

Celeste rose. Her face felt hot and her stomach fluttery. The moment had passed. She could not tell him about Michael now. 'Nothing,' she said. 'Perhaps I'll give Louise a ring some time.'

'Yes, do that,' he replied round the cigar, looking up at her. 'Girl talk. Fantastic therapy.'

Celeste simply wanted to leave the building. She wanted to be back at Porterfields, sitting composedly at her desk with her early-flowering Christmas cactus, her catalogues, her telephone and her view from the side window out across the corner of Berkeley Square. She wanted to be her own person again, even if, as Fabian implied, that was not much of a thing to be. She didn't hear Annette's good-bye, or Claire's, and she wouldn't have noticed the person coming up the steps outside if the two of them hadn't bumped shoulders. She was knocked off balance and staggered sideways. A large hand caught her upper arm and righted her. To her horror, tears of dismay sprang into her eyes. 'I'm so sorry, I was somewhere else entirely.'

'That's all right.' There was something familiar about the voice and about the hand, which now withdrew discreetly – but not before she'd noticed the gleam of scar tissue on the back.

'Oh good heavens,' she said. 'We've met before, haven't we?'

'We have, yeah.'

Joe Cook put both hands in his pockets. The jacket of his suit, caught by one button, gaped open to reveal a dark blue button-down shirt and a red and white paisley tie. 'Do you work here, then?' he asked, giving a small jerk of the head to indicate the whole building. He stood there on the steps as if he had all the time in the world, as if he operated to a different rhythm from everyone else. Celeste felt her own heartbeat slow and regulate, but remembering the circumstances of their last meeting she decided against the whole truth.

'No, but I've just been lunching with someone who does. I'm on my way back to work, as a matter of fact.' From habit she half-glanced at her watch and he noticed the involuntary movement of her wrist.

'Mustn't keep you, then.'

'Not at all!' She sounded, even to herself, eager and urgent. Joe Cook stood looking down at her. 'This is just such an amazing coincidence!'

'Yeah. Small world.' His voice was still flat and his face unsmiling, but Celeste had the pleasing sensation of having his undivided attention.

'So what brings you here?' she asked.

He swung his large shoulders slightly from side to side. 'Going to see the doc. About getting some new skin.'

'The doctor?' She felt a sudden cold rush of apprehension.

'My bloke says this Gervase is about the best there is for

226

what I want.'

Relief. She smiled. 'A new skin.'

Now there was the trace of a smile on his face, too. 'Just a few patches. Tell you what, if I could change the lot I'd trade it in for a thicker one.'

She looked up at him with real sympathy. 'I'm sure you must need it, in your work.'

'—murder, some nights,' he said, the missed beat standing, she realised, for an adjective he declined to use in front of her.

'Well,' she said, 'good luck.'

'Yeah.' Neither of them moved. Joe Cook glanced lugubriously into the carpeted hall, where Spiro was standing with folded arms, like a bouncer. 'Better go, my appointment's two-thirty.'

'Right,' she held out her hand. 'Good-bye. Or if this is anything to go by, maybe it's *au revoir*.'

'Yeah.' Instead of taking her hand he reached into his inside breast pocket. 'Yeah, why not?' He handed her a card. 'Give me a ring, I'm only in Alexandra Palace. We could have a drink. Finish the conversation.'

'Thank you, I may well,' said Celeste.

'Cheers.'

'Bye.'

She hurried down the remaining steps like a woman utterly consumed with the need to get back to work. Five minutes before she had been but now, as she sat in the back of a taxi, she was entirely taken up with calculating how long an interval she should decently allow before ringing Joe Cook at Flat 1b, 104 Prince Regent Road, London N22.

When she got back to Parsloe Mews that evening there was a sheaf of purple orchids propped on the front step. She took it in with her and pulled out the card from its envelope. It was from Freddy. 'My dearest Celeste,' he had written in his tiny, exquisite hand. 'Don't worry, I shan't be a pest, it's such bad manners. But neither shall I disappear. You see, I have complete faith in your judgement . . . F.' Celeste smiled as she arranged the flowers. For some reason she felt more kindly disposed towards Freddy now than she had a few hours earlier. She tidied the kitchen and set out the seafood salad and mayonnaise which she'd bought at Marks and Spencer's on the way home.

Alexa arrived home late, blazing with irritation about some office injustice involving a secretary and the deputy pictures editor who was known to be a bastard. Celeste removed a bottle of St Michael white from the fridge and poured them both a glass.

'That's nice,' said Alexa. 'What did I do to deserve this?'

'Absolutely nothing,' replied Celeste. She raised her glass. 'But it's not every day I turn down offers of marriage.'

CHAPTER FIFTEEN

After his meeting with Freddy Gervase, which had underlined the pressing need for resources, Joe Cook went to call on his agent, Victoria Cullen. Her office was in Great Marlborough Street, behind the London Palladium, and it always gave him a thrill to walk past the theatre and feel that in his small way he was part of the mighty ebb and flow of metropolitan show-business life.

Six years ago when he'd been taken on by Quality Artists, Victoria hadn't been able to get enough of him. In fact, without vanity, Joe could say that she had fancied him a bit. Most of her clients were singers on the club circuit, and her only two big names were old-style variety entertainers of advancing years, still well known and able to keep a pier theatre full for three months, but without TV potential. Victoria had assured Joe that he was a tonic, and that with the huge popularity of comics like Jim Davidson, who provided an antidote to all the smug, clever-clever alternative stuff, he stood an excellent chance of going places. Joe had set out his stall: he was aiming, eventually, for comedy of character. He wanted to sit on a stool, alone on the stage, or in front of a studio audience, and do a carefully-rehearsed ramble through the curiosities of life as he observed them. He wanted to do a grown-up show which adults could take kids to. A show where people laughed because they recognised the humour of the situation, not because they had to show how hard they were.

'Yes,' Victoria had said, 'but that is an incredibly difficult area

229

to get into. Let's play to your strengths for the time being, shall we?'

His strengths were his looks (at that time relatively unspoiled by nerves, nicotine and unsocial hours) and sufficient likeable charm to deliver blue gags without giving offence. This made him a good bet for office parties, stag- and hen-nights and sports club dinners. In the first couple of years with Quality Artists he got a lot of work of quite a reasonable kind, some of it even black tie. But there was no evidence of the great leap forward so confidently predicted by Victoria; and Jim Davidson, though making a fortune in the big cabaret clubs around the country, was rarely on television, where the prevailing comedy was anarchic and presupposed a certain set of attitudes in its audience. Joe felt his stuff becoming marginalised. The bookings became scarcer and the venues less smart. In order to keep the work coming, and to get the laughs, his act became bluer. He was on a slippery slope and he knew it. For a while Victoria kept up a pretence of optimism, but he was getting less co-operative and more impatient, and it was obvious she now had other clients who were a more promising investment. Every so often there'd be a smart gig, a classier audience – the stag at the Cableford Phoenix had been one of these – but their rarity only underlined the barrenness of the rest. And even with these, he was only too painfully aware that his audience were slumming. There was an extra dimension of humiliation in being paraded as an example of one's species before a bunch of high-earning, well-spoken punters out for a cheap thrill.

It was his intention, this afternoon, to advise Victoria of his new rationale for work: that from now on, for a trial six months anyway, he would only go for, or take, those bookings which were half-way decent, and he would introduce some new material into his act – clean it up, smooth it out, see if he could hold an audience with the kind of humour he really wanted to do. She couldn't object, since if the gamble paid off it would be to both their advantages, and if it didn't it was for only a limited period, so . . . As a matter of fact, he had no idea what would happen if it didn't.

He reached the building, the ground floor of which was taken up by a computer showroom, and pressed the buzzer for Quality Artists. As he waited he put his hands in his pockets and turned his back on the door. There was always a hiatus while Victoria's PA, Jane, stopped whatever she was doing and came to the speaker; and he didn't like to be seen to be too obviously waiting. He spent so much of his time doing it. Waiting for the phone, waiting for his cue, waiting to be called, waiting for cash . . .

'Yes?'

'It's Joe.'

'Sorry?'

'Jane, it's Joe Cook.'

'Come up, Joe.'

The door yielded and he closed it behind him and took the stairs with a measured tread. When he'd first come here he'd been able to take them two at a time, but it was a different story now. If he didn't pace himself he'd be buggered by the time he reached the second floor. As it was, he paused half-way up the last flight, his chest heaving. He wanted to compose himself before reaching the door, which would be ajar, and which was in direct line of Jane's desk.

He trudged up the remaining steps and pushed the door open. Straight across the narrow hall Jane sat in what appeared to be a large nest of playbills, bulging concertina folders of beige and pink card, piles of loose letters and documents, and boxes of papers and periodicals. Quality Artists were strangers to the silicon chip. There wasn't an inch of wallspace in either hall or office that wasn't covered by posters and photographs, many of them autographed by quality artists past and present. The massive untidiness of the place disturbed Joe. He liked order in an office. He found nothing stylish or cosy in this unbusinesslike shambles. He itched to get at it. He even suspected that it might have had a hand in his declining fortunes: an untidy place meant an untidy mind. From behind the closed door on the right came the sound of voices, animated, occasionally overlapping, Victoria's chirruping laugh.

Jane was talking on the phone, but she caught his eye and

made a childish opening and shutting movement with her free hand, which she then left sticking up in the air to indicate that she'd be right with him. Joe did not go into her office but remained in the doorway, hands in pockets. One thing his years in the unforgiving business of stand-up comedy had taught him was that you had to take charge. You had to impose your rhythm, your way of seeing things, your personality, on the people out there, not let them impose theirs on you. Once they did that you were lost. Almost unconsciously he applied these rules in his everyday life. By the time Jane put the phone down he had retreated out of sight and was looking through a copy of *Time Out* from the cluttered table in the hall. Jane craned forward over her desk.

'Joe?'

'Yeah?'

'Victoria's got someone with her at the moment, do you want a coffee or anything?'

'No, thanks.'

He remained resolutely out of sight, so Jane got up, as he had intended she should, and came into the hall.

'Oh, there you are. Look, I'm sorry to keep you hanging about – are you sure about the coffee? Or tea? We might even rise to a glass of wine . . .' She glanced about with a faint frown, as if the wine might be lying somewhere amidst the clutter.

'No, thanks. I'm fine.'

'All right then. Do come in and take a seat if you want to. She won't be long.'

Joe glanced at his watch, a man who had not got all the time in the world. 'Good.'

Jane went back into the office and he heard her lift the internal phone. 'Just to let you know Joe Cook is here.'

Joe threw the copy of *Time Out* back on to the table. Standing with his legs braced and slightly apart, arms folded, he surveyed the gallery of photographs on the wall in front of him. He'd seen them all many times before. Some of them were quite old: crinkly-haired, Brylcreemed men and Marcel-waved women, photographed at whimsical angles through gauze, and smiling those smiles peculiar to showbusiness mugshots, with either an unfocused brilliance or a heavylidded assumed intimacy. The well-practised signatures sped and leaped across the bottom corners of these photographs, accompanied by messages of confident spontaneity: 'All the best', 'Good luck always', 'Be happy', 'See you in lights'.

Joe's eye travelled along to the more up-to-date pictures. There were a couple of nearly-bands from the 1960s, several female singers, the two grand old variety artists still looking cheeky and cheerful but with less hair and more jowl, a gay conjuror with bleached hair, and a Michael Ball wannabee. Beneath this line-up were QA's handful of comics: a small angry black guy in a pork-pie hat, a couple of red-brick alternative types, all zits and crumpled jackets, and Joe himself. The first two were not smiling and had not signed their photographs. Joe had, and was. Gloomily, he reflected that the others were doing much better than he was in spite of their gracelessness in this area: a sign of the times. It wasn't a bad photograph of him, either, taken when he was looking his best, a big, confident sexy bloke with a come-hither grin and a twinkle in his eye. The sort any audience would relax with, and most women would fancy.

Joe entertained these thoughts in a spirit of realism, professionally and without vanity. He bent to look more closely at his younger and more optimistic self and as he did so became suddenly aware of his present-day reflection, large and ominous, caught in the glass of the photograph like a ghost. Bulky shoulders, hair beginning to recede at the temples, lines scored from cheek to chin and from nose to mouth. He drew back in dismay just as the door of Victoria's office opened.

'Far be it from me,' said Victoria, 'to put a dampener on ambition, but I think we're in fantasy land here.'

'That's right,' said Joe doggedly. 'Fantasy's the name of the game. It's the currency, isn't it?'

'Yes, yes, of course.' Victoria closed her eyes briefly and shifted in her seat. 'It is, yes, but we do have your career to think of.'

'Believe me,' said Joe, 'I think of little else.'

'Joe, the climate's not very welcoming at the moment. It really isn't the time to make a high-risk move like this. The chances are I might not be able to get you a single booking of the kind you want. As it is, you're keeping quite nice and busy.'

'Be honest,' said Joe. 'It's all crap.'

'It's a particular market, and you supply its needs admirably well.'

'Not the other night, down at that sergeant's mess. I died. I mean I really died. Dug a big hole, stood on the edge, blew my brains out and fell in.'

Victoria laughed, and he heard in her laugh a trace of the old warmth. She was a nice-looking sort when she got out of executive mode. Big glasses, short hair, nail extensions, great legs. He nudged his small advantage along a bit.

'It was bloody tragic, girl, no kidding. There was this sergeant from hell who tagged my final gag so I didn't even have a decent death-rattle. You've got to put up with all that shit. They're paying you so little they can do what they like with you. And what gets to you is they're so thick – half of them wouldn't recognise decent material if it blacked their eyes. I've had it up to here with the bastards.'

'Yes, I can see that.' Victoria sighed. 'And I do understand. I know it's tough, Joe, but it's work. Do you have any idea of the number of entertainers who are getting nothing at all? You at least are an item, you're known on that circuit. People actually ask for you by name. I've got a letter here at the moment as a matter of fact—' She began leafing through a pile of correspondence on her desk.

'Don't bother,' said Joe. 'I've thought about it, and I want to give this a go.'

Slowly Victoria replaced the letters. She sat back and removed her glasses. Without them she looked slightly older, and tougher. 'You forget Joe, it is I who have to "give it a go" as you put it.'

He didn't like the sound of that 'it is I'. That was a rank-puller to remind him of the correct grammar, just in case he didn't know. Whereas of course he knew, but no normal human being went around saying 'it is I'.

234

'Not necessarily. I'll get my head down too, get in touch with a few contacts, see what I can come up with – and still count you in, of course.'

'Big of you,' she said. He could see her hardening before his eyes.

'You know what I mean. Joint effort. If it works it'll be in both our interests, after all.'

'And if it doesn't?' Victoria replaced her glasses sternly.

He shrugged, favoured her with his best smile. 'Nothing lost. Business as usual.'

'But that's where you're wrong, Joe!' She brought down one hand hard on the desk top, at the same time leaning forward and glaring at him like a teacher grown impatient with a laggardly pupil. 'That's just where you're wrong. It won't be business as usual. You'll have deliberately disaffected the circuit that knows you, and some other bright young lad will be trying out your place for size. If he happens to be a client of mine, don't think I'll stand in his way.' Her eyes were flinty behind the fashionable specs. Joe believed her. 'I've got to tell you, Joe, this is not a good idea.'

He tried one more tack. Without speaking he took out his cigarettes and matches, put a cigarette in his mouth and raised his eyebrows for permission. She nodded, and pushed a minute ceramic ashtray towards the edge of the desk. When he'd lit the cigarette he leaned his forearms on his knees and looked up at her, in a subservient position, but relaxed, too, implying a touch of intimacy. When he did speak his voice held a hint of come-hither. 'Come on. It's a great idea and you know it. I'm not exactly lining your pockets with the stuff I'm doing at the moment, am I? All I'm saying is I want to move on, do better stuff, stand a chance of getting on the box, and I'm prepared to stand the risk. If you've got some sprig who can fill in for me, sweetheart, you go right ahead and use him. I'm big enough and ugly enough to look after myself.'

He smiled gently, winningly at her, and the corner of her mouth moved very slightly in response before she pursed her lips and covered them with her clasped hands. Two large rings glinted like knuckle-dusters on her long fingers.

He leaned back, took a drag on his cigarette, blew the smoke over his shoulder. 'We know each other pretty well, don't we?' She didn't answer. 'So indulge me. You got nothing to lose.'

She continued to gaze at him, cat-like, over her folded hands for a moment. He took another drag on the cigarette, very relaxed. She let the hands fall, palms downwards, on the desk in front of her, and examined her outspread fingers while she collected her thoughts. She was a clever, independent, feisty baggage, thought Joe, playing him at his own game. But she was also transparent. He knew what she was going to say and was already preparing himself for it.

'No way, José. It won't wash. You're not in a position to dictate terms and this agency's not in a position to carry performers and their clouds of glory.'

'Fair enough. So what are you saying?'

'I'm saying that perhaps we've reached the parting of the ways.' She gave him a quick, diamond-bright look and then picked up the letter she'd located. 'Unless, that is, you want to accept this.' She held it out, but he didn't take it, so she read part of it aloud. 'Building contractors in Ealing: benefit for the family of a colleague killed in a motor accident . . . entertainment suite at the Axe and Compass pub, et cetera . . . Actually, it sounds like a civilised engagement. A nice mixed audience.'

Joe took his time. He took the letter, scanned it, handed it back and stubbed out his cigarette. He would have liked to do the grand thing, to tell Victoria and Quality Artists to drop dead, to march out with his head up and his new image fluttering bright and proud as a banner.

'Yeah, all right,' he said, 'I'll do that.' He allowed himself a slight emphasis on the last word, to show he was making this one concession, out of respect for the widow and her fatherless children.

'Good,' said Victoria, sounding businesslike rather than delighted. 'Take my word for it, you're doing the sensible thing. In the meantime, if you want to work up some new material—'

'I've already got it.'

'Then if you want to let me have a tape of some of it, I'll give you an honest opinion and we'll see what we can do.'

'Yeah.'

Victoria got up and came round the desk to open the door for him. He didn't at once move to go, but left her standing there with her hand on the handle for a second.

'It was nice to see you, Joe. Drop in any time, you know that.'

'Sure.' He got up and walked past her and was almost out of the place when he heard her say: 'Times are hard, Joe.'

He turned and gave her a long, quizzical look. 'I noticed.'

'So don't get your hopes up.'

He was just going to say, 'I won't', but she closed her office door.

When Joe walked back past the Palladium the thrill had gone. This was not so much because he felt depressed but because he was deep in thought. There had really been no question, in view of his consultation with the surgeon, of calling Victoria's bluff. It was going to set him back something in the region of two grand to have the tattoos removed from his forearms – tattoos which had cost a mere fifty quid to have done in the first place. He had savings amounting to a little over that, previously earmarked for improvements to his flat, kitchen units and the like, but one had to prioritise. He could probably extend his overdraft a bit; he was a careful budgeter and rarely went to the limit of his facility. Just the same, he had not liked Victoria's attitude. Implicit had been the idea that he was a small-time smut artist with ideas above his station.

'Well, sod her!' he said aloud as he went down the steps into Oxford Circus tube station, causing two ladies in town for a day's shopping to scuttle out of his way in high anxiety.

Now he had yet another evening with no gig he was feeling much less bullish. His mother rang up and asked at once: 'What's up, love? You don't sound yourself.'

'I'm fine. Right as rain.'

'You look after yourself.' It was an order.

'I always do.'

'Get rid of those cigarettes.'

'Just like you did, eh?' said Joe. This was a familiar exchange. Margie Cook had been a heavy smoker since the age of fourteen, and gave up once a year with a born-again enthusiasm which generally lasted a month.

'It's different,' she said. 'I'm old. God knows I need at least one vice to keep me going, and there's no toyboys in this house.' She spoke cheerfully. Joe's father Roy, a butcher, had died five years earlier and Margie made much of her consequent sexual deprivation but Joe knew that she would die rather than look at, far less marry, another man. His parents' loyal and unaffectedly romantic marriage, ended just before their ruby wedding by his father's prematurely hardened arteries, had had a considerable influence on Joe, and on his sister, Cathy. In Cathy's case this influence had evinced itself in an almost manic determination to get laid by everything in trousers, behaviour which had earned only the most indulgent reproofs from Margie and Roy, but the keenest disapproval from Joe.

He believed in commitment. At thirty-seven he had had two long-term relationships, interspersed with the kind of one-night stands which no one else knew about and which he hardly liked to admit even to himself. Quick, messy, furtive operations, only rarely involving penetration, in the back of the van after a gig, or even in a pub toilet or backyard during one. The strippers were stuck-up mares, the adrenalin got to them and they were busting for it – but the second it was over they looked at you like something the cat brought in. Joe always regretted these happenings, but had become adept at wiping them out of the reckoning, just as a dieter blots out the memory of hurried, forbidden snacks. Joe believed in marriage, and had offered it to both his serious girlfriends who had declined, and not long after been off. In spite of having been unattached for the past eighteen months he was optimistic of being third time lucky.

'So,' said Margie, 'keeping busy?'

'Mustn't grumble,' said Joe.

'Going anywhere tonight?'

'No, as it happens. Going to have an evening in with the stereo.'

'Why don't you come over,' said Margie, who lived in

Highbury, 'and I'll stand us a Chinese.' She had no illusions about her own cooking and was the queen of the local takeaway emporia.

'Yeah, well, I'd really like to, Mum, but there's a couple of things I've got to do. Calls to make, things around the flat, you know . . .'

'Yes, darlin',' said Margie. 'I know.'

Joe always hated the moments following his mother's calls. He could picture her sitting by the phone, taking a drag on her Silk Cut and gazing into space, re-grouping her forces, adjusting to her loneliness, which he'd just added to by refusing the invitation. Still, he'd go over on Sunday.

He got up, put *Les Misérables* on the tape deck and went into the kitchen. He'd been looking forward to getting this sorted, some nice pine-fronted cabinets and possibly a washing machine. Going to the launderette was something he could live without, and he got through a lot of clothes. Many people thought what he did was a doddle, popping out of an evening to go through a set routine, and spending half the day in bed and the other half watching TV. But it was hard labour. You had to be ahead of the game all the time, jealously guarding new gags, praying your stuff wouldn't be used by the spot comic who was on before you, hoping some joker wouldn't tag you, improving your timing, psyching yourself up for the nightly power-struggle with the audience. Joe loved to listen to other performers, established guys, talking about their 'rapport' with the audience. He loved the sound of it; what he wanted more than anything was to feel a warm wave of affection and identification coming back to him from the darkness. The places he went to were lit like chippies so he could see every last drunken leering mug, and it was dog eat dog. When he got laughs he was winning, just. When he didn't he was dying.

Joe fed the cat first, and then himself: Kitty Supreme for her, two packs of supermarket stir-fry for him. He had taken on board the healthy-eating message, but found when he did eat healthily he needed a lot more of whatever it was. In his weight-training days he'd thought nothing of putting away a pound of steak, a large pile of chips, tinned peas (one of his passions) and onions fried to an aromatic, caramelised sludge.

He ate his supper at the table in the living-room with the stirring final choruses of *Les Misérables* ringing in his ears. When both tape and food were finished, he put his plate in the sink and sat down with his address book and his diary, which he opened to the blank pages at the back. The diary was a file design, filled in and kept meticulously up to date in his slanting well-formed handwriting. He turned the pages slowly, pausing here and there to consider a particular entry. By the time he got to the G's he had three. His eye passed over, and then returned to, the address and number of Mr Frederick Gervase. Gervase had told him that there was a new laser method which could just remove the colour from the tattoos: less radical, less scarring, and not so expensive, either. But Joe wanted them gone. He wanted clean skin, even if it had to be taken from somewhere else and soldered on. He rubbed his left forearm thoughtfully. He knew the design there so well he fancied he could feel it through his fingertips. Sometimes when a certain kind of person looked at him he was sure the vulgar, coloured graffiti beneath could be seen through his clothes. Tomorrow was the day he was to ring Gervase with his decision, but he'd made it almost at once. No matter what it took, he'd have the tattoos removed, and as soon as possible. And in the mean time he'd get on to some of these guys who claimed to know useful people, and find out whether or not they were all piss and wind.

It was while he was still thinking about the surgery that the phone rang. After a while he reached out and picked it up, his eyes still on the page and his mind elsewhere.

'Hallo.'

'Hallo, is that Mr Cook?'

He lifted his eyes. Who in hell called him Mr Cook? It could only be one of the public utilities – hardly likely at eight in the evening – or some cold-caller about replacement windows or smoke alarms.

'Who's that?'

'This is Celeste Gallagher. May I speak to Mr Cook?'

Very suddenly and clearly he saw her face in front of him, as it had been when they bumped into each other on the consulting room steps.

'Hallo there. Nice to hear from you.'

'You suggested I give you a buzz some time, and I was sitting here all on my own, so I thought . . .'

He smiled. Not many women would have admitted to being all on their own, or implied so guilelessly that their call was the last resort of the lonely.

'I'm glad you did. So how're you doing?'

'Fine!'

'What are you up to?'

'Nothing very exciting. Unlike you, I'm sure!' She laughed.

He could hear the warmth beneath the slight nervousness, the buzz she was getting from making this call. He held the receiver between his hunched shoulder and his jaw and lit himself a cigarette. 'Depends what you mean by excitement, doesn't it? If you call risking health, sanity and self-respect in front of a roomful of piss-artists three nights a week, excitement, then I've got plenty.' There was a pause. He'd shocked her.

Her voice was quiet and chastened when she spoke again. 'I'm so sorry, what an extremely silly thing to say.'

'No, it wasn't silly at all. Perfectly understandable after that little ruck at your brother's do.'

'That was most unpleasant.'

'Pretty standard. You handled it like a good 'un, though.'

'Thank you.'

'Listen, I owe you one. Why don't we have a drink some time?'

'That sounds lovely.'

He couldn't remember when a woman had last said to him that something sounded lovely. 'So how are you fixed?'

She laughed. 'My diary isn't black with engagements, if that's what you mean.'

'Go on,' he teased her, and went on before she could demur, 'what about tonight?'

'What a pity, I can't. I'm doing book-keeping tonight.'

'And you said you weren't in demand.' She laughed, but

didn't elaborate. 'Tomorrow?'

'Lovely.'

'I'll come and pick you up, shall I? Or would you like to meet somewhere?'

There was a tiny pause while she considered what was both the polite and the appropriate thing to do. 'I'm down in Paddington. Let's meet – you say where.'

He named a nice pub in Hampstead, music-free and off the beaten track, and suggested nine o'clock. He wasn't in funds to shout dinner at the moment.

'Right then,' she said. 'I shall look forward to that.'

'Me too,' he said. 'And by the way, the name's Joe.'

'Oh, I know!' she laughed with a kind of merry embarrassment. 'But I wasn't sure who else might be there!'

Joe considered this as he drove through the hilly north London streets to Hampstead the following evening. It was the remark of someone sufficiently worldly to see the possibilities, but direct, even naive enough to come right out and comment on them to his face. She was obviously not a lady accustomed to playing the dating game – or perhaps disinclined to. After the verbal fencing match with his agent, Joe found this a refreshing change. He had almost forgotten what it was like to have a conversation with a woman which was predicated on truthfulness and good manners. He winced at the recollection of his own heavy-handed comment about his work. Had boorishness become a habit with him? Had he become so brutalised by what he did that he could no longer conduct a civil exchange over the phone without whining and sounding off? If so, it wouldn't do. He had a bit of personal ground to make up here.

'With Freddy?' asked Alexa. 'He did ask you to call back.'

'And I will.'

'I see. Then who?'

Celeste looked down at herself. 'Do these shoes look funny with this?'

'No. Who?'

'Oh, someone I met when I went down for my brother's wedding,' said Celeste, 'and them bumped into again the other day quite by chance.'

Alexa raised her eyebrows. She was sitting on the sofa, cross-legged, nursing a tumbler of white wine, and a sheaf of cuttings from which she was attempting to distil the key facts concerning a leading American gay activist due to be featured in the Christmas edition of *Maxima*.

Now she pushed her glasses on to the top of her head and folded her arms. 'So is this just a diversionary tactic, or what?'

Celeste checked busily in her handbag for her car keys. 'Certainly not. I was asked out for a drink and I said yes.'

Alexa grinned. 'You're looking very smug. You're pleased, aren't you?'

'It beats doing Sandro's accounts,' said Celeste. 'What's my quickest route to Hampstead?'

'Hampstead already! Tell me about him.'

'I don't know a lot. His name's Joe Cook.'

'And what does Joe Cook do?'

'He's a comedian.'

'Aren't they all?'

'No, I mean he *is* a comedian. That's what he does for a living.'

'You're joking.'

'Not at all.' Celeste glanced at her watch, decided she was too early and sat down, determinedly ignoring Alexa's goggle-eyed reaction.

'I'm trying to wrap my mind round this. A comedian? A stand-up comic?'

'That's right.' Celeste couldn't contain a smile at the effect she was having.

'Full time?'

'Well – I suppose so. It's not a day-job anyway, is it?'

'Too right, it's not.' Alexa shook her head in wonderment. 'Should I have heard of him? Is he on telly?'

'No, you won't have heard of him. He's still working his way up.'

'Oh, yeah.' Alexa's tone became maddeningly sceptical.

243

'Many are called but almost none are chosen.'

'I imagine it's a highly competitive world. I know it is, from things he's said.'

Alexa dropped the cuttings and notebook on the floor and leaned forward with a show of almost uncontainable eagerness. 'What's he like? An abrasive Comedy-Store rebel or a tux and ruffles type?'

Celeste laughed. 'Neither.'

'The mind boggles.'

'Anyway, I'm off,' said Celeste, rising and slinging her bag over her shoulder.

'Bye-bye, God bless, you've been a lovely audience,' said Alexa, and put her spectacles back in place.

CHAPTER SIXTEEN

When she arrived at the pub, a shade flustered having missed a turning in Swiss Cottage, he was standing outside the entrance, feet slightly apart, hands in pockets. There were a couple of tables on the pavement and two or three couples were sitting there in the mild early autumn night, their faces lit like a de la Tour painting in the light from the pub windows. There was something chivalrous about Joe Cook's conspicuously solitary waiting for her out there, and she smiled as she hurried towards him.

'I'm so sorry I'm late, I did something silly on the way.'

'You didn't, did you?' She couldn't be sure if he was teasing her. 'No worries, I haven't been here long. Do you want to be in or out?'

She considered this. The pub looked bright and welcoming, but it was nice out here, too, with the lights of London sparkling in the distance, and a clear sky, fading from orange at the horizon to purple-black overhead, and wearing its constellations like the perfectly-displayed gems in the cabinet at Porterfield's.

'Let's stay out here.'

As soon as she'd said it she realised there was nowhere to sit, but Joe Cook was equal to the problem, finding and extricating one chair from the group near the door, and another from the public bar, and dragging forward an ornamental barrel that stood against the wall. He managed all this with a style she began to see as typical of him, combining physical ease and absolute lack of fuss – the second, she supposed, being the direct result of the first.

'There you go,' he said. 'What's yours?'

While he went to buy the drinks she sat contentedly in her coat, with her hands in her pockets and her collar turned up, and thought (as her father had so often done): 'At this moment I'm absolutely free. Nobody but Alexa knows where I am, or who with and they couldn't possibly guess. Joe Cook doesn't know me, and I don't know him yet, so I have a clean slate. Anything's possible.' She felt curiously safe.

Joe came back with a glass of wine for her and a pint of shandy for himself. He put his glass on the barrel and sat down on the hard slatted chair. It looked far too small for him but he managed to appear comfortable, sitting flat against the back, his knees splayed and his heels tucked, just touching, beneath the seat. Producing a packet of cigarettes he shook one out and offered it to her.

'I won't, thanks.'

'Mind if I do?'

'Of course not.'

'Thanks.' He took the cigarette from the packet using his lips in a manner which reminded her of the way she'd seen some high church communicants of Blaise's receive the host, direct on to the tongue. When he'd dropped his spent match on the barrel, he added: 'No of course about it these days. Some places you feel like a leper.'

'I share a house with a smoker,' Celeste explained.

'That right? Male or female?'

The question was obviously not, to him, a leading one, so she tried to match her tone to his. 'Female.'

'Old friends, are you? Or is it just business?'

She considered this. 'Neither, really. About four years ago I bought the house and advertised for a share, and Alexa answered it. But since then we definitely have become friends.' She remembered Pooter. 'We have our ups and downs, of course, but that's only natural.'

'I couldn't stand it,' he said.

She was surprised. 'Why not?'

He shook his head. 'Having someone else around, cluttering

the place up, using the kitchen and the bathroom. It'd drive me crazy inside a week.'

'I like it. Apart from the financial advantages, I enjoy the company. You need a few simple ground rules of course – just to provide a framework.' She realised she sounded a little pompous and took a sip of her wine.

He kept his gaze on the view. 'Do you think women are better at that?'

'Possibly.'

'Did that sound sexist?' Now he did look at her and something in his voice told her this was a straight question.

'A question can't be sexist, can it? My answer may have been.'

He lifted his head in a short, silent laugh. 'You're right.'

Emboldened, she asked, 'I suppose your act is, though? Sexist?'

He thought for a moment, dragging on his cigarette. He had not as yet touched the shandy. Finally he said, 'It's dirty.'

'Isn't that almost the same thing? After all, that sort of humour's very aggressive, and you're a man, so – it's going to be sexist.'

'Well, of course, when you put it like that.' He favoured her with the mere hint of a smile. 'But I'm not anti-women.'

'Of course not.' She found that she very much didn't want him to think she had been criticising, especially in an area of which she knew nothing. 'I should imagine it goes with the job.'

'It does, yeah.' He sounded gloomy, but added emphatically: 'That's one of the reasons I want out.'

'You want to give it up? To do what?'

'Don't get me wrong, I want to go on doing comedy. It's what I know. But different. There's only so far you can go with the circuit I'm on now, I'm not getting any younger and I'm tee'd off with doing nothing but smut.'

'I can see that,' she agreed. 'So what's the next step?'

'Well, for a start,' he said, pushing back his jacket sleeves to reveal densely tattooed forearms, 'I'm getting this lot removed. And the rest.'

'That's why you were going to see Freddy Gervase.'

He nodded. 'I don't rate all that change-what's-inside-first

247

stuff. Appearances count in my business. I've got to lose these, lose the earring, lose the stubble, lose some of this,' he slapped his midriff, 'and start looking like the sort of person you'd have round to dinner.'

She laughed at this. 'You mean me personally?'

'Not necessarily. That one would have to dinner.'

'Like royalty.'

'Like anybody.' He took a pull at the shandy, disposing of about half of it. 'Who do you know at the surgeon's, then?' he asked.

It no longer seemed appropriate to hedge. 'My brother is Freddy Gervase's partner.'

'Really?' He raised his eyebrows. 'Is that right?'

'Yes.'

'Your brother that was getting married back in the summer?'

'Yes.'

'You never said.'

'It hasn't arisen.'

'When I asked you, you said you were having lunch with someone who worked there. Was that your brother?'

She was taken aback by his detailed recall of their conversation. 'No. I'd actually been lunching with Freddy Gervase.'

Joe lit another cigarette. 'You're saying your brother's a plastic surgeon.'

'Yes.'

He whistled. 'He must make a pile.'

'Yes, I believe he does. They only do cosmetic work.'

'Doesn't seem right, does it,' he said ruminatively, 'just to be making rich people prettier, when there are people really shockingly disfigured who could do with the treatment.'

She was taken aback, both by the moral tone of this observation and by its simplistic assumption that the treatment of the one group prevented the treatment of the other. 'But you're not rich,' she said. 'Are you?'

'You're joking.'

'There you are, then. You said it yourself, you want to change your life. You feel, rightly or wrongly, that the tattoos hold you back, that they are a disabling influence. So you've decided that it's worth spending money on their removal. To help you make your new start.'

'Yes, ma'am.'

'I'm sorry if I sounded preachy, but so did you.'

He shook his head, and there was a look in his eyes that made her glad it was dark and he couldn't see her blush. 'You sounded okay to me.'

'It's just that it's not all silly women wanting to improve on nature.'

'Silly men, too, hm?'

'I didn't mean—'

'Forget it, only taking the rise.' He drained his glass and gestured with it towards hers. 'Other half?'

'Thank you. Here, let me.' She reached down for her bag but he pretended not to hear her and was already on his way. The moment he reappeared, she said, 'Don't think I'm defending my brother in all this. He has the basest possible commercial motives for what he does. But Freddy's a very decent, genuine person, with an excellent reputation as a surgeon.' I protest too much, she thought, it must be guilt. Freddy is so staggeringly suitable.

'Glad to hear it.' Joe Cook's reply held more than a trace of irony.

'The plastics argument is rather like the one that says if you pay pop stars less, you could give nurses more. There's no correlation between the two. Fabian and Freddy may just as well do what they do. There's surprisingly little professional jealousy or disapproval, provided the work is good. Anyone unskilled or slipshod soon gets a reputation in the profession.'

'Such as?'

'Well – I shouldn't mention names really, but I have heard Fabian utter harsh words about a Mr Reeves. He has rooms out in Hertfordshire somewhere.'

'Likely to stick your finger back on in the wrong place, is he?' said Joe. 'Might even be handy.'

'Good heavens, nothing as awful as that. He's just not as painstaking as he might be. And he charges less. So you pay for

249

what you get.'

He favoured her with his hint of a smile. 'And you reckon I'm in safe hands, do you?'

'Yes,' she said. She looked away for a moment. He was teasing her and she was embarrassed to think that he might see how much she liked it. 'You're in safe hands with Freddy.'

'And your brother?'

She looked him right in the eye now. 'I've never heard anything to make me think otherwise.'

She was startled when he burst out laughing, shaking his head and rubbing the side of his face as if the laughter had taken him by surprise and he was trying to bring it under control. 'I'm sorry,' she said, smiling in spite of herself. 'Did I say something funny?'

'Funny? No, no.' The laugh began to subside and his eyes rested on her with a kind of merry relish as if he were seeing something in her that she didn't even see herself. 'Nice one, Celeste.'

It was the first time he'd used her name, and it seemed as intimate as a kiss on the lips.

He walked her back to her car. It was beginning to get chilly but he seemed in no hurry to go. He leaned, arms folded and ankles crossed, against the bonnet as she unlocked the door.

'Good little motors, these.'

'Yes. It does for me. And of course my parents are outside London, so it's handy to be able to nip up the motorway to see them at weekends.'

'Reliable?'

'It seems to be. Actually,' she added with a touch of modest pride, 'I did a course once, so I am in a position to judge.'

He had been looking down at the car, but now he glanced up. 'What course was that, then?'

'Car maintenance. Only at the local night school, nothing particularly—'

'Car maintenance?'

'Well, yes. I mean only—'

'So you're a motor mechanic?'

'No, of course not, just—'

'You're a one-off, aren't you?' He gave her a grin of pure delight which was at once mirrored on her own face.

'I don't know.'

'Take it from me.' He pushed away from the car, and stretched. She was keenly aware of him towering next to her. It was like being in the protective shade of a large tree.

She opened the driver's door. 'It's been a lovely evening.'

'Lovely,' he echoed.

'Thank you.'

'My pleasure. We could do it again some time.'

'That would be—' she checked herself. 'Yes, I'd like to.'

'We could have dinner. Or anything.' He gave a small shrug. 'I'm easy.'

'As the actress said to the bishop.' She got into the car.

He chuckled as he leaned in through the door. It pleased her to hear him laugh, and to know that she had been the cause of it.

'Hey, watch it. That's my territory.'

She pulled the door shut and rolled down the window. 'Now you're talking.'

'How's that?'

'That's what I'd really like to do,' she said, astonishing herself with her own boldness. 'See you work.'

'You mean come to a gig?'

'If that's possible. If I'm allowed.'

'Course you're allowed. But I'm not sure you'd want to.'

'Why don't you let me be the judge of that?' She smiled, in case she had sounded sharp. 'Honestly. I'm so interested. I can't think of anything I'd rather do.'

He looked away for a minute and then ducked his head to look her straight in the eye. 'We're not talking classy venues here, you do understand that.'

'Yes.'

'Your brother's do, for instance – that was top of the league for me.'

'Yes. I understand what you're saying.'

'And the material I do—'

251

'Yes. Yes. Joe.' He was leaning on the opened window and on an impulse she put her hand on his and exerted a brief, light pressure, making her point. 'I'm really not bothered about what you say. I'm not so naive that I can't imagine the sort of jokes you have to make at a stag night.' She glimpsed from his expression that something she said had demonstrated just such a naivety, but she pressed on. 'It's not what you say I'm interested in, it's how you say it.'

He stared in at her and she looked back steadily. She felt that she was being examined and assessed.

'Okay.' He tapped the door and straightened up. 'But I'd better choose something that isn't wall to wall animals, and there isn't that much going right now . . . I'll give you a call if something comes up.'

'Thank you. I'd appreciate that.' She thought she might have sounded as though she were motivated more by prurience than a genuine desire to see him, so she added: 'But call me anyway, won't you.'

'I'll do that.'

'Good-night then.'

'Night. Safe journey.'

As she rolled the window up and pulled away from him she felt sure that her journey would be safe.

Bruno had stayed up late. So late, in fact, that the sky was turning grey and the first few birds were making tentative sounds in the wet, black garden. He was inordinately pleased to have stolen this march on the rest of the world. At a quarter to four he raided the fridge and ate a sandwich consisting of two slices of ham spread with mayonnaise and wrapped round a quarter of a pound of Wensleydale and some Webb's lettuce leaves. He felt monstrously hungry and hyper-alert in a way that he had not experienced since his days as a student when, after parties where all the bottles were emptied into a slop-bowl and the contents dished out with a ladle into pint glasses, he rolled free of the embrace of some unknown and by now rather smelly girl and walked home through echoing streets washed

252

clean by the night.

Before leaving he went upstairs and glanced in at Elodie, who lay in a characteristic position, half-turned as if running, one arm thrown up. Her profile on the pillow was veiled by her hair. She took a sleeping pill these days and was out for the count from midnight until about seven, when she began to rise little by little out of a deep, warm bath of sleep. Suddenly interested, Bruno walked over to the side of the bed and stared intently down at his wife. He examined minutely the texture of her neck, the slight flutter of her slackened lips, the just-visible scattering of liver spots on the back of the hand which lay on the pillow. These small signs of age – fewer and less marked than in many younger women – seemed to blur her outline, as though someone had taken his old, clear image of her and unkindly smudged it. He took a hank of hair between his finger and thumb; he could never quite reconcile himself to the fact that hair was a dead fibre, that his handling of it created not the slightest ripple on the surface of Elodie's profound unconsciousness. The individual hairs were fine and silky but it had always seemed to Bruno that there were an unimaginable number of them, an uncountable shifting, sifting mass like grains of sand on a beach or stalks in a hayfield. Lauren's hair was very different, a springing thatch composed of thick, wiry, separate strands. If he parted her hair, he fancied he could see the base of each one, bedded stoutly in its follicle in her smooth white scalp like the hair of a child's doll. Elodie's hair – he peered at it – had been allowed to lose its colour, which it had done haphazardly, some hairs remaining blue-black, others turning stark white, some mottled like cat's fur. Lauren's had been maintained expensively and continuously at the same level of lustre for as long as Bruno could remember. Standing in the dim light, with his wife's hair in his hand, he tried to extract some neat kernel of truth from this comparison. He was sure that somewhere in this matter of the hair there was, if not an answer, at least a pattern which would explain why he had fallen so completely out of love with Elodie. Still fingering the hair he glanced up and caught sight of his own murky reflection in the dressing-table mirror. He looked sinister, half-stooped over the bed, the dark hair like blood trickling from his hand, his face pale and furtive. He looked, thought Bruno, like a murderer. Not entirely displeased with the idea, he let his wife's hair fall back on the pillow and walked briskly from the room. Ten minutes later he was driving through the village at speed, in the direction of the motorway.

Lauren was not amused. 'Don't be ridiculous,' she said. 'I'll make us some coffee and then you can go back.'

'You don't understand, do you?' he replied. 'I've left.'

'Oh, I understand all right.' Lauren pushed back the sleeves of her towelling robe and took two white fluted mugs out of the dishwasher. 'I understand all too well. That's why I'm sending you packing.'

'I wish,' said Bruno, 'that you wouldn't adopt that schoolmarmish tone. It doesn't suit you and frankly at your age it's a rather dangerous game.'

Lauren put the mugs down by the kettle and stared at Bruno, her arms folded. Her face, unmade-up, was early-morning pale and harsh. 'Don't fudge the issue. Grow up and go home.'

Bruno slapped his jacket pockets for cigarettes, failed to find any and walked across to his coat which lay on the sofa.

'And don't smoke in my apartment.'

'It's your apartment now, is it? What happened to poor old Chrétien?'

'You want coffee before you go?'

'Thank you.'

He took his cigarettes out on to the balcony and lit one. The morning was grey and sharp; a helicopter buzzed in from the south carrying some moneybags to his City office. In the middle of the river a convocation of seagulls rose and fell around a slick of floating refuse. It was a quarter to seven. Very soon Elodie would begin the series of small sounds and stirrings that accompanied her rise to wakefulness. She would find, first of all, that he was not in bed beside her; then, that he was not in the house; finally – at about midday he estimated – that she wasn't sure where he was. The only thing he regretted was that he would not be there to see her reaction. She had been indifferent for so long, would she be indifferent to this, too, and just carry on in her dreamlike way?

'Coffee,' said Lauren, 'and put that thing out before you come back in.'

He threw his half-smoked cigarette over the balcony rail, his tiny contribution to the gulls' smorgasbord. Back inside he gazed appreciatively at the black, smoking coffee, the glistening white mug, the white and silver cafetière, the dense posy of blue anemones in a square glass pot on the white table.

'This is very nice,' he said.

'Make the most of it, it's not for long.'

'No, you're right.'

Lauren looked at him over the edge of her mug. 'I'm glad you've seen sense at last.'

'About what?'

'About not staying here.'

Bruno beamed. 'But I was never going to stay here.'

'I beg your pardon.'

'You were obviously under a misapprehension, my dear.'

'Don't my dear me, Bruno, for God's sake. Stop playing games and tell me what's going on.'

'I told you I'd left, which was true. But I never told you I was staying here. That, for some reason, was your assumption.'

'Okay. So where are you going?'

'Over the Channel.'

'So it's running-away time, is that it?'

'Not in the least.'

'That's what most people would call it.'

Bruno's bland smile grew yet more affable. 'I am not most people.'

'No,' said Lauren, upending the cafetière and pouring herself a second half-cup. 'That's true. Christ, you're a vain bastard, Bruno. Do what you like with what's left of your life – it could not interest me less – but tell me, do you ever think of Elodie in all this?'

'Naturally, since it's her I'm getting away from.'

He was gratified to see Lauren's eyes widen in shock. 'You jerk.'

'I don't know what you mean. If I still cared about her I'd be there. But I don't, and neither do I flatter myself that she cares for me, or has done for years.'

'She's always worshipped you, for some reason which escapes me—'

'Ah! No!' Bruno's voice was suddenly harsh. 'That's just where you're wrong. I worshipped her. In the beginning I did, I worshipped her, no other word for it. And unfortunately there's nothing more squalid and repellent than worship that's gone off. It leaves a smell, can you believe that? A sort of rancid stink, like prawn shells in the dustbin.'

'You're ashamed.' Lauren leaned towards him across the table with a gleeful expression. 'That's what it is. You're ashamed and embarrassed because you worshipped her and she'll always have that over you.'

'Naturally,' said Bruno, 'you're perfectly entitled to your opinion.'

'You're a prize shit, you know that?' said Lauren, a note of awe creeping into her voice. 'Now I know where your sons get it from.'

'Everything they know,' agreed Bruno complacently, 'they have learned at my knee. And I can't say I'd noticed any deleterious effect on your attitude towards me.'

'I beg your pardon?'

'Prize shit I may be, but that has never prevented you, as the vulgar saying goes, spreading the welcome mat.'

Lauren stood up, leaned over the table and poured the dregs of her black coffee into Bruno's lap. The coffee was no longer hot and he watched with a sort of satisfied detachment as it pattered on to the well-worn corduroy of his crotch.

'And now,' said Lauren in an unexceptionably conversational tone, 'I'm showing you the door.'

As Bruno crossed the bare, dark landing with its suggestion of unoccupied spaces – the area that was still discernibly a warehouse – he heard her explosive burst of laughter, and his own rose to join it like an echo as he ran down the black metal stairs to the street.

*

Tessa heard Blaise come in. Her whole body went into instinctive overdrive, heart racing, skin prickling, breathing shallow. She was gripped by absolute dread. Dread of her husband, and dread of what she had to tell him.

He came into the room, stooping slightly through the low door. In this ancient, low-ceilinged space his height made him appear imprisoned and dangerous.

'Hallo,' she said. 'How was the chapter meeting?'

'Perfectly regulation.' He went to the sideboard. 'But I am going to enjoy this drink. You?'

She shook her head. She was sitting – perching, she felt – on the rather uncomfortable upright chair near the telephone. There was nothing in her hands. She was doing nothing. Their lunch of home-made soup and bread and cheese was ready in the kitchen. Surely he would immediately deduce she had been talking to someone on the phone.

But, 'They're good men,' he said. 'And most of them are nice men. One or two of them are people with whom under any normal circumstances one might establish a friendship.' He let the implied condemnation hang in the air.

Tessa watched as he took a mouthful of whisky and his face seemed first to darken and then to relax slightly.

'I should have said that we – or you, anyway – *were* friends with them,' she said, and wondered, 'Why don't I tell him, why am I prevaricating like this?' But she knew that she was hypnotised by him, allowing him to dictate to her even when that wasn't his intention.

His gaze came to rest on her abstractedly, as though his thoughts were elsewhere and he had only just noticed her.

'Blaise,' she said, 'I was talking to your mother on the telephone.'

'How was she? I've been rather remiss in that department recently.'

'As a matter of fact she rang me. But it was you she wanted and I said you'd call back.'

'I will do, later. I've got a breather before evensong.'

257

Tessa said: 'I think she'd like you to call right away if it's possible.'

'Naturally it's possible,' said Blaise, 'but not ideal. It's much better if I can speak to her at what passes for leisure. She's getting older, she likes to talk at length and she is becoming rather repetitive—'

'Blaise,' said Tessa. 'Your father's gone.'

'Really? Where to this time? I hadn't realised he was off anywhere.'

'Neither had your mother. He was gone when she woke up, and he didn't leave a message and she has no idea where he is.'

'But it's only' – Blaise glanced at his watch – 'ten past one. Wherever he is at the moment, it'll involve lunch. Has she tried the publisher? And the club?'

'I don't know . . .' Tessa saw now that she had allowed Elodie's anxiety to infect her. She had asked none of the sensible questions and elicited no useful information. What on earth could there be to worry about?

'I must say, I think the panic's a bit premature,' said Blaise. 'But perhaps I'd better give her a ring and allay her fears.'

He came over and stood near the phone table. Tessa could smell his particular scent, now overlaid with a faint whiff of Scotch. She slipped out of her chair, being careful not to touch him.

'Are you going to do that now?'

'I might as well.'

'Yes,' agreed Tessa. 'I think she needs her mind setting at rest.'

As I do, she thought, on her way through to the kitchen. She moved around very quietly, not listening to Blaise, but conscious of the interrupted flow of his voice beyond the heavy half-open door of the sitting-room. When he was silent for a long period she remembered all too clearly the agitation in Elodie's voice, the fearful certainty that some long-awaited disaster had at last taken place. Cutting a fresh piece of butter into the dish, her hand shook so much that the knife rattled. She tried to breathe deeply, and take control of herself. If there was a problem, which there probably wasn't, it was not hers and she was not the cause of it. But she did not like to be the harbinger of bad news. 'Fears duly allayed,' said Blaise. 'That does smell nice.'

Lightheaded with relief, Tessa served the soup.

They were about half-way through it, eating steadily and in a not unfriendly silence, when the phone rang and Blaise answered it, this time picking up the receiver from the wall phone near the kitchen door.

'Hallo – oh, hallo. Yes,' he said. And then, lifting his chin and staring at some point in the middle of the ceiling: 'Go on.'

Tessa looked at his soup spoon, lying abandoned in what remained of his leek and potato soup. She was suddenly certain that he would not finish, and she couldn't either. She picked up their dishes and carried them over to the sink. Blaise was standing completely still, listening to whoever it was on the other end. Except for the brusque informality of his greeting she might have deduced, from her husband's attitude of irritation and attention, that the caller was the bishop.

She did not run the tap because of the noise. Instead she continued to clear the table, glancing at Blaise as she did so. Her former anxiety rushed back. His face had the dark, still, concentrated expression that she hated. It was always, always, a bad sign. A small pulse of pain, like a distant drumbeat, started up between her eyes.

'I simply can't take this seriously,' he said, in the tone of one taking it very seriously indeed. 'It's farcical.'

There was another long silence during which he turned to the wall, one hand on the back of his head, the middle finger tapping. His mood, so far from communicating anything farcical, was an almost palpable emanation in the room with them, a third presence prowling about and likely to pounce. Desperate to defend herself against it, Tessa now began to fill the sink. The taps were ancient and erratic, and the water spurted out and hit the bottom with a sound like snare drums.

'Please!' It was not a request but an order, shouted over the noise. Hurriedly Tessa turned it off.

'Sorry.' Her face was burning.

'All right,' said Blaise to the caller, '*all right*. You've

259

made your point. Have you spoken to anyone else? Don't worry, I'll do it. Yes, whatever needs doing. And in the mean time, if you hear anything more perhaps you'll let me know. Good-bye.'

He replaced the receiver and remained standing there for a moment, facing the wall. When he turned his expression made Tessa flinch. 'I would say it was incredible,' he said. 'But that wouldn't be true. It's all too terrifyingly credible.'

'What?' she said. 'Who were you talking to?'

'Lauren Lalande.' He made his aunt sound like a stranger. 'My father called on her this morning.'

Tessa felt a rush of relief. 'Good. So she knows where he is.'

'No.' Blaise left the room. She heard the faint clink of the decanter and he returned with a measure of whisky. He approached the sink and she stepped swiftly out of his way as he topped the glass up from the tap, muttering 'Damn!' as the water splashed on to his jacket.

'I'm sorry,' said Tessa, 'I don't understand.'

'Join the club,' replied Blaise.

'What's happened?' She was being forced to interrogate him, something he disliked and which she generally made a point of avoiding. He seemed to want the information to be wrung from him.

He shook his head and made a short, sharp grunting sound of annoyance.

'Where's Bruno gone?' she asked again.

'I don't know.' He snatched a deep gulp of the whisky. 'She doesn't know. Nobody knows. But he has definitely gone. He has left my mother.'

Tessa gasped. 'Blaise, no – surely not!'

'Nothing more certain. Apparently he turned up at the Lalandes' flat early this morning, not merely unrepentant but positively cock-a-hoop, boasting about how it was the best thing for all concerned.'

'So Elodie was right. She must have sensed something.' Blaise didn't answer. He knocked back the rest of his drink and put the glass in the sink.

'What I have sensed,' he said, 'all my life, now I come to

260

reflect on it with something of a new perspective, is that my father is not just egocentric but amoral, which is a peculiarly dangerous and unstable combination.' He directed a cold, challenging look at Tessa, as if daring her to contradict him. 'Now, predictably enough, the rest of us are left to clear up the mess he's left behind while he runs away to be a cabin boy or whatever his brave new life entails.'

'I'm so sorry,' Tessa said.

'It's not your fault,' snapped Blaise. He often said this when she expressed sympathy, and by means of this deliberate misinterpretation made her feel that much of what happened *was* her fault, that she was a useless, passive, cause of trouble.

'I know that,' she said with a sturdiness she did not feel. 'I'm sorry it's happened. Sorry for poor Elodie. And for you, of course. What will you do?'

Blaise looked at his watch. 'I must call my mother back before the diocesan finance lot arrive.'

'I'll put them straight in the study and ply them with coffee,' said Tessa. 'Don't hurry, say whatever needs saying, make any arrangements, she's going to be so—'

'And then this evening,' went on Blaise, moving towards the door. 'I'll contact Celeste.'

Blaise spent twenty minutes in the kitchen, talking on the telephone to his mother, with the door shut. The afternoon had closed in, and Tessa lit the fire in the study. There was insufficient draught and it smoked and sulked before conceding a few pale flames. In the meadows below the window the cattle seemed turned to stone, and there was no one walking along the lane or down the footpath. In the distance the last two gypsy vans lay like maggots on the downy grey of the fen bridleway.

There was a brisk rattle on the door-knocker and Tessa went to let in the first of the finance board. But Blaise was there before her. As he opened wide the door his smile was warm and welcoming and his shoulders open and relaxed. 'A very good afternoon to you both,' he said. 'Just the weather for sitting inside in warmth and comfort and discussing an extremely healthy profit . . .'

Tessa nodded across the hall at the visitors and went into the kitchen to fill the coffee pot. She heard Blaise's voice as he showed them into the study, and heard them laugh, content, as people so often were, simply to be with him.

She set the things out on the high-sided butler's tray. What was it Blaise had said? A dangerous and unstable combination.

Celeste sat in Michael's office with the files and paperwork pertaining to several years of culinary artistry and creative budgeting spread out before her on the old-fashioned rolltop desk. It was nine p.m. The office was like that of some raffish gumshoe in a 1940s movie, complete with branching hatstand, parchment-coloured roller blind, hanging overhead lamp and portable typewriter. Downstairs, the sixteen or so mid-week diners burbled contentedly. Along the landing Michael was under orders to remain in bed, his Shaw biography resting on the adjustable lectern which had been Celeste's coming-home present to him, his white wine in the green Lalique goblet which had been Sandro's.

Since Michael's return from hospital Celeste had discovered that she enjoyed these evenings over the restaurant, with a useful job to do and the business of the house going on around her. She liked to feel that she was freeing Sandro to do what he was good at, and that she was in some small way bearing Michael company by being up here, within hailing distance. At intervals she would get up and go along to the bedroom and perch on the edge of the bed for a while, reporting on her efforts. She had not as yet discovered anything to interrupt her slow and painstaking progress towards clear water.

'I apologise,' said Michael, 'if it's a dog's breakfast, but what with me firing on one cylinder and the littl'un's complete inability to focus on figures, things have got rather neglected. If you can just bring things up to date I can take over.'

But of course she'd told him he could do no such thing. Once things were up to speed she could simply drop in and keep them that way, it would take no more than an hour a week, she was happy to do it.

And indeed she was. But then she had a different

perspective on life these days. Alexa's testiness, an unreasonable customer at Porterfield's, a persistent amiable siege from
Freddy, and a lunch with Louise at which the latter had
become stupendously drunk – none of these had caused her to
break stride. She remembered her mother, pregnant with
Sandro, explaining her lack of a coat with the then-
incomprehensible remark 'but I have internal heating'. When
Celeste thought about that remark now, she understood it.
Now she, too, had internal heating, and she had traced its
source to Joe Cook.

They had met once more in the week since their drink in
Hampstead. He'd driven down in his van and they'd gone to
the cinema in Bayswater. The film, about a wartime childhood,
had enchanted Celeste but Joe had reservations.

'It's well made,' he conceded over a Chinese meal
afterwards. 'It's well done, but it's got no reality.'

'I thought it had,' she said. 'It was real on an emotional level.'

'How would you know?' he asked. 'You weren't alive then.'

'Neither were you.'

'And you're not that class.'

'Not being working class has nothing—'

'They weren't working class. They were lower middle.'

She was surprised by his insistence on such a nice
distinction. 'Does it matter?'

'Yeah. I'm lower middle. It's dying out.'

'I see. But the point I'm making is that childhood is a
separate country, and the way we remember it is separate
again. We look at it through lots of filters and from different
angles, we project all kinds of interpretations on to it,
retrospectively.'

'Is that how you remember yours, then?'

They'd finished eating and his eyes were lowered,
concentrating on a roll-up.

'Well, no,' she said. 'But then I'm not making a film about
it.'

'But if you were, you'd use all these retrospective filters and
what have you?' He leaned his elbows on the table and blew the
first mouthful of smoke sideways over his shoulder.

'I wouldn't have to, I can see everything as if it were yesterday.'

He nodded. 'Me too. That's reality.'

For the first time with him she'd felt a little uncomfortable, as though he had unintentionally brushed against the secret hiding-place of some shameful object.

'But if I were fictionalising it,' she persisted.

He shook his head. 'Then you'd put a gloss on it. Let's face it, most of it doesn't bear looking at.'

She'd laughed then, and asked for another beer, admitting (but only to herself) that he was right.

Since that evening, when he'd taken her back to Parsloe Mews but refused an invitation to coffee ('Your flatmate in? Perhaps I'd better pass.'), she'd spoken to him on the telephone twice and received a note. The note was actually a postcard, headed with his name and address printed in blue (she pondered the significance of this). His handwriting was round, regular and easy to read. It confirmed, rather formally, his invitation to her to attend something described as a 'benefit wake' at the Axe and Compass in Ealing in four weeks' time. It gave the address, telephone number and route to the venue, indicated that men would be in lounge suits, and explained that he would meet her at the entrance to the entertainment suite at the rear of the pub. It concluded: 'This is a mixed gig so I'm keeping my fingers crossed, but I'd still bring your smelling salts if I was you, Yours, Joe.'

At all times his manner, like his note, had been friendly and polite. Once or twice he had held her upper arm as they crossed a road, and on one occasion he'd put his hand on her shoulder when she said something that made him laugh. She knew that the elation she was experiencing was out of all proportion to anything that was happening, but she felt neither deluded nor guilty. The internal heating warmed and illuminated her. She was glad to be of service, and her evenings spent scanning Michael's scaffolding of figures were imbued with a sense of the rightness of things. Joe was working tonight, but she was going to ring him at midnight when he got back. She loved to listen to him talking about the animals and the hecklers and the strippers and the dodgy customers, and to feel, crackling down the line, the adrenalin which was his chosen drug.

She sat up and stretched her arms above her head. From downstairs there came a soft explosion of laughter. She pushed her chair back, intending to go and visit Michael and see if he wanted anything, but the phone rang. The telephone was shaped like an upturned hand, so that it seemed to grip her own hand when she lifted the receiver. It was the only object in the room – in the house, even – which she thought of as gay.

'Hallo?'

'Celeste. It's Blaise.'

'Blaise! How did you—'

'I spoke to Alexa and she told me you were there. How is Michael, by the way?'

She lowered her voice. 'Stable for the moment, that's about all.'

'That's tremendous.' She wondered if he'd heard her. 'Look, I know you're busy, and I wouldn't have disturbed you if it weren't extremely important.'

'What can I do?' she asked. As she listened to what her brother had to say, she felt the edges of her happiness begin to shrivel and curl. Not only the bad news and its worse implications, but his voice and his unassailable authority struck home to some old, tender, private place where she was utterly unprotected.

'Yes,' she said. 'I understand. It's all right. I'll go.'

And as a few moments later she wearily tidied the desk and turned off the light she remembered her conversation with Joe Cook and thought how true it was that the past remained close, enmeshing the present in its cruel and clinging detail.

CHAPTER SEVENTEEN

Elodie sat at the kitchen table. In front of her was a metal colander containing four pounds of Brussels sprouts, which Celeste had suggested she might prepare 'if she wanted something to do'. Elodie had always found sprouts (despite their name the most English of vegetables) curiously intimidating. She had rarely either cooked or eaten a sprout that was satisfactory, and the smell of them, even five minutes after a meal had ended, made her feel ill. To be confronted with this mountain of small green cannonballs, in her own home, was the final evidence that her world had fallen apart. She looked across at Celeste, who was busy at the sink, doing things with potatoes and carrots. From the Aga came the fatty, not-yet-appetising smell of a shoulder of lamb beginning to cook.

Celeste glanced over her shoulder. 'Okay, Mother?' Elodie nodded. Celeste sighed. 'A silly question, I do realise that.'

'No, really,' said Elodie. 'I'm quite all right.' She picked up the kitchen knife which Celeste had laid beside the colander. To her left stood a large saucepan. It seemed that everything – the sprouts, the colander, the knife, the saucepan, even Celeste – was waiting with close attention for her next move.

'You don't have to do that,' Celeste told her.

'But I want to,' said Elodie. She knew that it was a case of what Celeste might prefer. Celeste was terribly tense and worried, and had organised this family lunch to cheer her up and set her back on course. Was it so much to ask that she play

266

her part by preparing a few sprouts? She knew that Celeste's agitation was far greater than her own. Hers, in fact, was non-existent. The fact of Bruno's defection, which she had absorbed immediately, as though it had been written on the pillow, had engendered in her only a kind of dazed relief. He had left a letter which Celeste had read aloud to her, not referring to his reasons for leaving but making it clear that apart from his royalties he would be making no more claims on their joint finances or property. She wasn't happy, exactly, but she felt as she had done during childhood illnesses when the magic thermometer endorsed her symptoms and she was able to lie back in bed with a book, officially afflicted.

With a hand that moved slowly and heavily, she picked up the first sprout.

Celeste scraped and scrubbed at the potatoes and carrots. Her hands were red with cold in the muddy water, her neck and shoulders were beginning to ache. This, she reflected, was her punishment for having become smug and complacent. Her concentration had slipped, and look what had happened. Internal heating indeed. Here in the cluttered, draughty kitchen at Hartfield she felt chilled to her bones in spite of the Aga. She suspected that the cold came from inside, that it was a chill of the spirit and not of the flesh. Just when some sea change had seemed to be taking place in her life the tide had turned, and powerful atavistic forces had sucked her back.

She put the two saucepans containing the vegetables on top of the Aga, and opened the oven to look at the joint. A rude blast of heat slapped her face. The shoulder of lamb spat sullenly. She closed the door.

'Coffee?'

Elodie shook her head.

Celeste didn't know how she should be treating her mother. Elodie seemed almost serene, it was impossible to tell what she was thinking. The outward manifestations were not unlike the slightly haughty self-containment of her youth – the straight back, the uptilted chin, the slow, graceful movements – except that now her gaze was blank and faraway. Celeste presumed that her mother was in shock, from which she would emerge in her own good time.

If Elodie had been distraught, Celeste would have known what to do about it. She would have talked, and listened, and sat up late, and poured medicinal cognacs, and discussed her father exhaustively. It might even have been a purging experience. As it was, she was at a loss. And the fact that Bruno's whereabouts were still not known didn't help. Like an unburied corpse he lurked on the fringes of her mind, gone but impossible either to forget or to confront. Celeste had always managed to swallow her father, metaphorically speaking, whole and intact, rather as a python swallows a live rabbit, but this latest – and surely final – piece of bad behaviour had stuck in her gullet. Damn, damn, damn them all, she thought, blinking rapidly as she basted the joint and slammed the door shut, and damn especially the lifelong family conspiracy which decreed that she should have to shoulder these problems not of her making.

By one o'clock, the joint was fragrant in its log-jam of roasting potatoes, a blackberry and apple crumble puddled with its own purple juice stood on the hob, and the offending sprouts were coming to the boil.

Elodie had been moved into the library. She walked there under her own steam, but the impulse had come from Celeste, who could envisage her mother sitting at the kitchen table indefinitely. She had lit the fire, and Elodie sat by it, accepting such attention as came her way. She might have been said to be holding court, except that her manner was not so much regal as slightly bemused. She seemed not to know what all the fuss was about.

'It was nothing personal. I think he flipped his lid,' said Lauren.

'Do you?' asked Elodie earnestly. 'Poor Bruno.' But when Chrétien voiced the disobliging opinion that recent events constituted no startling aberration but were simply the latest step in a lifetime's self-indulgence, she inclined unhappily in that direction too. 'Oh dear, you're very probably right . . .'

When Blaise, Tessa and the children arrived, Lauren and

Chrétien retired not very gracefully to the icy drawing-room, there to conduct a sustained and fluidly bilingual row. The door was pushed shut against the prevailing draught with a surly hydraulic hiss and the confrontation lashed against its far side like sleet on a window.

'Idiot!' hissed Lauren. 'Don't you know better than to trash all those years of marriage?'

'It wasn't marriage I was trashing,' said Chrétien coolly, 'but her husband. She shouldn't feel guilty.'

Celeste, in and out of the library with drinks and nuts, wondered what she had ever hoped to achieve by this gathering. Molly and Nathan were clearly bored and disgusted by the whole thing. One grandparent leaving another was almost as bad as parents sleeping together, the clear evidence of passions and resentments not at all in keeping with the humbleness of old age. Two years ago the situation would not have unsettled them, they would have continued their parallel and separate existences, cocooned by childhood, even a little smug that this disaster did not touch on them. But now Molly in particular was in the wings, about to enter the luridly-lit stage of adult emotions, and here were these people whom she had always known, strutting and fretting and hogging the space which she yearned to occupy.

'Don't I get a kiss?' asked Elodie.

Nathan lurched forward and bumped his face against hers, but Molly couldn't manage it and Tessa made anxious 'don't mind her' faces at anyone who would look.

Blaise was less lenient. 'Molly, don't sulk. Give Granny a kiss. I think she deserves one, don't you?'

'For God's sake, Dad . . .'

'Don't use that expression, please.' Blaise's voice was velvety but penetrating, the voice that could carry the prayer of St John Chrysostom right into the corners of the Abbey and make the hairs rise on the back of the neck, and scatter the proud in the imagination of their hearts.

Unfortunately Molly was too full of her own personal and tumultuously complicated feelings to be either thrilled or frightened by her father.

'Why not?' she barked. 'I meant it. You should do things for God's sake, shouldn't you? And I was not sulking. If I don't feel like kissing anyone, why should I? What's the point?'

Celeste glanced anxiously at her mother, but Elodie seemed to have lost interest in the discussion and was gazing absently into the fire, the rim of her glass held just beneath her lower lip.

'Will you go out of here, please, Molly?' said Blaise. Nathan at once charged for the door and his heavily-trainered feet could be heard slapping across the kitchen floor. Molly hesitated. Tessa took her arm and looked with head bent into her face, whispering something emollient. Celeste watched in dismay. They should never have brought the children. She saw Molly's self-destructive longing to take issue with her father, to leap wildly across the divide and risk everything. Even her clothes displayed her agony. She wore unflattering loose jeans and a thin black jumper, the cuffs gone frilly and hanging to her knuckles, and her feet were comical in massive black lace-up shoes: the clothes of a child wishing to be grown-up but not wishing to be a woman.

Molly wrenched free of her mother and left the room. The door of the kitchen slammed mightily.

Tessa made a small galvanic movement to follow.

'Leave her,' said Blaise. 'Just leave her.'

'Don't worry,' said Celeste, 'I'm in and out, I'll make sure she's okay. There's coke in the fridge.'

'Right,' said Tessa, looking pink and on the verge of tears. Blaise sat down on the arm of the chair and took one of Elodie's hands in both of his. She turned and looked up into his face with what Celeste could only have described as a radiant smile. A smile such as she herself might have been capable of only a very few days ago.

'I think actually . . .' said Tessa. She moved towards the door. Blaise, reflecting Elodie's smile, glanced up at her. 'I just want to get something from the car,' she blurted out.

Celeste followed her out into the hall. As she left the library Elodie was saying, 'It's so lovely to see you, Blaise, and the family.'

To which Blaise replied, in his voice of milk and honey, 'Don't be daft, *maman*, you couldn't have kept us away. All I want is for you to be happy.'

And more of the same, presumably, followed. Celeste found that her teeth were clamped together, almost grinding. She paused in the hall and took a deep breath.

The library door swung open and Lauren emerged, carrying her glass. She wore a suit of simple and immaculate cut – Celeste imagined it might be Armani – in the palest eggshell tan, and her hair was like spun gold. The hand encircling her tumbler had perfect, gleaming scarlet nails and her tights gave her slim legs a glamorous sheen. She made Celeste feel irredeemably dumpy and scruffy.

'I do apologise for our little domestic, Celeste,' she said with unapologetic composure. 'It happens to the best of us. Could I fetch myself another of these?'

She disappeared into the dining-room. Celeste, gazing enviously after her, jumped as Chrétien put his hand on her shoulder.

'She misses him, you know. Your father. She may well be the only one that does.'

On her way to the kitchen Celeste reflected that when it came to inscrutability the French had the orientals beaten into a cocked hat.

She checked the lunch. Fabian and Louise had still not arrived. The sprouts were on the point of turning soggy so she drained them and put them back on the hob. She wanted to turn on the hotplate on the sideboard, but her aunt and uncle were now conducting their exchange in the dining-room, on a more muted level which suggested that an entente might be imminent, so Celeste didn't like to go in.

She stood by the sink with her arms folded, staring out into the garden. It was one of those still, grey autumn days when the spire of the church seemed to rise out of the village like a raised periscope, spying on its surroundings. Tonight was the night she was supposed to be going to watch Joe Cook perform but she had left a message on his answering machine to say that there was a family crisis and she wouldn't be able to make it. She had left Hartfield's telephone number but she hadn't heard from Joe, and now she wondered whether she ever would. There was a deep reserve, almost a formality, in him which she sensed would not take kindly to being messed about. He might have misconstrued her message; for obvious reasons she had not been very specific; he might think she was being simply casual with the arrangements. Oh Joe, she thought, if you only knew!

The back door opened and Tessa came in, with the scoured and scraped look of someone who has been crying.

'Hallo,' said Celeste. 'Where are the children?'

'In the loft over the garage. Do you suppose it's safe?'

'Probably not, but we've all played in it since long before people worried so much about safety. How's Molly?'

'Taking it out on her brother.'

'Poor Molly.'

'Yes.' Tessa sighed and slumped down in one of the chairs at the kitchen table. 'I wouldn't have dragged them along today, but there wasn't anyone about at our end that I could farm them out with. Molly's missing her disco class to be here.'

'Surely,' said Celeste, 'you didn't have to come.'

'I suppose not.' Tessa twiddled her wedding ring which was quite loose. 'But Blaise thought I should be here.' She paused and added: 'We did talk about it.'

'It's sweet of you to make the effort,' said Celeste gently.

Everyone was round the dining-table and Celeste was tranferring the lamb from roasting tin to carving dish when the swish and crump of fast wheels on gravel announced the arrival of Fabian. He slammed the outer back door and walked into the kitchen, tossing his car keys in one hand. 'Am I late, or is it just that the young and the elderly were demanding to be fed?'

Celeste glanced at the clock. 'It is nearly two.'

'My God, the end of life as we know it. Any chance of a drink?'

'There's wine, we're about to eat.'

'A pox on wine.' He began opening cupboards and banging

them shut so that they bounced open again. 'What have you done with the fire-water?'

'It's on the side in the dining-room.' Celeste stabbed roast potatoes and laid them round the joint.

'What did you do that for? Ah, what have we here?'

'It's Mother's cooking brandy.'

'That'll do.' He took a glass off the draining-board, half-filled it, swallowed the contents and poured another, smacking his lips.

Celeste pushed her hands into the oven mitts. 'Where's Louise?'

'Yes, it's a shame, she couldn't come,' said Fabian. 'She's a bit off-colour. You know.'

'No.'

Fabian swallowed the second brandy. 'Women's stuff. What do I know, I'm only a doctor.'

Celeste picked up the meat dish. 'Can you open the door for me?'

'Hang on.' He held the handle of the door and leaned back against it so that she was effectively trapped, holding the heavy dish. 'What's the word on the old man?'

'There is none. We don't know where he is.'

'And how's Mother?'

'Why don't you go in and ask her. Look, will you open the door before I drop this?'

'I don't know what I'm doing here, I've got fuck-all to contribute.' Fabian opened the door. 'Ah, there you all are.'

About ten minutes into lunch Blaise proposed a toast.

'We all know why we're here.' ('Buggered if I do,' said Fabian to Lauren and received a punch in the ribs.) 'We're here to be with *maman*, and to show that we love her, and decide what's best to be done.' He glanced down at Elodie and she took his hand and pressed the back of it to her cheek. Fabian cleared his throat disgustingly.

'Perhaps it's only fair,' went on Blaise, 'to think of Father as well on this occasion, since we must presume he has some demons of his own to confront, and is obliged, with only himself to blame, to confront them alone . . .'

Blaise went on to say that the important thing was that they were still a family, and that Elodie was the centre of it, and that he, and all of those present, were willing and eager to do all they could to support her . . .

Celeste glanced round the table. Fabian was pouring himself the last of the red wine. Lauren was listening attentively, her eyes fixed on Blaise's face. Chrétien was sitting with head bent, staring down at his folded arms. Tessa was maintaining an anxious surveillance of Nathan who was fiddling with his digital watch and almost certainly about to activate the alarm.

Molly had eaten virtually nothing and her face was a mask of suppressed misery and rage. When the telephone rang in the hall she was out of her chair in seconds. 'I'll get it!'

Blaise raised his glass and they drank to Elodie. As they all sat down again Elodie murmured, 'Thank you all, this is so sweet of you.'

Molly flung open the door. 'It's Uncle Sandro for Celeste.'

'Thanks. Excuse me for a tick.'

As Celeste went out she heard Tessa say, '*Aunt* Celeste.'

'Hallo, Sandro?'

'Celeste – look, I'm really, really sorry that I couldn't make it. You do understand, don't you?'

'Of course. It's not that important, honestly. Just a token gesture for Mother's sake.'

'I still can't believe he's done a runner. I can't imagine what he'll do with himself. Where will he go? Who on earth would have him?'

'I don't know, none of us does.'

'What happens if he turns up again with his tail between his legs?'

'Lauren's the only one who's seen him and she doesn't think that's very likely.'

'That's funny too, isn't it? Him going to their place, what do you make of that?'

'I think he sees her as a sort of friendly outsider – not judgemental.'

'This may not be the moment to mention it but I've always wondered if—'

'Sandro, how's Michael?'

'Oh, God,' Celeste heard the self-pity creep into his voice, 'not good. But holding. They've changed the nurse, and this one is such a little Hitler, she makes me feel completely redundant and treats Michael like a five-year-old.'

'That must be wearing,' Celeste agreed. 'But if she's kind and competent, I suppose that's all that matters.'

'I can't bear to see him like this,' went on Sandro, changing tack seamlessly, 'so thin and weak when he used to be so fit. He used to tease me about my size, he could pick me up with one arm. Now I could do the same with him.'

'It must be awful,' said Celeste. 'I don't know what to say.'

'There's nothing to say,' said Sandro. 'His brother came the other day, you know, Malcolm, the great grey homophobic suit, the one who can't stand me, and I've got to say it's entirely mutual.'

Celeste thought of Michael, caught in the cross-currents of this mutual loathing. 'So how did it go?'

'He behaved as if I wasn't capable of looking after him, as if I was some sort of irresponsible gadabout who kept a disorderly house. He as good as implied that it would be better if Michael went to stay with them in New Malden, Lester, can you imagine? Michael cooped up in that revolting metroland villa with Malcolm and Donna. You haven't met her, but take my word for it that Donna is the woman for whom velour leisurewear was invented. What she can do to green vegetables has to be seen to be believed. At least here there is some chance of the invalid appetite being tempted—'

'Sandro, I'd better go. I'll give them all your love, shall I?'

'Yes, of course, and especially *maman*. Give her a big kiss, and perhaps you can persuade her to come and have dinner on the house some time? Did you see our write-up in *Maxima*?'

'I didn't, but I'm sure Alexa will show it to me when I get back.' There was a sudden raising of voices in the dining-room, not quite a laugh nor a cheer but a concerted exclamation of approval. 'Look, Sandro, I think I should get back to the others.'

'Celeste, just before you dash off—'

'Yes?'

275

'Does all this mean that you won't be able to look over our books? I hate asking you, but you know what I'm like, and Michael's really not up to it.'

'Don't worry,' said Celeste. 'I'll be in to check the books.'

'Lester, thanks awfully,' said Sandro. His voice sounded quite different. 'You are an absolute star.'

When Celeste went back into the dining-room she knew at once that she had entered in the slipstream of some recently delivered piece of news. Elodie's chair was pushed back as though she had just returned to it, Chrétien was uncorking a new bottle of wine, the other adults were smiling (though Celeste noticed that the smiles differed in intensity and warmth) and even Molly looked relaxed and eager as though her attention had at long last been wrested away from her internal conflict. Nathan looked if anything even more disgruntled.

'Celeste,' cried Lauren, 'get a load of this. Fabian's going to be a daddy!'

'That's wonderful,' said Celeste dutifully, 'congratulations.'

Tessa was stacking plates and Fabian was lighting himself a cigar, puffing with the sensuous concentration of someone performing fellatio. For a moment Celeste thought he'd had the grace to avoid her eyes, but when he glanced up his own were sharp and challenging.

'It's nothing serious, I hope, with Louise?' asked Blaise.

'No, no. Only queasiness. She had a bit of a hard week at work so I told her to take a day in bed, doctor's orders.'

Tessa, carrying plates, paused at his shoulder. 'It's such a bore – in the early weeks you feel like death and you don't get a shred of sympathy, then when you're like a blue whale you feel wonderful and everyone treats you as an invalid.'

'She'll be fine,' said Fabian, shaking his match and dropping it on his side plate. 'She's as strong as a carthorse.'

'Now, Fabian,' said Elodie, 'you must look after your wife and indulge her a little during pregnancy.' Celeste saw that there were tears, the first she had seen, in her mother's eyes.

Fabian raised an eyebrow. 'Who's here, after a punishing

week adjusting the human frame? And who's tucked up in bed with a good book?'

'I'll make coffee,' said Celeste. 'Why don't you all go through into the library, I banked the fire up.'

A little later Blaise announced he was going for a walk, and would Celeste and Fabian care to join him? Celeste interpreted this as an order and stood up at once, but Fabian demurred.

'I'd so much rather not, Blaise. You know my views on exercise.'

'It'll do you good.'

'I ought to be getting back to the wee wifey.'

'If I were you,' said Blaise, 'I'd leave her in peace for as long as possible.'

'Okay.' Fabian stubbed out his cigar. 'If you're determined to organise a crocodile I'll come, but I refuse to go anywhere which involves a change of dress.'

Lauren was playing cards with Molly and Nathan. 'Have a nice time, give my love to the Great Outdoors.'

Chrétien was reading the newspaper and wagged a finger in farewell. Elodie, her head tilted back on her chair, appeared to be asleep. Tessa was looking along the bookshelves. Celeste caught her uncertain glance in their direction.

'Bye, darling,' said Blaise, ending uncertainty. 'We shan't be long. I need to be on the road by four-thirty at the latest.'

In deference to Fabian's hand-made brogues they went not across the Craft but up the drive and along the lane away from the village. The dank, deserted winter fields stretched away on both sides, broken here and there by the interrupted remnants of ancient hedgerows. There were few trees. What relief there was was man-made – pylons, telegraph poles, a combine harvester abandoned like a dinosaur skeleton in the middle distance. The surface of the road was covered by a slick of mud, straw and horse-droppings.

'Christ,' said Fabian. 'Why am I so co-operative?'

'I wanted us to be able to have a quick word,' said Blaise. 'What is your reaction to *maman*'s state of mind?'

'She seems remarkably chipper to me. Who wouldn't be?'

'Celeste? You've seen more of her.'

Celeste sensed that much might depend on her answer. She chose her words carefully. 'I agree she's not as upset as you might expect, but then she may have anticipated this. And she may also be in shock. What concerns me is that she really isn't herself, and hasn't been for some time.'

'What you're trying to tell us,' said Fabian, 'is that she's going slightly barmy.'

'I wouldn't put it anything like as strongly as that.'

'But is it what you're getting at?' asked Blaise. 'Because if it is, she shouldn't be living on her own.'

When she looked back on this conversation Celeste could see that from that point onwards she had been on a hiding to nothing. If she had hoped, by voicing her anxieties about their mother's frame of her mind, to enlist her brothers' support, then (she reflected grimly) she had gone about it in absolutely the wrong way. It was as if by putting her fears into words she had taken on responsibility for them. Fabian suggested that they acquire some kind of paid live-in help; the accommodation was still there, and cash was no particular object. Blaise agreed that this was certainly one avenue worth pursuing, but he could not accept that there was anything fundamentally the matter with Elodie; she had been dancing attendance on their father for as long as anyone could remember, and would need time to pick up the threads of any kind of independent life.

Celeste ventured the opinion that they should consider selling Hartfield; it was a great barn of a place quite unsuitable for one elderly lady living on her own.

'She's a hard woman,' said Fabian to Blaise. 'She wants to sell off the family seat.'

'I don't want to,' said Celeste, 'but we have to look at what's practical.'

Fabian grimaced. 'Since when has practicality been a consideration in this family? It's never exactly been the old man's strong suit. He could turn up tomorrow and start behaving as though nothing had happened.'

'I don't think so,' said Celeste, 'and anyway, he's forfeited all rights in the matter.'

Blaise cut in. 'You're both overlooking the obvious fact that if *maman* is in shock, or a little confused – and she does after all have some justification – then to suggest a move would be absolutely disastrous. She needs continuity and stability, not an upheaval, and our immediate task is to provide that stability.'

From there it was only a short step to establishing that it would not be impossible for Celeste to extend her stay (she had been due to return to London the following afternoon) for at least another week. She could after all commute quite comfortably; it would enable her to keep an eye on Elodie, and by the end of that time Bruno's whereabouts might have been established and the situation might be clearer.

'You're so good at this kind of thing,' said Fabian.

'I don't think so,' said Celeste, with feeling.

'That's not the point,' put in Blaise. 'I cannot simply uproot myself from the Abbey to be here, and it's important that *maman* stays on her patch at present. Obviously you have your commitments, Fabian, all the more so now that Louise is expecting.'

'I'm confining my role in the antenatal period to that of nanny-finder general,' said Fabian. 'Who the hell does that rust-heap belong to?'

Joe Cook had been contemplating his next move for some time. He was in the habit of deliberation. In his job you had to be ahead of the game if you weren't going to get ripped off or publicly humiliated. All the swift decisions he had to make in front of an audience were based on many hours of laborious contingency planning. It was something of a luxury to have an objective towards which he could work in peace without the fear of public failure. The objective was as yet vague, but the process was both intriguing and pleasurable, and the very worst that could happen was a little wasted effort.

He had set in train various contributory factors. He had arranged with the doctor to have his arms cleaned up in a month's time when the last handful of QA bookings spluttered to a halt. He'd blown a few quid on an exercise bike and a season ticket for the local pool. And – he still couldn't get quite used to it – he'd had a haircut, short all over.

When he'd found the message from Celeste Gallagher on his machine he'd tried to call her at the house in Paddington, and when her flatmate answered – one of those knowing women with a voice bent double with suppressed amusement – she'd given him the mother's address and number.

He'd tried the number once, and it had rung for ages. He had the idea someone had picked it up as he rang off. Going to the house was a move he intended to look like an impulse, but he had thought about it carefully. He was *concerned*, that was the thing: concerned enough to drive out and see how she was, even just before a gig. And in truth he was concerned. He thought he'd read her pretty well, he was a fair judge of character, he had to be. This girl was dependable and straight, a person of her word, probably prided herself on it. She was unlikely to be flannelling him. And she most likely reckoned that her rather cryptic reason for cancelling would put him off and spell the end of their – whatever it was. Normally, she'd have been right. Dealing with agents and social secretaries you got to smell an iffy excuse a mile off. But he believed her, and he intended to show it. The time had come for surprise tactics.

As he'd driven through the village about three-fifteen he'd had a few qualms. He came out of London for gigs – often much further than this – but generally speaking it was to towns. Driving along the main street, its few small shops tight shut on a Saturday afternoon, he had the uneasy feeling that, like the Eastwood figure in a spaghetti Western, he was the stranger in town and everyone knew it, and was watching him. A townie to his toenails, the dead quiet unnerved him. On the other hand, his curiosity was piqued. Here was another side to Celeste Gallagher. His notions of country life were stereo-typical. Did she perhaps wear green wellies, own a labrador, ride a horse?

There was a woman waiting in the bus shelter at the far end of the village and he pulled up to ask her the way. Yes, she knew the house – it was where that writer lived, the one who was so peculiar and rude and drove the Rolls-Royce. She gave him some directions. Before he pulled away, Joe asked the name of the writer and the woman said she couldn't remember but thought it was something Irish or Scottish. Gallagher, suggested Joe. That was it.

He knew there was a risk involved in turning up like this. He was forcing the pace. However well she behaved (and he couldn't imagine her behaving badly) she would effectively either play along, or show him the door. It was make or break.

On the north side of the village he turned left, on the woman's instructions, into a lane bordered on one side by terrifyingly empty fields and on the other by a meadow with a track running through it. Mud spattered up off the road surface and he thought glumly that he was going to have to run the van through a carwash on the way back.

The meadow on his left gave way to woods, which the woman had mentioned. Joe slowed down. The entrance to the house was advertised by a temporary-looking but obviously aged sign, painted in black on a board and resting against a tree trunk. He turned into a mossy drive, so sharply curving that the house wasn't visible at all. Bumping along at a snail's pace he came upon it rather suddenly, as though it had stepped out of the woods into his path with the express purpose of giving him a fright. He leaned forward over the steering-wheel and gazed up at the tall windows, the sharp angles of the roof, the general air of haughty neglect. He was at the edge of a small circular sweep. Of labradors and horses there was no sign, but to his right was a big yard with several cars in it – no Rolls-Royce, but a dark blue Jag, a Volvo estate, Celeste's red Metro, and a long black sporty number which made his mouth water.

He went first to the front door. It was sheltered by a high, ornate stone porch in a poor state of repair. The tiles under his feet were sunken and uneven and there was a snail intrepidly climbing one of the columns. It was like the entrance to a mausoleum. There was no knocker or bellpull and when he tried to flip the letter-box it was either sealed, or jammed through long disuse. He walked round into the yard in search of the back door, touching the long bonnet of the sports car as he passed. When he looked up and saw that someone was watching him from the doorway he nearly jumped out of his skin.

She was a tall, dark woman with her hair scraped back. He couldn't have put her at any particular age except that she wasn't young. From her thin, unmade-up and rather haunted face Celeste's eyes stared back at him.

'Yes?' she said.

Celeste moved ahead of her brothers, and almost ran through the back door, pulling off her coat and dropping it over the back of a chair in the kitchen. The library door was half-open and for a split second she was able to take in the scene before she became part of it.

Tessa and Lauren were on the sofa and Elodie was in the chair by the fire. All three looked as if they had seen, if not a ghost, at least an alien or extra-terrestrial being. The expression on all their faces was one of stunned fascination thinly veiled by politeness. Molly and Nathan were still at the table in the window, each holding a hand of cards which did nothing to conceal their smirks.

The object of their attention stood in front of the fireplace with one elbow on the edge of the crowded mantelpiece, rolling a cigarette.

Celeste smiled. 'Hallo, Joe,' she said. 'It's so lovely to see you.'

PART THREE
1988

Hell hath no vanity like a handsome man.

Coco Chanel

How a little love and good company improves a woman!

George Farquhar, *The Beaux Strategem*

Burning for burning, wound for wound, stripe for stripe.

Exodus 21:25

CHAPTER EIGHTEEN

On the second Saturday in February 1988, Joe was booked to do the cabaret for P.J. Wainright and Sons' St Valentine's dinner dance at the Mulberry Hotel in Croydon. It was a respectable do for a reputable firm, its male and female employees and their partners. There was to be a band, Bahama Brass, rather than a disco, and the tickets specified lounge suits. Joe was the only act and would have a clear half-hour spot for which he would be paid £150. It was a definite step in the right direction.

And not a moment too soon, reflected Joe, slapping on Aramis and running his palms over his hair. Things had reached the point where he'd have gone down on his knees for a session at the lorry parks. Since he'd taken time out to have his arms done the previous November, Victoria had been as good as her word and stopped putting his name up for stags, hens and sports clubs. She had also proved her point by not getting him anything else, though whether this was deliberate or caused by an unforgiving market Joe was unable to say. He hadn't seen or spoken to anyone at Quality Artists since Christmas, and didn't give a toss if he never did again. With Celeste Gallagher's help he'd do it without them.

After that one extraordinarily successful change of gear when he'd turned up at her house and given her family the heebies, he'd let the clutch out with excruciating slowness. The knowledge of the control he had over her made him very, very careful in the exercising of it. He didn't want to foul everything up. Besides he liked her, she was okay. He'd got their association to the point of a nice, warm working friendship and he was holding it there like a hill start, until the right moment presented itself.

Underpinning their relationship was the carefully fostered notion that he was indulging her, rationing out little peeks into his dirty unsuitable world, while always being sure to deprecate it. He didn't whine, or give the impression that he thought himself better than he was. She wouldn't go for that. He made it plain that he was pursuing a strategy of his own in his own way. He was civil and asked about her work, and about her mother. She had been back in town for a while, but at Christmas she had moved into the country house to keep an eye on Mrs Gallagher whom Joe liked, but who was undoubtedly going the tiniest bit ga-ga, with good cause, as far as he could see. A bigger bunch of headbangers than her family would have been hard to find. The little brother who was a chef in town didn't sound so bad, and had been through a tough time recently. But when he tried to picture the father, the one who'd done a runner, his brain overheated. Naturally it hadn't improved their humour to discover what type of person Celeste was associating with. One thing Joe did slightly regret was the indirect effect he might have had on her mother's mental state. She'd had enough to contend with, what with the runaway husband and Sandro's boyfriend, without being caught in the cross-fire occasioned by his arrival.

He'd been very careful not to give the brothers anything to complain of. It was a real pleasure to watch them both, the sky pilot and the surgeon, squirm. He knew that if he provided the least pretext they'd give him the heave-ho and it wouldn't be worth retaliating, he'd have to withdraw gracefully. As it was, they were grinding their teeth with frustration.

Celeste was a lot less cautious than he was; in fact he had to put the brakes on or she'd have been downright indiscreet. She was really carried away with the idea of helping him. She'd positively pressed the down payment on him for a new car, and he'd had to insist that it was all kosher and businesslike with an agreed rate of interest. Then there was the constant offer of the use of the empty flat upstairs at Hartfield if he'd had to travel out that way and wanted to shorten the night drive. He'd held out against that for ages, but now he'd used it twice, all very proper with a key left under the water-butt outside. No matter how late he'd been he made a point of being gone by six, putting one of his business cards in the kitchen letter box with 'Thanks a million' scribbled on it. He was sure the brothers didn't know about the arrangement, and he wanted it to stay that way. After he'd had the op Celeste had been solicitous, dropping round to leave goodies from Marks and Spencer, and a note ('Dear Joe . . . love Celeste G', as if he knew other women called Celeste) offering to do anything to help. He'd called her up to thank her for the food and she'd pressed the offer once more, so in the end he'd asked if she'd mind picking up a bit of dry cleaning for him just to keep her happy.

He found her a real study. She had tremendous stamina. She was only doing three days a week at the jeweller's shop in town at the moment, but apart from this she ran the house, had redecorated the upstairs flat, she cooked and drove her mother around on her days off, and still spent one evening a fortnight doing the books for her brother's restaurant. She did everything without any fuss and seemed to expect no support from the others, which was just as well. He himself never commented on this. She was loyal – even the mad professor was rarely referred to unkindly – and he wasn't going to be the one to undermine that loyalty.

She never ceased to surprise him, either. Once, when he still had the van, he'd driven into town on his way to a gig and they'd had a drink together when she left work. When they came out of the pub the van had refused to start. She'd been tactful, helped him check all the usual things, tried to jump-start it using her own car, and then suggested that it could be a faulty connection with the ignition. She turned out to be right, and because he hadn't got time to wait for the AA then, she'd shown him how to fire the engine so he could get to his booking and ring them from there. He'd been impressed. As well as that she'd arranged and paid for him to make a cassette of his best stuff, and she'd redesigned his business

287

cards and stationery. He could picture her in Victorian times in a long skirt and pith helmet taking Jesus and medicine to the natives in darkest Africa. Occasionally he wished he wasn't using her.

He took a final glance at himself in the mirror and switched off the bathroom light. Tonight wasn't one of those occasions.

Celeste was happy, and a little guilty about it. She caught the happiness in herself from time to time, like one of those patterns which it's easier to see with one's peripheral vision. She had once read that definition of happiness about it being something that happened when one was too busy to look for it, and she supposed that must be true because when she listed the things there were to worry about they seemed endless.

Now that she was back at Hartfield the others were keen not to rock the boat and she was well aware that this unspoken trade-off provided her with more autonomy than she might otherwise have had. There hadn't been too much interrogation about her friendship with Joe (though Fabian lost no opportunity to be snide) because they still thought she was there on suffrance and she did not disabuse them. Not that Blaise and Fabian had ever been martyrs to conscience as far as she was concerned. But it was pleasing, just this once, to have a private agenda of her own which she could follow while apparently following theirs.

In early December Michael had died. He was admitted to the hospice four days earlier. Celeste went there every evening, and read him the political sketches, the restaurant and theatre columns and the football coverage. Sandro went in the mornings and according to Sister Hope was 'extremely distressed'.

'I know,' said Celeste. 'They've been together for several years and my brother has tended to be the emotionally dependent one. Well, dependent in every way, really.'

'He cries and cries,' said Sister Hope with a rueful little smile. 'It's very hard on Mr Shand.'

'Isn't that quite a common thing with the people who are closest?' ventured Celeste.

Sister Hope was emphatic. 'No. Not here. The hospice almost always provides serenity, at least a modicum of inner peace, for the residents and their families. The freedom from physical pain seems to provide a balm for the spirit as well. But not in your brother's case. It's unusual to come across someone so determinedly distraught.' Celeste felt that she had been gently rebuked.

That evening she waited for Sandro in the hall of the hospice. When he saw her he at once went into her arms and pressed his face into her neck. She could feel his tears moistening the collar of her shirt. She took him to one side and sat him down. 'I know how horribly difficult this is for you, but we must all try to keep our composure, for Michael's sake.'

He stared at her, red-eyed, his breathing ragged with recent weeping. 'Keep our composure? But this is tearing me apart! I've never known a pain like it.'

'I don't suppose,' said Celeste sternly, 'that he has, either.'

'I know, I know, believe me I think about it all the time. If there were any justice it would be me that's going, not him, he's such a good person and I'm so completely and utterly worthless . . .'

Celeste put her arm round his heaving shoulders. She weighed up the pros and cons of a stiff wigging and decided that in the short term, which was all they had available, it would only ruin this evening's visit.

She stroked the back of his head. 'Don't be silly. You know that's not true, and you have nothing to reproach yourself with. But you must remember that Michael loves you and it will be a comfort to him to know that you are able to cope.'

Sandro wiped his eyes on his sleeve and sniffed noisily. 'Brave and calm?'

She nodded and stood up. 'Brave and calm.'

When Michael died the following afternoon it was he who was brave and calm, consoling his friend to the last according to the acerbic Sister Hope.

Sandro immediately began to panic about the administrative panoply of death, and all that needed to be done which he had neither the time nor the strength to do. He needn't have worried. The Shand family mobilised organisational forces of unstoppable speed and efficiency, and with only the most token reference to Sandro put in place a full church funeral for the following Monday.

The whole thing, in Celeste's opinion, was hell. Or perhaps purgatory would have been a closer analogy – the sense of being in a nightmarish no man's land, where nothing made sense and there was no relationship between the outward event and the emotion it was supposed to express. Sonorous middle-class hymns, mealy-mouthed prayers and an unctuous and evasive eulogy by Malcolm were punctuated by the discreet sniffs and gulps of a congregation wallowing (Celeste thought) in guilty sentimentality warmed by more than a trace of relief.

The church, a stern, charmless structure of yellow and grey brick, stood on what was, thanks to unsympathetic town planning and chronic traffic congestion in New Malden, effectively a roundabout, accessible on foot only by means of a pelican crossing or a depressing underpass. The vicar, understandably determined to make the most of such a large funeral, took everything at a snail's pace, and with much fussy enunciation. Celeste had more than once glanced along the pew at Blaise, but if he found anything irritating in the delivery he was keeping it to himself, his face grave and placid beside Sandro's swollen, ravaged one. Not for the first time she realised what a gift her older brother had. Not oratory, but something more grand and indefinable, an ability in church to give all sorts and conditions of people what they wanted, so that each one present felt they had been spoken to personally and blessed in an individual way. Without doubt if he had been taking this service – with only a fraction of the good intentions and precious little more first-hand knowledge – they would have felt Michael's presence with them, the particularity of the man, his value and preciousness, a sense of the life that he and Sandro had shared, now gone. There would still have been sadness, but it would have been rooted in a specific reality. This dim, formalised gloom placed a dead hand on grief and sought to impose a spurious respectability on the glorious untidiness of life. Celeste had cried, but for all the wrong reasons.

The Shands were out in force as if to prove to the world at large, and to the considerable contingent of gay men present, that they were open-minded people who could accept anything. The Gallaghers seemed to advertise the notion, so common among the English middle classes, that funerals were men's work. Only Celeste and her brothers were present. There had been no way of notifying Bruno and Elodie had elected not to come. Tessa had remained behind with Molly, who had tonsilitis, and Louise was suffering from what Fabian disparagingly referred to as the vapours (later diagnosed as toxaemia and requiring several days' bed rest in hospital).

Celeste's eye was magnetically drawn to Sandro and Michael's friends, with their air of concentrated aloofness. It seemed to her that they behaved with a grace lacking in everyone else. Amid the glaring inappropriateness of the ceremony they alone were earthed, surrounded by a quiet forcefield of shared experience. At the end of the service they embraced Sandro with a warmth and solemnity which his own family could not match. Celeste felt humbled. At the graveside – to which they had to travel half a mile by car, there being no churchyard on the traffic island – these friends stood grouped together, listening to the words of the burial but not looking at the narrow hole into which Michael was to be lowered. By their very presence they succeeded in dignifying the otherwise dismal proceedings.

Over elaborate canapés and a passable Australian white at Malcolm and Donna's house, Fabian quizzed Celeste about Joe.

'How's Mr Cook? Wowing strippers all over the home counties?'

'I doubt it. He's not going for those sorts of bookings any more.'

'Aiming higher – of course! He's had all those tattoos removed.'

'I thought these things were meant to be confidential.'

'Of course they are, but I keep my ear to the ground and my eye on Freddy's appointments book.'

'You're incorrigible.'

'I hope so.' Fabian moved alongside and leaned towards her. 'And by the way, he was talking about you.'

'Really?'

'Oh yes. He continues to cherish hopes. God knows why. It must be the age-old allure of the unattainable.'

'It must, mustn't it.'

Fabian put his glass down, making a face as he did so. 'I'd bang my granny for a proper drink. And I'd still like to know why you turned him down.'

'I don't want to discuss it.'

'Aha! A definite note of disgruntlement. Could it be that you're beginning to regret the decision?'

'No.' It was with the greatest difficulty that Celeste maintained her composure. 'I like Freddy enormously. We're friends, and I very much hope we're going to remain so.'

'Your trouble,' said Fabian, 'is that you expect too much of marriage. You should adopt a more pragmatic approach. So tell me, what's Cook to you, and you to Mr Cook? Spot of rough trade?'

She ignored this and made to move away but his hand, which she realised must have been positioned for just such an eventuality, tightened on her arm.

'I don't want to talk to you, Fabian.'

'Be a sport, I'm fascinated. What goes on?'

'Nothing. And even if it did it would be none of your business.'

'Not my business when my gently-reared sister takes up with a yob?'

Celeste blinked. Fabian delivered these verbal slashes with a glancing offhandedness which made them twice as painful, and usually in circumstances so public that one could scarcely protest or defend oneself.

'I'm not bothering to answer that.'

'I only asked.'

'You didn't "only" anything!' Her voice rose. She brought it under control and continued in a fierce whisper. 'You never do! You have to be insulting and insinuating. Why don't you go back to Louise and see how she is?'

Fabian drained his glass. 'I know how she is. That's the trouble.'

This time Celeste got away from him, and didn't know where else to go but to Blaise, who was talking to Michael's mother. She was perfect Blaise-fodder – a gentle, kindly, slightly baffled woman of about seventy, trying to make sense of the situation in which she found herself, and in pain. She was talking, Blaise was listening, his head bent and held slightly to one side, eyes downcast, as if the better to absorb and reflect upon her words. When Celeste arrived he laid the fingers of one hand lightly on her arm to indicate that she would have his attention shortly.

'. . . only wish we'd been less inhibited about going to visit,' Mrs Shand was saying. 'We somehow always felt that it might be an intrusion, that they might feel spied on. I know it sounds foolish but we're of a different generation.'

'It's a perfectly natural response,' said Blaise, 'and you have absolutely nothing to reproach yourself with. Family life is not the easy and spontaneous thing some people make it out to be, but a hard, complex business, especially these days. And Michael,' he added with a hint of sweet confidentiality, 'was a shining testament to the success of yours.'

Celeste wondered, 'What would he know?' but Mrs Shand's eyes shone with grateful tears. His mission accomplished, Blaise turned to her. 'Celeste – have you met Michael's mother?'

'Earlier, yes.'

'Well, it's been lovely to talk to you,' said Mrs Shand. 'And now I really think I should try and talk to some of Michael's friends.'

Blaise smiled. 'That sounds like an excellent idea.' He turned to Celeste. 'What a very nice woman, but I don't imagine any of this is easy for her.'

'Well,' said Celeste abrasively, 'her son has died.'

'I wasn't referring to the most obvious cause.'

'No.' Celeste glanced over her shoulder to where Sandro, red-eyed and haggard, was introducing Mrs Shand to a red-haired man in a black suit, white tee-shirt and braces. 'When they put that announcement in the *Telegraph* about a long illness bravely borne, they definitely weren't referring to little bro.'

'What would you expect?' said Blaise. 'Everyone has to cope in their own way. Not everyone has the prop of faith. And Sandro was never cut out to be a stoic. I must say,' he added, 'that I think you are doing absolutely the right thing in helping out with the accounts.'

Celeste felt the slight but firm pressure of this remark. 'Sandro will eventually have to employ a book-keeper of some sort.'

'Yes, of course, but these things take time. And as you've pointed out yourself he's been knocked for six, hardly in the frame of mind to make arrangements in the foreseeable future.'

'Perhaps,' said Celeste, 'you could have a word with him. Help him get to grips. He has a lot of respect for you.'

'I will do that, of course,' agreed Blaise. 'But unfortunately I'm at several removes. And what I know about the restaurant business could be written on the back of a postage stamp.'

'Me too,' said Celeste.

She considered these things as she drove to meet Joe at the Mulberry Bush in Croydon. She wasn't sure how much longer she could keep the disparate threads of her present life separate and untangled. There was a phrase Alexa was very fond of: 'making a commitment'. Celeste felt that any day now she was going to have to make a commitment. She was going to have to come clean, stand up and be counted, or perform one of those threatening activities which involve taking an irrevocable and public step. She knew she occupied a place in Joe Cook's life which was rather more than that of a casual acquaintance – though she herself was far from sure what that place was. She often wondered how he categorised her to his friends, if he had them. She had never encountered any, beyond a few work acquaintances. But while she burned with curiosity, he seemed endlessly able to keep at a certain distance and never step across a line which he had drawn and which was invisible to her. She wanted him to cross it, but so fixed and ineluctable was his curious personal etiquette that she had no idea how to do so.

The Mulberry Bush was an old pub which had been burnished, enhanced, added to and extended so that it resembled a miniature theme park. On the corner of an unassuming residential street it glowed and twinkled, busy with beams, carriage lamps and diamond-paned windows, its car park spread before it like the welcoming lap of some jolly tapster.

Celeste parked at the front (Joe had delivered a stern lecture on the inadvisability of ladies parking in corners) and went into the saloon bar. The clientele at this hour on a Saturday evening was chiefly young and male in an anticipatory mood, pacing themselves, either going to meet someone, or hoping to get lucky, knowing that time and the long night were on their side.

It was a raw, foggy evening, but the Raleigh Room (as the saloon bar was called) was hot. Gas flames in a black iron fire-basket flickered in the savage central heating. The P.J. Wainwright function, the barmaid told her, was in the restaurant at the back. She found Joe waiting in the corridor. He wore his suit (she was fairly certain now that he owned only one) and looked scrubbed and trimmed. When he kissed her cheek she was buffeted by aftershave.

'They're a nice crowd,' he said. 'All ages, but smart.'

Celeste glanced through the glass panels of the door. Men in suits and women with impeccable coiffures and smart frocks were grinning and talking energetically, well on the way to having a good time.

'They look all right,' she agreed. 'How are you feeling?'

'Not bad. A bit lost without my gear.' He referred to his PA equipment, which had occupied the whole of the back of his old van and taken an hour to install.

'You don't need it, Joe. And especially not at a do like this. You don't want to shout them down, you want to make them listen.'

'Thanks, boss.'

'I was quoting you.'

'Yeah, I know, it's a good theory. Let's hope it works.'

'Why don't we go and have a drink?'

They went back to the Raleigh Room and sat at a corner table.

Celeste had a glass of wine and Joe had a large tomato juice with Worcester sauce, a slice of lemon and a lot of ice. She felt absolutely happy to be there. His lack of talkativeness didn't bother her, she'd got used to it and knew it was nothing personal.

'How's the new material?' she asked.

'I'll answer that afterwards.'

'It'll go down a storm,' she said, using one of his expressions. 'And when you've got the laughs with it once, you'll be able to build on it.' She placed her hand over his and gave it a squeeze. 'Remember they're here to enjoy themselves, they *want* you to succeed.'

'Yeah.' He glanced up at her with an expression which told her – nicely – how little she knew. 'Yeah.'

When they went back to the dining-room he was noticeably edgy, clearing his throat and pulling at his jacket. Celeste had noticed before that he did his tie up a little too tightly so that the ends sprang away from the pinched knot. She resisted the urge to loosen it. 'By the way,' he said. 'You look nice.'

'Thank you. So do you.'

He glanced through the door. Bahama Brass, six men dressed like bellhops in blue blazers and white trousers with a blue stripe were in place on the dais at the far end of the room. They seemed to be about to take a break, stashing their instruments and shuffling music together.

'Better go,' he said.

'Yes, you should. Am I allowed in?'

'I said you were from my agent's. I hope you don't mind.'

'No, that's fine.'

'Just slip in at the back.'

They had this exchange, or something like it, every time she accompanied him to a job. She took nothing for granted. 'Don't worry, they won't know I'm here.' She patted his shoulder. 'Go get 'em, Joe.'

There was a warm rush of noise and the smell of food and drink as he opened and closed the door. She didn't follow at once but watched as he made his way round the side of the room. Nobody looked his way. There was obviously some kind of comfort break in progress for several women came out past her on the way to the cloakroom, and others went through a door beyond the bar to where there must have been a private Ladies. One of the male diners went over and spoke to Joe, shook his hand, slapped his bicep, pointed out one or two features near the dais, held up five fingers. Joe disappeared through the same door that the bandsmen had used.

In fact it was considerably more than five minutes before Joe began. When everyone had returned to their seats the same man who had greeted Joe made a speech, which from Celeste's observation of the audience's reaction alternated between the hilarious and the affecting. Joe's entrance was on this man's coat-tails, the applause as much for the act just gone as for the one being introduced. Guessing that he might get off to a shaky start, she decided to slide in and sit down at the back during his first big laugh.

It didn't come. She watched him, Joe Cook the man transmogrified into Joe Cook the entertainer, as he did his job. With the sound turned down, as it were, from her position behind the door she could still tell what he was trying to do. His body language was absolutely readable. His walk took on a hint of swagger, but he stood still a good deal as well, pacing himself and his audience, making them come to him, favouring them with his Golden Joe smile, the one that was on the wall in Quality Artists. He was taking it leisurely, not bringing them to heel but inviting them to walk his way, doing all the things he'd explained to her. He was really trying.

But it wasn't working. The audience were smiling, some even chuckled from time to time, but others looked indifferent, if not downright bored, and as a group they had not bonded, they had not become Joe's creature to do with as he wished. They were hearing him out and no more. Two women quite close to the door were actually conducting a covert conversation – discreetly, with heads averted, but a conversation nonetheless. If they were doing it, then how many others?

Celeste glanced at her watch. Joe was only half-way through his time-slot and if he wasn't actually dying he was not making the right impact. She opened the door, slid in and sank on to the chair by the raffle table. Such was the inattention that several people looked round at her. The room was buzzing, fidgety.

'. . . what?' said Joe, 'you don't believe me? It's true, honour bright.' He gazed disingenuously at them, taking them into his confidence, but they were not to be drawn. He had embarked on his five-minute module on marriage, the one he'd intended to end on, so at least he'd decided to cut his losses.

'Now which one of you gentlemen,' he asked confidingly, approaching the front few tables, 'enjoys a game of snooker? Come on, don't be shy, it's only us. Who enjoys a spot of cue-work on the green baize? Eh? You sir, good, I'm glad someone's honest. Sign of a misspent youth, you know, girls . . .'

The men on the nearest tables were responding quite well, smiling and acknowledging the playfully accusing looks from their wives, but Joe had got their attention at the expense of the rest, who were beginning to talk amiably amongst themselves – about snooker, about wives, about anything. He needed to open out again, embrace the room, imprint his authority on it before it was too late.

He stepped back. 'Yes, snooker's got a bad reputation. I don't know why – couple of fellers in bow ties and fancy waistcoats bending over a table with their arses in the air, beats me. Still, it can come in handy, this bad reputation. Saved my bacon one time, tell you what happened . . .'

He took the story a fraction too quickly. He was nervous and it was beginning to show. The words he took at the same pace but the pauses, the grace notes, he was stifling.

'So she looked me up and down, and spotted this white mark, this chalk mark, on the pocket of my trousers. "Oy," she says, "don't give me that. You've been down at that flaming snooker hall again!".'

There was a broken laugh and a scattered round of applause. Celeste had the impression that they were clapping because they assumed that was the end. Joe beamed and lifted a hand. She prayed that he would say, 'This has been Joe Cook and you've been great company,' but to her horror he seemed to have taken heart from the applause, and began again.

'Sometimes, though, you just got to say sorry, isn't that right? You know you've been a bugger, you know you don't deserve her, so the next night you buy this thumping great big bunch of flowers . . .'

Celeste's heart sank. She could not believe that he had lost his presence of mind so much as to be telling this joke, to this audience, on this occasion. Just before closing her eyes she caught sight of a man looking at his watch.

'. . . so she folds her arms – because they do that, don't they? Like this. Doesn't matter what they look like, they're all Ena Sharples when it comes to making you grovel. She folds her arms, and she says, "What's this?" And I say, "It's a peace offering, beautiful aren't they? But not half as beautiful as you." So she goes tap, tap with the foot, da-dum da-dum with the fingers. You know, fellers, you've seen it, and you girls, you've all done it, and she says: "I suppose I'm expected to open my legs for those?" and I'm standing there all innocent and I say, "Why? Aintcha got a vase?" '

In the Ladies Celeste kept her eyes and ears open and her mouth shut. The band had struck up and no one was much interested in the cabaret now it was over. Joe had not been so terrible as to cause a furore, but he had been guilty of poor judgement and the womenfolk of P.J. Wainwright and Sons, veterans of many such occasions and only too conscious of the value of hard-earned cash, knew it. The few burbles were hard-nosed and dismissive. Most of the women had already forgotten, and were looking forward to their evening's dancing and drinking.

Celeste stood at the basin, washing her hands. Next to her was a woman touching up her make-up with a friend hovering, handbag in hand, at her side.

'No, you can't tell,' said the one at the mirror. 'I think Charlie got him through an agency, and he was reasonable. If that's how you go about it, you're bound to wind up with a pig in a poke from time to time. It's got to be word of mouth, hasn't it, unless you want to spend a fortune.'

She stepped back and smoothed her dress over her hips. Celeste went to the hand-drier.

'It's a shame, though,' said the friend. 'He was nice. I mean *nice*. I wouldn't have said no—'

'Peggy!' admonished the first woman. 'Get your hormones under control before they do something we'll all regret.'

'I bet I'm not the only one,' said Peggy sturdily. Celeste was already warming to her. 'It beats me why someone like him does it. What a way to make a living.'

'If it *is* a living.' The two women began moving towards the door. Peggy held it open for her friend. The last remark Celeste heard was Peggy's.

'There's no justice,' she said. 'He was no worse than a lot you get in these summer seasons and pantos, and a lot dishier than most.'

Celeste met Joe in the public bar – one or two of the Wainwright party had temporarily evaded their social responsibilities in favour of the Raleigh Room's draught bitter – and bought him a whisky mac. She didn't say anything. She no longer found silences awkward: they could be as purposeful as the pauses in a comic's patter, those pauses which Joe had filled in, fatally, this evening.

He rolled a cigarette, lit it, gulped at his drink as though it were syrup of figs, and said dourly, 'Another one notched up to experience.'

'They weren't hostile,' she said carefully. 'Far from it.'

'Yeah, well, they were nice people, weren't they? But nice people being polite are no different from a rabble getting mouthy, worse in some ways because you got no comeback with them.'

'I only heard the last ten minutes, but you seemed to be doing everything right. They just weren't receptive.'

'Doing everything right?' For the first time he looked at her with an expression of pure scepticism. 'I had a chance to get off with a bit of credit and I blew it. Like a complete – fucking – bozo. I totally blew it.'

'You mean that last joke. Yes, it was a mistake.'

He shook his head. 'I'm not paid to make mistakes, I'm paid to get it right.'

Celeste felt there was nothing she could offer here. 'What happened?'

'The snooker gag went okay. I was cutting the act short anyway, I thought I could make a bit of ground up with one more gag.' He shrugged. 'I picked the wrong one.'

'They weren't particularly shocked. In the Ladies I didn't hear anyone say they were disgusted or appalled.'

'Better if they had been,' said Joe gloomily. 'Disgusted and appalled means they remember you.'

'Actually,' said Celeste, 'I know of at least one person who will.' She told him about Peggy, not making more of it than was necessary to cheer him up. As she talked, he rolled his glass back and forth between his palms. 'So there you are,' she concluded. 'She was charmed by you.' On an impulse, her confidence greater because his was weakened, she placed her hand on his forearm. 'Me too.'

He looked up at her and covered her hand with his own. 'Thanks, Celeste.'

Outside in the car park he walked her to her car and stood close behind her as he always did while she found her key and unlocked it. The twinkling red bonhomie of the Mulberry Bush now seemed in poor taste, like a grinning drunk cadging for attention. Celeste turned with the key in her hand.

'I think—' she began.

He put his arms round her and lifted her slightly as he kissed her. She had never known a pleasure like it, the keener for being utterly unexpected.

'Don't,' he said.

CHAPTER NINETEEN

Celeste's life changed with that kiss, just as Joe had intended it would. It represented both release and capture, power and vulnerability, an ending and a beginning. Her happiness now was like a great glad shout reverberating through her life, a shout that rang in her ears even when she was at work, or driving the car, or cooking Elodie's supper or checking the accounts at Fare Do's. That this was love she had not the slightest doubt. It was like nothing she had experienced before, and if very occasionally a prim, niggling internal voice enquired where it would all end, she stifled it.

Their love thrived on contradiction – on obvious and mutually acknowledged differences, beneath which a serene visceral closeness was always present, like the steady pulse of an athlete. This sense of a secret sameness which no one else could guess at was heightened by the extreme discretion with which they conducted themselves. Celeste realised that such a state of affairs could not continue indefinitely, but she was exhilarated by it. By April she was ready to make things happen.

Elodie could no longer make anything happen, but she wasn't unhappy. Celeste was living with her now, and if she went out in the evening the nice Mrs Hodgkiss, Wendy Potton's replacement, came in to keep her company. Mrs Hodgkiss was a widow with her own little car, who liked nothing better than to spend an evening or two a week at Hartfield, knitting in front of the TV.

There were some developments which in her increasingly confused state she did not fully understand. Celeste had a friend, Joe, who seemed very much at home in the house, and who came and went at will. When Blaise rang he often asked if Joe had been, but something in her son's tone flustered her, and the subject would be dropped. Celeste had told her that she would soon be giving up her job in London altogether and working from home. Elodie hoped the house would not be turned into an office, but she looked forward to having Celeste around all the time.

This evening Celeste was in London. She had told Elodie where she was, and also left a note on the kitchen table: 'I'm having dinner with Fabian and Louise. If you need to get in touch with me you can leave a message at the club, and I'll call you back.' There followed a telephone number, but Elodie did not anticipate using it.

Mrs Hodgkiss had a meeting and couldn't be there till eight o'clock. At seven o'clock Elodie ate the macaroni cheese which Celeste had left in the oven for her, and then went for a walk around the house. She turned no lights on, but she was used to the dark and knew the house like the back of her hand. She moved slowly and in perfect silence. Nothing could possibly happen to her, even if someone broke in, because they wouldn't know she was here.

She went upstairs. None of the curtains were drawn, and the gallery was dusky and restful. She felt the friendliness of the house when it was left to its own devices. She went into the bedroom which had been Fabian's when he was a boy, and stood there, remembering. Then the door had generally been closed, either on a scene of bloody banishment resulting from a misdemeanour, or wedged with a chair by Fabian himself. Now it stood wide open and the room was bare and neat. It was the room Nathan slept in when he came to stay, so some items from the distant past had been dug out and reinstated – a framed painting of a Spitfire on the wall over the bed, a leaning row of books including Biggles and P.G. Wodehouse, and a rug patterned like an aerial view of a football pitch. These items were directly traceable to Bruno's brief and long-ago attempt to

303

create a 'boy's room'. They had been hopelessly ill-judged then, and were even more so now. Elodie stood by the door and wondered when the grandchildren would come next. They were growing up, were less interested in being with her. She wondered if they realised that she understood. She longed to say to them, 'Please don't worry, don't feel you have to say or do anything, I know how it is.' She bored herself, so how much more must she bore them?

She went along the passage and into the small room which had been first the baby's room, more recently Iphigénie's. The memories that crowded in on her here were so mixed and powerful they made her head swim, memories of being called upon and needed, of having things that must be done and only by her.

The spare room was where Celeste slept. She had offered Celeste a nicer bedroom, but she had chosen this one. The room was, as always, very tidy. There was no sign of occupation except for Celeste's dressing-gown on the back of the door and her slippers by the double bed, a few bottles on the dressing-table. Of course Celeste still had the house in London, so only a small proportion of her things were here, but just the same this looked like a room without secrets. Elodie was not so sure. She sat down on the bed and closed her eyes.

Freddy Gervase was at a cocktail party at the Chelsea home of one of his former patients, Mrs Miriam Fallah. Mr Fallah (absent on this occasion) was an Iranian businessman of fabulous wealth who had provided his wife with an unlimited budget with which to improve on nature. Freddy had been only too happy to oblige, and Miriam was now a walking tribute to his skills, a fifty-year-old with the contours and texture of a woman half that age. Happily for the practice, the Fallahs had a trio of nubile daughters, and had entrusted Freddy with the sacred task of ironing out any little faults and blemishes in Ghitti, Shahnaz and Sima, and rendering them prime properties on the marriage market. 'Jammy bastard,' Fabian had commented on seeing the invitation. 'It beats working.'

At the party Freddy was fawned upon by all four Fallah females, but it was nonetheless work. He was not, nor ever had been, a man on the make as Fabian was. He had no problem, as the Americans would have said, with the commercial aspects of the job. He was a highly-qualified professional who would provide (within reason) whatever people wanted that they were able to pay for. He saw his patients in no other light but a strictly business one. His famous languid charm and *soigné* appearance were a defence, a means by which he contrived to treat everyone the same.

The Fallahs' house, like its owners, was large and overtly opulent and smelt faintly spicy, like a souk. Freddy was the focus of more flattering attention than he could manage. He stood beneath a portrait of a racehorse and felt like a sacred cow. Like a man who has lived for too long on *foie gras* and *châteaubriand* and who craves the simple goodness of a boiled egg with Marmite soldiers, he thought longingly of Celeste. There was a candour in Celeste's eyes and a plainness in her speech that he found delightful. Freddy was a far more straightforward man than most of his female patients could have dreamed, and not a passionate one, and in Celeste Gallagher he saw perfect wife material. Their infrequent telephone conversations and even less frequent meetings, the civilised friendship which she professed to want, were not enough.

He had spoken to her earlier that day to see whether she might be able to accompany him to the party, but she'd explained she was dining with Fabian and Louise.

'I have a feeling,' he'd said, 'that I am going to need you quite desperately.'

'Really?' she replied. 'Get away with you. Besides, they need me quite desperately too.'

'You surely don't expect me to believe that. Fabian's never needed anyone in his life.'

'Louise, then. Anyway they asked me ages ago.'

'You'll be sending me out to face the enemy alone.'

She'd laughed kindly. 'You must tell me all about the encounter afterwards.'

Freddy sighed.

'Mr Gervase,' purred Miriam Fallah, 'I want you to meet a very special friend of mine, Karen Eichelberger.'

Freddy beamed obligingly upon the glossy Manhattan matron being paraded for his inspection, and thought how nice it would have been to have Celeste's honest and nourishing presence to go home to.

'We've been meaning to do this for bloody ages,' said Fabian, 'haven't we, darling?'

'I suppose so.' Louise smiled apologetically. 'It should really have been at home. But these days after work I'm completely bushed, so taking you out was the only way to guarantee you a decent dinner. Whether or not this mausoleum was the place to get it is another matter.'

'How dare you,' said Fabian. 'The castle pudding here is second to none.'

'Not everyone wants to eat institution food.'

'Nor do they have to. Ours is an extremely adventurous menu. When they did that consumer guide to London clubs we were second in the league table.'

'Come on, Fabian, that's hardly the most exacting test.'

'Look,' Fabian's face was red, except for a paler aureole around his mouth, 'if you didn't want to come here you only had to say.'

'As far as I'm concerned,' said Celeste, 'going out for dinner anywhere is a treat.'

'You should never have given Freddy the bum's rush, should you, Lester? He was winding up for the longest and most expensive courtship since Solomon and Sheba.'

For Louise's sake, Celeste laughed. 'I didn't give him the bum's rush, as you put it. We're on perfectly good terms.'

It had been a long evening, during which Celeste sometimes thought she'd only been invited as at best a lightning conductor, at worst a referee. It was almost a relief to have the fire directed at herself for a moment. She felt angry and affronted, chiefly with Fabian. One could hardly direct blame at anyone so strikingly pregnant as Louise. She was in her last month, and had lost weight everywhere except in the voluminous swell of her belly. She looked barely strong enough to carry such a huge burden around with her. Though she was as immaculately turned out as ever, there were grey-blue hollows beneath her eyes, and her long hands, on which the expensive rings looked loose and heavy, trembled slightly. She had picked at her food, drunk four glasses of wine, and smoked several cigarettes with a defiant flourish.

Fabian had been his bullish self throughout. Now he pushed his chair back and grasped the edge of the table as though about to overturn it.

'Fancy a nightcap?'

'Well, I really think . . .' began Celeste, glancing at her watch.

'Don't worry about Lou. You'd be bloody glad to pop it, wouldn't you?'

Louise stood rather unsteadily. 'Come on, Celeste, wouldn't a brandy be nice?'

Celeste had no option. She was securely caught between their locked horns. On the way down the broad, darkly-carpeted stairway to the downstairs Drawing-Room (the only room other than the dining-room where ladies were allowed) Fabian asked her, 'Still seeing our smutty friend Mr Cook?'

'How dare you speak to Celeste like that?' demanded Louise.

'Very easily, since it's the plain truth. Isn't that right, our Lester?'

'I don't have to discuss it with you.'

'Are you and he an item?'

'Yes.' Celeste didn't allow herself time to think. 'We are.'

Fabian had been walking slightly ahead and was at the foot of the stairs. Now he stopped and turned round. His face was alight with the intense, dangerous curiosity that she remembered from childhood. 'Is that so? Is that really so?'

Louise swept past him. 'As Celeste very rightly pointed out, it's nobody's business but hers.'

'And Mr Cook's, presumably.'

The 'Mr' was deliberately patronising, but Celeste was not going to invite Fabian to use 'Joe'.

'And what,' went on Fabian, following both women into the downstairs Drawing-Room, 'are we to understand from that?'

307

'Whatever you like. You used the term.'

'But you agreed to it. So you must have your own idea of what it means.'

'Just that we're a little more than friends.' She dropped her eyes before Fabian's disbelieving stare. A vivid picture of Joe's face looking up at her, and his hands reaching for her breasts, made her feel hot.

'Ah, do I detect a not terribly maidenly blush?'

'Give it a rest, Fabian, for God's sake,' Louise told him, 'it's well beyond a joke.'

'If you'll excuse me,' said Celeste, 'I think I'd better go.'

'No, Celeste, you mustn't, please! Apologise, Fabian.'

'What for? A perfectly standard fraternal josh about her latest swain?'

'You were stirring and you damn well know it!'

'Look, it's all right. Please don't wrangle over me.' Celeste subsided as a stony-faced waitress approached them.

Fabian ordered without looking at her. 'Brandy, ladies? Two brandies and a malt, if you please.'

Celeste wondered, but decided not to ask, whether Fabian was driving home. Louise leaned towards her and asked about Parsloe Mews. 'I think it's incredibly noble of you to drop everything to hold the fort at Hartfield. What are you going to do about the house?' While Celeste answered Fabian grew fidgety, turning around in his chair and tapping his fingers together. At last he interrupted.

'Would you excuse me for a second? I saw a friend upstairs that I wouldn't mind a word with.' He was out of the room with his quick, stalking stride almost before they'd answered.

'Thank God for that,' said Louise.

'Is something the matter?'

Louise gave a bitter little laugh. 'How long have you got?'

'As long as you want. We could arrange to—'

'He's got some new female or other.'

'Louise, I'm so sorry.'

'Not half as sorry as me. Look at me.' She spread her arms and gazed down at her belly. 'He got me into this, in every sense. Expensively-educated children are part of his game

308

plan. And then when I am the largest mammal to walk the earth he kicks sand in my face. Not that she's by any means the first, but this one hurts because I can't fight back.'

Celeste, not knowing what to say, remained silent. If they had been anywhere else but here she might have gone to Louise and put her arm round her shoulders. But the Drawing-Room – a large dim basement furnished and decorated in shades of subaqueous green – cast a dampener on spontaneous intimacy. The only other people here were a young man and an elegant old lady, presumably his grandmother, in the far corner.

The drinks arrived. When the waitress had gone Louise pushed Fabian's to one side, as if to banish him completely from the conversation.

'How are you – I mean otherwise?' asked Celeste.

'A walking casebook, so my doctor tells me. A drinking, smoking, stressed-out nightmare. It's a miracle the sprog is alive, according to him. Maybe it would be better if it wasn't.'

Celeste let this pass. 'Did you consider giving up smoking?'

'What do you think? You're literally bombarded by anti-smoking propaganda from the moment of conception. But since it was quite likely the poor little thing was going to be addicted to Havanas anyway, I thought what the hell?'

Celeste wasn't sure she saw the logic of this. 'So long as you're all right.'

'I'm far more interested in talking about you,' said Louise. 'Now that public enemy No.1 has gone, tell me about the man in your life.'

Involuntarily and, as she saw it, foolishly, Celeste smiled. 'What would you like to know?'

'Everything. Remember I'm the only one who hasn't seen him, and I'm utterly fascinated. Anyone who can attract so much hostility by doing nothing must be interesting.'

'Oh, he's interesting all right,' said Celeste. For the first time, she enjoyed the sense of holding all the conversational cards.

Louise picked up her brandy glass and leaned back. 'Are you in love with him?'

'Yes.'

'How wonderful to answer as simply as that! Love at first sight?'

Celeste had thought about this. 'I believe it was, although I didn't recognise it.'

'And when did this thunderbolt strike?'

Celeste, enjoying the sense of a sympathetic audience, indulged herself. To Louise's appreciative gasps she described the night before the wedding, the dates, the gigs, the tension, the kiss . . .

'So what is the current status of this affair?' asked Louise. 'Is it his place, or yours? Or Hartfield?'

'Usually his place, or Hartfield. I hardly ever go to Parsloe Mews these days.'

Louise shook her head. 'I can't tell you how impressed I am. I mean, it's like hiding British airmen in France, for God's sake. If the palace guard find out, they are going to go absolutely spare.'

Celeste shrugged. 'What about? I am over thirty after all, and I was the only one prepared to go back to Hartfield to look after Mother.'

'Yes, and there's nothing fuels resentment quicker than obligation. One whiff that your man is having his wicked way with you under the family roof and they'll be descending on the place like crazed hillbillies, shotguns and all.'

'Just let them try!'

The young man and his grandmother had left their seats and were walking towards the door. Although tall and erect, the old lady was a little unsteady and was using the backs of chairs to support her. Her grandson, bringing up the rear, kept a tactful distance. When she reached Celeste and Louise she paused.

'How nice to hear some really sprightly conversation instead of the obligatory hushed tones.'

'I hope we weren't disturbing you,' said Celeste.

'Far from it. This place is so perfectly ghastly, don't you think? I don't remember disliking it quite so much when I used to come here with my husband, but disaffection began to take hold when my son was a member, and now poor Giles has to put up with my endless carping.'

'Not at all, Gran,' said Giles gamely.

'I shall say good-bye. It takes me hours to get up the stairs, so please ignore me.'

'Good-night,' said Giles.

Celeste watched them as they made their way out of the door and to the foot of the stairs where there was some gentle wrangling about who should go first. In the end Giles went ahead, blurting out something about hailing a cab, and the old lady followed, one step at a time, leading with her right foot.

Celeste heard Louise sigh heavily.

'Are you okay?'

'I was thinking, in forty years time that will be me.'

'You could do a lot worse,' said Celeste. 'She was nice.'

'But only think, she's been coming here with one man or another for donkey's years, and hating it.'

'She didn't have to.'

'There, if you'll forgive my saying so,' said Louise gloomily, 'speaks the woman who has taken up with a vaudeville artist.'

When Mrs Hodgkiss arrived Elodie went downstairs and sat with her in the library. They talked for a little while, but it wasn't long before the television went on, and the knitting came out. Elodie had no real objections to either television or knitting, but these days she had no concentration. The programmes seemed to exist in another dimension to which she did not have access. Mrs Hodgkiss made every effort to include her in her own enjoyment of whatever it was she was watching, with many exclamations along well-will-you-look-at-that lines, but Elodie could make no sense of it.

'I think, if you'll excuse me, Mrs Hodgkiss, I'll go upstairs.'

Mrs Hodgkiss looked genuinely dismayed and concerned. 'Oh, dear, are you sure? Can I bring you something? A cup of tea?'

'No, thank you, I shall probably have a bath, and then . . .' She let her intentions, vague even to herself, hang in the air as she headed for the door. Mrs Hodgkiss's attention was already back on the screen.

311

'You'll let me know if there's anything at all, won't you?'

'Yes, of course.'

'Good-night, then, Mrs Gallagher.'

Elodie went back upstairs. She ran herself a bath and lay half-floating in the hot water, like a foetus, warm and wet and silent, protected by the many layers of the house. That reminded her of Louise's baby. It would be nice to have another grandchild but she entertained no great hopes of seeing very much of it. She scarcely saw Louise now, and she couldn't imagine Fabian fondly parading his offspring for her benefit, especially now that she wouldn't be any use as a babysitter. Perhaps Celeste would look after it sometimes and that would be an opportunity to hold the little one. Her hand moved to her breast. Even in the hot water it felt cold, neglected. The touch reminded her of Bruno. He had truly loved her once. More than she had ever loved him. And now she had no alternative but to believe he truly despised her, as she had never despised him. What had she done wrong? She lay in the bath and wept hot tears which trickled down her face and neck and eventually found their way into the cooling water.

'Louise? Oh my God, Louise!'

Celeste stood up and leaned over her sister-in-law. Louise was staring up at her, but her concentration was elsewhere. Her lips were pressed tightly together and her eyes were focused on her body's alarming inner landscape.

'Louise, what's the matter?' But she knew what the matter was. She gazed wildly about at the greenish gloom of the downstairs Drawing-Room. The hush was absolute. They might have been the only people in the building, and this the only building for miles around. Louise's hand clutched hers with the imperative strength of panic.

'Get somebody, Celeste! Please get somebody!'

Celeste patted her hand. 'I will, don't worry, you'll be fine.'

'I'm going to have the baby, Celeste!'

'No, you're not – not here, anyway. Isn't this the first contraction?'

'Yes. I don't know . . .' Louise's grip loosened as the pain ebbed. 'It was a bastard! I must have been in labour without noticing. God knows what's going on.'

'Isn't it early?'

'A couple of weeks. Look, Celeste, can you please contact someone. Where the hell is my husband when I need him?'

'Don't worry, I'll go and find him. Or perhaps I should help you up the stairs first.'

'No, I don't think I could manage.'

'But you have to get up them some time, and presumably it will be more difficult the longer you leave it.'

'Yes, but I need help! If you could just *find* someone as I keep on asking you to do—' Louise began breathing heavily again, eyes closed, knees sagging apart. Celeste dithered. 'What shall I—?'

'Go, go, go, go . . .'

Celeste ran out of the room and raced up the stairs. At the top she was confronted by a dilemma. She was in the long, lofty hallway of the club. Straight ahead were the tall glass and mahogany doors leading into the porter's lodge, beyond which the traffic of St James's glided back and forth like shoals of gleaming fish in an aquarium. To her right was the dining-room where they had eaten dinner. Everywhere else was a no-go area. On the left was something labelled The Writing Room, its door uncompromisingly shut. Between the dining-room and the main entrance was the grand, slightly battered staircase which led to the exclusively male upper reaches: a second dining-room, the library, the weightily named Higher Drawing-Room, and God knew what else.

Panting, Celeste sped along the hall, dragged open the heavy doors and approached the porter. He was young, dark, and Spanish.

'Excuse me!'

'Yes, madam.'

'My sister-in-law has been taken ill in the downstairs Drawing-Room. Her husband – my brother – is somewhere in the building, but I don't know where. Is it possible to have him paged?'

'We can't page anyone here,' said the porter, with more than

313

a hint of perverse pride. 'But I can try to locate him.'

'That would be helpful,' said Celeste. 'It is *most* urgent.'

'And the member's name is?'

With infuriating deliberation the porter lifted the receiver of the old-fashioned black telephone from its cradle, and ran his finger down a faded, handwritten list of internal numbers pinned to the wooden pannelling of his lair. Three calls drew a blank. On the fourth he covered the mouthpiece and told Celeste: 'Mr Gallagher is in the closed clubroom.'

'Well, will you please tell him he is urgently needed downstairs. His wife needs him. It is absolutely vital!'

The porter kept his hand over the mouthpiece and betrayed a hint of a frown, as though Celeste were behaving with quite unusual crassness. 'I understand, madam, but the closed clubroom is exactly that. There is no telephone.'

'Then perhaps someone could go in and tell him. And then call an ambulance.'

'It isn't quite as simple as that, madam—' began the porter, but already Celeste was gone.

She raced up the stairs so fast that two elderly gentlemen on the way down only registered the scandal when she was past. When one of them eventually managed a querulous 'Hey!' she leaned over the baniser and asked, 'Please could one of you direct me to the closed clubroom?'

'It's to the right at the end,' replied one of the men meekly.

'Don't be an idiot, Piers, she's in flagrant breach of club rules!'

'I do beg your pardon, but she seemed . . .'

Celeste left them wrangling and ran along the passage. The carpet up here was dark red. Gilt-framed paintings marched along the walls. Through a couple of doorways startled faces noticed her.

At the end of the corridor was a window overlooking St James's. There was one, unmarked door to her right. She did not knock, but opened it. Fabian and another, younger, man were standing in the middle of the room, rather too close together, like actors on television. On a table to one side stood two glasses and a large brass ashtray, on the lip of which a

314

lighted cigar rested.

'Fabian!' said Celeste. 'Will you please come at once, it's Louise!'

He was on her like an animal pouncing, his face dark with rage. 'You are not allowed in here!'

'I don't give a damn. Will you come at once, please? I'll go and help your wife.' She realised that she felt elated, as well as angry. A small, muttering crowd had gathered behind her. She leaned round Fabian and addressed the younger man who was looking satisfactorily thunderstruck.

'Do excuse me. My brother's wife has gone into labour in the downstairs Drawing-Room.'

When she returned to the basement the waitress was in attendance, much animated by this unusual turn of events. Louise was now paying attention to her body's demands only, and Celeste felt no compunction in speaking over and about her.

'Did you call someone?' asked the waitress.

'The porter's called an ambulance. I hope. And her husband should be on his way down. I went and fetched him,' Celeste couldn't resist reporting, 'from the closed clubroom.'

'You never did!'

'Yes. The porter was being positively obstructive, so I simply went upstairs and walked in.'

'You didn't!'

Louise emerged from a contraction. 'Would you please do something to help me, instead of conducting a mother's meeting!'

'Yes. Come on,' said Celeste, 'we must try for the stairs now. Fabian's on his way.'

'Bully for him!'

They hauled Louise to her feet. Celeste could feel the heavy, urgent weight of the pregnancy, more separate than ever now, a vital force asserting itself with a splendid disregard for the regulations of the club.

They had to stop twice on the stairs from basement to the hall, and then a third time at the top. On this occasion Louise slid from their grasp and sank down with her back against the wall,

315

her legs spread in a wide vee-shape in front of her. A small audience of startled members soon gathered. The porter came to say that an ambulance was on its way. The waitress instructed Louise to breathe deeply and tap the rhythm of 'Humpty Dumpty' with her fingers. Fabian elbowed his way through the onlookers. His apoplectic look was balm to Celeste's soul.

'You took your time,' she said.

'Oops!' said the waitress. 'I think it's coming.'

It was not uncommon for Elodie to wake in the night. Sometimes she got up and fetched a glass of water, as she had done so often for children and grandchildren; sometimes she walked about the dark house, and even went in and gazed at Celeste as she slept; sometimes she lay in bed and listened to all the nocturnal stirrings and creakings.

But tonight something had disturbed her. It was the sound of muted voices downstairs – Mrs Hodgkiss and someone else, a man. There were discreet good-nights, and then the back door closing and the unmistakable sound of water rattling into the kettle. Elodie got out of bed and walked barefoot out of the bedroom, along the gallery and down the stairs. Just before she reached the half-landing the man came out of the kitchen and crossed the hall, pausing for a moment as if checking that he was alone. Then he went on, not into the library but into the drawing-room, turning on the light and leaving the door open behind him.

She went down the remaining stairs. She didn't need to go any further because the man was standing just inside the door, examining the contents of the porcelain cabinet. He was a big heavy man, but he handled the delicate ornaments lightly and sensitively, turning them upside down to check maker's marks. In one hand he held a thin stalk of cigarette, and as she watched he tapped this on the edge of the chinoiserie bowl of dried lavender that stood on the table next to him.

He turned his head and looked straight at her. Not abruptly as if he'd been startled, but quite slowly. Then he smiled, replaced the jug he'd been looking at, closed the cabinet and put his free hand in his pocket.

316

'Hallo there. How long've you been standing there?'

'Something woke me up,' she replied.

'I'm sorry, expect that was me saying good-night to Mrs H.'

'I expect so.'

'Can I get you anything?' He turned the light out, stepped into the hall and closed the door.

He was such an unlikely friend for Celeste. A name popped into her head. Freddy. What had happened to Freddy?

As if reading her thoughts he said: 'Celeste's car wasn't outside. I'll hang on and see her if that's all right. I wouldn't want to leave you on your tod, anyway.'

'Thank you.' She started up the stairs. 'Good-night.'

'You going back up, then? Good-night. Sleep well. No more disturbances, guaranteed.'

She didn't look back, but she knew he was watching her all the way along the gallery. Then she heard his long, stalking tread move into the kitchen. She climbed into bed. A sense of purpose, the first to come her way in years, seized her. Tomorrow she would write to Blaise.

CHAPTER TWENTY

Blaise was rigorous about Lent. All the vain things which charmed him most – and there were many – he eschewed. He gave up alcohol, and all sweet things and set himself a personal study programme to which he adhered obsessively. Over the Lenten period he invariably lost weight and his face became pale and drawn. The ladies of the diocese commented on it with tremulous admiration. Their admiration was something Blaise had no intention of giving up.

He made a point of an exquisite petty humility, nowhere more apparent than when he was on the roads. He would give way, and motion people into queues, and stop to assist others who were changing tyres or pouring water into hissing radiators. The black cassock which replaced his suit during Lent looked especially striking as he pumped a crank on the hard shoulder, and he enjoyed the look on people's faces when he got out of the Volvo and advanced towards them, cassock fluttering.

But today he had only been on the dual carriageway for ten minutes before a police car appeared in the rear-view mirror, driving far too close and flashing its lights. Blaise pulled over to let it go past. It moved in behind him, and flashed again. A German lorry swung out into the overtaking lane, passed both the police car and the Volvo and cut back in with dangerous sharpness. To Blaise's astonishment this manoeuvre went unchallenged, and the motorised behemoth drew away. The police flashed their lights again. The driver of a red

318

Volkswagen Golf made an insulting clear-off gesture at Blaise as he passed.

Blaise moved into the slow-lane, and on to the hard shoulder. An officer in a yellow oilskin jacket approached his window.

'Excuse me, sir, but have you any idea what speed you were driving at just now?'

'As a matter of fact, officer, I haven't. I'm in a hurry, that I do know.'

'You certainly were, sir. Our monitor showed you were doing over a hundred miles per hour for the past ten miles.'

'Really? You astonish me.'

'It astonished us, sir.' The policeman was quick on his feet. 'I'm afraid I shall have to book you for exceeding the speed limit. There's a little bit of paperwork involved – could I possibly join you in the car?'

'That won't be necessary. I'll get out.'

Blaise had no intention of making the policeman's work any easier. He climbed out of the driver's seat and slammed the door. He was by a couple of inches the taller of the two. The traffic whizzed and howled past. Blaise could imagine how they looked, the officious bright yellow of the policeman's jacket, the austere darkness of his cassock. 'In that case,' the officer said, replacing his notebook in his pocket, 'perhaps you'd come into the police vehicle. It's a bit windy out here.'

By the time Blaise was on his way again his temper, which had been inflamed to begin with, was fanned to a furnace. Keeping within the speed limit required a real effort. Every time his concentration lapsed, his foot went down. When this eventually led to a near-miss with a van, he turned into the next service area and bought himself a coffee.

Elodie's handwriting was difficult these days, a spidery net which covered the page with no break between words, but the message had been lucid enough:

'I am worried about Celeste's friend who is often here at night. He seems to be very interested in our things. I'm sure it's nothing, but I wonder if you could have a little word with Celeste? I don't want to seem ungrateful when she looks after

319

me so beautifully, but it worries me having a strange man in the house at night. He is always very friendly and polite and I have no cause for alarm except that I came across him examining the porcelain in the drawing-room cabinet . . .'

There had been a good deal more, mainly about Celeste's kindness, and the men who had come to cut down the dead elm and at the end, in a different coloured biro, a reference to the birth of Louise's baby. But Blaise had scarcely read it. All he could think about was that coarse, insinuating man under what he regarded as his roof, his rightful inheritance, picking over his stuff and in return for what? Blaise's mouth tightened just thinking about it. He had noticed a sea-change in his sister. She was more assertive, less reliable. It had been in all their interests when she had agreed to return to Hartfield for the time being, but with this bizarre infatuation she had become a downright liability. It was embarrassing at the best of times when a well-bred woman conceived a misbegotten passion for some oik, but when the woman was your sister . . . Blaise had simply been waiting for his chance to put a stop to it, and now the chance had come.

Celeste had taken Elodie to visit Louise and the baby at the private clinic in St John's Wood. They picked up Sandro on the way. He was looking less wan, and was carrying a shock of spring flowers tied with ringleted yellow ribbon.

'How are you coping?' she asked as they moved down West End Lane in a queue of traffic.

'Not too bad, considering. Life has to go on, doesn't it?'

'My poor darling,' said Elodie, her face averted.

'You do know,' said Celeste, 'that I've handed in my notice at Porterfield's? After the end of this month I shan't be working there.'

'Where are you going?' asked Sandro. 'Somewhere exciting?'

'I'm going to work from home, from Hartfield. I'm putting Parsloe Mews on the market.'

'It's me, I'm a horrible burden,' murmured Elodie.

'No you're not, Mother,' said Celeste briskly. 'But the thing is, little bro, I simply shan't be able to continue with your

320

book-keeping. You're going to have to find someone else.' She glanced at him in the rearview mirror.

He gave her shoulder a quick squeeze. 'Don't worry about it, Lester.'

'Are you sure? You must have someone to help, the business side really isn't your thing.'

'You don't need to tell me. But I have a lot of kind friends.'

'Good.' She glanced at him again. His face was quite untroubled. He leaned forward so that his face was almost next to Elodie's.

'Isn't it lovely, *maman*,' he said, 'about Louise's baby? When one door closes another opens, it's really true.'

Celeste, her gorge rising, kept her eyes on the road.

Louise, in a snowy Edwardian-style nightdress with lace insets, looked frail but beautiful. The baby, Marcus, looked only frail, having weighed scarcely five pounds at birth. Elodie picked him up at once and sat crooning to him happily in one of the armchairs by the window. Sandro arranged the flowers and Louise picked with long, unsteady fingers at the smocked romper suit Celeste had brought.

'Thank you, it's sweet.'

Celeste was determinedly cheerful. 'I bet Fabian's chuffed,' she said. 'A son, and born in the hall of his club!'

Louise smiled thinly. 'He'll never forgive me for that.'

'Nonsense, it was all rather exciting.'

Louise looked up. 'He won't forgive you, either.'

Celeste shrugged. 'I couldn't care less. And you must make jolly sure he pulls his weight.'

Sandro sat down on the other side of the bed. 'I'll drink to that. I'm really looking forward to seeing Fabian pushing the pram in the park on Sundays.'

'Don't hold your breath,' said Louise. 'The nanny's organised. She's been in to see Marcus already. Her name's Hilary, she's from Birmingham, and she loves our baby more than we do.'

'What a terrible thing to say,' said Elodie, getting up and putting Marcus in his mother's arms, 'nobody can do that.'

Louise looked down at her son like the child caught with the parcel when the music stops.

When they left the clinic Sandro took a taxi back to Fare Do's because Celeste wanted to collect some things from Parsloe Mews. It was four o'clock in the afternoon, bright and windy. The tops of the trees marooned in London squares fluttered and lashed like flags. The cobbles in the mews were still greasy from an earlier shower.

Celeste switched the engine off. 'Do you want to come in, Mother? I could make you a cup of tea. But I'm not going to be long.'

'No, you carry on. I'm quite happy.' Elodie folded her hands as though switching herself off. Celeste knew she could sit like that for hours, perhaps not even thinking.

Celeste unlocked the front door and went in. She was only picking up some lighter clothes and a few writing things she'd left in her room. She intended to contact Alexa in a few days' time to discuss the sale of the house. To her complete surprise, as she went up the stairs, Alexa appeared on the landing.

'Celeste! You gave me the fright of my life!'

'Sorry. I didn't expect you to be here. I've come to collect some clothes, I shan't be long. I've got my mother in the car.'

'Oh, fine!' Alexa smiled brightly. She was dressed in black leggings and a loose fuchsia top, with pink and black striped socks and no shoes. She was fully made-up but her hair was disarrayed as though she had pulled the clothes on in a hurry. 'Anything I can do to help?'

'No, thanks,' said Celeste. She went into her bedroom, opened the wardrobe and began scooping things off the shelves and hangers. 'But I must have a talk with you some time, Alexa. I want to put the house on the market.'

'God!' Alexa leaned one hand on the doorjamb and clasped her forehead with the other. 'What a bombshell! You really know how to discombobulate a person, Celeste.'

'You can have first refusal, of course.'

'Of course, of course!' said Alexa wildly. 'I've only got a down-payment to find and a mortgage to arrange and a tenant to organise!'

'There's no panic,' said Celeste, taking a case from the top of the wardrobe and folding the clothes loosely into it. 'I wouldn't even have mentioned it today, only here you are. I'll give you a ring and we can have lunch and talk about it properly. I don't want to foist anything on to you.'

'Thanks,' said Alexa. She turned away and started down the stairs. 'I'll pop out and pass the time of day with your mother.'

When Celeste emerged with the case and a carrier-bag containing books and writing things, Alexa opened the back door of the car so that she could put them on the back seat. 'Sorry if I was a bit off. Give me a buzz, and let's have a proper talk.'

'I will, don't worry. I wouldn't dream of doing anything without consulting you. And I meant what I said about first refusal – and preferential terms.'

They bumped cheeks, and Alexa walked round with her to the driver's door, casting a quick glance up the road as she did so. 'I appreciate it.'

As Celeste turned the car Alexa stood behind her and directed the operation. It was impossible to escape the impression that she was sending them on their way as fast as she could. She waved merrily as they bumped back up the mews towards the main road. As they paused to turn out, a black Ferrari approached from the direction of Praed Street and slowed almost to a standstill to make the tight turn into Parsloe Mews. The bumper missed theirs by a millimetre. Celeste was ready for Fabian's look of bored contempt, and gave him her warmest and most welcoming smile before moving out into the traffic.

When they got back at six, Blaise was waiting for them. He was sitting at the library table, with several of Bruno's dog-eared manila business folders open in front of him. He refused a drink, but Celeste poured herself and Elodie a glass of sherry.

'How are mother and baby?' he asked. 'Tessa and I are going down on Saturday.'

'They were fine,' said Celeste. 'The baby's very tiny but then he was a couple of weeks early, and Louise—'

'*Maman*, would you mind if I took Celeste into the drawing-room for five minutes to talk about some dull business matters?'

'No, of course not.'

He kissed Elodie's cheek. 'Thank you for your letter, by the way. I always enjoy getting them.' Celeste glimpsed the anxiety that slipped over her mother's face. She braced herself.

In the drawing-room Blaise closed the door firmly. 'Celeste, this relationship has to stop.'

She stiffened. 'I beg your pardon?'

'Please don't be disingenuous, you know perfectly well what I mean.'

'I hope very much that I don't.'

'This man, Cook. It's absolutely not on. It was bad enough when I simply thought it was a temporary aberration conducted elsewhere. But now I gather he's coming here – spending the night here – and making some kind of inventory of our possessions.'

'What?'

'You heard me. *Maman* found him going through this cabinet the other night when you were out somewhere' – he made it sound as though she had been soliciting in Soho – 'and she's quite distressed about it. As I am.'

Celeste glared. 'I've spent all day with Mother and I can assure you she is not in the least distressed. On the contrary, she was in rather good form. But she is getting confused; I think she may have incipient Alzheimer's. She's definitely not a reliable witness.'

'Don't sidestep the issue. She was perfectly clear about this, and what I am saying to you is stop wasting your time and energy on this character.'

'Please don't tell me what to do, Blaise.'

'I already have done. And I'm in deadly earnest.'

Celeste folded her arms. She was still standing by the door so that Blaise, in the centre of the room, flanked by the matching French sofas, appeared slightly stranded. She had learned some things from Joe.

'Me too,' she said.

Blaise put his hand to his brow. 'Celeste, I don't want us to argue over this.'

'Really? You do surprise me. What did you expect me to do, touch my forelock and say yes, your honour, of course I'll do just as you say, and only be friends with the people you approve of, and only have sex with dull professional gentlemen—'

'Celeste!'

'That's what you mean though, isn't it? You're a crashing snob, Blaise, and so is Fabian.'

'That is totally untrue. My objection to this man is that he is taking advantage of you, and of all of us, sneaking around our family house, picking over our private things.'

'You only have Mother's word for that, and she's in a world of her own most of the time these days. If you want to know, Joe is wonderful with her, but half the time she can't even remember his name.'

'She remembers seeing him examining the porcelain.'

Celeste shrugged. 'What if he was? I expect he was admiring it. He likes nice things and there aren't that many in his life.'

'There might be, though, mightn't there?' said Blaise. 'If he took up with you.'

Celeste left the room. She was trembling with shock and indignation. She didn't rejoin Elodie but went into the kitchen and sat down at the table with her head in her hands. All she wanted was to be with Joe, held in his arms and protected by his love. For he did love her. He did! The fact that he had held back initially made her all the more convinced that his feelings were genuine. He had been so anxious not to display those very ulterior motives of which Blaise had accused him that he had been prepared to wait indefinitely. Blaise had gone into the library, but now she heard him crossing the hall. She swiped hastily at her face with her sleeve.

'Celeste?' He sounded conciliatory, but she couldn't trust herself to answer. She continued to think of Joe; it was like keeping her hand on a talisman.

'Celeste, I do hope you see that it's you I'm thinking of. I honestly believe that you're making the most terrible mistake.

325

You may well be physically attracted to this man, but when that wears off, which it surely will, you are suddenly going to discover the gulf that exists between you and by then it may be too late.'

Without looking at him, Celeste said: 'Do shut up, Blaise.'

He pulled out a chair and sat down next to her at the table. She had her hands held like blinkers on either side of her face and all she could see were his hands, loosely linked. A gold signet ring, a watch with an expanding gold strap, and an inch or two of wrist covered in dark hair, disappearing into the black sleeves of his cassock.

'I have to go back home tonight,' he said, 'much as I should like to stay.'

'Good.'

He sounded pained. 'There really is no need to be childish.'

'It's how you treat me.'

'If that's how it appeared, then I apologise. It certainly wasn't my intention. On the contrary I intended to make an appeal to your maturity.' Celeste did not respond to this, so he continued: 'What are your immediate plans?'

'I'm going to stay here. I'm selling the mews house whatever happens. And leaving Porterfield's. I want to be more independent and work from here.'

'Doing what?'

She twitched her shoulders. 'I'm a very competent PA. I'm prepared to bet there are a lot of people in an area like this who would be prepared to pay for a good secretarial service.'

Blaise's hands withdrew from the table. 'And what exactly lies behind all this?'

'What do you mean?'

'I mean, do I detect the hand of Joe Cook in these plans?'

'What if you do? I'm a free grown-up woman, Blaise, and I don't have to get my entire life approved by you, or Fabian, before I live it.'

'Of course not,' said Blaise. He pushed his chair back and stood up, a tall, black, severe figure looking down at her. 'But this is our house, and we reserve the right to withhold that approval.' He replaced the chair so that its back was pressed tightly against the table's edge. 'I'll go and say good-bye to *maman*, but I'll be in touch soon. And I do advise you to think extremely carefully about everything I've said.'

Joe had never heard her so upset.

'Hey, darling, steady on, take it easy. Nothing's ever that bad. What they been saying to you?'

Between near-hysterical sobs she explained to him.

'Is that all? You can understand it, they reckon I'm after the family silver. But we both know I'm not, so that's okay.' He paused for another torrent of distress. It wasn't like her at all, she'd really let the bastards get to her. 'The only thing they got that I'm after,' he said, 'is you.'

She told him, in that sweet, open way of hers, that she felt exactly the same. He knew it to be the unvarnished truth.

'Tell you what,' he said, 'come and meet my mum. You'd really like her.'

'What about my mother?' demanded Celeste.

'You can bring her too, if you want to. If you'd rather not, fix for Mrs H to be there. Come down Sunday afternoon, okay?' After another five minutes or so she was a lot more composed and had agreed to the Sunday invitation. Joe put the phone down and lit a roll-up. Whatever their motives, the brothers were doing him a favour. Celeste was a woman whose affections would only grow stronger under pressure. And she was great in bed. Really warm and passionate, lots of talk, a real giver. He had another gig coming up next week, the first one in a month, things were pretty desperate, but he had some new ideas. It was an office party, all girls, and he had a notion how he might play it. It was something Celeste had told him after the P.J. Wainwright disaster. If he could get this one half-right, he'd make his next and biggest move, and sod the brothers.

Celeste liked Joe's mother. It was just as well, because Joe absented himself from the proceedings in order to work on some loose tiles in the bathroom.

'He's good like that,' confided Margie. 'Quite handy and gets on with it, unlike his father who was a real *mañana* man.'

'Mine too,' said Celeste, 'it used to take him hours to change a plug. He was completely cack-handed.'

'A good marriage doesn't depend on these things, but they can be the death of a bad one,' said Margie. 'But I could never complain because I can't cook, so there you go.'

'This cake is wonderful,' said Celeste.

'Of course it is. I bought it down the market.' Margie cut to the chase. 'You're seeing a lot of each other, are you?'

'Yes, we are.' Celeste fell victim to the smile and the blush that now seemed always to be lying in wait for her.

'Taking precautions, I hope?'

'Of course.'

'Only I know the kind of company my son keeps in his working life.'

Celeste said: 'He seems rather solitary to me.'

'A loner, yes. All he wants is to make it, and get on the telly. He never will,' said Margie wearily. 'Have you ever seen his act?'

'Yes, I have.'

'So what do you reckon?'

'I'm not an expert.'

'You're a bright girl with my boy's interests at heart. Give us your opinion.'

'I think his material is a bit old-fashioned' – this got a hearty laugh from Margie – 'but he's very charming and attractive to women, and he could make more of that.'

'Have you told him that?'

'Not the bit about the material being old-fashioned. But about the charm and the sex appeal . . .' she smiled helplessly. 'Naturally.'

'He's lucky to have you, Celeste, I hope he appreciates how lucky.'

'It's not luck.' Celeste longed to say the words, and now she said them: 'I'm in love with him.'

To her astonishment Margie's eyes filled with tears. 'You told him?'

'Of course. Of course I have.'

'And he loves you?'

'Yes.'

'Is he going to marry you?'

'He hasn't asked,' said Celeste, and then added untruthfully, 'I haven't even thought about it.'

On the way back to Joe's flat where her car was parked, she was unusually quiet.

'Coming in?' he asked.

Sex with Joe had been a revelation to her, and still was. She thought of herself as inhibited, but in bed with him she was abandoned. When he told her things about herself and her body she believed him. He said it was sexy that she wore conservative clothes and plain white 'nurse's underwear' as he put it, he said that was far more exciting than black lace and suspenders. He told her she had the greatest boobs he'd ever seen bar none, and all her own, too. And he loved her skin, which was pale and velvety. She was beautiful in his eyes. And he was the man of her dreams, literally. A man who could pick her up in his arms and carry her to the bedroom and who felt solid and muscular between her thighs and under her hands. He liked sex to be slow and drawn out, there was nothing peremptory or selfish about Joe.

Afterwards they lay together, with Celeste on her side, snuggled against his chest. He would make a roll-up behind her head, and then light a match on his thumbnail and inhale deeply.

'So you liked her, did you, my old dot?'

'Yes, very much. She's lovely.'

'She's all right. You don't want to go for dinner, she's a dog cook.'

'She told me.'

'What else did she tell you?'

'Nothing.'

'Go on, what did you talk about all that time I was gone?'

'You, of course.' Celeste raised her head and took his nipple between her teeth. 'I told her I loved you.'

He groaned and reached his arm back to stub out his cigarette. 'You're a wicked woman, Celeste.'

As she was leaving he said: 'I've got a booking on

Wednesday, do you want to come?'

'Of course. What sort of thing is it?'

'Office party, all women, but one up on an out-and-out hen. I'm thinking of trying a different sort of line.'

She felt a small shock of apprehension at this. She wasn't sure she could bear to see him fail again.

'I'll be there.'

When she got back Elodie was sorting through old photographs, and was at her most animated. She seemed entirely to have forgotten the business with Blaise.

'Did you have a nice time?' she asked.

'Very nice,' Celeste assured her. 'And how have you been?'

'I've been looking through these,' said Elodie. 'I am going to make up some proper albums so that the grandchildren can see their family as it used to be.'

'She's been very busy, haven't you?' said Mrs Hodgkiss, putting on her coat. 'Busy all afternoon.'

Celeste saw Mrs Hodgkiss out, then came to stand beside Elodie. 'You need the magnifying glass for some of those old pictures,' she told her. Elodie nodded. 'I'll go and get it,' said Celeste. She went into the drawing-room. There was a polished mahogany medicine chest that stood on a table next to the porcelain cabinet. The chest contained all kinds of bits and pieces including ivory lace bobbins, odd chess pieces and the magnifying glass.

As she lowered the lid of the chest Celeste's eye was caught by something in the bowl of dried lavender next to it. She thought it was a dead moth. But when she'd picked it up between her finger and thumb it turned out to be a cigarette end.

She stared at it for a moment, and then took it back with her into the library and threw it on the fire.

TWENTY-ONE

Watching Joe work that Wednesday evening, Celeste knew she was witnessing a miracle. She realised that though she loved him and had always believed in him, she had also been guilty of underestimating him. His talent was more complex than she could have imagined. He had reinvented himself.

She had offered to drive this evening because he was nervous. The venue didn't look promising. The seventy or so female staff of Bobkits, a children's clothing company, were holding their party in a hired hall on the outskirts of Luton. Every effort had been made to make the place more sympathetic – the oblong tables were covered with long primrose cloths, and laid with pale green paper napkins and centrepieces of spring flowers; bunches of white, green and yellow balloons bloomed on the curtain fittings and cross-beams; the hired caterer and her teenage staff were attempting to work wonders in the badly-lit and ill-equipped kitchen. But nothing could hide the fact that this was a jerry-built box of a building, too big for the occasion, with scabby paintwork, stained floorboards, and khaki curtains stiff with dirt and tobacco fumes. On a small platform at one end stood the speakers and light show of the disco which would come later.

Celeste dropped Joe and parked the car. When she found him again it was in a small room next to the kitchen. Most of the space was taken up with stacked spare chairs, a broken snooker table and cleaning materials. Joe was standing in a

331

corner with his travel bag at his feet, nervously cracking his knuckles.

She went over to him and kissed his cheek; he was never responsive just before a gig. 'How are you?'

'Shitting bricks.'

'They seem a nice audience,' she said truthfully, and added less truthfully, 'I'm sure you'll be fine.'

'You reckon . . .' He sounded absent-minded. Celeste took her cue and left him to it. She went out of the hall and round to the rear entrance where his car was parked. Just inside there was a small room containing an upright piano and the meter box, and a flight of four steps leading on to the platform. By perching on the top step she could get an interrupted view of the hall in between the pieces of disco equipment. The noise level had risen considerably. The Liebfraumilch was flowing, the melon, noisettes of lamb and pears *Belle Hélène* were going down, and the girls were enjoying themselves.

The disco-owner got on to the stage from the other side and began fiddling with some wires. He jumped when he saw Celeste. 'Hallo, what are you doing there?'

'I'm a friend of the comic, Joe Cook. Am I in your way?'

'No, love – no problem. Sure you're all right down there? Wouldn't you be better off going in at the back?'

'No, this is fine, thanks.' Celeste had decided in advance that on this occasion she would keep a low profile.

She needn't have worried. Within two minutes of Joe's entrance, following the sort of diffident introduction guaranteed to kill confidence stone dead, she knew he was going to win. Gone was the must-grab-em-early dash to the front and the rapid withering fire of short gags to bludgeon them into submission. Instead he almost ambled to the front of the hall – she thought he was never going to get there – and he must have paused on the way because although she couldn't hear his voice she saw the women craning their necks and there were several low, pleasurable bursts of laughter. She noticed the disco-owner, changing a plug on the far side of the stage, smiling to himself.

When Joe did come within her range of vision, his jacket was unbuttoned and he had one hand in his pocket. He looked completely relaxed. As he began to speak he fetched two chairs and set them down facing the audience.

'I'm afraid I've got to apologise,' he said, 'only I haven't had any time to get my act together for your do, so – er – I've got the names of one or two ladies who said they'd help me out. Hang on a minute . . .' He went through a charade of searching his pockets, taking the opportunity to remove his Jacket. 'Here we go.' He produced a piece of paper from his hip pocket. 'Olga, keen disciplinarian? No? Carole, artist in PVC? She here? Sorry, wrong piece of paper, that was last week . . .' A murmur of relieved laughter greeted this. He found another piece of paper. 'This is more like it. Do we have Tracy Dawning, sales assistant *extraordinaire*? We do? Tracy! You're first on my list. Thank you so much for agreeing to help, you're about to make an old hand very happy . . .' This time the name was greeted by shrieks of laughter and loud applause accompanied Tracy's reluctant but giggling progress to the front. Joe took her hand, kissed it gallantly, dusted off a chair seat with his handkerchief and sat Tracy down before sitting next to her.

'That's lovely, Tracy. You look nervous. Don't be nervous. It was very kind of you to put yourself forward like this – are you a forward sort of girl as a rule?'

It was simple stuff, but he was making it work for him. The audience craned and moved their chairs to get a better look. Of course Tracy – and the three others he called out after her, he'd been doing his homework – didn't have to say a thing. He had prepared a patter, and a whole mass of new or newly-worked material, which could be fitted around the answers to his questions. He made use of the girls without ever humiliating them, and managed to make the performance feel like a series of private conversations upon which the rest of the hall eavesdropped. Even the disc-jockey stepped forward and stood there with his screwdriver in his hand, smiling appreciatively.

Joe's line was self-deprecating and confiding. He appeared to allow his guests to steer the exchanges, but Celeste knew the amount of work that had gone into this, so that he could pick up on the slightest cue for a particular joke or observation. At every stage he had to keep in mind five or six possible options, and then embark on the chosen line as though it had only that very second occurred to him. And the whole thing was performed with an ease and low-key charm which the Bobkits girls found irresistible. He ran to a little under time – twenty-four minutes – and then thanked them for being such sports and helping out, begged them not to tell his agent what a dead loss he'd been and left to rapturous applause.

When Celeste went to the main entrance of the hall it was impossible to get to Joe. He was besieged by a group of about a dozen women, including Tracy Dawning and the rest of his 'helpers', wanting to know where he'd got the information, asking for his autograph and enquiring whether he did birthdays, fund-raisers, lunch clubs . . .

Celeste went out and sat in the Metro, listening to the radio. Relief and pleasure over Joe's success was tempered with some consternation. Where had all that come from? He hadn't put a foot wrong, only she could guess at the effort and planning that had gone into such a radical change, and the courage involved in taking such risks in performance. Joe was no alternative comic, raised in the hairy world of improvisation. He was a man with a prepared act, who ad-libbed successfully enough when he had to, but had spent years perfecting a public persona who walked, talked and behaved in a certain way. Tonight he'd jettisoned that. Celeste had seen the Joe Cook she knew – or thought she knew – being himself, and making it work.

He flung his bag in the back and crashed into the driver's seat, alight with success, high on the kind of adrenalin rush that Celeste had never before witnessed, let alone experienced. She was a little in awe of it.

'Fancy dinner?' he asked. He reversed at speed and shot forward towards the road. 'Let's blue the lot, I got three more bookings from that.'

'You were absolutely wonderful, Joe.'

'I was, wasn't I?' he agreed. 'It worked!' He took both hands off the wheel and slammed them down again, making the car swerve.

Over pizza he explained to her. 'What I did before at that other gig wasn't enough, I was hedging my bets. When things didn't go my way it was too easy to slip back into the old stuff. I had to take the risk and go for it.'

'I was so proud of you,' said Celeste. 'Afterwards, it was like the star's dressing-room.'

'Yeah.' He smiled briefly. 'But there's a hell of a lot of graft to go yet. I may have worked out a better formula but I won't get anywhere without a decent agent, PR, contacts, and a couple of hundred seriously lucky breaks.'

'When she had dressed and was about to leave his flat later that night, she took a cheque from her handbag and handed it to him.

'Joe, will you accept this? It's not a fortune, but if you can use it towards anything, please do. With my love. I'm going to sell my house in London and then there'll probably be some more, but for now – do take it.'

Without looking at the cheque he pushed her hand aside and took her in his arms. 'Keep your money. You know I don't want it.'

'Please, Joe.' She tried to press the cheque into the breast pocket of his shirt, but he tweaked it out of her fingers, scrunched it up and dropped it on the dressing-table.

'Forget the handouts. There is one thing you could do for me, though.'

'What's that?'

'You could marry me,' he said.

Suddenly she realised she'd been half-expecting this. Her heart leaped, but she didn't give him an answer. She told him she couldn't make such a big decision there and then, that there were too many uncertainties in her life. He said *she* had uncertainties, where did that leave him, for God's sake? But though it hurt, she was firm. There were a lot of things she had to sort out – a new job, family commitments, the sale of the house – she couldn't consider marriage just now. But, she added, when she did he'd be the first in line.

She left him looking crestfallen. The screwed-up cheque still lay on the dressing-table where he'd dropped it.

This was her final week at Porterfield's. Everyone was terribly sorry she was leaving; she'd been there a long time and was something of a fixture. The word 'institution' was even mentioned by one of the younger secretaries. Henry had arranged a little party for her at six o'clock on Friday, just the staff and some of the customers with whom Celeste had had dealings over the years. And of course, added Henry in his suavest manner, if there was anyone whom Celeste herself would like to bring? She declined; she'd arranged to meet Alexa for dinner afterwards to discuss the sale of Parsloe Mews.

She had no qualms. When she remembered how important this job had once been to her, how it had represented order and security and her place in the world, she was astonished.

'Won't you be sorry to leave?' asked Fiona, who had stood in for her on the days she wasn't there and would now be replacing her full-time.

'Not in the least. I wouldn't be going otherwise. After all I jumped, I wasn't pushed.'

'That's what I can't understand,' said Fiona. 'To leave a place like this these days and with nowhere else to go to, it's either very brave or quite mad.'

Celeste smiled. 'I do have some capital. I'm lucky, I realise that. I can afford to freewheel for a bit.'

'Won't you be bored, stuck at home with your mother? I don't mean that to sound beastly, it's just that I'd go bonkers if I had nothing to look forward to but that.'

'I shall manage,' Celeste assured her.

On Wednesday she had lunch with Freddy. It was a quick affair, three-quarters of an hour in a pub as he was on his way between the consulting rooms and the clinic. When, in response to his interrogation, she told him of her plans, he smiled wistfully. 'My goodness, you are busy.'

'I decided I was stagnating.'

'You look frightfully well. Anything but stagnant.'

'Thank you.'

'Tell me . . .' he frowned down into his glass. 'I realise you're fully entitled to say it's none of my business, but is there – anyone else?'

'You're quite right, it is none of your business,' Celeste said gently.

'*Mea culpa.*' Freddy held up a hand. 'Not another word.'

'I suppose Fabian has said something.'

'How well you know him. He did indicate that there was some other fellow who had very understandably become enslaved by you.'

She laughed. 'I can assure you, Freddy, that absolutely no one is enslaved by me. And that includes you.'

'He implied,' went on Freddy, 'that it would not be entirely unrealistic of me to continue to entertain hope . . . '

'I'm afraid,' said Celeste firmly, 'he was wrong. You of all people should know that Fabian likes nothing better than to tie people in knots. Have you looked at the time? You'd better get going, or you'll be late.'

The party on Friday was, as one might have expected, very nicely done. There was no question of Porterfield's laying on wine-boxes, crisps and peanuts. There was champagne, smoked salmon sandwiches and real caviar on tiny rounds of rye toast. Henry called Celeste to his side in order to propose the toast, and spoke warmly and sincerely of her excellent qualities and the sense of loss occasioned by her leaving.

'Some of you may not realise,' he said, 'that the calm, collected and wonderfully efficient young woman who greeted you as you arrived here to conduct your business was also the ravishing model featured in many of our catalogues. To display superb jewellery to advantage one needs a model who radiates breeding, quality and class. Celeste, for many years you have brought your own discreet style to all that you do for us here, and we thank you warmly for it and wish you the very best for the future. You deserve it.'

As the assembled company raised their glasses to her, Celeste fought down an urge to raise two fingers to them.

*

'I couldn't believe you really meant this place,' said Alexa over her menu. 'I rang and checked in case there was another restaurant with the same name.'

'My treat,' said Celeste. 'You must have whatever you like.'

'Don't worry,' said Alexa, 'I shall.'

They ordered two crocks of *moules*, each with a different broth, and then one of the house specialities, a large pan of vegetables dauphinoise, baked in cream and nutmeg beneath a still-blistering golden crust of cheese.

Celeste ordered red wine. 'I dare say it's completely the wrong thing to do, but this feels like a red wine occasion.'

'You are in good form,' said Alexa. 'How was your office farewell?'

Celeste described the occasion, with advantages. Alexa laughed uproariously, and Celeste sensed that the laughter was fuelled in part by relief that all was well and no finger-wagging about to take place. It was curious how foolish everyone suddenly seemed. They all underestimated her.

They moved on to discuss the disposal of the house and when Celeste repeated her offer of preferential terms in lieu of the otherwise necessary solicitors' and agents' fees, Alexa said she was interested and would come back to her within a week when she'd finished massaging her bank manager and building society.

'Let's talk about something more interesting,' said Celeste at the pudding stage. 'How is your social life?'

'Toddling along,' replied Alexa guardedly. 'And what about yours? How's the comedian?'

'He proposed to me,' said Celeste.

Alexa dropped her jaw. 'Men are always doing that! It must be because you're a proper lady that they want to love, cherish and honour, and all that crap.'

'It must be, yes,' agreed Celeste. She scraped up the last of her butterscotch tart and turned the spoon over in her mouth the better to lick out the sticky deposit.

'And are you going to?'

'I don't know, I haven't decided. I've been put off marriage

338

by my brothers.'

'Really?' Alexa lit a cigarette.

'I have never seen two more unhappy arrangements in my life,' went on Celeste. 'Blaise's wife is terrified of him, and Fabian's has him on toast.'

'You don't say.' Alexa raised her eyebrows. 'You do surprise me. I scarcely know either of them, of course, but from what I've seen of Fabian I'd have thought it was the other way round.'

Celeste shook her head. 'He has endless fancies, but she knows about all of them and rules him with a rod of iron.'

'If that's the case, it sounds like a perfectly workable relationship,' suggested Alexa.

'It's the law of diminishing returns,' said Celeste. 'He needs more and more extra-marital attention, which boosts his ego less and less, and she enjoys the power she derives from ignoring him. Where's the fun in that?'

Alexa looked doubtful. 'Is marriage meant to be fun?'

'If it's not,' said Celeste, replenishing their glasses, 'I want no part of it.'

'I'll drink to that,' agreed Alexa. But as she did so her expression was thoughtful.

It was midnight when Celeste began the drive home, and she was well over the limit. She took the back route north through West Hampstead and pulled up outside Fare Do's. There were a couple of diners still at their table, but most of the lights were out and the 'Closed' sign was up. She rang the bell for the flat.

It was answered by a red-haired man in stockinged feet, jeans and a black baseball cap. He looked familiar. 'Hi.'

'Is Sandro about?'

'He's still in the kitchen.'

'Do you think I could go down and see him? I'm his sister.'

'I know. I saw you at the funeral.' He opened the door and motioned her to come in.

'I'm so sorry,' she said as she followed him through the restaurant. 'I should have remembered, only I wasn't at my

339

best that day.'

'It was fairly horrendous,' he agreed.

Down in the kitchen Jack was washing up, and Sandro was leaning against the worktop, smoking. He had recently removed his bandanna and the mark could still be seen on his forehead.

'Lester! How are you? What a nice surprise. You met Danny? Danny, this is my sister Celeste, the one the whole family depends on.'

'We met,' said Danny. 'I'll go back up if that's okay.'

'Sure, yes, we might even join you in a moment.'

As Danny left, Celeste said: 'I only came in to beg a black coffee. I over-indulged at dinner and if I get stopped I've had it.'

'Lester, that's not like you!' Sandro put the kettle on. 'Celebrating?'

'In a way.'

Sophie came down with the last set of cups and Sandro said that provided everything was straight upstairs she and Jack could go. 'And tell your parents, Sophie, that I'm really sorry you're late again.'

He poured two mugs of coffee. 'Shall we go up?'

'No, I like it down here.'

They sat down at the table. Sandro beamed at her, but there was always something untrustworthy about his moods, and she was not encouraged.

'Who's Danny?' she asked.

'Danny Shea, he's a sound engineer with London Weekend.'

'Is he living here?'

'As a matter of fact, yes.'

'As long as you're happy,' said Celeste.

'We are. And it doesn't mean,' added Sandro touchily, 'that I cared any the less about Michael.'

'Of course not.' Celeste drank her coffee.

'You should be pleased, anyway,' went on Sandro. 'Danny's the reason I no longer have to pester you with my accounts.'

'Good for him,' said Celeste. 'But I still think it would be a good idea to pay a professional. You can't afford to get into financial trouble.'

'We're fine! Business is great and Danny's good for me – he understands about food, about how I feel about cooking, what this place means to me. He's really supportive. More in a way than Michael ever was.'

'I see.' Celeste stood up and put her coffee mug in the sink. 'Thanks for that.' She bent to kiss Sandro. 'I'm happy if you're happy, little bro, you know that.'

She continued her careful drive home thinking about Danny Shea who had been in, as Joe would have said, like Flynn.

The following morning she despatched Mrs Hodgkiss and Elodie into the village to shop, a shared activity which they enjoyed. Mrs Hodgkiss had to go and pick up one or two things for herself anyway, and liked the sense of importance which came from giving Mrs Gallagher a lift in her red Fiesta. Celeste indicated that they could have a coffee at the pub, and gave Mrs Hodgkiss the cash to cover it.

When they'd gone she settled herself at the library table and began to make phone calls.

She began with Blaise, and got a harassed Tessa.

'. . . there doesn't seem to be a moment. Easter's always a nightmare – that doesn't sound very Christian, I'm sorry – and then after Easter it's a long hot summer of fêtes and fun days. The church is terribly good at marking out the calendar so that there is never a free moment. I'm sorry,' she said again. She sounded on the verge of tears. 'Is it Blaise you're after, because he's in his study.'

'I wouldn't mind a word with him in a minute or two,' said Celeste, 'but maybe I could ask you something first.'

'Not about this man of yours,' said Tessa, 'I'm bound to silence.'

'I wasn't going to.' Celeste wondered what had been going on. 'It's nobody's business but mine anyway. I wanted to find out whether you could possibly have Mother to stay for a week or two. You know I've left work and there are quite a few things I have to sort out. What do you think?'

341

'I don't see why not, provided Blaise has no rooted objections.'

'I'm sure he won't,' said Celeste firmly. 'She is his mother after all. But since you're the one who does all the work—'

'Don't let him hear you say that!'

'Since you're the one who does all the work, I wanted to ask you first. How is he, by the way?'

'Oh – you know.'

'No.'

'Terribly busy, taking too much on as usual, and I'm no help to speak of. I'll go and tell him you're on the line. Hang on.'

There was an interval during which she listened to Tessa's retreating footsteps, followed by silence, and then the receiver being lifted in the study. However, Blaise did not speak until Tessa had replaced the phone in the hall.

'Celeste.'

'Blaise, I wanted to let you know that I've been thinking a lot about what you said the other night.'

'Yes? I'm glad to hear it. With what result?'

'Much of what you said was absolutely right.'

'Thank you.'

Self-satisfied pig, thought Celeste. She said: 'In fact, I'm grateful to you for taking the initiative and stepping in before I made an even greater fool of myself.'

Blaise's voice, which had been stern, was suddenly warm and caring. 'If your elder brother can't do a little thing like that for you, who can? I love you, Celeste, and I care a lot about what happens to you and what you do with your life and your energies . . .' Celeste held the receiver away from her ear for thirty seconds. '. . . Celeste? Are you still there?'

She cleared her throat. 'You mustn't say such nice things, I'm in a rather delicate emotional state.'

'Of course. I apologise if I was hard on you, but one has to be cruel to be kind. And *maman* was genuinely frightened and we can't allow that.'

'That was the other thing.'

'Yes?'

'Can she come to you for a while? I seem to have got myself

into a bit of a mess one way or another, and it would be nice to know she was in safe hands while I straighten things out.'

'Is that all? Of course she can!' said Blaise in the rich, warm tones with which he delivered the Blessing. 'Bring her tomorrow if you like, the spare room's always there. I'll brief Tessa, it's no trouble at all.'

'I did mention it to Tessa.'

'Even better. She's not busy at the moment. She'll be able to buzz *maman* around in the car a bit, she'll enjoy it.'

Celeste arranged to drive Elodie up on Monday when, Blaise assured her, Tessa would be at home all day. She wasn't worried about Elodie's reaction; these days she liked to be told what to do.

Next on Celeste's list was Quality Artists. According to Joe they worked, as much as they ever worked, on Saturdays.

'Hallo, may I speak to Victoria Cullen please?'

'Who shall I say it is?'

'Celeste Gallagher.'

The voice, young and female, became wary. 'May I say what it's about?'

'Yes,' said Celeste, 'you can say it's about Joe Cook.'

There followed a short, muffled silence and then a different voice came on the line. 'Victoria Cullen.'

'Miss Cullen, my name's Celeste Gallagher. You don't know me, but I wanted to call and say how impressed we were with your client, Joe Cook.'

'Joe Cook . . .' Celeste heard the rustle of pages. 'I'm delighted. Which booking was this?'

Celeste, who knew perfectly well that the booking had not come through Quality Artists, said: 'The Bobkits staff party in Luton. Last Wednesday. He was quite splendid. Any number of people said how much they enjoyed him, and how he made the evening. He was utterly charming.'

'He is, isn't he?' agreed Victoria. 'He's been with us for some years.'

'He's got several engagements coming his way as a result of the other night,' said Celeste. 'You'd better be prepared for the onslaught.'

343

'Thank you.'

'You definitely have a star on your books.'

'Thank you,' said Victoria again. She sounded shell-shocked.

'Byee,' said Celeste.

Her final phone call was to Fabian and Louise's number in St John's Wood. Louise answered.

'Celeste, wonderful woman! I'm stir crazy. I've fed the brute, made coffee for Hilary, arranged flowers, done pelvic floor exercises, made two terrines for the freezer and listened to Loose Ends. What now? Actually, Hilary's off at lunchtime so I shall take the buggy to Regent's Park and play at being a mother.'

'Where's Fabian?'

'Working. He's got two rhinoplasties and a breast augmentation at the Farefield. Sod him, I say. He has actually been around the past couple of nights so he must be between women. He picked the wrong moment. I can't imagine ever being interested in the male member again.'

'When do you go back to work?'

'Aeons, I can't remember. End of May? Something like that.'

'Why don't you come out here for the day some time? Next week or the week after – I'm taking Mother up to stay with Blaise and Tessa for a bit so I shall be all on my own. I'll cook lunch and we could have a good natter.'

'Do you want the caravanserai,' asked Louise, 'or just me?'

'Just you. Let Hilary earn her keep.'

'You're on.'

Last on Celeste's list was a handwritten letter to Max Lindberg at Repton Lyle.

'Dear Max,' she wrote. 'This is not a business letter, but a request for help. It occurred to me that spring royalties must be due, and I wondered whether you would be sending them here as usual, or whether my father (being nothing if not canny) had left you an address at which he could be contacted. My mother has aged a lot in the months since he left, and I am concerned about her and anxious that the family should make a real effort to reunite before it's too late, if not permanently then at least so that we are not completely lost to each other. We haven't heard a word from my father since he left, and I simply didn't know where to start.

'If you can help in any way I should be enormously grateful. Of course, if he has been in touch and insists on confidentiality then I must respect that. I don't wish to put your long personal and professional relationship under any strain. I do hope there is some help you can give us, and I very much look forward to hearing from you, Yours sincerely, Celeste Gallagher.'

She posted the letter at once.

That evening Joe called.

'What goes around comes around,' he said. 'I heard from QA this afternoon, and they're finally getting off their backsides.'

'That's terrific, Joe. Did they say why?'

'Not in so many words. But she mentioned having had some positive feedback about that do the other night, and it must have made her gag that it was nothing to do with them.'

'It certainly must,' agreed Celeste.

'She said she'd definitely put some stuff my way. There's some conference coming up, one of those piss and wind things on communications or whatever, and they want someone to keep the wives happy on Saturday afternoon. She's going to recommend me for that.'

'You'd be good at that – keeping wives happy,' said Celeste.

'Wouldn't I just,' said Joe. 'How about you being a wife?'

'You never know,' said Celeste. 'I might.'

At the end of the week she received the bank statement she had ordered. It covered the period that had elapsed since her last one, and gave details of all transactions up to the previous day. It showed that the cheque for a thousand pounds which she had given to Joe had been paid out the previous Thursday. In the same post was a letter on Repton Lyle's distinctive letterhead. A verbosely sheepish Max Lindberg wrote that he had only recently been in receipt of an address for Bruno

Gallagher, but had been asked not to divulge it. He hated being put in this invidious position, but perhaps it would be best if she sent a letter to her father care of the publishers and he, Max, would be sure to send it on.

CHAPTER TWENTY-TWO

'You must get in touch with her,' said Lauren, handing Celeste's letter back to Bruno. 'She's right and you know it.'

'What do you mean, she's right?' Bruno waved the letter away petulantly. 'You talk as if she had access to some absolute moral criterion.'

'Let me put it another way. What *you* did was wrong. You did the family a violence' – Bruno snorted – 'yes, a violence, whether that's how you care to look at it or not, and Celeste is offering you the chance to make some kind of restitution.'

'Violence? Restitution? I honestly do not know where you dredge up this meretricious, pseudo-psychological tosh.'

'From an area in my brain not apparently present in yours, known as the conscience,' said Lauren. 'I feel I must bear some of the guilt in all this.'

'Fine, go ahead, bear all of it if it'll make you feel any better.'

'Write back and agree to a meeting. It's the least you can do.'

'I refuse to be treated as the prodigal parent. I will not be forgiven. I will not allow my children to let bygones be bygones. I want to be rid of the whole shooting match – I thought I *was* shot of them! I made it perfectly clear that I wanted nothing from them, except not to be pestered. They're not exactly church mice, any of them. And Elodie has the house, the savings, the investments, her pension, and their continued support for what it's worth. Mind you, I notice that my wife, whom one might suppose to be the most aggrieved party, has not put her name to any of this. She was glad to see the back of me. Why Celeste can't let sleeping dogs lie I cannot imagine.'

'She's trying to reunite you with her and the boys, not with Elodie. You don't deserve Celeste,' said Lauren, folding the letter and replacing it in its envelope. 'None of you do.'

They were eating lunch on Bruno's verandah in the village of Dornier-le-Bois, fifty miles south of Paris. A friend of Max Lindberg who worked at the Commission in Brussels had initially lent Bruno a cottage in the village and having got used to it he'd decided to find something more permanent and stay.

Max's friend told him there wasn't much accommodation going in Dornier that hadn't already been snapped up by the Eurocrats, but there was a small religious community on the edge of the village. It couldn't quite be dignified with the title of monastery, but it was self-sufficient and it sometimes had rooms available. The drawback was that lodgers were expected to contribute to the running of the place, and that, presumably, would not be in Bruno's line.

Bruno was not so sure. He had long experience of his profession's ability to freeload. The words 'writer' and 'author' had near-magical door-opening qualities, and he was prepared to bet that even the monks of Dornier-le-Bois would be susceptible.

He had set off on foot to the *manoir Dornier*, with its apron of scrubby vineyard, its arthritic orchard of cider apples and its rutted fields scattered with wall-eyed goats. He dressed with uncharacteristic care in a sort of scuffed but cleanly *style anglais* calculated to commend itself to the holy men.

As he trudged up the long, poplar-lined drive he mentally rehearsed his approach.

The community was presided over by two monks whom Bruno instantly suspected of having an arrangement. Brother Paul was in his early sixties, handsome and ascetic with swept back white hair and a flawless skin. Brother Luke was a choleric Irishman with a wheezy laugh that generally degenerated into a cough.

In his dreadful accent Bruno explained his situation – that he had come to live in Dornier-le-Bois in order to work. He was a published writer of some stature – here he produced a couple of his works – and a professor, but had recently lived in the real fear of not being able to write any more. It was a creative person's worst nightmare, and one he had to confront alone. He needed to get back to basics and rediscover the wellsprings of his creativity. The brothers nodded sagely. Bruno said he had heard that it was possible for outsiders to join the community in return for some labour. Had they ever considered a writer in residence? They hadn't, but were interested in hearing about it. Bruno explained that the person concerned, preferably a full-time writer with a work in progress, would live on the premises and provide an insight into the mysterious writing process. If he himself were to perform such a role, he added modestly, there were other perspectives he might be able to give, such as discussion of the various moral questions addressed in his books, and a grounding in conversational English. He would not insult them, he said, by pretending that he was a practising Christian. A lively agnosticism was the most he could admit to.

This was his trump card. If Bruno had read the brothers correctly, their own faith did not bear too close an inspection. They were opportunists who had fallen foul of the organised church. The presence of a writer in residence might attract more people to the farm, people of a somewhat higher calibre than was at present the case.

Bruno's reading proved correct. He moved in. He was allotted a large ground-floor room which had once been a byre. There was a fireplace, and rudimentary wiring: a light-bulb hung from the distant beams on a long strand of flex and moved in the slightest breeze. With this came three meals a day and complete liberty.

His duties were not arduous. He impressed upon the brothers that the keynote of his role was availability – anyone could come to him at any time and he would answer their questions. It would not be appropriate to teach in any formal sense, since writing was such a secret and subjective art.

The other members of the community found this perfectly acceptable. Apart from the brothers there were an elderly

Belgian brother and sister; a group of six New Age travellers – Bruno thought of them as hippies – of whom two, Jez and Mia, were English, and the rest Danish; a sad and silent Anglican priest; and two neat, clean young French couples who radiated virtue and kindliness. None of them claimed to be writers *manqué*, but they were curious about Bruno and occasionally called in on him to chat. Mia, Bruno soon discovered, was willing to do considerably more than chat, so that was another aspect of life taken care of. He had rarely been more content. He was comfortable, he was a focus of exactly the right amount of attention, he had no responsibilities, and he was writing. The book was a diary, something he had always rubbished when produced by other authors as being the soggiest depths of indulgence. But they got published, and appeared to sell in gratifyingly large numbers. He was calling his *Twelve Months' Solitary*, and it would chronicle (with a few permissible embellishments) his self-imposed exile at the *manoir Dornier* – part idyll, part incarceration – surrounded by a group of real-life characters who could out-Murdoch Iris with one hand tied behind their backs. The book would give ample scope for reflection, observation and analysis as well as a robust commentary on daily life in the community. It would have the timeless popular appeal of home thoughts from abroad, with the bonus of a topical European dimension. He had no doubt of its commercial potential and it was extraordinarily easy to write.

It was Lauren who first sniffed him out. She had met Max Lindberg's friend on a previous occasion and had made a direct approach. Not knowing of any reason to do otherwise, he'd given her a direct answer, and she'd driven down from Paris to Dornier that weekend. Her life and Chrétien's were now at such a civilised distance from one another that no excuse was needed for such an independent venture.

Bruno hadn't been displeased when she turned up, unannounced and unapologetic. She was often critical but rarely judgemental – until today.

'You know what you ought to do,' she said now. 'Take the initiative. Don't go back over there like a whipped pup. Be the wise old man of the sea. Ask them to you.'

'What? Here?'

'Of course here. Where else, you great noodle? If they see you in this crazy place, writing and disseminating knowledge or whatever the hell it is you do they might even be quite impressed.'

'You haven't been listening, have you? I said I don't give a fuck what they think!'

'They might even find it in their hearts to forgive you for the thoroughly shitty way you've behaved.'

'I don't care, you silly cow, I tell you I don't care!'

At this point Mia came round the corner. She wore a cheesecloth sundress, a Popeye Doyle hat and brown boots without laces. The ensemble made her pale skinny form look even paler and skinnier. Her dingy orange hair hung in points around her face. 'If you're not working, can we talk?'

'He's got company,' said Lauren crisply.

'Excuse me,' said Bruno, 'but the most crucial of my terms of residence is that I should always be accessible to enquirers.'

'Right,' agreed Mia.

'Right,' said Lauren. 'And I got here first.'

'Your attitude is just so hostile. Where do you get off on that?'

'I guess I was born that way.'

'That's sad for you.'

'Not really. I like it.'

Staying where she was, Mia crouched down, arms resting on her knees, fingers trailing in the dust. 'I'll wait.'

Bruno said hastily: 'No, Mia, don't, because I don't know how long we'll be. You wouldn't want someone listening when we – talk, would you?'

With the same studied neutrality she stood up. 'You'll come and find me.' It was a statement.

'Of course. As soon as I've finished here.'

Mia advanced and stared at Lauren. 'Life's not a trade-off. You want to loosen up.'

Lauren gave her a crocodile smile. 'No I don't, believe me. I pride myself on being really, really tight. Tough shit, honey.'

Mia wandered off, her loose boots making a clopping sound.

'That wasn't very friendly,' said Bruno.

Lauren turned slowly and gave him a look, eyes wide and eyebrows raised. 'No. But friendly is your area, huh?'

Bruno scratched vigorously, beginning under his armpit and ending up at his crotch. Finally he said: 'Okay, okay, I'll write to Celeste if it'll make you happy, but for pity's sake get off my back!'

Celeste made a particular effort to imagine what she would like for lunch if she were recently delivered of a sickly baby, cheated on by her husband, and bored to tears. It was quite hard, since she herself felt so alarmingly free, fit and vital. But the day before Louise's visit the weather turned unseasonably warm and made her mind up for her. She made a cool, white soup with mint, cucumber and yoghurt; salad niçoise, with garlic bread; and fresh fruit salad. She then decided the fresh fruit salad was a little too virtuous, and made an option of chocolate mousse.

Louise's white Toyota jeep drew up on a wave of Brian Ferry just after one o'clock. Celeste was pleased to see how much better she looked than when they'd last met. Her hair was newly cut, bobbed at the back with a smooth, angled fringe that fell in a point over one eye. Her face, though still too thin, bore the discreet gloss of perfectly applied make-up, and her clothes! Her clothes, thought Celeste, who had recently begun to notice such things, were blue-chip, five-star, drop-dead wonderful. She wore a Ralph Lauren fantasy of Englishness – a supple hacking jacket trimmed with chocolate suede at the collar and elbows, a fine blond cashmere polo-neck sweater, skin-tight cream breeches and narrow boots the colour of conkers.

'You look fantastic,' said Celeste.

'Thank you.' Louise accepted a glass of muscadet. 'There are some compensations to being Mrs Fabian Gallagher and the day before yesterday I availed myself of all of them in South Molton Street.'

'You're obviously feeling better.'

'Well . . . Hilary's not such a bad sort, and even young Marcus is beginning to look and sound a bit more human. The trouble is, I feel combative.'

'I'm sure that *is* better.'

'Yes.' Louise twirled her glass. 'You're dead right.'

Celeste let this lie until amost the end of lunch. She had the pleasant sense of having provided exactly what was needed. Louise was positively sparkling by the coffee. Mrs Hodgkiss, arriving to wash up, spoke to Celeste in the kitchen. 'She's so gorgeous! Is she on the telly?'

'Not the telly, no. She's in publishing.'

'An author?' Mrs Hodgkiss's fertile imagination was immediately off on another equally erroneous tack.

'No, she's on the marketing side. But she's not working at the moment because she's just had a baby—'

'A baby!' cried Mrs Hodgkiss. 'And look at her figure!'

It was warm enough to sit outside to drink their coffee. Louise linked her hands behind her head and stretched her long, boyish legs out in front of her, the conker-coloured boots gleaming in the sun.

'So how's Fabian?' asked Celeste.

Louise closed her eyes. 'I take it you mean is he still playing fast and loose?'

'Among other things.'

'The answer is I've got no idea. Conjugal rites have been resumed. But since those are about the only times I see him, he could be doing God knows what the rest of the time – and probably is.'

'You don't seem terribly bothered,' said Celeste.

'I'm not.' She opened her eyes and looked directly at Celeste. 'He's not entirely to blame. I never loved him. I should probably never have married him.'

'Why did you?'

Louise gave a long shrug. 'I was hypnotised. The three R's – rude, rich and randy. No basis for marriage, take my word for it.' She put down her coffee-cup on the ground, took a wafer-thin gold lighter from her bag and lit a cigarette. Celeste said:

'So do you regret marrying Fabian?'

'Honestly? Yes.'

Celeste realised she was in one of those rare situations where almost anything she cared to ask would receive a completely truthful answer. It would be all too easy to abuse it. 'Is that,' she asked, 'because of Fabian, or because you wish you'd never married at all?'

'Both, in a way. Fabian's no different now from what he's always been. I knew he was a blackhearted bastard and to his credit he's never attempted to conceal it. I suppose somewhere in my heart of hearts I thought he'd change. That was a big mistake. One always imagines that when one does something oneself it will be different, that you'll confound all precedent and stun the world. But that's pure vanity.'

'Surely,' said Celeste, 'you can't be looking forward to years and years of marriage, feeling the way you do? It would be like confronting a life sentence.'

'I imagine the time will come, as it does with millions of people, when we'll face the fact that we've "irretrievably broken down".'

'And when's that likely to be?'

'I don't know,' said Louise. She stretched luxuriously. 'Something will come up.'

If Celeste had scripted the lines herself she could not have provided an answer that suited her own purposes better.

In a different way, Tessa had been equally obliging at the beginning of the week. While Elodie was upstairs unpacking, and Blaise was closeted in his study with the diocesan legal adviser, Tessa had taken Celeste into the garden to show her some new developments, and had promptly burst into tears.

'Oh, Tessa!' Celeste had put her arm round her shoulders and led her to a seat near the wall. 'What's the matter? Aren't you well?'

'No, no, it's not that.'

'Then what? Please, you must tell me, or I shall feel awful leaving Mother here and knowing you're like this.'

'It's nothing, honestly. I'm so sorry, I do apologise.' Tessa took a well-compressed sheet of kitchen towel from her sleeve and dabbed at her face. 'How awful to do this to you, I am *such* an idiot.'

'You're not an idiot at all. Quite the opposite. You're always so busy and organised and capable, that's why—'

Tessa burst into tears again. This time Celeste asked no more questions until the storm had abated.

'Do you want to talk about it?' she asked. 'Or would you rather not?'

'I feel so awful,' responded Tessa, hiccuping, 'because whatever I say it will sound as though I'm being beastly about Blaise.'

'I'm sure it won't,' said Celeste. 'And even if it does, it doesn't matter.'

'But you're his sister,' wailed Tessa. 'What must you think of me?'

'Only that at the moment you seem extremely unhappy and I'd like to help if I can.'

'The thing is—the thing is—' began Tessa. She looked in serious danger of crying again, so Celeste prompted her vigorously.

'Yes? What is the thing?'

'I'm absolutely useless. It's a full-time job being a clergy wife and Blaise is so brilliant and ambitious, I feel all I do is hold him back.'

'Hold him back?' Celeste was incredulous. 'A jumbo jet couldn't do that!'

'But I'm no help. I can't cope. And the worst thing is . . .' Tessa gulped before continuing. 'I'm not sure what I believe any more.'

'About what?'

Tessa looked shocked. 'About God – Christianity.'

'Of course, I'm sorry.'

'I really don't know if I care any more.'

Celeste settled a thoughtful look on Tessa. 'We're still talking about God here, are we?'

'Yes,' Tessa sniffed. 'Why, what else were you thinking of?'

'It's a case of what else *you* were thinking of.'

355

'Honestly, Celeste, you can't imagine how ghastly it is living with someone like Blaise and knowing that you can't match up to their ideals. I feel such a traitor. So unworthy. And it seems to be getting worse and worse. I know how disappointed he is. He gets really angry sometimes, which isn't like him.'

'Isn't it?' asked Celeste.

'Well, he gets passionate about things – spiritual things – like Jesus in the temple. I've always felt Blaise would overturn tables given half a chance, he feels so strongly about God. Perhaps that's it, perhaps in some mysterious way he knows that I've lost my faith. I've never said anything but perhaps it's just there in my face, like when you stop loving someone, it's the same thing really after all.'

'Yes,' said Celeste, 'I suppose it is.'

'Oh dear.' Tessa gave a long tremulous sigh. Blaise opened the door and called:

'I have to take Mr Payne over to the Abbey for a few minutes. Celeste, if you're gone when I get back, safe journey. And good luck with your plans.'

He came forward, arms extended, palms uppermost, his face wearing his best never-fear-I-believe-in-you smile. Celeste felt like a sinner, perhaps also afflicted with leprosy or boils or something equally horrific, being invited to begin a new life. She did not rise. Blaise laid his hands on her shoulders and bent to kiss her cheek.

'Au revoir,' she said.

Blaise turned to Tessa. 'Don't forget the international youth convention begins on Monday, will you?'

'I won't.'

'Only we need to make absolutely sure the volunteers are familiar with the school kitchens if we're going to avoid last year's shambles.'

'Yes, of course.'

'Bye. See you shortly.' He bent, laying one hand on his wife's wrist, and kissed her cheek. As he walked away Celeste saw the imprint of his fingers on Tessa's arm, the white turning to fiery red as she watched.

They heard the men's voices in the hall and then the sound

of the front door closing. The look on Tessa's face prompted Celeste not to wait any longer. 'If you are really this unhappy, Tessa, don't you think you should do something?'

Tessa shredded the kitchen towel with rapid, squirrel-like movements. 'I wouldn't know where to begin.'

'You can't go on like this.'

'Oh, I don't know.' Tessa smiled weakly. 'I'll come round. We've been married for fifteen years, you know. I expect it's only hormones or something.'

'I don't believe that, and neither do you.'

The tears oozed once more. 'Please, Celeste, what do you want me to say? This is all so awful. We shouldn't be having this conversation.'

'On the contrary,' said Celeste firmly, 'we should have had it years ago. If you're miserable married to my brother – and, frankly, who wouldn't be? – then it's time to stop being a martyr.'

'Is that how I seem?' Tessa sounded utterly despairing. 'Perhaps you're right.'

'I am.'

'But doing something about it is another matter altogether. What I need,' said Tessa, rising and looking down at Celeste with a watery smile, 'is divine intervention.'

On her way back to Hartfield Celeste, like Mary, pondered these things in her heart and came to the conclusion that the Divinity had already intervened, and given her permission to go forward.

Her father seemed similarly well disposed. The next day she received a letter from France, typewritten on an A4 sheet and sellotaped into a re-used airmail envelope. It was postmarked Paris, but the address at the top was Manoir Dornier, Dornier-le-Bois.

'As you know,' he had written, 'I have absolutely no interest in "healing rifts" and "reconciliation". That is why I left. But if you feel it would make a difference to anyone else I'm of a sufficiently open mind to go along with whatever daft scheme you have in mind. If you and your brothers want to come and see me here, then do. But if you're expecting an affecting scene of some sort you'll be disappointed.'

That evening Celeste poured herself a large gin and tonic with plenty of ice and sat in the cracked leather armchair by the library window. Patches of acid new green were showing on the Craft. The church tower was shrouded in scaffolding and plastic sheets while essential maintenance was carried out. It looked awkward and off-guard, like a woman caught in curlers.

She lifted her glass in its direction. The tower was nothing but old stones and crumbling mortar. But she was alive, and could shape destinies.

CHAPTER TWENTY-THREE

Celeste followed Sandro round the supermarket, pushing the trolley. It filled up at an alarming rate with items which she could not help mentally costing – cream, brandy, butter, exotic cheese and fruit, chocolate, back rashers and French cigarettes. They had already been to the butcher, where Sandro was understandably a favoured customer, and had come away loaded with pheasant, pork tenderloin and fillet of Scotch beef. The wet fish shop had yielded turbot and fresh mussels.

She blenched at the bill, which Sandro paid by credit card.

'Part of the anti-health food backlash?' She nodded at the provisions as he unloaded them into the boot.

'Come on, Lester, don't be po-faced. This is supplies. A lot of it goes into the freezer, we take weeks to use it up. That home-made ice-cream you're so fond of isn't exactly light on the saturated fats, you know.'

'I suppose not.'

As they turned out into the traffic, she added: 'As long as the incomings are staying out in front.'

Sandro patted her hand. 'We've taken you off the case, remember?'

'You're absolutely right,' she agreed, 'it's none of my business.'

Nonetheless, she couldn't help thinking that it was at least in part her business. And her few months overseeing the books of Fare Do's had left her in no doubt that even in Michael's day Sandro's extravagance had bitten deep into the restaurant's profit margin.

'How's *maman*?' asked Sandro, bouncing to a halt at a roundabout. He drove mainly on the brake.

Celeste withdrew her hand from the dashboard. 'She's with Blaise and Tessa. I needed some time to sort myself out now I'm moving out of town.'

Sandro shot forward across the path of an oncoming dormobile. 'I must say I think it's incredibly noble of you to do this.'

'Not really,' said Celeste. 'In fact I'm thinking of going to Paris for a couple of days myself.'

'Paris?' echoed Joe incredulously. 'On your own?'

'Yes. I'm going to visit relations.'

He propped himself up on his elbow and lay looking down at her. 'Can't I come?'

'Not this time. Family matters.'

He brought his face down to hers. 'I wish I was family.'

Celeste pushed him gently away. 'No, you don't. You don't like my family.'

'You know what I mean.'

'I do, yes, but I told you I need time to think about that.'

A little later, when Celeste left, Joe stood at the front door of the block and watched her as she unlocked her car and got in. A change had taken place. There was something different about her, a spring in the step and a tilt to the chin. She was almost – he felt around for the word – sassy.

And there was something else. The realisation of it made his senses reel. He had fallen in love with her.

Just before she drew away from the kerb she turned and waved to him. Still stunned, he lifted one hand, palm outwards, impassive as an Indian brave. But when he was back upstairs and had closed the door of the flat behind him, he went to the bathroom and stared at his reflection in the mirror. His eyes were shining like a kid's on Christmas morning.

'Get you,' he said. 'You silly sod.'

Celeste hired a small Renault at Charles de Gaulle and spent the night with Chrétien and Lauren. It was a long time since she had seen them, let alone visited them at home, and they had both aged. Chrétien, after all, was now in his early sixties, and Lauren only a few years younger. His hair was greyer and thinner, his face greyer and fatter; his wife looked much the same, but at a greater cost than before. Both were almost excessively polite to one another, which made Celeste suspect that these days they were only rarely together. After dinner, which was cooked and served by a pale, voluptuous Corsican maid named Elvira, Chrétien got out a road map and gave her exhaustive directions for the drive to Dornier-le-Bois the following day. While this was going on, Lauren retired to the study to do some work.

'It doesn't look like much of a place,' said Chrétien, squinting at the map through half-moon glasses. 'I find it hard to imagine my brother-in-law confined to a religious commune in a place that size.'

Celeste studied the tiny print that marked her father's whereabouts. 'We can be sure of one thing,' she said. 'Wherever he is and whatever he's doing it'll be because that's exactly what he wants.'

Chrétien went to bed at half-past ten and Lauren made herbal tea for Celeste and herself. 'It's such a treat to see you here,' she said, and then added, carefully, 'Celeste. I've got a confession to make.'

'What's that?' Celeste was becoming used to hearing confessions.

Lauren smoothed her skirt along her thighs with impeccably manicured hands. 'Perhaps you can guess.'

Celeste thought she probably could, but didn't feel inclined to play the game. 'I'm not even going to try.'

'I have known where your father is. For some time.'

'Oh,' said Celeste, 'is that all.' How interesting, she thought, all these years and she's still not going to come clean.

Lauren glanced quickly at her. It was the first time that Celeste was aware of having her aunt at a disadvantage.

'You don't seem to mind.'

'I don't.'

'I imagined you'd be furious with me – for not letting you know, for keeping his secret.'

'Not at all. I always supposed someone would know. After all, it's no fun to walk out on everyone and not to enjoy the effect you're having.'

Lauren smiled. 'You know him quite well, don't you?'

'Perhaps I'm like him.'

'Oh, come on!'

'No, I mean it. I never thought so myself, but since he went away I've felt closer to him, if that makes any sense.'

'Sure, sure . . .'

'So what's he up to?'

'Playing the writer with a past. Enjoying a little afternoon delight with a hippy. Working on a book. Like a pig in shit.'

'It sounds,' said Celeste, 'as though he did exactly the right thing.'

Lauren laughed out loud. 'Celeste, you're unbelievable. What are you, a saint?'

No, thought Celeste, on her way south out of Paris at eight the following morning, most emphatically not any such thing. To prove it to herself she drove rather too fast, flashing past the grim procession of commuters coming in the opposite direction. It was raining and the suburbs looked grubby and desolate. She was glad to be getting out.

She had reckoned on the journey taking two and a half hours, but by nine-thirty she was so far ahead of herself that she stopped in a small town square and bought coffee and a *croque-monsieur*. The rain had eased and the sky was lightening. The day ahead began to take on an inviting aspect. She had written to Bruno announcing her intention of visiting him, and the date, but had deliberately posted the letter so late that there would be no time for him to reply.

The eponymous woods of Dornier-le-Bois had long since disappeared. The village now stood alone and clearly visible on gently rising ground, surrounded by arable fields and long, whimsically winding cart tracks that resembled the closing scene of a Disney cartoon. A crooked cluster of higgledy-piggledy roofs gleamed wetly in the sunlight. There was no jarring new development – even the road along which

Celeste drove was scarcely more than a track, full of potholes and occasional shocks of hardy weeds. The village itself was something of a disappointment. The lack of development was soon explained: this was a desolate place. The church windows were broken and the overgrown graveyard was scattered with litter. There was one shop, but the window was coated with grime and the door closed. The houses were unkempt and the old people sitting and standing in the street had hostile faces, pinched by low expectation.

At one corner of the central *place* was a telephone box and a stone drinking fountain, both far gone in dilapidation, probably because there was usually, as now, a large group of teenagers piled on, in and around them.

Celeste pulled up, rolled down the window and brandished her map with a quizzical smile. The teenagers drew closer, like brown bears drawn to a picnic basket.

'*Manoir Dornier?*' enquired Celeste brightly. '*Où est-il, le manoir Dornier?*'

This acted upon the teenagers like folding money. There were smiles and hoots and joshings and an English-speaking youth, with zits peeping through his stubble like fieldmice in corn, was pushed forward.

'You're going to be a monk?' he enquired facetiously.

'I'm looking for my father,' replied Celeste.

'Your father is a monk?'

'No, he's an author.'

This seemed to strike a chord. The words '*auteur*' and 'Rolls-Royce' were bandied about. The young braves were now crowding the car, leaning on the bonnet and roof and in imminent danger of bending the wing mirrors.

'Excuse me,' said Celeste. 'You know him?'

'Your father has a Rolls-Royce?' asked the youth.

'Yes.'

'We have seen it. He takes the monks for journeys. And the girl.'

Celeste decided she had heard enough.

'So which way do I go?'

The youth waved an arm, and several others joined in with

enthusiasm. When Celeste glanced in her rear-view mirror they were looking after her, apparently much enlivened by the exchange.

The *manoir Dornier* had once been the manor farm, focal point of the village. All that now remained of its former status were the twin rows of poplars which lined the rutted drive. Half-way up a young couple were trudging along, toting between them a string bag full of vegetables. At Celeste's approach, the young man raised a thumb and jerked it in the direction they were going. Celeste slowed, and pushed open the passenger door. 'Jump in.'

'Great, thanks.'

The girl pushed the seat forward and scrambled into the back. Her scrawny pallor was exaggerated by the baggy threadbare shirt and skirt she wore. The young man climbed in next to Celeste, grasping the string bag in his arms. He was equally thin, but a tan made him appear more robust. His black hair was worn in a shock of corkscrew curls which flopped over his forehead. This, combined with the bright beady eyes he directed at Celeste, gave him the look of a large poodle.

'Are you coming to join us, or just visiting?' he asked.

'Visiting. I've come to see my father, Bruno Gallagher.'

'Oh, the Professor!' The young man threw a look at his companion. 'He's your father?'

'Yes.'

There was a short silence and then the girl said, in a small voice, 'He doesn't look old enough . . .'

Celeste realised that this was the girl whom Bruno took on 'journeys': remembering Lauren's reference to 'afternoon delight' she inferred that most of these journeys were not undertaken in the car.

She let the couple out at the front of the manor. A verandah ran right round the house, a twentieth-century construction grafted on to a mediaeval building. One or two recent replacement windows gave a cross-eyed look to the place. There was the distant sound of pots being clattered, and the chug of a tractor in one of the fields below.

'Do I have to check in with anyone?' she asked.

The girl shook her head. 'Just go round the end of the house, his room's on the corner at the back.'

A shade self-consciously, Celeste locked the car, and then walked round the house as instructed. At the side she had to pass through some wooden outbuildings where chickens squawked and made heavy weather of getting out of her way. A young woman milking a goat smiled and said, '*Bonjour.*' When she emerged from the sheds she at once saw her father, sitting in a canvas director's chair at a round gate-legged metal table, writing. He wore a beige jumper frayed at the neck and in holes at the elbows, and dark green cords. His bony ankles, sockless, disappeared into black and white trainers.

He turned round. 'Celeste,' he said, betraying not a hint of surprise. 'I was just thinking about you.'

'Were you?'

'Wondering when you'd show up.'

'And here I am.' She sat down opposite him at the metal table and glanced around. 'How are you? This doesn't look terribly comfortable.'

'It may not be luxurious,' agreed Bruno, 'but I've never been more comfortable in my life.'

'And of course you still have the Rolls.'

'One needs some sense of identity, and that car has become my trademark.'

'So I hear.'

'Apart from the fact that it has wonderfully comfortable seats and a radio which picks up the BBC, it helps me to know that I can flee at any moment. Not that I have the least intention of doing so.'

'I'm sure. No strings, no commitments, no responsibilities.'

'How did you guess?'

'It's no secret.'

Bruno raised his eyebrows. 'Oh-oh. Straight out of the knife-box, as my sainted mother used to say. And anyway it's hardly fair, since I've agreed to this God-awful family reunion or whatever it is you have in mind.'

'Not a family reunion, it's far too late for that. But it would be helpful to' – she chose her words carefully – 'reconcile the past

365

with the present.'

'Christ! You sound like Lauren.'

'You should know.'

He looked momentarily flustered. 'What's that supposed to mean?'

'You've had plenty of time to study her speech patterns.' Celeste felt she could afford to be generous, and added: 'You've seen her more recently than the rest of us.'

Bruno's relief was obvious. 'The woman's a bloodhound, she tracked me down!'

'So I believe.'

'God knows why, she has that obsessive American *need to know*. I've always found it peculiarly off-putting. They make things their business.'

You bastard, thought Celeste. She said: 'Maybe we should all have tracked you down. But the rest of us decided it wasn't worth it.'

'That's a low blow, Celeste.'

'I've changed my mind, though. We owe it to each other to make some sort of contact.'

Bruno picked up a battered packet of Gitanes from the table, and lit one. 'So what's the plan? Pistols at dawn, *déjeuner sur l'herbe*? Solicitor's office?'

'Don't be silly, this isn't legal, or financial.'

'Then what is it?'

'It's a clearing of the air,' said Celeste, 'a closing of the circle.'

'Jesus wept,' moaned Bruno. 'And there's me thinking I'd just broken out of the sodding thing.'

On leaving the bank, Sandro just made it back to his car before allowing the sob which had been filling his throat to break out. He clasped the steering-wheel and lowered his head on to it, inadvertently giving a blast on the horn which stopped several passers-by in their tracks. Hastily he sat upright and dashed at his eyes with his sleeve. A figure appeared at the window, tapping.

Sandro rolled the window down. 'Yes?'

'Waiting limited to twenty minutes here.'

'I'm sorry . . . I'm not feeling too good . . . a little overcome . . .' Sandro gave the traffic warden his most soulful look, his voice breaking with emotion. She gazed stonily back at him.

'In that case I should get yourself home. You can't hang around here any longer.'

Sandro drove back to West End Lane in what he assured himself was black despair. Mr Turville, his bank manager, usually the most obliging of men, and one who had always taken the liveliest interest in the progress of Fare Do's, had suddenly decided to cut up rough. The overdraft extension for which Sandro had asked was not very great, and Danny had told him that its provision was more or less a rubber-stamp job. 'You're obviously a good investment,' he'd pointed out, 'you've proved that.'

Mr Turville had not agreed. Sandro, who had always liked his burly authority and pleasantly avuncular manner, now saw that both had been merely patronising. Today Mr Turville had been cold and rude, using words like 'unwise' and 'present climate' and 'curbing expenditure' and – worst of all, this, in Sandro's view – 'for your own good'. How dare he? Sandro had only rarely accompanied Michael on his twice-yearly visits to the bank, but he had never noticed Michael receiving such treatment. The tone of those exchanges was always calm and measured, with a sensible man-to-man atmosphere which Sandro had found captivating. It was because of this that he had gone to the bank in such good heart today, buoyed up by precedent and by Danny's encouraging words.

When he got back to Fare Do's there was no one there. The only message on the answering machine was from a customer enquiring about a lost diary. The lilies in the bay window were beginning to curl: they had always been Michael's preserve, he was good with flowers, and décor. Danny knew what he liked, but such things were not his bag, nor was Fare Do's his baby. Sandro saw this now, and realised for the first time how terribly alone he was, the sole creative spirit behind this enterprise, and with the financial ground about to be pulled from under his feet. The restaurant, lily white and holly green with its great bowl of dying flowers, was like a backdrop expressly designed for the enactment of his misery. He sat down in the bay window and rested his head in his hands.

Joe drove out to Hartfield on Tuesday, the day Celeste was due back from Paris. He wanted to be there to greet her, and to tell her he loved her – this time without shame. He also wanted to arrive a bit early and mooch around the house on his own.

Joe had often fantasised about living at Hartfield. The knowledge of how much the brothers (bunch of tossers) would hate it gave the fantasy an extra edge. Now he could almost envisage being a real, organic part of the household, a husband and father, a bit of a local celebrity and pillar of the community, perhaps making cash donations to the PTA, the local hospice, doing his bit at charitable fundraisers in the village hall. The vision was so intoxicating he had to restrain himself – it was still a long way off. Before any of that could happen he had to make a go of his career, a real go. He wanted at the very least to be a name, someone with a public identity. In recent weeks that had begun to seem within his grasp. He had no qualms about having cashed Celeste's cheque – she wanted him to get on, that was for sure. And now there had been this shift in his own feelings guilt was no longer an issue.

He arrived at Hartfield and parked on the verge in the lane. This was both because he did not wish to advertise his arrival to Mrs Hodgkiss, and because he liked walking down the drive between the trees and seeing the house come gradually into view. He liked everything about it. He lusted after it. It was wasted on Celeste's family. But then of course it was the go-hang mentality of the English upper classes which created houses like this, with their thrown-together grace and ramshackle elegance.

He took out his key and let himself in. The house was absolutely still – no hoover, no running tap, no sound of footsteps bustling about upstairs. He remembered now that Mrs Hodgkiss's car had not been in the yard. He walked through the kitchen, across the hall and into the library. This was the room he most coveted – books without dustjackets, paintings covering the walls and jumbled together anyhow in a display of conspicuous profligacy, furniture that seemed to have grown organically and become barnacled with its own cushions and rugs. Untidiness here didn't bother him. The ampleness of everything was what he craved.

When the telephone rang it startled him.

'Hallo?'

'Hallo – I'm sorry, I think I may have the wrong number. Who is that?'

Joe recognised the voice of the younger brother. 'Is that Sandro?'

'Yes.'

'This is Joe Cook, Celeste's friend.'

'What are you doing there?'

Joe had never met Sandro, but he knew enough about him not to take offence at this. In fact he felt sorry for the poor little blighter.

'I just got here. I'm waiting for Celeste, she gets back today.'

'Gets back? From where?'

Joe shook his head. None of them ever knew what the others were doing. 'She's been to Paris.'

'Has she? I suppose she was visiting Chrétien and Lauren.'

'I wouldn't know. Was it her you were after, shall I give her a message?'

'I don't know.' Sandro heaved a huge sigh. 'No, I need to speak to her myself.'

'We haven't met,' said Joe amiably, 'but I've heard all about you. I keep meaning to come and eat at your restaurant.'

'You should.' Sandro's voice warmed slightly. 'You wouldn't regret it.'

'It's a deal. And I'll tell Celeste you called, shall I?'

'Please. It's extremely urgent.'

Fabian was tired. Exhausted, in fact. Well past the point where a large Bell's and a cigar could make the slightest difference. It was one of those rare occasions when he actually relished the idea of getting back to his large, comfortable, well-appointed flat, being served dinner by his beautiful (and much recovered) wife, and glancing in on his sleeping infant. On the way back from Portland Place he shot across two red lights, swore at some black youths in an Austin Princess and gave his offside front tyre a nasty bang against a kerb. It was eight forty-five. His shoulders were stiff and there was a fierce, nagging pain spreading upward and outward from the base of his neck. He had a horrible feeling he might be going to need glasses.

A few weeks ago, feeling as he did, he would have gone to call on Alexa. She had been an exceptional find – pleasingly emancipated but tractable. It could never have lasted, but it was galling to have the whole thing ended by her. She seemed to develop a sudden paranoia about being found out.

The hall when he entered was in darkness, but the kitchen light was on. He went through and sniffed: there was no smell of cooking. A sheet of notepaper lay on the kitchen table. There was no preamble: 'Hilary is in her room, but it's her night off. I've gone to dance class with some chums. One must suffer to be beautiful. Food in fridge, and remember *you're in charge*. L.'

Fabian swore viciously. The fridge yielded mackerel pâté and he morosely married it with melba toast and wolfed down a few slices. Then he took off his jacket and poured himself half a tumblerful of Scotch. In the drawing-room he removed his shoes and lay down on the cream leather sofa, staring out over the park. He began to feel better. But just as his shoulders started to unknot there was a series of small staccato coughs and Marcus cried.

Tessa woke up abruptly in the night. She thought for a moment that someone had called her name, she was tingling all over from the effects of the adrenalin rush. She sat up in bed, breathing rapidly, staring into the dark and trying to orientate herself. Then she remembered that the children weren't here. On the other side of the bed Blaise was profoundly asleep, his face grave and untroubled.

Tessa put on her dressing-gown and slippers and went across the landing to her mother-in-law's room. Elodie too was asleep, with her long dark hair spread around her. Softly, Tessa went downstairs. The ancient house creaked and breathed around her as she stood by the window. She looked at her watch. It was three-thirty. Another hour and the first blackbird would be singing and the fens would be rising from their rippling sheet of mist.

She felt suddenly, unaccountably, optimistic.

CHAPTER TWENTY-FOUR

'As a matter of fact, I could use a couple of days on my own in France,' said Fabian to his brother on the phone. 'Louise is a prize rectal ache at present. Now she's back at work I hardly see her. Our sex life's shot to pieces.'

'It sounds like a typically modern predicament.'

'Something you would know all about, of course.' There was a sneer in Fabian's voice.

'There is still a pastoral side to my work.'

'Do me the courtesy of not treating me like some dough-brained villager.'

'That wasn't my intention.'

'I dare say not, but you're hardly part of the psycho-sexual hurly-burly of marriage in the eighties. Up there at the Abbey, securely immured in the ivory tower of the Anglican hierarchy, your union vetted and blessed by the bishop—'

'That's not true.'

'Either that or you were astonishingly lucky in dear Tessa, a woman programmed to be a clergy wife if ever I saw one. Or is that your doing, Blaise?'

'Shut up, Fabian.'

'Is it all evidence of your famous ability to mould people to your will? Just how often does one have to beat them to achieve results like that?'

'Enough!' Blaise's voice was very loud, then very soft. 'Enough.'

'Touched a nerve there, didn't I? You forget, I know you and your little ways.'

There was a pause. 'You should do, certainly. Which is why I'm surprised at your determination to provoke me. I'll make allowances for the fact that you and Louise are going through a sticky patch.'

'Into each life a little rain must fall. Currently we have a shit storm.'

'I'm sure you'll weather it with your customary fortitude.'

There was another pause, broken by Fabian in a lighter tone. 'So how do you want to play it, this trip?'

'I suggest we take one car.'

'The Ferrari?'

'I know it gobbles petrol. I'll chip in.'

'Naturally. But there's no need. I run the car I can afford.'

Blaise ignored this. They made arrangements for an evening crossing.

'Dinner the other side, and a night at some civilised little hotel,' said Fabian. 'If it wasn't such an enticing prospect I might be tempted to ask myself why in God's name we're traipsing over the Channel to see the old man on Celeste's say-so.'

'I suspect,' said Blaise, 'that Celeste is that rare thing, a thoroughly good person.'

'You do?' responded Fabian. 'What about the comic?'

Joe had gone down a storm. As soon as he'd finished, with a great warm tide of laughter and applause breaking round him from the assembled ladies, he made for the door, but of course he was waylaid. Not many autographs this time – these were smart women – but they were still softened up. The organiser, a real darling in a plaid jacket and black miniskirt, asked if she could have her photograph taken with him for the in-house magazine, but he could tell by the way she tucked up to him and flicked her hair off her face that she'd be ordering a print for herself. He could do nothing wrong. He remembered names, he pressed flesh – but with a preternatural sense of how far to go so as to leave them wanting more – he smiled and joked and charmed them half to death. What was more, as he eventually emerged into the hotel corridor he realised that he hadn't even broken into a sweat. Where was the soaking, stinking shirt that had clung like the memory of a bad dream after gigs in the British Legion Halls and lorry parks? He felt clean, and fit, never better.

Celeste was waiting for him in the bar. She looked gorgeous in a black suit with a high-necked white blouse.

He kissed her. 'That's sexy. Like one of those old-fashioned riding outfits.'

She pushed his drink towards him. 'So how did it go?'

'Fantastic. I feel great. Shall we have dinner here?'

'Whatever you like.'

'Can you stay the night?'

She shook her head. 'I must get back to my mother before I go to France at the weekend.'

'The rooms are really nice.'

She smiled. 'I only said I wouldn't spend the night.'

They decided on dinner in the restaurant, but they went up to his room for an hour before that. The conference wives were beginning to congregate with their husbands in the bar, and the burbles were music to his ears. When they spotted him one or two waved, and the organiser blew him a kiss and called, 'You were wonderful, we're going to recommend you to all our friends!'

Celeste put her arm through his. 'I'm not recommending you to anyone. I'm guarding my monopoly.'

Upstairs, Joe's elation was too great for him to take things slowly, but Celeste too was in a funny mood, soft and acquiescent but thoughtful, as though she were looking down at the two of them from a great height.

'I love you—' he gasped as he sank down beside her, his head on her shoulder.

'I know,' she replied. Her voice, unlike his, was quiet and controlled, her breathing even.

He cuddled her, kissing her breast. He felt her hand stroking the back of his head lightly. 'What's the matter?' he asked.

'Nothing.'

'You seem, I dunno, a bit down. Out of it.'

'Down? Not at all, quite the reverse. But I may be out of it.'

He glanced up at her. 'Why?'

'I've got a lot to think about, Joe, with the family. How my mother is. The prodigal father. Sandro.'

'Sandro will be okay,' said Joe comfortably. 'His sort can always find someone to pick up the pieces.'

'That's true.'

'You worry too much,' he added. 'You can't be responsible for everyone, all the time. Give yourself a break.'

'Don't worry,' she replied. 'I intend to.'

Over dinner Joe gave a blow-by-blow account of his performance and the audience's response to it. 'It was mega,' he said. 'If I can keep going like this I'll make that snooty Victoria eat crow.'

Celeste smiled. 'Poor Victoria.'

'Poor nothing. She's always had me marked down for a smut-and-snigger merchant and she wasn't brave enough to back me up when I wanted to change.' He took her hand and lifted it to his lips. 'You were, though. You're the best.'

'Thank you.' Her tone was one of cool detachment. To his surprise he found himself turned on by it. He wanted her again, fiercely. 'Stay the night, Celeste. It's a special night.'

'I'm sorry, Joe.' She glanced at her watch and he cursed himself for having mentioned it. It was suddenly very important to him to pin her down, to make her commit herself.

'Marry me then!'

'What, here? Now?' She was teasing him.

'I want to be with you all the time.'

'Do you?' There was that distance again, not unfriendly but as if she were looking at him through glass. His sense of urgency increased.

'How often do I have to say it? You gotta believe me.'

She laid her napkin on the table as if bringing a meeting to a close. 'I'll think about it seriously, Joe. And I'll give you an answer when I get back from France.'

'I can wait – just so long as it's yes.'

She smiled at him and touched the back of her hand to his cheek. He felt immensely reassured. His life was coming together at last.

*

'Freddy? It's Celeste.'

'What a delightful surprise. Don't tell me you've reconsidered.'

Celeste ignored this. 'I wondered whether you might be able to come and have dinner with me towards the end of the week. I can't come into town, but there's quite a nice pub near us.'

'Name the place and time and I shall be there.'

In fact Celeste was at the Five Bells first, and was sitting at a table on the far side of the restaurant when Freddy arrived and crossed the room towards her with his long, leisurely stride, a figure of impeccable elegance and urbanity. She noticed the split-second admiring glances of several of the women at other tables.

'My dear Celeste.' He bent to kiss her on the forehead. 'This is so nice.'

'Good.'

He sat down opposite her. 'May I order you a drink?'

'You may not. There's champagne coming.'

'Champagne! Is there no end to it? What are we celebrating?'

'Nothing, I just thought a treat was in order.'

'I can't help feeling there's something afoot.'

'You have a very suspicious nature, Freddy.'

'I do not, I'm a natural optimist.'

The champagne arrived and was poured. Freddy lifted his glass. 'Here's to friendship, and the future. May it bring the fulfilment of all our dearest wishes.'

Celeste clinked her glass against his. 'Yes, I'll drink to that. I hope you don't mind I've already ordered for us. It's only a small menu here but they do try to use local produce. We're going to have their watercress soup and then pheasant.'

'It sounds wonderful. I must say you are extraordinarily attractive in this masterful vein. It's not a side of you I've seen before, though of course I've always suspected it was there.'

'Is that so?'

'I'm unusually perceptive.'

'And so modest!'

'I'm a man of many parts. Would you like to hear about the faintly bizarre circumstances in which I found myself last weekend?' Freddy proceeded to describe, with great irreverence, the two-day conference on prosthetics which he had attended at a luxury hotel in the Scottish borders.

Celeste tried to sound disapproving. 'Should we be laughing about something like this?'

'These occasions and the people who attend them are insufferable. They're chiefly about marketing. I limit myself to two a year, one in the spring and one in the autumn, and I apply rigid and unvarying criteria – the quality of the golf, and of the cellar.'

'You're a hard man, Mr Gervase.'

'Not hard, simply realistic. You should know the difference, having had a lifetime's experience of a genuinely hard man.' He gave her a teasing glance.

'You mean Fabian.'

'Who else?'

'Actually . . .' Celeste placed her knife and fork together carefully. 'It was Fabian I wanted to talk to you about.'

'I see.' Freddy's look became wary. 'What's he been up to now?'

'I wouldn't know. But I wonder whether you fully realise the sort of man he is.'

'We've worked together for several years. I think I know him well enough. Are you quite sure you want to go on with this conversation?'

'Absolutely sure. Because I don't believe you do know him well enough, Freddy.'

'And you think it's necessary?'

'Yes.'

'Then fire away.'

When she'd finished Celeste could tell that she had hit home. The irony had left Freddy's expression and he looked pale and solemn. She almost regretted having spoilt a delightful and convivial evening. Almost.

Freddy raised a hand in the direction of the waiter. 'Would you care for a brandy?'

377

'No, thank you.'

'Do you mind if I do?' He waited until it arrived, and then said, 'You make your brother sound like a monster.'

'I didn't mean to. A monster is larger than life; Fabian's personality is incomplete. Where other people have a section marked 'moral code', he has a black hole.'

'I shall take your word for it. Though it doesn't seem to affect his work. He's popular with the customers.'

'Of course, because blackness is compelling. People are drawn to it in the same way that when they stand on the edge of a cliff they want to jump over it. It may be inexplicable to the rest of us, but it's real.'

Freddy spread his hands on the edge of the table, as if on invisible piano keys. He looked up at Celeste from beneath his brows in a manner she imagined he must have used with innumerable querulous patients. 'I must say that professionally speaking I have no cause for complaint.'

Celeste met his gaze steadily. 'Maybe. Not yet.'

'Why did you suddenly experience the urge to tell me all this?'

'Because I'm embarking on a new phase in my life, and I want to start it with a clean slate.'

'Many people might see such a course of action as stirring up trouble.'

'Is that how you see it?'

'I know you better than that.' Freddy smiled gallantly. 'Tell me, this new phase of yours – does it by any chance include marriage?'

'I think it's highly likely. Certain, in fact.'

Only she would have noticed the tiny flicker of disappointment disturbing the smile. He raised his brandy glass.

'I hope he realises how lucky he is. And I wish you both all the good fortune in the world.'

'Thank you.'

'As to this conversation, I intend, unless circumstances dictate otherwise, to pretend that it never took place.'

'You can try,' said Celeste, 'but I shan't let you.'

*

She suggested to Sandro that he come out to Hartfield for Sunday lunch. Elodie was extravagantly pleased to see him.

'Darling, how lovely! It's been such ages since I saw you!'

'Not so very long, *maman*. We went to visit Louise in hospital, remember?'

She relieved him of the proffered bouquet of jonquils and narcissi. 'And these are so beautiful.'

'They're for both of you,' Sandro pointed out a mite sheepishly, casting a sidelong look at his sister, who was basting a shoulder of pork on top of the Aga. 'I brought these as well.' He produced a prettily-wrapped parcel and put it on the kitchen table. 'They're handmade chocolates from my lady in Swiss Cottage.'

'They're gorgeous, you do spoil us,' said Elodie, removing the wrapping and helping herself. Sandro took off his black leather jacket and hung it on the back of a chair. Celeste saw how nervous he was.

'How's Danny?' she asked.

'He's away at the moment with an outside broadcast. So your invitation was especially welcome.'

'Provided you can put up with my cooking,' said Celeste drily. 'I opted for pork because it's impossible to overcook it.'

'It smells wonderful,' Sandro assured her eagerly. He fetched a vase from the cluttered shelf in the back passage, filled it with water and began arranging the flowers. Elodie took another chocolate and wandered out of the kitchen. Celeste poked simmering carrots with a fork.

'There's some wine in the fridge, help yourself.'

He took out the box and set it on the edge of the draining-board. 'You?'

'Thanks.'

As she took her glass, she said: 'So the finances are rocky.'

Sandro's tenuously maintained composure collapsed in disarray. 'God, Lester, I wish I understood! Business doesn't seem too bad, but when I went to see the bank manager he refused to extend my overdraft and implied that I'd been overstretching myself. Well, more than implied. It was all most unpleasant, he made me feel like a criminal and as good as told me I had to get my act together.'

Celeste gazed at her little brother as he stood there with arms folded, shoulders hunched, his wineglass clutched in his fist. Though his face was pale, the lower half was already slightly shadowed by the black stubble that had to be shaved twice a day. He was a baby to have such a virulent and tenacious beard. His hair was rough and tousled, his eyes reddened. She felt a wave of impatient tenderness.

'And are you going to?'

'What?'

'Get it together.'

'Well, of course I'd try, if I only knew how! Christ! I can't tell you how much I miss Michael.'

Celeste drained the carrots and replaced the saucepan on the Aga. 'Yes, he was good at the business side of things.'

'You make me sound such a selfish bastard.'

'Really? I didn't mean to.'

'Look – I don't suppose you could help at all, Lester?'

Celeste stirred the apple sauce. 'In what way?'

'I know you've already been terrifically generous putting money into the business in the first place, but I'm sure this is just a temporary glitch. Danny says—'

'Yes, what does Danny say?'

'He says that it's only a liquidity problem. You know, just a cash-flow thing.'

'Hmm. That much is painfully obvious.' Celeste put the lid back on the apple sauce. 'And I'm quite sure it's worth investing more in the business.'

'You do?' His voice was full of a pathetic gratitude. 'Oh, Lester, you are a brick.' He embraced her unaffectedly, kissing her cheek with the warm, moist abandon of a puppy. She loved him for it – but he had to learn.

'I'll think about it and give you a ring when I get back.'

His expression became pleading. 'You do understand why I can't come, don't you? Only with things as they are . . .'

She touched his cheek. 'You're forgetting something, Sandro. You weren't invited.'

Celeste took the jetfoil across the Channel the day before her brothers were due to go. The day was golden, and soft with the real balminess of summer – but that was no more than she expected. She had not the slightest doubt that this venture, treated with a kind of disparaging indulgence by Fabian and Blaise, would be an unqualified success. She had the cleansed, pleasantly smug sensation of the child who has finished her prep ahead of time and tidied her desk. She could take the next step with perfect confidence.

Tessa had been only too delighted to come down to Hartfield with the children to keep Elodie company. On the phone she said that it would suit her beautifully because she had some serious thinking to do, though she sounded anything but serious. Celeste had told her she must treat it as a holiday, the children were welcome to bring friends, and suggested that Louise might come out for lunch one day and bring Marcus to visit his grandmother. Tessa thought this, too, was a wonderful idea, and said she would arrange it.

Before leaving Celeste went to considerable pains to leave the house as pretty and welcoming as possible, with fresh flowers everywhere, champagne and smoked salmon in the fridge and criminally expensive peaches in the fruit bowl. Together she and Mrs Hodgkiss made up the beds with the old-fashioned embroidered linen sheets which smelt of lavender, and Mrs Hodgkiss swept and laid the grates both in the library and in the drawing-room because the evenings were still chilly. She laid in a stock of silly treats for her nephew and niece – corn for popping, Coke, crisps, and fun-size chocolate bars.

As she set out along the Autoroute des Anglais, south from Calais, it gave her real pleasure to think of Hartfield as it would be that weekend, warm and scented, sheltering the women and children of the family.

She was booked in at a hotel in the market town of Caillon, less

381

than two miles from Dornier, but well before she got there she stopped in a village that straggled along the main road. She found a *quincaillerie* where she purchased a small hacksaw and some twine, explaining in her laborious French about the problems her father was experiencing with the branches of a neighbour's tree overhanging the fence and stealing his light. Ah, neighbours! agreed the man behind the counter. She rolled the hacksaw in a jumper and put it on the floor of the car behind the driver's seat, before driving on and arriving in Caillon in the late morning. In a small *supermarché* she bought two bottles of wine, some local cheese and charcuterie, salad and bread. She then drove to the Hotel Lamartine, checked in and unpacked in her room. The pink handkerchief sachet was these days filled with pot pourri, and she hung it up in the old-fashioned wardrobe near her new silk dress. The sun was high in the sky when she drove up between the poplars to the *manoir Dornier*. The fields on either side of the road were brilliantly lit. Her confidence was like a high, steady note, ringing in her head.

She parked the car against the wall where there was a mean sliver of noonday shade, and walked to the main entrance. The panelled double door stood open, but she jangled the black iron bell-pull before entering. In the dim hallway stood a table covered with a cloth, on which stood a large crucifix, the dying Christ twisted in a sinuously naturalistic death agony. In front of this monstrosity a Bible lay open on a shallow lectern. Celeste walked over to the table and looked down at the open pages. An embroidered bookmark had been laid across the left-hand page to highlight a text, but it was a different one entirely that caught her eye.

'I hope you are finding something to sustain you,' said an Irish voice.

She looked up. A tall, pear-shaped man was standing framed in an open door to her left. The room behind him was extravagantly untidy, the floor strewn with newspapers, a coffee mug and full ashtray on the corner of the desk.

He walked across to her. He wore a monk's habit in a fierce shade of gingery brown, so loose at the neck that it was almost off one shoulder, and tattered espadrilles. What remained of his hair had been shaved to stubble. As he advanced towards her she caught a strong whiff of BO.

'Hallo there!' He greeted her like some amiable Dublin chat-show host. 'Welcome!'

'Good morning,' said Celeste. 'I'm Celeste Gallagher. Bruno Gallagher's daughter.'

'Ah, the Professor!' The monk shook her hand. 'I'm Brother Luke.'

'How do you do.'

'So you've come to visit your father, that's good, that's very good. A great many of us here are exiles of one sort or another.'

'In my father's case,' said Celeste tartly, 'the exile is entirely self-imposed.'

'And isn't that the worst kind!' lamented Brother Luke.

Celeste ignored this. 'Two of my brothers are coming over as well, so he will have no excuse for feeling neglected.'

'Better still!' said Brother Luke, in whose speech the exclamation marks sprang up like dragon's teeth wherever a sentence ended. 'Even as dedicated a writer as your father needs diversion from time to time.'

'We'll be taking him out to lunch tomorrow. We're staying in a nice little hotel in Caillon.'

'But why aren't you staying here? We welcome travellers!'

Celeste tried to imagine Fabian picking his way through the chicken shed to Bruno's quarters, and Blaise gazing down at the mawkish crucifix. 'Thank you, but we'd rather be independent.'

'The historic English position,' said Brother Luke with a hint of acerbity. 'Never mind, you will join us for our communal lunch today!'

'As a matter of fact I brought a few things with me.'

'Contributions are most gratefully received.'

'No, you misunderstand me. My father and I have a great deal to talk about. We must have some time alone.' Mentally gritting her teeth, Celeste settled a beseeching look on Brother Luke. At once he laid a large, moist hand on her shoulder.

'Of course, of course, I understand. Sure, and what else is a family for?'

She decided not to tell him.

Bruno was initially grumpy, but grew more tractable under the influence of Celeste's wine and the promise of lunch in a hotel the following day.

'It's a bit like a holiday camp here,' he said, who had never been near such a place in his life. 'Much store is set by togetherness. Fellowship.' He pronounced the word like the name of some disgusting disease. 'I manage to avoid it most of the time but meals are a three-line whip.'

'I should have thought it was the least you could do, seeing as how you're living here buckshee. And you a self-confessed heathen.'

'They don't mind that,' said Bruno. 'They like it. It makes them feel pious, gives them something to work on.'

'And do they? Work on it?'

'They tried to begin with. But I made it abundantly clear I was not in the market for conversion. I told them my eldest son was a sky pilot and they seem to think that's the next best thing.'

After lunch she made Bruno take her for a walk around the Manoir. It was hot, and very quiet. Clearly the early afternoon was sacred to the siesta. Through various open windows inert forms could be glimpsed, both separate and entwined. At the back of the house was a stone barn, now used as a chapel. Mutterings from within indicated devotions in progress.

'Monkish practices,' commented Bruno. 'They're in and out of there like weather men.'

'You'd expect them to be, wouldn't you?'

'I suppose so,' he conceded ungraciously. As he spoke a tall, silver-haired man, with film-star good looks and an immaculate cream robe, moved out of the dark of the barn into the doorway. He smiled and called a greeting to them in French. Celeste started to reply, but Bruno grabbed her elbow.

'*Bonjour! Bonjour!*' he barked rudely and wheeled her away in the opposite direction. She shook free. 'What are you doing? Stop that, for goodness sake, I'm not a child.'

'I don't want to be cornered by that poor man's Douglas Fairbanks,' muttered Bruno. The blind outer wall of the chapel was now behind them to the left, and on the right was a deeply rutted expanse of dried mud on which stood a tractor, a minibus with a crucifix hanging lopsidedly in the window, and Bruno's Rolls.

'Your car,' exclaimed Celeste, going over to it. 'Your lovely car – it looks so out of place here.' She touched the bonnet, which was covered in a fine film of farmyard dust. As she did so a chicken burst from beneath the Rolls and flapped away with much agitated squawking.

'So everyone keeps telling me,' said Bruno, joining her and blowing moodily on the windscreen. 'That doesn't stop them asking for rides in it.'

'Do they?' Celeste remembered the 'journeys'. 'Do they really?'

'Constantly. For people who claim to have given up the world for a life of prayer and contemplation, they are almost obsessively interested in the combustion engine.'

'And do you take them?' asked Celeste mischievously.

'Sometimes.' He did not sound in the least guilty. 'If I have reasons of my own for going out.'

'But most of the time it's just standing here,' said Celeste. 'I don't suppose that's doing it much good.'

Bruno pushed the front tyre with his foot. 'No problems whatever. For one thing, you may have observed that the weather's not exactly inclement. And for another, these things are built to last. Bloody should do at the price.'

'It's an old car, though,' said Celeste, walking round it. 'When did you last have it serviced?'

Bruno clasped his hands in his armpits and shrugged. 'I don't know. Don't interrogate me. It goes a treat. I'm the envy of all I survey around here, I can tell you. It was the best day's work I ever did, investing in a Roller. You're never alone with a Rolls. I consider that and my ungodly cast of of mind to be my two chief qualifications for this extremely cushy post.' As he walked on towards the goat paddock a scrawny yellow-eyed cat jumped on to the bonnet of the Rolls and from there to the roof, and spread itself luxuriously on the hot metal.

When they got back to Bruno's room the girl Mia was there, sitting on the verandah with her back against the wall, her thin legs with the big boots sticking out in front of her. Celeste was reminded of the cat, with its mixture of scruffiness and sensuality.

'Hi,' she said, still sitting.

'Hallo, my dear,' said Bruno.

'Hallo again,' said Celeste.

'You've met?'

'Oh, yes,' said Celeste. 'The first time I came I gave Mia and her friend a lift.'

'I do that from time to time,' said Bruno.

'I need to talk to you, Professor,' murmured Mia. She put her head back against the wall so that her sunhat flipped up like a lid. Bruno turned to Celeste.

'I generally give Mia a bit of time about now.'

'Oh, don't let me stop you,' said Celeste. 'I'll tidy up this stuff. Is there a fridge anywhere here that I can put the leftovers in. It's a pity to waste them.'

'They got one in the main kitchen,' offered Mia.

'And without wishing to be rude,' added Bruno, several decades too late, 'we should try to have some peace and quiet.'

'Fine!' said Celeste brightly. 'I'll find the fridge, and then I'll be off. We'll come and fetch you tomorrow at about twelve.'

As she went away with the remains of the pâté and cheese in a carrier-bag she could hear the muted sounds of Bruno imparting knowledge to his pupil.

The kitchen, when she found it, was archaic and deserted. Another cat lay on the butcher's block table, flanked by catering-sized tins of dried soup. Cardboard cartons full of potatoes and greens stood on the floor in one corner. The fridge was a hulking 1950s monster, the colour of buttermilk, with the chrome trimmings of a Cadillac and the engine noise of an ocean liner. Celeste put the remains of lunch in the fridge, where it shared a catacomb of greyish ice with butter, margarine, cheese, some frostbitten salad and a large glass bowl of opaque beige liquid which she took to be pancake batter.

When she closed the door, reflecting that on the whole she

was glad not to have accepted the invitation to lunch, the Douglas Fairbanks monk was standing waiting for her, with an amused smile curving his sculpted lips.

'I wonder what you can be doing?' he asked in charmingly accented English.

'Just putting away some groceries. Do feel free to use them.'

'Thank you. I accept. Everything here is common.'

A Freudian slip, thought Celeste. 'So I understand. By the way, my name is Celeste.'

'*Céleste*,' said Brother Paul, giving the word an extra final syllable, his mouth shaped like a kiss. 'An 'eavenly being.'

'Only by name, I assure you.' She laughed playfully. 'I wonder – might I be allowed to go into your chapel for a few minutes?'

'*Bien sûr*.' Brother Paul made a courtly gesture, accompanied by an inclination of the head. 'You can go out of this back door, and straight across.'

He stood aside, not quite as far as he might have done, and Celeste slipped past him, breathing in. He smelt, inappropriately, of hyacinths.

'It is only very simple,' he called after her.

'That's all I need,' Celeste assured him.

She walked away, oblivious to the unpriestly look of appreciation resting on her backside as she did so. Brother Paul had always liked dark, curvaceous women.

Inside the chapel it was cool and dim. Inside the door on a wooden milking stool was a stoneware jug filled with wild flowers. There were several rows of battered canvas and metal chairs like the one in Bruno's room. The altar was a plain trestle table, and the crucifix made of wood, on a rather hideous black marble plinth. In the wall above the altar was an arched window of plain glass, obviously of quite recent origin since there was a border of new plaster round the edge. The building still had a barn-smell of feed, and straw and soil.

Celeste walked up the central aisle and sat down on one of the canvas chairs. She clasped her hands, and closed her eyes. Suddenly self-conscious, she glanced over her shoulder, but there was no-one there so she knelt, feeling the hard chill of the stone bite into her kneecaps.

Once more closing her eyes she began to pray, reflecting as she did so on the biblical text which had caught her attention in the hall. It was from the Apocrypha, Ecclesiasticus, Chapter 25: 'Neither give a wicked woman liberty to gad abroad.'

When she got back to the Hotel Lamartine she went straight up to her room. The hotel was a typical old provincial establishment, with a patchwork of mismatched wallpapers, a serpents' nest of noisy pipes, and uneven floors which emitted occasional loud reports. But Celeste's room did have a bath, into which it was just possible to step with the bathroom door closed. She ran herself as much hot water as the antiquated system would allow and luxuriated in it for half an hour, washing her hair and shaving her legs as though she were about to see Joe. When she got out, still wrapped in a towel and with her hair rubbed into a wild afro, she asked for an outside line on the telephone and dialled his number.

Rather to her surprise she got through at once. It rang for almost a full minute before he picked it up, but she was patient. She knew he never answered immediately, on principle; she had seen him leave it even when it was resting on the arm of his chair.

'Hallo.'

'Joe, it's me.'

'Hallo, sweetheart!' His voice lit up. 'Where are you calling from?'

'From the hotel.'

He paused, and she knew he was lighting a cigarette. 'I wish I was there with you.'

'Yes.' She caught sight of her reflection in the mirror and combed her fingers through her wet hair. 'I know. But this has to be just me and my brothers.'

'They don't appreciate you. How's your dad?'

'The place where he's living has to be seen to be believed. It's run by mad monks and there are chickens roosting under his Rolls.'

'When are you coming back?'

'Soon.'

'Can't be too soon for me.'

'You've got a booking tonight, haven't you?'

'Yup. Polytechnic staff do in Walthamstow. Mixed, which is going to be more tricky.'

'Don't worry, Joe. You've cracked it.'

'Victoria rang up. They're doing another of those comedy showcase series on telly. Mainstream stuff, not alternative, but unknowns like me. The queue'll be round the block but she reckons it's worth giving it a go.'

'I'm sure it is,' said Celeste warmly. 'What a break that would be, Joe.'

'Yeah.' Another pause. 'I do love you, girl. It's killing me with you over there.'

'I love you too, Joe. Always.'

After that she called Hartfield. A woman answered the phone, but Celeste did not at once recognise the voice as Tessa's.

'Celeste, it's you! I'm sorry I was such a long time coming, but we're all having a wonderful time. This was such a good idea of yours.'

'I'm so pleased,' said Celeste, 'I thought it would be. How's Mother?'

'A bit wandery, but basically in better form than she's been for ages. I've decided,' added Tessa almost playfully, 'that it has something to do with having no men around.'

'I think it has everything to do with that.'

'Who needs them, anyway?'

Celeste smiled to herself. 'Good question.'

'When my two are back at school, Louise and I are thinking of taking off on one of those Nile cruises together, how about that?'

'It sounds wonderful.'

'You must come too, of course.'

'No,' said Celeste. 'It's sweet of you, but I don't think you'd want me.'

Next Celeste wrote a letter to Sandro. It was a firm, friendly, businesslike letter, affectionate but brooking no argument. She went straight out and slipped it into the letterbox in the wall of the *bureau de poste*. Back at the hotel she changed into her new dress, a wonderful emerald silk shift from Monsoon, and went downstairs to dinner. She chose a table on the terrace and sat there proud, composed and bookless, eating four courses and drinking a bottle of wine. Solitary though she was, she felt neither lonely nor pathetic, and she was keenly aware of the looks, flirtatious or admiring according to gender, which drifted her way. She had perhaps been happier, but never more content. If she had had to choose one mood to retain for ever, it would have been this.

When her brothers arrived next morning Celeste was pleased to see that she had successfully stolen a march on them. Not only was she the organiser, the one with the plan, but she had already seen Bruno in his new surroundings, she was familiar with the area, and was rested and fresh, whereas they were travel-stained and a touch querulous. It was another hot day and they'd been delayed by a lorry shedding part of its load on the outskirts of Mons. They looked large and heavy, slower in some way, whereas she herself had lost weight – she felt light and agile, like a winged insect that could flit around them and never be caught.

'You must go and have showers and rest for a bit,' she said. 'And there's a lovely small swimming-pool in the garden.'

'I really should phone Hartfield,' said Blaise without much enthusiasm.

'Don't worry, I spoke to them last night. They're having a lovely time.'

'I need a drink,' growled Fabian.

'The bar's through there.'

'How is Father?' asked Blaise.

'Very well, as you'll see for yourselves. He's coming at one o'clock. By the way,' she added mischievously, 'you'll have to watch your back.'

'How so?'

'I think he's developing a taste for the religious life.'

Fabian left his case by the desk and disappeared in the

direction of the bar. Blaise turned to her. 'What are you going to do?'

'It's a lovely morning, I'm going to walk over to Dornier. I'll get a lift back with Father. He could do with the moral support, he's quite nervous about all this.'

Blaise raised his eyebrows. 'Nervous? That'll be the day.'

Celeste laughed. 'He is! He has good reason to be.'

When she arrived, unannounced, Bruno was standing in the middle of his room dressed in a check suit, scraping something off his jacket lapel with his thumbnail.

'What the devil are you doing here?' he exclaimed churlishly on seeing her.

'The others have arrived, so I walked over.'

'You're mad.'

'Not at all, it's only a couple of miles.'

'And eighty in the shade.'

'I like the heat.'

He pointed at her. 'That's rich I must say. I've made some kind of effort and you're in blasted jeans. You don't even wear jeans!'

'I do now.' She looked down at herself. 'I bought these the other day. What do you think?'

'They don't suit you.'

'You're just not used to me in them. Don't worry, I'm not going to wear them for lunch. I'll nip up and change when we get back.'

'Don't go to any trouble on my account.'

'I won't, it's strictly on mine.'

They walked round to where the Rolls was parked.

'You've been cleaning it,' she remarked.

'Mia did it, for a small consideration.'

Celeste went round to the driver's door. 'I think you show her more consideration than she deserves. May I drive?'

'Certainly not.'

'Please. These are such quiet roads.'

'No!'

She leaned her folded arms on the roof and grinned at him. 'I'll be good as gold.'

'I don't doubt it, it's your most distressing quality.'
'And anyway' – she lifted one hand – 'I picked up the keys.'

Back at the hotel she dropped him at the door.
'Thanks for letting me drive. It was a treat.'
'I didn't have much option.'
'You go on in,' she said. 'And I'll park this for you in the shade somewhere. You'll find them on the terrace or in the bar. I'll join you when I've changed.'
'I'd much rather—'
Celeste leaned across him and pushed the door open. 'Go on, Father. Don't be such a baby.'

She parked the Rolls next to her own car in the shady and secluded corner between the overgrown garden wall and the lean-to the hotel staff used for their bicycles. She opened the Metro and unwrapped the hacksaw. It was perfectly private but even so she knew she had to be lightning quick. When she slid out from beneath the Rolls she got into the Metro and changed her dirty T-shirt for the clean sweatshirt which had been wrapped round the saw. She rolled up the saw in the T-shirt and replaced it on the floor behind the driver's seat. Then she took a small plastic container of razor blades from the pocket of her jeans and returned to the Rolls for a moment, before locking it. Within five minutes she was going up in the swaying lift to her room.

When she came back down after changing her jeans for a dress, the three men were sitting in the bar, drinks in front of them. The only other patrons were some workmen in overalls and an elderly couple studying a guidebook. Bruno and Fabian had the graceless, hangdog air of small boys told to stay put and keep quiet. Blaise was talking.

'. . . it's amazed all of us with its success, we've gone from being a somewhat demoralised loss-making concern to being one that's not just in profit but is literally packing them in. It's a classic example of people placing more value on something they've had to pay for.'

'That operates on an ascending scale,' said Fabian, rolling his cigar between his finger and thumb. 'Take my word for it.'

Celeste looked down on them benignly. 'What are we talking about, the Church of England?'

'Might as well be,' said Bruno. 'You never see a vicar on a bike.'

'The Abbey,' said Blaise. 'Charging the public has been a phenomenal success.'

'You know it's funny,' said Fabian, 'but I always had you marked down for someone who was dedicated to keeping the riff-raff out.'

'You've misunderstood me,' explained Blaise with deadly gentleness. 'It's as if people are more reverent, more awed, because we are asking them to pay. It seems to dignify them in some way.'

'Jesus wept,' said Fabian.

Bruno glanced tetchily up at his daughter. 'Any chance of lunch in the foreseeable future?'

'Of course,' she said gaily. 'Now, in fact.'

She led them through on to the terrace. She had reserved a table near the stone balustrade, overlooking the small town garden with its creeper-covered walls, and its round, greenish pool. She had already ordered the wine, and a platter of hors d'oeuvres arrived as they sat down.

'You simply must allow Fabian and me to pay for this,' said Blaise.

'Certainly not. This is my day.'

'Every dog has one,' said Bruno rudely.

'You'll get no objections from me,' said Fabian. 'Things are looking up. Shall we have the other bottle?'

Celeste realised how calm and placid she felt: they had no power to ruffle her now. 'It's on its way.'

'I can't help feeling,' put in Bruno, 'that you're all here to get something out of me. If so, I ought to say that you've had a wasted journey.'

'We don't want anything out of you,' said Celeste. 'What a cynical idea.'

'It's such a comfort,' observed Fabian, 'to have a father who can be relied upon to behave atrociously.'

'Now, come on,' said Blaise. 'None of us is blameless.'

Fabian grunted. 'Ain't that the truth.'

'We have to let the past go.'

'What on earth do you mean?' Bruno looked wary. 'I don't intend making a habit of this sort of thing.'

'Damn right,' said Fabian.

'You're doing this to satisfy a whim of mine,' said Celeste. 'And don't think it's not appreciated. But I don't know so much about letting the past go. We're the products of our past, aren't we? Unless we acknowledge that, we can never be free of it.'

Blaise gave her a look of polite interest. 'That sounds worryingly like a rationale for predestination.'

'Believe me, it's not.' She beamed. 'I'm for free will, one hundred per cent.'

'This is all getting a bit metaphysical for me,' complained Bruno. 'Grub's good though, it beats the monkish fare into a cocked hat. Am I allowed pudding?'

'You're allowed anything,' said Celeste.

It was four o'clock when they got up from the table. Bruno knocked his chair over. 'An excellent lunch. I enjoyed that.'

'We can tell,' said Fabian.

'I was thinking,' said Celeste, 'that you ought to see where Father lives, at the *manoir*.'

'Naturally,' said Blaise, retrieving the chair. 'We could drive him home perhaps.

'Suit yourselves,' responded Bruno. 'The place is stuffed with staring lunatics already, so you won't attract attention.'

'Just for that,' said Fabian, 'I'll come, but I've driven enough for one day.'

'I'll drive!' volunteered Bruno. 'The little beauty's parked outside – somewhere – isn't that right, Celeste?' In response Celeste took the keys from her pocket and jingled them. Fabian gave Bruno a strafing look. 'Do me a favour, you're rat-arsed.'

Celeste turned to Blaise. 'Why don't you drive up there? It's not far. I'll come over in the Metro in an hour or so and pick you up.'

He took them from her and tossed them up and down in his

hand. 'Why don't you come?'

'She should,' said Fabian, 'as the architect of this bizarre event.'

Celeste laughed. 'Sorry.' She glanced at her watch. 'I'm expecting a phone call.'

When they had gone, Celeste went up to her room, kicked her shoes off and lay on the bed with the window open, listening to the gentle buzz of the town coming back to life in the late afternoon. Her call, she calculated, would come through in about half an hour. She felt calm and lazy and actually dozed for a few minutes until the telephone woke her. It was Brother Luke, in a state of almost comic agitation. 'My dear, I don't know how to tell you this, Jesus, Mary, I do not, but—'

'Don't worry,' she said. 'I'm coming now.'

The ambulance overtook Celeste on the Dornier road and its team were in attendance when she arrived. It was not a pretty sight. The Rolls had left the unmade road leading up to the Manoir at speed, and lay up against one of the sentinel poplars, blazing fiercely, when she arrived. All three occupants had got clear somehow, with the help of the tractor driver who had been working nearby. Bruno was the least seriously injured, with whiplash, cuts and bruises, and a seismic attack of shock. A large pool of vomit at his feet testified to the lunch he had so greatly enjoyed at Celeste's expense. Fabian, who according to his father had been lying full length on the back seat, had a broken leg and multiple fractures to the right arm. His normally high complexion was a greenish grey, and his eyes dull with speechless panic. Blaise had gone through the windscreen. He had sustained several broken ribs, and appalling lacerations to the upper body, neck and head. His face looked as if someone had tried to rub out his features with a cheese grater, and reduced it to a dark, sticky blur.

Celeste was utterly composed. She dealt with everything, answered questions, and travelled in the ambulance to the hospital fifteen miles away. Blaise's condition was the most serious, but none of the men was declared to be in danger, and she declared her intention to return to England to break the news to the others the following day. Brother Paul predicted dreadful consequences of this stony English control, but Brother Luke was of the opinion that Celeste would have to come out of it in her own time, and suffer, if need be, a delayed reaction.

When she returned from the hospital by taxi late that night he bent her ear over cocoa, served by a red-nosed Mia, in his study.

'My dear, I only hope you're not feeling guilty at all over this terrible, terrible business.'

'Guilty?'

'Because you must not. Very often the one who escapes injury feels that in some way he or she has done so at the expense of the others.'

'It's all right,' said Celeste peacably. 'I don't.'

'You don't feel very much now because you're still numb, if you'll forgive my saying so. When the numbness wears off, there will be pain, and it is then you must be sure not to blame yourself.'

Celeste put down her mug on the desk. 'It's very kind of you to be concerned, but I don't think that's going to happen. They're all alive. As we speak, they're being cared for in hospital. They're going to get better. What have I got to feel guilty about?'

As she put this rhetorical question she smiled at Brother Luke, and he realised for the first time that Celeste Gallagher was a remarkably good-looking woman.

Brother Paul and Brother Luke persuaded Celeste to stay at the *manoir* overnight, and to accept a lift to the hotel with Zac in the mini-bus the next morning, but none of them could prevent her from embarking on the long drive home.

Nor could they possibly have guessed at Celeste's mood as she sped away from Caillon in the black Ferrari, borne on a tide of *Carmina Burana*, at full blast.

For the return crossing she exchanged her jetfoil booking for a ferry ticket because she wanted to sleep – which she did, like a baby. As soon as she reached England she headed for London, and Joe's flat. She could not stop until she'd completed everything, every part of the plan.

As she zoomed north she spared a thought for Sandro, who would about now be reading the letter she had posted him from France. In it she had explained her urgent need to reclaim her stake in the restaurant. The most important investment he could make, she assured him, was in time and effort. The talent he most certainly had, and with Danny's help she was quite certain he would be able to repay her and see a reasonable profit in one year's time. She had wished him all the luck in the world but explained that her mind was not to be changed.

She hoped Danny was around. The tears would flow this morning.

Joe's delight in seeing her was so genuine and heartfelt that she experienced a powerful shock of realisation, like an amnesiac recalled to an earlier life. All this was hers to call upon. How had she deserved it?

'So,' he said, when he'd finally released her and made them both coffee. 'How did it go?'

'Very well,' she said.

'And it was worth it?'

'Oh yes.'

He smiled at her fondly. 'You and your ideas. You're barmy, you know that?'

'Thank you.' She smiled at him over the rim of her coffee-cup, but now he reached out and took it away from her.

'Celeste . . . You said you'd think about us while you were away.'

'I did.'

'About getting married.'

She let him take her in his arms again. She wanted to savour the sweetness of this. He put his hand to her breast and held it gently, almost reverently. 'God, but I love you.' His voice broke with desire, he pulled at her T-shirt and slipped the hand inside, sighing with pleasure. 'I want you all the time.'

Not without difficulty she took his hand from her body and returned it to him with the gentleness of a mother restraining a child. He looked puzzled.

'What's up?'

'I know you love me, Joe.'

'Good,' he reached for her again but she caught his wrist quite strongly; lowered it, patiently.

'And I love you, too. And I owe you so much.'

'You don't owe me anything!'

'More than you can possibly imagine, more than you'll ever know.'

'Shucks, what can I say? So what's the problem?'

'There is none,' she said. She got up and stood looking down at him, fit and free in her grubby jeans and loose T-shirt, her eyes bright, her hair a wild dark halo.

'So?' He grinned up at her – a new, confident, expressive Joe, the man she loved.

'I promised you an answer, Joe,' she said, 'and here it is.'

This time as the Ferrari glided down the hill between the plane trees and the parked cars she played a tape of her own, and it was the gravelly purr of Nat King Cole which made her eyes mist with tired, sentimental tears.

> *'You may not be an angel, 'cos angels are so few,*
> *But until the day that one comes along*
> *I'll string along with you . . .'*

POSTSCRIPT
1989

Where's the man could ease a heart
Like a satin gown?

Dorothy Parker, *The Satin Gown*

'All wickedness is but little to the wickedness of
a woman.'

Ecclesiasticus 25:19

Reader, I married him.

Charlotte Brontë, *Jane Eyre*

Many people might have thought the bungalow on the cliffs at Peacehaven ugly and tasteless. Celeste could think of several to whom she was related who would have had no compunction in calling it 'common'. But she knew as she walked up the path that none of the obvious things mattered. It wasn't important that the front garden was paved with pink and white slabs, with tiny areas picked out in pebbles so that shrub roses (also pink and white) could sprout through. Neither did it matter that there was a bijou pond with a gnome, and an urn of simulated bronze complete with verdigris, from which water trickled and tinkled, driven by some unseen electrical pulse. Neither these nor the open-work low wall made of pebbles bedded in plaster, nor the ruched nylon net curtains, nor the brass knocker fashioned like a zephyr with fat cheeks, bothered Celeste in the least. On the contrary, she found them comforting and eloquent of order.

When the door opened there was a pleasant warm waft of scented cleanliness and baking of the sweet, tea-time variety.

'Hallo, Mrs Dove,' she said.

Evadne was having none of that. She opened her arms and drew Celeste into them, and rocked her lovingly from side to side, half-laughing, half-crying.

'Bless you, my precious, for coming! It's the best thing that's happened to me in years! Now come in and sit down and tell me all about everything, I want every detail.'

The inside of the bungalow was just as Celeste had expected, and hoped. Spotlessly clean, pin-neat, painstakingly pretty, with all Mrs Dove's 'nice things' set out and highly polished. Celeste saw that Evadne was like Joe in her ordered approach to her surroundings.

'Is Mr Dove in?' asked Celeste cautiously as she sat down on the plump, pale grey, buttoned sofa. Even after all this time the 'Mr' felt awkward, and Evadne had no intention of bothering with it.

'Dove died,' she said, with a comforting, never-mind expression. 'Three years ago. Cancer,' she added, and then mouthed richly, 'colon,' accompanying the word with a delicate gesture, her scarlet-tipped hand tapping her backside.

'Oh dear,' said Celeste, 'I'm so very sorry. I always remember Dove . . . as being . . .' She felt herself floundering. Dove had been such a silent background presence. 'He was absolutely splendid,' she said finally.

'He was a good man,' agreed Evadne, pouring tea. 'But you wouldn't have wished a dog the sort of suffering he was going through at the end. I was glad when he went.'

'I can understand that,' agreed Celeste. She sipped her tea. Evadne looked at her, shaking her head and smiling, unable to believe that she was really there. Evadne herself had scarcely changed, though she must by now have been in her seventies. She was still upright and curvaceous, and impeccably groomed, her hair a whipped and frosted tribute to the local salon, every nail glossily red to match her lips, her green and blue checked cotton shirt perfectly matching her green cotton trousers and moccasins. Celeste found that she still loved her in a way she had loved only one other. Evadne Dove was someone to respect and admire and who asked for nothing back. Someone who took life on and made something of what little it offered her.

'I'm afraid I have some bad news too,' she said carefully. 'Though not as bad as yours, about poor Dove.' Evadne's expression changed to one of keen concern.

'What's that? Not your lovely mum, I hope.'

'Actually no. I told you my father left.'

Evadne nodded. 'And a good riddance.'

'Perhaps. Anyway, Mother's fine, though she's very confused now. We had to settle her in a retirement home.'

'Of course,' Evadne nodded. 'Best thing for everyone, she'll be safe there.'

'I told her I was coming to see you, but she couldn't really take it in.'

'Course not. So what's the bad news?'

'My father and brothers were in an awful car accident last summer. In France.'

Evadne's hand flew to the side of her face. She opened her eyes wide, then closed them. 'No!'

'It was dreadful.'

'Little Sandro?'

'He wasn't with them.'

'Thank God!' Evadne took a hankie from her sleeve and dabbed at her nose. 'And the others – are they all right, now?'

Celeste chose her words carefully. 'They're recovering.'

'But whatever happened?'

Celeste sighed, collecting herself. 'The three of us had gone over to France to visit my father, and we'd taken him out to lunch in the hotel where we were staying. After lunch Fabian and Blaise wanted to go back with him and see where he was living, and Blaise had had the least to drink so he drove the Rolls—'

Evadne shook her head. 'He loved his Rollers, your father.'

'Yes. Anyway, what we believe happened is that Blaise's epilepsy was triggered by trees lining the road, and he went out of control. They hit one of the trees. Fabian had a lot of broken bones, and poor Blaise's seatbelt failed and he went through the windscreen.' Evadne gasped. 'Fortunately Father only had minor injuries and he and a tractor driver managed to pull the others clear before the car went up in flames.'

Evadne's eyes filled with tears. How, thought Celeste, could anyone be so forgiving? 'I can't bear to think about it. I never realised epilepsy could come back like that. Surely he never even had a fit since he was a kiddie.' Her voice caught and she put her hand over her mouth. Celeste put her cup down and moved along the sofa to lay a comforting hand on her knee.

'It can, unfortunately, at any time. An epileptic can never honestly say they're a hundred per cent cured, although we did all think Blaise was. *He* thought he was. He'd been through the statutory period without drugs and been completely clear. Otherwise of course he wouldn't have been allowed to drive at all. But it's the only reason we can think of why the car just careered off the road like that. At any rate it was a write-off and' – she patted Evadne's knee – 'I thought you'd want to know.'

'How are they both now?'

'It hasn't been a good year. Fabian's wife left him, and his right arm's in poor shape – going back into plastics is a long way off still. Blaise had to have a lot of remodelling done on his face. We put him in touch with a man called Patrick Reeves who has quite a reputation, but it's not been entirely successful. Tessa, his wife, has been an absolute brick of course, but she's working full-time now and the job at the Abbey was too much for him in his present state, so he's been moved sideways.'

Evadne gave her nose a brisk blow. 'Your poor mother. Is this what brought on the senility?'

'No, she'd deteriorated long before the accident.'

'And at least Sandro's well, is he, and happy?'

'I don't think he has time to think about it,' said Celeste. 'The restaurant got into financial trouble, and he's working all the hours that God gives to clear his debts. It's going to be another year or two, I'm afraid, before he gets out from under. He's even got a proper grown-up ulcer.'

'Poor lad.'

They sat for a second in respectful silence.

'I do have some happy news too, though,' said Celeste. And it was pure pleasure to see Evadne's face light up in happy expectation. 'I'm married.'

An hour later Evadne accompanied Celeste out of the front door. 'You will come again, won't you?' she asked, clasping Celeste's shoulders and kissing her cheek.

'Of course. And I'll ring up. We can talk.'

'Give my love to your mum if you're able, and to that little monkey, Sandro.'

'I will.'

'I'm ever so sorry you've been having a bad time, all of you. I know I left under what you might call not very happy circumstances, but I never harboured a grudge. They were only boys. I can't imagine Blaise with that lovely face of his all smashed up.'

Celeste squeezed her hand. 'Don't worry about Blaise. He has his faith, remember. And Fabian will rebuild his life, I'm sure.'

There was a trace of the old sparkle in Evadne's smile. 'She left him, did she? That must have hurt more than the broken bones.'

They walked arm in arm to the gate. Evadne's smile changed to a frown of disapproval as she caught sight of the rusty Austin Princess parked in the drive next door. 'That thing is an eyesore. Belongs to the boy, and he says he's going to do it up, but I see no sign of it.'

Celeste surveyed the car critically. 'It's not worth doing.'

'He says it is. He reckons with a bit of work and a respray he can make a profit on it.'

'Yes, and the next person who drives off in it will have a nasty accident,' said Celeste. 'It only takes something like a damaged brake pipe, and you're driving around in a deathtrap.'

'Anyway,' said Evadne comfortably. 'It's not my problem if he wraps himself round a lamp-post.'

'No,' said Celeste, 'it certainly isn't. Look, here's my husband come to pick me up.'

'Oh!' exclaimed Evadne, putting her hands to her cheeks. '*Very* nice!'

As they drove between the ranks of bungalows, down the road towards the sea, Celeste said, 'She hasn't changed a bit.'

Freddy glanced at his wife, the sleek, expensive, poised Mrs Gervase, her magnolia skin set off to advantage by a perfectly-tailored lilac suit.

'Is that so?' he said. 'Well, you have.'

She turned on him that look of burning self-satisfaction which he found utterly irresistible.

'I know,' she said.